THE LONG CHAIN

ARCANE CASEBOOK 3

DAN WILLIS

Print Edition – 2019

This version copyright © 2019 by Dan Willis.

All rights reserved. No part of this book may be reproduced or transmitted in any form or by any electronic or mechanical means, including photocopying, recording or by any information storage and retrieval system, without the express written permission of the copyright holder, except where permitted by law.

This novel is a work of fiction. Names, characters, places and incidents are either the product of the author's imagination, or, if real, used fictitiously.

Initial Edits by Barbara Davis
Edited by Stephanie Osborn

Cover by Mihaela Voicu

Published by

Dan Willis
Spanish Fork, Utah.

1

SECURITY

Alex Lockerby got off the crawler rail at Empire Station and crossed the platform to Empire Tower. Not quite a year ago, Sorcerer Andrew Barton had launched his new elevated crawler line and now rails ran all over the city. Wherever they went, however, Empire Tower was where they began, the center of a vast network connecting areas beyond the outer ring directly with the city's core.

Empire Station took up the third floor of the tower, with the crawlers passing the building on the north and south sides. A glass enclosure had been built along those edges to keep passengers out of the weather as they boarded and disembarked. Inside was a terminal to rival Grand Central Station, with marble floors, a café, a barber shop, a newsstand, and rows and rows of stained oak benches.

On the east wall were the elevators that could take people down to the street below, or up to the public observation deck far above. What most patrons didn't know, however, was that there was another elevator on the west wall, inside the security station. This was the building's main elevator that led to the power plant, the living quarters, and the corporate offices of Barton Electric. It was this elevator for which Alex headed as he crossed the immaculately polished floor.

An enormous clock on the far wall showed the time as just after noon. Normally at this time of day, the terminal would be filled with light, but today the city was beset by a persistent haze that had the terminal lights on already.

As he went, Alex pulled his cigarette case from his inside pocket next to his rune book and flicked it open. The case was made of engraved brass and held about half a pack's worth of smokes. Pulling one from the end, he tucked it into his mouth, then lit it with the spring lighter he kept in his trousers pocket.

The security station on the west wall was a decent-sized room, large enough for a guard room and a lockup in the unlikely event someone needed to be detained. A frosted glass window ran along the front of the space with a pair of double doors in the exact center. A bored-looking man in a blue security uniform sat behind a counter made of cherry wood, stained and polished to a deep maroon color. The counter always reminded Alex of a bar, complete with a brass foot rail running along the bottom edge.

"How are you today, Mr. Lockerby?" the bored guard said as he noticed Alex's approach. He was a large man, like most in his profession, with broad shoulders, a broad smile, and an accent that was all Brooklyn.

"Hi-ya, Joshua," Alex said, returning the guard's smile. "I need to go up; the boss is expecting me."

Joshua pulled out a clipboard from behind his counter and handed it to Alex.

"You know the drill," he said, then turned to open the glass door with a key.

Alex wrote his name and time of arrival on the visitor log, then handed it back as Joshua held the door for him. A few moments later, Alex was ascending up almost a hundred stories to the main office level of Barton Electric.

The elevator doors opened on a visitor lounge that was larger than Alex's whole office. A bank of telephones covered the right-hand wall, with a long mahogany bar opposite. At the far end of the space was an elegant podium where a man in a tuxedo stood. When he saw Alex, he hurried forward.

"Hello, Alex," the man said in a proper British accent. "Have you made any progress with this case?" His smile was warm and friendly but there was worry in his voice. "Mr. Barton is most put out by this affair."

"Don't worry, Bickman," Alex said, clapping the man on the arm. "I think he's going to like what I've discovered."

When professional valet Gary Bickman had been set up by his former boss as the scapegoat in an insurance scam, Alex had gotten him hired on with Andrew Barton. Barton was a Sorcerer and one of the famous New York Six.

Actually Sorsha talked Barton into hiring on the suddenly-out-of-work valet, he reminded himself.

Bickman looked relieved that Alex had potentially made a break in the case. Alex had worked for Barton before and found him driven and exacting. He could only guess what working for the Lightning Lord full time would be like.

The valet led Alex into the private elevator behind his podium and up to Barton's palatial office. It was only half the size of the terminal downstairs, but that still made it enormous, and with a ceiling that went up three stories, it was imposing. A bank of floor-to-ceiling windows lined the back wall, giving a grand view of Central Park, north of the tower, barely visible through the haze. Barton's desk was four times the size of the one in Alex's office, with a marble top about a foot thick and a massive steel frame to hold the weight.

Alex moved to the desk and dropped his hat on top of a stack of papers. A dozen contraptions of wood and metal covered the desk, along with reams of paper and rolled-up blueprints. Alex knew from experience that they were models of the Lightning Lord's various projects. They were all interesting, but Alex turned away from the desk. If Barton got started talking about them, Alex would be here all afternoon.

Along the left-hand wall were row upon row of pictures, certificates, and other awards. As Alex strolled along, looking at them, he found Barton's Master's Degree from Yale, a commendation from the New York Department of Power, and a handwritten note from Teddy Roosevelt.

The pictures were mostly of Barton with various famous people: Abbott & Costello, Clark Gable, Humphrey Bogart, and Mary Astor were easily recognizable. Alex finally stopped in front of a picture of the sorcerer with a beautiful blonde woman in a sequined gown on his arm. She had an enormous smile that simply radiated personality. Alex was certain he'd seen her before, but he couldn't place the face.

"Figures you'd find the prettiest girl in the bunch, Lockerby," Barton's voice came from behind him.

Alex turned to find the man himself coming through the door on the far side of the office with Adam Duncan, his head of security, in tow. Barton had turned to Alex when Duncan failed to find out who had been scrawling threatening messages on the walls of the residence floors right below where they now stood. The graffiti was directed at Barton's new accountant, a man named Thomas Whitley. Like all key members of Barton's staff, Whitley had been given a suite in the building. What made Whitley a target was the fact that he was colored.

It looked like someone didn't want a colored family moving into their neighborhood. While that wasn't an uncommon reaction, Barton was having none of it. He'd hired the best accountant he could find and what the man looked like couldn't have mattered less.

"I hope you've got something for me, Lockerby," Barton went on, crossing the floor to where Alex stood. "Another message was found this very morning and if you and Duncan here," he jerked his thumb over his shoulder at the security chief, "don't catch this guy soon, I'm going to fire both of you."

Alex put on his most reassuring smile as he pulled a sealed envelope from his pocket and held it up.

"Not to worry, Mr. Barton," he said. "I have the answer to all your questions right here."

A disbelieving look crossed the sorcerer's face, but he reached out for the envelope just the same. Before he could grab it, Alex pulled it away and turned back to the picture of the blonde woman.

"So who is this?" he asked as if Barton wasn't fuming at being denied the envelope. "She looks familiar, like I should know her."

"That's Jenny Leavitt," Barton explained, putting his hands on his hips as he gave Alex a hard look. "She was a big Broadway star back in the day. Everybody wanted her."

"How'd you let her get away?" Alex asked, suppressing a smirk. He expected Barton to be angry, but instead the Sorcerer's face turned wistful.

"Not for lack of trying," he said. "She left the stage and married some stiff. His family came from old money. That was back when I wasn't as successful as I am now."

"What happened to her?"

Barton shrugged.

"She did modeling work for years, magazine covers and such, but she doesn't even do that anymore. Her husband went into politics and spends a lot of time abroad." He took a deep breath and turned back to Alex, his business demeanor returning. "Now, if you don't mind." He reached across Alex's body and yanked the envelope from his hand. "Let's see what you have for me."

He crossed to his titanic desk and extracted a silver letter opener from beneath a stack of correspondence. With a deft motion, he sliced open the envelope and extracted a folded piece of paper from inside.

"If this is supposed to be a joke, I'm not amused," he said, once he'd opened the entirely blank page. He dropped it on his desk and looked at Alex, awaiting an explanation.

"No joke," Alex said, crossing to the desk. "This is how your vandal is leaving his messages." He withdrew his red rune book and flipped to the last page where a mildly complex rune had been drawn. It had five nodes and two rings of symbols, one on the inside and one out. In the center there was a symbol that always reminded Alex of Stonehenge. "This is a curing rune," Alex said, tearing the page from his book.

"Is the paper sick?" Barton asked, still not amused.

"It's not that kind of cure," Alex explained. "This rune speeds up the drying process. Historically it's been used by painters to dry their paint, or by bookbinders to cure their glue."

"What has that to do with a blank piece of paper?" Duncan said, speaking for the first time. He was a tall, heavyset man but spoke in a mild voice that belied his appearance.

Alex licked the back of the rune paper and stuck it to the blank sheet.

"This," he said, sticking the lit end of his cigarette to it. The rune paper vanished in a puff of smoke, leaving the rune behind, hovering in the air. It pulsed with an azure light, slowly at first, but then faster and faster, until finally it popped like an overpressure balloon and vanished.

All eyes turned to the paper where, very slowly, two words were starting to appear.

Security Ink.

"What the devil is security ink?" Barton demanded. He looked at Duncan, but his security chief just shrugged.

"It comes in several flavors," Alex explained. "The most common is disappearing ink. You write a message and over time it fades and disappears. It's the kind of thing governments or high security places use so their messages don't get out."

"Is there a kind that goes on invisible and then appears later?" Duncan asked.

Alex tapped the side of his nose.

"Got it in one."

"So whoever's been doing this has been writing his messages hours before anyone can find them," Barton said, crumpling the paper in his hand.

"I'd guess as much as twelve hours before," Alex said. "That's why no one is ever seen writing the messages."

"Not bad," Barton said, though he still looked cross. "So, have you figured out which of my employees is actually doing this?"

Alex pulled a second envelope from his pocket and handed it to Barton.

"If this one is blank, Lockerby, you'd better be able to outrun lightning," he said, slicing it open with the silver opener. "Who is Fredrick Patterson?" he asked after reading the page within.

"No one by that name works here," Duncan supplied, helpfully.

"Funny story about that," Alex said to Barton. "I talked with all the people on Thomas Whitley's floor, and while some of them aren't excited about him living there, no one was angry enough to threaten him. I started to wonder if maybe the messages were being left by someone else."

"Fredrick Patterson?" Duncan said.

"His name appears in the visitor logs the day before each of the threats was found," Alex said.

"That could be a coincidence," Barton said.

"That's what I thought," Alex said, his smile getting wider. "But since he was the only consistent visitor, I figured I'd better check him out."

Alex paused for effect.

"And what did you find?" Barton growled at him finally.

"Turns out, Mr. Patterson used to be the head of security for Abernathy Machine Works, until they went bankrupt three months ago." He turned to Duncan. "Ask me how he got that job?"

"All right," Duncan said, playing along. "How?"

"The previous head of security was fired after he couldn't stop a series of thefts on the property," Alex said. "By a strange coincidence, Fredrick Patterson's brother worked there at the time and recommended Fredrick for the position."

"So you think it was an inside job," Barton guessed.

"Patterson was a good fit for that job," Alex went on, ignoring the Sorcerer's comment. "Turns out he ran the MP's office at Fort Benning when he was in the Army. He got that job when the former sergeant failed to find out who kept writing rude messages on the commandant's office door."

"I'm sensing a pattern here," Barton said, glancing at his head of security.

Duncan nodded.

"Looks like this Patterson fellow wants my job."

"And he'd have got it, too," Alex said, indicating Barton. "Your boss threatened to fire you ten minutes ago. As long as Patterson kept up with the messages, sooner or later you'd be out."

"So how did he expect to get this job?" Barton asked. "Has he got a brother working here as well?"

Alex shook his head.

"Better," he said. "He's dating a woman who lives in the building, Amy Carter."

Barton looked confused, but Duncan groaned and put his hand to his forehead.

"Who is she?" Barton asked.

"My secretary."

Alex pointed at Duncan.

"So, Patterson gets you out of the way," he said, then turned to Barton. "Then Miss Carter tells you all about a candidate who'd be perfect for the job."

"Was Miss Carter in on it?" Barton asked.

Alex shrugged.

"No idea," he said. "But I'm sure Duncan here can get to the bottom of that."

"But what about Whitley?" Barton said. "Are you saying none of this was about him?"

"No," Alex said. "He was just a convenient target for Patterson's plan. When Miss Carter told him about Whitley, Patterson saw his chance."

Barton stood looking at Alex for a long minute, then he smiled and nodded.

"Good work," he said. "You're more annoying than I like, Lockerby, but you get results." He turned to Duncan. "Go find out what your secretary knows about this and put that Patterson fellow's name on the security watch list. I don't want him in this building again."

Duncan promised to handle it and, shooting Alex a grateful look, he withdrew.

"What do I owe you?" Barton asked, fishing his wallet out of his jacket pocket. It was made of alligator leather and bulged with cash.

"Six days' work at twenty-five dollars a day," Alex said.

"You said that some of my people weren't thrilled to have Whitley living in the building," Barton said as he fished three fifty-dollar bills from his wallet. "Who are they?"

Alex reached for the cash, but Barton pulled it away, just as Alex had done with the envelope earlier.

"I can't recall," Alex lied, not wanting to get involved. "But if you really want your new accountant to fit in around here, have him throw a party."

Barton raised a skeptical eyebrow.

"And how is that going to help?"

"Tell him to invite everyone in the building," Alex explained. "Then make it known that you plan to attend."

"Why?"

"So no one will skip it," Alex said, as if it were the most obvious thing in the world. After all, who'd miss a party when the big boss was going to be there?

"Again," Barton said. "Why?"

"Arrive late, after everyone is there, then take Whitley around and introduce him to everyone. Talk your other employees up to Whitley and talk him up to them."

Barton nodded after a moment.

"So they'll understand why I hired him, and he'll know why I hired them," he said.

"It'll give them some common ground to build trust on," Alex said.

Barton handed over the cash, but held on to it when Alex tried to take it.

"You're pretty smart, Lockerby," he said. "I could use someone like you around here. Why don't you come work for me?"

Alex grinned at that but shook his head.

"You wouldn't like that, Mr. Barton," he said. "I'm annoying, remember?"

Barton chuckled and released the money.

"I guess you're not as smart as I thought," he said. "Or just too damn independent."

Alex shrugged, pocketing the cash.

"Take your pick," he said, depositing his cigarette butt in the ashtray on Barton's desk.

"Hey," Barton said as Alex turned to leave. "If you're dumb enough to turn me down, maybe you're dumb enough to botch things with that gorgeous redhead. You still seeing her?"

"Jessica," Alex said with a nod. "And I may be dumb, but I'm not stupid."

"Too bad," Barton said with a chuckle and a shake of his head. "Well, phone me if you change your mind," he called after Alex. "Or if Jessica comes to her senses."

2

THE RUNEWRIGHT DETECTIVE

Alex caught a northbound rail crawler from Empire Terminal, and fifteen minutes later, he got off only three blocks from his office. The only real problem with Barton's new sky bugs, as most people called them, was that he simply couldn't add new rails and their millipede-like passenger cars fast enough.

Normally Alex favored the cars with an open upper deck. He liked the view of the city and the feeling of the wind in his hair. Being mid-September, the weather had lost the scorching edge of summer, which would have made for a very pleasant ride.

Except for the fog.

When he went to see Barton it had been a hazy mist that made everything look like a photograph taken through a dirty lens. Now, however, it had thickened quite a bit. Whereas before, Alex could see well beyond a block, now his vision was half that. Fog in the city wasn't unknown, but it only happened on rare occasions and usually when the weather shifted suddenly from hot to cold or vice versa.

Alex shrugged as he lit a cigarette for his walk back to the office. The weather had been nice, and he hoped the fog wasn't a herald that it would shift suddenly. He liked riding in the open sky bugs.

His office was in a squat professional building on the mid-ring side of the outer ring border. It was cheap but still looked respectable, which was all Alex asked of it. The building didn't have an elevator, so he had to climb the stairs to his third-floor office, but he didn't mind. It reminded him that he was still alive, and he'd take that any day.

As he rounded the railing on the third-floor landing, he caught sight of his office door. He'd come a long way from the basement hole in Harlem where he'd started out. The sign read, *Alex Lockerby, The Runewright Detective*, and had the runewright ink bottle and quill symbol in the bottom right corner in case anyone doubted his bona fides.

A year or so back, Alex had helped catch the infamous Ghost Killer, and during the investigation the tabloids had dubbed him the Runewright Detective. The idea that he had such a public *nom de guerre* embarrassed him initially, but after the case was done, he got a steady stream of clients looking for the Runewright Detective, so he decided to embrace it.

"How did it go with the Lightning Lord?" Leslie asked as he let himself in. Leslie Tompkins had been his secretary for almost a decade now. She kept his calendar, screened his clients, and handled the money. Alex often reminded himself that if he didn't keep solving cases, she'd probably go into business for herself.

"Case closed," he said, crossing the outer office and depositing the hundred and fifty on her desk.

Leslie flashed him a dazzling smile. She used to be a beauty queen in her youth, and even though Alex knew she was in her forties, time had been very good to her. She wore a loose shirt covered with a form-fitting blue vest and a matching skirt. Her eyes were naturally gray, hazel to be exact, and they had a tricky way of matching any dark color, so today they were blue. Leaning down, Leslie opened the bottom drawer on the left side of her immaculate desk and pulled out a heavy steel box with an intricate rune engraved on the lid.

"Open sesame," she said, knocking on the box.

The rune flashed orange for a moment, then the box top popped open with a ringing clang. Inside the box were a pad of paper, a roll of bills secured by a rubber band, and a pencil.

Leslie noted down the cash Alex had given her on the pad and totaled the sum, then she unwrapped the bills and counted them out, checking the amount against the note pad.

"Any new prospects?" Alex asked as she counted.

"On your desk," she said, not missing a beat. "A couple of record searches, someone looking for their grandmother's missing wedding ring, and I even found you a lost dog."

Alex smiled at that. There had been a time when the best he could do was tracking down wayward pooches. Now it was a rare treat.

"You take good care of me," Alex said, turning toward the door marked *Private* that separated his office from the reception area. "Did you find the title for that disputed building?" he called over his shoulder.

"Yes," Leslie said, irritation creeping into her voice. "I was at the records annex going through their storage room for hours. My blue jacket is covered with fifty years of dust and muck."

"I'll whip you up a cleaning rune," he promised.

"Before five," Leslie called back. "Remember, I'm going out of town right after work."

Alex was of two minds about that. During the Ghost Killer case, he'd sent her out to Suffolk County to look up some land records. Ever since then, she'd had an on-again, off-again relationship with the County Assessor, one Randall Walker.

"So how is Randy?" he asked, more out of a desire to be polite and supportive than any real interest.

"He's wonderful," Leslie said with a contented sigh that made Alex turn. She stood holding the strongbox but not moving to put it away, and her face had a wistful expression.

"What's all this?"

Leslie jumped as if he'd startled her and hastily put the box back in her bottom drawer.

"I didn't want to say anything," she explained as she stood up, her cheeks a little pink. "Not until I was sure, but...I think Randy is going to propose."

A million thoughts cascaded across Alex's mind. Chiefest among them was the question of how he could possibly run his office without

Leslie. With a Herculean act of will, he managed to keep those thoughts off his face. Instead he smiled.

"That's great," he said. "I'm happy for you."

Leslie blushed, but she chuckled as well.

"Liar," she said. "But thanks."

"If he does propose, tell him he can't have you until you've helped me find a new secretary," Alex said in a gruff voice but with a smile.

Leslie saluted at him.

"Yes, boss."

Alex turned and entered his office, shutting the door behind him. As Leslie had promised, a small stack of folders sat in his in-box, potential clients waiting for him to take their cases. Hanging his hat and coat on the stand beside the door, he crossed to his desk and sat down. He stared at the folders for a while, then pulled open his right-hand drawer. A bottle of decent, single-malt scotch lay inside with two glass tumblers, but he didn't reach for them.

His thoughts wanted to focus on Leslie, on what he would do if she left, but instead they turned to Jessica. They'd had their own on-again, off-again relationship. The only difference was that they were never officially off. Jessica just never really had time for him. He hated that, but it was impossible to be angry. Jessica and her mentor, Dr. Andrea Kellin, spent most of their time working on a cure for Dr. Kellin's daughter, Linda. Linda had polio and spent her days in an iron lung at a sanatorium upstate.

"How am I supposed to compete with that?" he asked his empty office.

He shut the desk drawer and reached for the stack of folders.

Half an hour later, Alex set the folders aside and rubbed his eyes. Leslie was right, these were all good clients. He'd call most of them tomorrow and officially take their cases. The lost dog he'd try to do on his way home.

A wave of exhaustion washed over him and he rubbed his eyes with suddenly-trembling hands. Pushing back from the desk, he opened the center drawer and withdrew an engraved silver flask. Unscrewing the lid, he took a swig of the bitter liquid inside and forced it down.

"Yuck," he said, just as he had every time he'd had to drink Dr. Kellin's rejuvenator. It tasted awful, but it kept away the bouts of exhaustion and shaking. In recent months, they'd gotten more frequent. Alex hadn't told anyone, because there was nothing to be done and they'd only worry. He was dying and he knew it. He'd made peace with it.

Maybe it's a good thing Leslie is leaving, he thought.

Alex replaced the lid on the flask and shook it. There wasn't much of the rejuvenator left and it sloshed. Dr. Kellin had given him enough to last for two months. This batch had barely made it five weeks.

"Well at least that gives me an excuse to go see Jessica," he said, tucking the flask back into the drawer. His trembling had almost completely subsided, and his mind was able to focus again. Dr. Kellin might be a strange old bird, but she knew her alchemy.

The intercom on his desk buzzed and he pressed the talk button.

"Yes?"

"There's a Miss Karen Burnham here to see you about a missing person," Leslie's voice came through the little speaker.

Alex picked up the folders he'd been perusing, squared them, then dropped them back into the in-box.

"Send her in," he said.

A moment later his office door was opened rather hesitantly by a girl who couldn't have been more than twenty. She had long, straight, black hair that hung down past her shoulders and brown eyes in a pleasant, if unremarkable face. Her clothes were functional — a simple blouse and a knee length skirt with black flats. Despite the blandness of her appearance, Alex could tell that the clothes were of good quality, which meant the girl had money, she just felt no desire to show it.

"Mr. Lockerby?" she asked.

Alex wondered who else she thought he could be in his otherwise empty office, but he smiled and nodded in his most reassuring way.

"Won't you sit down, Miss Burnham," he invited, standing and indicating the comfortable, padded chair in front of his desk. "Why don't you tell me who's missing?"

She looked startled, but then seemed to remember that Leslie had told Alex the reason for her visit.

"It's my grandfather," she said. "He didn't come home last night, and I can't find him anywhere."

"He lives with you?"

The girl grinned and shrugged.

"Actually I live with him," she explained. "He lives in the west side mid-ring. I moved in with him to take an internship with Harrisons; they're an advertising agency."

Alex nodded; he'd heard of them and they were, by all accounts, a reputable firm.

"So your grandfather didn't return last night," Alex said. "Does he usually go out in the evenings?"

Karen looked embarrassed and shrugged.

"As far as I know he never goes anywhere," she said in a small voice. "He's usually tinkering in his workshop behind the house. Sometimes he loses track of time, but he always comes in for dinner. I cook for him."

"Did something disturb him recently? A letter maybe, or a phone call?"

Karen shook her head.

"He doesn't get mail or calls," she said.

"You said he spends time in his workshop," Alex said. "What does he do there?"

Again, Karen shrugged.

"He has lots of lab equipment," she said. "But I don't know what he's doing."

Alex raised an eyebrow at that. Lab equipment wasn't the kind of thing you expected to find in a backyard workshop.

"Is your grandfather an alchemist?

"No," Karen said. "He's an engineer. He used to work for Dow until a few months ago."

"Was he fired?"

"No, he retired. They threw a big party for him and his boss tried to convince him to stay. It was the only time the two of us ever went out." She started shaking and pulled an embroidered handkerchief from her handbag, pressing it to her eyes. "Please, Mr. Lockerby, I need to find him. Can you help me?"

Alex wanted to ask a few more questions. The more he got to know someone, the better chance his finding rune had to locate them, but it was clear Karen Burnham was barely holding herself together.

"I will," Alex said. "I have a finding rune that can locate your grandfather, assuming he's still in the city."

She looked up, wide-eyed at that, but Alex went on.

"I'll need something personal of his to help the rune find him. Something he treasured or something he used every day."

Karen reached inside her blouse and removed a silver wedding band on a chain.

"This belonged to my grandmother," she said, slipping the chain over her head and handing it to Alex.

He held it up and examined it closely. There wasn't a stone or any engraving, and the ring had clearly seen its share of wear.

"He gave this to you?" Alex asked.

She nodded.

"Years ago, when I was ten."

"How long ago did your grandmother die?"

"Before I was born."

Alex handed the ring back.

"Is something wrong?" Karen asked, fear in her voice.

"That ring has been out of your grandfather's possession for too long," he explained. "I need something with a more recent connection."

Karen looked at the ring in her hand with a distraught expression.

"Don't worry," Alex said, soothing. "I can still cast the rune for you once we get a better catalyst. I charge twenty-five dollars for the rune, and I'll knock off ten if it fails to find your grandfather — but that doesn't happen often," he added quickly. "Is that all right?"

After a moment, she nodded.

"How will I know what to bring you for the rune?" she asked. "I don't want to waste any more time."

Alex opened his left-hand drawer and pulled out a notepad and pencil, passing them to Karen.

"Put your address down there," he said. "I need to prepare a fresh finding rune, but that won't take too long. I'll meet you at your grandfather's house in an hour or so."

She scribbled down the address and passed the notebook back, then she stood, and Alex escorted her from the office.

"As soon as I'm done writing a few finding runes, I'm going over to the west side to cast one for Miss Burnham," he told Leslie as he headed back to his office. "Do me a favor and call Iggy; tell him I might be late for dinner."

3

THE DOCTOR IS OUT

The home of Leonard Burnham was a modest two-story domicile on a quiet street in the center of the West Side mid-ring. A walkway of pea gravel ran from the street to a small porch complete with a rocking chair. A coat of sturdy blue paint covered the exterior boards of the house, with the shutters and the trim painted white. All the paint appeared to be in good shape and well maintained. The grass had been recently cut and there weren't any weeds, but the shrubs showed signs of not having been trimmed in some time. Heavy curtains covered the windows, revealing nothing of the interior.

A gravel driveway led to an empty carport on the left side of the house, and Alex could see a tall, barn-like structure behind it. Alex started up the drive, but motion off to his left caught his eye. When he turned, a woman in a pink bathrobe and curlers ducked back, out of a neighboring window.

Nosy neighbor. Maybe she saw something.

"Mr. Lockerby," Karen Burnham's voice broke over him as he turned to investigate the neighbor. The gravel crunched as Karen ran across the drive to him and Alex abandoned his designs on the curler-wearing neighbor. "I was worried you wouldn't come."

"Nonsense," Alex said, setting down his investigator's kit and greeting her with a smile. He nodded toward the barn behind the house. "Is that where your grandfather spent his time?"

"His workshop," she said with a relieved nod. "I've been wracking my brain to think of something to use for your rune Mr. Lockerby," she went on, speaking so fast her words ran together.

"Call me Alex," he corrected her.

She blushed and pushed her hair away from her face, behind her left ear.

"Alex," she said, "I don't know what to use. Grandpa wasn't the kind of man who held on to things. Would his toothbrush work, or a comb?"

"They'll do in a pinch," Alex said. "But most people don't have any kind of special attachment to those kinds of things, even though they use them every day." He pointed toward the workshop. "If that's where your grandfather spent his time, we'll probably be able to find something useful there. Do you mind?"

"No." Karen shook her head, and started off toward the building.

The workshop wasn't as tall as the house, but it was bigger than a simple shed, with a peaked roof and several large windows that appeared to have been papered over with newsprint. A large carriage door stood slightly ajar in the middle of the building and it was at least ten feet high. It reminded Alex of a boathouse, except they weren't anywhere near the river.

Like the front yard, the back lawn had been cut and the entire area from the back patio to the privacy fence that ran around the property looked well kept.

Karen reached for the wrought iron handle of the carriage door, but Alex waved her off.

"Allow me," he said. His gesture was only partly chivalrous. If Karen's grandfather hadn't gone missing of his own volition, there might be evidence inside.

The door opened, rolling aside on a well-oiled mechanism. The room beyond was a stark contrast to the house and the lawn. It was chaos. Tools, papers, and bits of metal and wood littered the ground and covered every other horizontal surface.

Two workbenches lined the back wall, each covered with debris, and a separate table stood on the right side of the space. This table was relatively free of random equipment, mostly because it held what looked like an alchemy lab. A complex network of glass beakers, rubber tubes, and gas burners were strung together in an impressive-looking apparatus that gave no clue what it might be used for. A metal sink stood behind the table, along with rows of metal shelves, stuffed to overflowing with all manner of mechanical parts.

A space large enough for a car was mostly empty on the left side of the workspace, and a series of pictures and awards hung on the wall.

Alex whistled, stepping carefully as he made his way into the room. The workshop was one giant contradiction. The lab setup looked like something Jessica and Dr. Kellin would use, but the tools that littered the workbenches and the floor were the kind an automotive mechanic might own.

He bent and picked up one of the discarded papers. It was dirty and there was a clear shoe mark on it where it had been stepped on. Complex formulas covered the paper on both sides, but they'd been viciously crossed out. Since the math made no sense to Alex, he dropped the paper back on the floor and made his way toward the lab. Before he could arrive, however, he noticed that a broken jar lay on the ground by the workbench and there were drops of dried blood on the table and the ground.

"Stop," he said, holding out his hand in warning.

Behind him, Karen froze.

"I think maybe your grandfather didn't leave of his own free will."

"It's not like that," Karen said, dismissing Alex's concerns. "Grandpa's workshop always looks this way. He's very neat and tidy, except when he's working."

"Okay," Alex said, trying to reconcile the pristine yard and the workshop that looked like it had been hit by a hurricane. "Still, there's some broken glass over there and what looks like blood."

"Grandpa got excited by something he was working on last week," Karen explained. "He dropped a jar and cut the palm of his hand. I had to help bandage it."

The Long Chain

"Okay," Alex said, shaking his head. "Did your grandfather go out last night or did he disappear from here?"

"I..." Karen began but then she hesitated. "I honestly don't know. When I got home from work, I went up to my room and changed, then I made dinner. I didn't think to check on grandfather until after that."

So, he might have gone out and gotten lost, or someone might have come in and taken him.

"Is there something in here you can use to find him?" Karen asked.

Alex looked around. Most of what was in the room were utilitarian objects. Sure, Karen's grandfather used them all the time, but they held no special sentimentality. He walked over to the paper-covered workbenches. All of the papers held complex math and strange drawings; it reminded Alex of hieroglyphics and made about as much sense to him. A battered and ink-stained slide rule lay across some of the papers, and Alex picked it up. Clearly Leonard Burnham had used it often, but still, it was just a tool. What Alex needed was something special.

Setting down the slide rule, Alex turned his attention to the array of photographs and documents along the left wall. Most of the pictures were of a sturdy-looking man with brown hair and a thin mustache, who Alex took to be Leonard Burnham, in various locations. Several showed him in Europe during the Great War, but he was always in civilian clothes, never military. In many of the older pictures, a blonde woman accompanied him. She had thick glasses, freckles on her nose, and a vivacious smile that lit up her face.

"That's my grandma," Karen said, coming to stand just behind him. "They met at Vanderbilt University."

"That's where he did his undergrad work," Alex said with a nod.

"How did you know that?" Karen asked.

Alex pointed back at the beginning of the wall where several certificates hung.

"That's his diploma," Alex said. "A Bachelors Degree in Mechanical Engineering."

"I told you he was an engineer," Karen said, her voice growing impatient.

"But you didn't tell me he was a doctor."

When she didn't answer, Alex turned to find Karen looking at him quizzically.

"He also got a PhD in Chemistry from Harvard," Alex explained, pointing to a second mounted diploma.

"Oh," Karen said, her cheeks pinking. "That kind of doctor."

"He sounds like quite a guy, your grandfather," Alex said, turning back to the pictures. "Here's four awards from Dow for his work there and..." Alex leaned close to read the fine print on an official looking citation. "This one is from the Army. It says he developed a new process for making gas mask filters during the war."

"I...I didn't know that." Karen said in a small voice. "Grandpa doesn't talk much about his work."

"You should ask him about it," Alex said, pulling a heavy frame off the wall. He turned it so Karen could see the official certificate encased inside. Next to it was a gold medal on a crimson ribbon. "This is the Nobel Prize for Chemistry. That's impressive, all by itself." Alex looked around at the disheveled workshop. "I don't know what your grandfather was doing in here, but I bet it was something amazing."

Karen just stared at the award. She might be living in her grandfather's house, but it was obvious she didn't really know the man.

"Please," she said, looking up into Alex's eyes. "We have to find him."

Alex pushed past her, carrying the mounted Nobel Prize with him to the cleanest of the workbenches.

"And we will," he said, setting the award aside and beginning to clear a space. "I should have noticed right off, but his Nobel Prize was hung right in the center of the wall. Clearly it was important to him."

"So you can use it to find him?" Karen asked, her voice full of hope.

Alex nodded and kept removing tools and papers from the workbench. When he had a large area cleared, he retrieved his kit and opened the battered valise. From inside he withdrew his rolled-up map of Manhattan, his brass compass, and a worn cigar box.

Setting the valise aside, he unrolled the map, then took four dark-green figurines from the cigar box. They looked like chess pieces, though each had the head of an animal. These Alex placed on the corners of the map to weigh it down and prevent it from rolling up while he cast the rune. Adding his compass to the center of the map, Alex then laid the framed Nobel Prize carefully on top.

With everything in readiness, he took out his red-backed rune book and turned to where he'd added the finding runes. The book was really just two covers that were held together by a spring clip in the spine. New pages could be easily added by removing the clip and pressing the pages over two metal posts that would keep them from falling out once the clip was replaced.

Taking hold of one of the delicate sheets of flash paper, Alex gently tore it free from the book, then snapped the book closed and set it aside. He folded the paper into quarters, then laid it on top of the glass that framed the award.

"All right," he said, taking his brass spring lighter from his trouser pocket. He flicked it to life and then touched the flame to the flash paper. It erupted in a flash of fire that left a slight scorch mark on the glass of the award and an orange rune hovering in the air above it. Alex couldn't see it, but he knew that the compass needle underneath the frame was spinning around. Gradually the hovering rune began to spin as well until a moment later it pulsed and vanished.

"Is that it?" Karen said, her voice barely a whisper. "Did it work?"

Alex lifted the Nobel award off the compass and set it aside. The compass beneath was trembling but fixed, pointing in a direction that was not north. He looked up into Karen's anxious face and nodded.

"Watch," he said, then he began to slide the compass along the map. As he moved it, the needle moved as well. He moved the compass in the direction the needle pointed until suddenly it flipped around, pointing back the other way.

"What happened?" Karen gasped.

Alex pulled the compass back and began circling an area of the map. As he did, the needle turned as well, pointing in toward the center of the circle.

"That's it," Alex said. "Your grandfather is there."

Karen let out a pent-up breath that came out as a gasp of relief and a nervous laugh.

"Is he okay?"

"I can't say," Alex cautioned. "But that's near the stockyards and the docks. It's a rough area after dark."

Alex picked up the compass, breaking its link with the map. As he did so, the needle swung around, pointing south.

"Do you have a car?" he asked.

Karen shook her head. Her breathing was coming quickly, and her face was pale.

"Take a deep breath," Alex told her, putting a reassuring hand on her arm. "The compass will take us right to your grandfather, but I need you to stay calm. Go inside and call for a taxi while I pack up my stuff. I'll meet you out front in a few minutes."

"Okay," she said, taking a moment to breathe.

Alex released her arm and Karen hurried from the workshop. Slipping the compass into his jacket pocket, Alex replaced the jade figurines into the cigar box, rolled up the map, and returned them to his kit. Last of all, he pulled out his handkerchief and wiped the soot mark from the front of Dr. Burnham's award.

He glanced around at the chaos that enveloped the workroom as he hung the Nobel Prize medal back in its place. He wondered that even a man as obviously talented as Karen's grandfather could get any work done in such a mess. When Alex was young, he never really had much in the way of possessions, and Iggy had impressed on him the need to keep his workspace clean and orderly, the results of his medical mind.

Alex picked up his kit and headed for the door. Before he left, however, he looked back at the workshop. Something about it bothered him, something beyond its state of disarray, but in all the chaos, he just couldn't put his finger on it.

Shrugging, he turned and shut the carriage door. With any luck Karen would have her grandfather back soon and Alex could ask him about the workshop then.

The corner nearest to where the map had said Dr. Leonard Burnham could be found was occupied by a lumber yard. Or at least it had been the last time Alex was in this part of town. Now the old yard was gone and a plain, three-story brick building had been erected in its place. Several ragged people were loitering about on the sidewalk, but no one attempted to shoo them away. The sign over the door read, *Brotherhood of Hope*, and the compass was pointing right at it.

Alex felt his jaw tighten as he read the sign. The Brotherhood of Hope had been the name of Father Clementine's mission, where he fed the poor and destitute. It had been disbanded two years ago in the wake of the father's death. The bishop of the local diocese had thought it a waste of Church funds.

"This way," he said to Karen, shoving two dollars at the cabbie as he jumped out.

"What is this place?" she asked as they approached the building.

"It's a Catholic mission," Alex explained, forcing his anger down. "A soup kitchen for the poor."

"Why would my grandfather be here?"

Alex just shrugged.

"Maybe he knows someone here."

He led her through the front doors and into a large lobby. Alex could smell the aroma of cooking wafting in from a pair of double doors to the left. Visions of his own youth with Father Clementine sprang, unbidden, to his mind, stoking his anger. If the church wanted to keep using the name of Father Clementine's mission, they should have left it where it was.

A middle-aged nun in a pressed wimple sat at a desk against the far wall. She smiled when they walked in, but her look faltered when she got a good look at Alex and Karen. Clearly they were not here in search of charity.

"May I help you?" she asked.

"Yes," Alex said, putting on a smile. "We got a report that this young lady's grandfather was here."

The nun's severe look softened as she looked at Karen, but it hardened right back up again when her gaze returned to Alex.

"What's his name?"

"Leonard Burnham," Karen supplied.

The nun consulted a clipboard for a long moment, then shook her head.

"I'm sorry, but we don't have anyone by that name here right now."

"He's a bit eccentric," Alex said. "He might have given a different name." He pointed toward the double doors. "We'd like to take a look, just to be sure."

The nun appraised him stoically. It was clear she wanted to send him packing, but the look of hope and dread on Karen's face was obviously giving her pause.

"Just a moment," she said, rising from her seat. "I'll call Brother Williams to escort you."

She turned and walked through a door behind her desk.

"Why would my grandfather give a false name?" Karen hissed at him.

"I don't know," Alex said, pulling the compass from his pocket and holding it out so that she could see it. "But according to my finding rune, he's in there. No doubt about it."

The nun returned with a paunchy man in a black cassock. He wore a simple wooden cross on a cord around his neck and his face was open and friendly.

"I hear you're looking for someone among our parishioners," he said.

Brother Williams might look friendly, but Alex recognized his choice of words. He'd said parishioners, not patrons. If Alex and Karen were police or process servers, Brother Williams would claim sanctuary for whomever they were seeking. Many of the city's forgotten people were wanted by the police, usually for stealing food or other necessities, and if the Mission were seen as helping the authorities, those people wouldn't come. Their goal was to feed the less fortunate, not to take sides.

"This is Karen Burnham," Alex said. "Her grandfather went missing yesterday and she hired me to help find him."

"And you are?"

Alex pulled one of his business cards out of his jacket pocket and passed it over.

"Alex Lockerby," he said. "I'm a private detective."

"Lockerby?" Brother Williams said, his brow suddenly furrowing. "Not Father Clementine's ward?"

Alex grinned at that despite his irritation.

"Guilty," he said.

"I'm so sorry about his loss," Williams said, clearly meaning it. "They don't make many men like that."

Brother Williams handed Alex back his card and motioned them toward the dining hall.

"Let's see if we can find your missing man," he said. "Then maybe you'd like me to show you around the new Brotherhood of Hope."

"How about that?" Alex said, fighting to keep his voice calm. "What's the idea of using that name?"

Williams looked stricken for a moment, but that quickly shifted to concern.

"We meant it to honor Father Clementine," he said, pushing open the double doors.

The room beyond was twice the size of the dining hall at the old mission, and that one had been in an old skating rink. Rows and rows of tables were laid out with benches and chairs where more than a hundred ragged men and women were eating. Along the far wall were counters where nuns dished out food.

"Grandfather!" Karen shrieked, and took off running.

Alex recognized Dr. Burnham before she reached him. He was thinner and grayer than he had been in the photographs on the workshop wall, but that was all. Alex started to step forward, but Brother Williams grabbed his arm.

"I was afraid he might be the one you were looking for," he said in a low voice.

Alex looked at Dr. Burnham as Karen stood, talking eagerly to him. Nothing registered in his face; it was as if he was looking at a stranger.

"What's wrong with him?" Alex asked.

"One of the local policemen found him wandering the streets last night," Williams said. "He was confused but didn't seem to be in any danger, so they brought him here. He doesn't remember who he is."

4

EXAMINATIONS

An hour later, Alex helped Dr. Burnham out of a taxi and across the gravel walk to his front door. For a man in his seventies, he seemed strong enough, but he walked with an unsteady wobble that required him to hold on to Alex's arm for balance. There was a dark purple bruise on his cheek, cuts on the backs of his hands, and his clothes were stained and dirty.

"I'll get the door," Karen said, running ahead of them. She produced a key and let them in, switching the light on as Alex and her grandfather came through.

"Home," Dr. Burnham said in a dazed voice. He hadn't spoken much since they found him, and so far there was no sign the he recognized Karen at all. Alex took his declaration that this place was home as a good sign.

"His bedroom is up the stairs on the left," Karen said, heading for the kitchen.

"Where's that doctor you called?" Alex asked, guiding his charge toward the stairs.

"Right here," a new voice came from the door.

Alex turned to find a middle-aged man with slicked back hair and a jowly face standing in the doorway. He wore a tweed suit and carried a black medical bag in the same style as Alex's crime scene kit.

"Dr. Higgins," Karen exclaimed, relief filling her voice. "Come in."

Higgins hadn't waited for an invitation. He was already stepping around Alex to get a look at Leonard Burnham.

"Leo?" he questioned, when Burnham didn't react to him. "Can you hear me?"

Leonard nodded, then turned to Alex.

"Is this a friend of yours?" Leonard said.

Dr. Higgins looked at Karen.

"Does he remember anything?"

All Karen could do was shrug.

"I think he knows this is his home," Alex supplied. "He seems dazed."

"Leonard," Higgins said in a loud, clear voice. "I'm a doctor and I need to have a look at you."

He held up a finger and had Burnham look at it while he moved it around, then asked Burnham a series of random questions. When he was satisfied, he looked at Alex.

"Go ahead and take him upstairs," he said. "Have him lie down. I'll be up in a minute."

Alex did as he was told while Higgins talked with Karen. A few minutes later he came up and Alex was banished back downstairs.

"What did he say?" Alex asked when he got back to the front room. Karen was pacing around like a tiger in a cage, biting the fingernail on her right ring finger.

She shook her head and kept pacing.

"I'm sure he'll be fine," Alex said, not out of any genuine intuition but rather from a desire to be encouraging.

"Oh," Karen said, looking up at him. "I'm sorry. I need to pay you." She went back into the kitchen and came back with her handbag. "In all the excitement, I forgot." Withdrawing a leather wallet from her bag, she counted out a few fives and some ones, then handed the stack over. "Twenty-five, you said?"

Alex nodded and accepted the money.

"Thank you for finding him," Karen said, her voice wavering.

Alex could tell she was on the edge of hysterics. He put a hand on her shoulder, causing her to look up at him.

"Why don't you sit down," he said, leading her to the sofa. "The doc will be a few minutes."

Karen looked as if she wanted to protest, but sat in spite of it. Alex sat down on the far side of the couch and offered her a cigarette. By the time the doc came down the stairs, Karen had smoked three to Alex's one. She practically leapt up when Higgins reached the parlor.

"How is he?" she demanded.

"He has a concussion," Higgins said.

"How did that happen?"

Higgins shrugged.

"There's a pretty nasty bump on the back of his head. If I had to guess, I'd say he fell and hit it."

"What about that bruise on his face?" Alex asked. "That looks like he was in a fight."

Higgins looked Alex up and down with an expression of obvious disdain.

"Leonard Burnham is a man of quality," the doctor said in an indignant voice. "Men of quality do not go around getting into fights."

"No," Alex admitted. "But sometimes a fight shows up anyway."

"Are you questioning my medical opinion?" He turned to Karen. "Is this a friend of yours?"

"I'm a private detective," Alex said, stepping close to Higgins so he could glower down at the shorter man. "Miss Burnham hired me to find her missing grandfather, which I did."

"And now that your job's done," Higgins fired back, "I'd say it's time you were on your way."

"Don't worry," Alex said, leaning down to pick up his hat from the coffee table. "I'll go, just as soon as I'm sure Miss Burnham and her grandfather are out of danger."

Karen, who had looked uncomfortable during the whole conversation, went white.

"What do you mean, out of danger?"

"Your grandfather has cuts on his hands and bruises on his knuckles," Alex said, turning to her. "The technical term for that is 'defensive

The Long Chain

wounds.' It means he used his fists in a fight." Higgins opened his mouth, doubtless to reiterate the absurdity of Leonard Burnham being in a fight, but Alex kept going right over him. "The most likely explanation for that is that he was out somewhere and got jumped. But he wasn't dressed up, he's wearing old work clothes. No thug looking for cash is going to jump somebody dressed like that, which leaves only two options." Alex held up his hand and ticked off his index finger. "One, he ran afoul of someone truly desperate, and since he still has his belt and his shoes, we know it isn't that one." He ticked off a second finger. "Or two, someone attacked him who knew he had money."

"What makes you think my grandfather has money?" Karen demanded. She wanted to appear angry, maybe outraged, but her voice broke when she said it, betraying her fear.

Alex fixed her with a steady look.

"This house is immaculate," he said. "The lawn is cut, the porch is swept, there's no peeling paint." He waved around at the parlor. "There's no dust anywhere and this floor has been swept. The only space that's not tidy is the one place your grandfather probably wouldn't allow anyone but himself. He's a slob, you have a demanding internship, and yet the rest of the property is well cared for. Clearly, he pays people to do that. Then there's you," Alex said. "Your internship probably pays less than being a waitress, and yet you didn't balk at paying my fee, and you aren't worried about what Dr. Harris here will charge you. Clearly your grandfather has money. The question is, who knew about it and how much did he usually carry?"

"This is preposterous," Higgins scoffed. "No one is stalking Leonard. He doesn't go around with wads of cash in his pockets. It's far more likely that Leo bumped into something in his workshop and then fell down."

"I'm sure the doctor is right," Karen said, taking a deep breath to calm herself. "I'm glad you're looking out for us, Alex, but we'll be fine, really."

Alex held her gaze for a moment, then shrugged and put on his hat.

"Do you think Dr. Burnham will regain his memory?" Alex asked Higgins.

"It's impossible to say," he replied, then turned to Karen. "But with rest and good care, I'm hopeful."

Alex withdrew one of his business cards from his jacket pocket and passed it to Karen.

"Glad I could help, Miss Burnham," he said. "If you feel you need me for anything else, don't hesitate to call."

She thanked him; Alex wished her good night and stepped out into the fog and the darkness.

By the time Alex climbed the steps to the brownstone belonging to his mentor and landlord, Dr. Ignatius Bell, it was well after seven in the evening. Normally a trip from the West Side to the brownstone would only have taken half an hour but with the fog thickening toward the pea-soup variety, it took him forever to find a cab. Then, of course, the cabbie had to go slowly to avoid hitting other cars. The trip had taken over an hour.

Alex sighed as he pulled out the brass pocket watch in his vest that served as his key to the building. Fog and slow cab rides were just two of the many parts of his life that were well beyond his control. He pushed the watch's crown and the lid popped open. Inside the watch, a complex series of runes activated, pushing at the protection runes that kept the brownstone safe.

Reaching out, Alex opened the door and stepped inside. As he did so, he snapped the watch closed, reenabling the protection runes and sealing the front door. He passed through the vestibule and into the house proper, hanging his gray fedora on a peg along the wall by the stairs.

"Well, here you are," Dr. Bell said as Alex stepped into the library. The library was in the front of the house and consisted of a room filled with tall bookshelves on either side of an impressive stone hearth. The fireplace held a grate for burning coal, but with the warm weather, it was covered by an ornate brass screen that resembled a peacock. Two comfortable, wing-backed chairs stood opposite the fireplace, separated by a tall end-table. A Tiffany lamp cast a good light for reading down below its shade and dappled, multi-colored light above.

In the far chair, book and cigar in hand, sat Dr. Ignatius Bell, late of His Majesty's Navy. He was a somewhat grizzled man in his seventies with deep set eyes and a bottle-brush mustache. His real name, of course, was Arthur Conan Ignatius Doyle, creator of the world's most famous fictional detective, but only Alex knew that. The thought made Alex glance up at the bookshelf to the left of the hearth, at the thin red book on one of the upper shelves. It was the Archimedean Monograph, the most sought-after book of rune lore in the business. It was also what forced Iggy to flee his home and family and change his name. Powerful and dangerous people wanted that book. Governments wanted it, and here it sat, on a shelf in Iggy's library, hiding in plain sight.

"You seem melancholy," Iggy said, shutting the dime novel he'd been reading. Pulp mysteries were a passion of his...for obvious reasons. "No luck with the girl and her missing relative?"

"Not at all," Alex said, dropping down into the second chair, glad that Leslie had remembered to update Iggy. "I found him, but he'd been in some kind of scrape and got hit on the head. When I left, he still didn't remember anything, not even his name."

"Well, that's not good," Iggy said. "Head wounds can be tricky. He might be okay with a couple days' rest."

"That's what his doctor said," Alex confirmed.

"Then what's the problem?"

Alex shook his head and sat back in the chair.

"Something about it bothers me," he said. "Not sure what." He stood and walked over to the hearth, looking down at the screen. "It's probably just the fog; it's got me on edge."

"Well, you know I always tell you to trust your instincts," Iggy said. "What's bothering you? What do you think?"

"Doesn't matter what I think," Alex said with a chuckle. "The girl got her grandfather back, I got paid, and that's the end of it."

Iggy sighed and puffed on his cigar.

"I suppose it is," he said. "Did you see the paper?"

"The war between China and Japan is heating up," Alex said. This was one of Iggy's favorite games. When he'd first trained Alex to be a detective, he'd stressed the importance of remaining up on what was going on in the world. The most random or innocuous bit of data might be relevant in the right context. To train Alex to observe and remember, Iggy went through the day's paper and would quiz Alex on what he found. Over the years it had grown into a game where each of them tried to find something so obscure the other would have missed it. Lately neither one of them could trip up the other.

Iggy made a sound of agreement.

"The Japanese are butchering them, if the reports are true. Roosevelt even recalled our ambassador to the Emperor."

Alex had seen that, but hadn't really paid too much attention.

"David Hendricks," Alex said.

"Henderson," Iggy corrected.

"Skinny guy with glasses and a pencil mustache," Alex supplied, remembering the photograph that accompanied the article. "What about Edison Electric?" Alex asked, changing the subject. "Do you think they'll be able to stop Barton from putting up his power relay tower in Brooklyn?"

"No," Iggy chuckled. "Barton's got too much money and too much pull. That lawsuit is the best Edison can do, but it will keep Barton wrapped up in court for a year or two."

"Too bad for Brooklyn," Alex said. He returned to his chair and wearily sat back down. It had been hours since he'd had a swig of the rejuvenation elixir and he could feel the exhaustion building.

"Yes," Iggy agreed, puffing on his cigar. "Once Barton's towers go up, everything will change. Speaking of change, what do you think about this weather?"

"It's making my cabs run slow."

"And?"

Alex turned to Iggy and found the doctor looking at him expectantly.

"And what? It's just fog, we've had fog before."

"Except the weather reports in the paper called for clear weather."

Alex laughed at that.

"So? When is it news that the weather report is wrong? If the weatherman at the *Times* was a baseball player, he'd be traded to the Braves."

"It's news because the experts can't explain it," Iggy said.

Alex looked back at his mentor with a skeptical expression.

"Are these the same 'experts' who predicted a cool summer?"

"Point taken," Iggy said, opening his pulp novel. "You look tired. I left you a sandwich in the icebox."

"Thanks," Alex said, pushing himself out of the chair. "But I think I'll just turn in."

"Eat something first," Iggy said, his nose now stuck in his book.

Alex didn't argue. Iggy was right, he needed to keep up his strength. He made his way to the kitchen and found the sandwich Iggy had made him, roast beef with mustard on rye bread. Iggy had cut it into halves and left it on a plate. Alex took one of the halves and went upstairs.

His room, like his office, was on the third floor. It was a simple affair with a bathroom, closet, desk, bed and reading chair. Alex hung up his clothes, then went into the bathroom to splash some water on his face. He felt tired, exhausted really, but he wasn't prepared for the face that looked out at him from the mirror.

"I look like a damn raccoon," he muttered, noting the dark circles under his eyes.

He finished washing his face, then went to his chair and sat, ignoring his sandwich. He poured himself a shot from the bottle on the table. In the past, that had been cheap bourbon, but these days it was decent whiskey. He took a sip, savoring the taste, then set the glass aside.

His mind drifted back over the events of the day. Try as he might, however, he couldn't focus. It was as if the fog outside had permeated his brain. He resolved to stay up for a while, eat some of his sandwich and think about Karen and her grandfather. Maybe he could figure out what it was that bothered him about that whole affair. As he sat, trying to will himself to think, however, his eyes slid closed and all thought of cases, clients, roast beef, and whiskey vanished from his mind.

5

ALCHEMICAL MATTERS

Alex arrived at his office half an hour early the next morning. The life energy he'd sacrificed saving the city two years ago caused him to be tired almost all the time, but ironically, he still couldn't sleep very long. Thank heaven Iggy, on his way to bed, had come by to check on him and seen to it that Alex had gotten into bed, himself; he'd be feeling a lot worse if he'd slept the whole time, slumped in that chair. As it was, his shoulders and back were tight and stiff.

"At least you're still on this side of the dirt," he muttered as he let himself into the waiting room with his key.

He went into his office and picked up the stack of client folders from his in-box, then went out to Leslie's desk and sat down. Since she had gone to see Randall out in Suffolk County, Alex would have to cover the front office. He didn't mind, but he recognized that as good a detective as he was, he was no Leslie — that required different skills. Still, he managed to put on a pot of coffee and log the money Karen had paid him into the cash box before he started making calls.

Alex started with the lost dog, and to his utter disappointment, the wayward pooch had been found and returned to the owner. He continued that way, calling through the stack of clients, taking down their particulars and advising them on how he could help. When he set the last folder aside and sat back, the clock on the wall showed it to be almost noon. The time had passed quickly, but now that he had stopped, Alex felt the ever-present weariness washing over him.

Standing, Alex retrieved the flask of rejuvenator from his office. A quick swig replenished him, and the nearly empty flask reminded him that he'd need to go see Jessica for more. That thought made him smile.

Since it was lunch time and he was done with his calls, Alex decided to go across the street to the five and dime and get a sandwich. He had just put on his jacket when the office door opened, and Dr. Andrea Kellin walked in. She was an older woman, in her sixties if Alex had to guess, with a rather severe face and gray hair that she kept twisted behind her head in a bun. She wore a cream-colored jacket over a blue blouse that exactly matched the color of her eyes, along with a dark skirt. Her face was stoic, but that was usual for her; what was not usual was the hollow look of her cheeks and her bloodshot eyes. Clearly the push to perfect her daughter's cure was taking its toll.

"Hello, Alex," she said, shutting the door behind her.

Alex looked at her, somewhat confused. Except for the time Iggy brought her to the office, Alex had never seen her outside of her own shop, north of Central Park.

"Hi-ya, Doc," Alex said with a grin. "What brings you out my way?"

"Do you have a few minutes?" she asked, not returning his smile.

Alex took off his hat and put it back on the stand beside the door, then motioned toward his office.

"Always for you, Doc," he said.

"I've been wrestling with myself all the way over to see you," Dr. Kellin said, once she'd sat down in front of Alex's desk. "I'm not sure what I should do."

Alex sat down at his desk and pulled out his note pad.

"What's the problem?"

"I have a friend," Kellin began. "His name is Charles Grier and he's an alchemist, one of the best in the business. I've known him for years."

She paused for a moment and Alex let her gather her thoughts. He noted that she didn't introduce her friend as a doctor. Many alchemists got a medical degree, like Dr. Kellin, but it wasn't a requirement.

"I...I've been working hard on my polio formula and I need a certain catalyzer. It's very difficult to make and I usually get it from Charles, because he's one of the few alchemists who stocks it. I've been by his shop three times in the last week, but it's been closed. That's very unlike Charles. I'm worried something has happened to him."

"Have you called his home?" Alex asked. "Maybe family or friends?"

Dr. Kellin shook her head.

"I don't know where he lives," she admitted. "And he doesn't have any family that I know of. If you could just make sure he's okay, I'd rest easier."

Alex gave her his warmest smile and nodded. He owed Dr. Kellin a lot. She made the rejuvenation potion for him, something he understood was quite expensive to make. She did it as part of a trade agreement with Iggy, where he put runes on some of her equipment to make it more efficient, but Alex suspected the rejuvenator cost more than any benefit she got from Iggy's runes.

"Of course I will, Doc," he said, handing her his notebook. "Just put down the address of Mr. Grier's shop and I'll see what I can find."

She took the notebook with a grateful smile.

"Thank you," she said.

Alex checked the address as she handed the notepad back; it was down on the South Side mid-ring, past the core.

"I've got to grab something to eat," he said. "But I'll go take a look right after that. I'll call you as soon as I know anything."

Dr. Kellin nodded and rose. She started to turn but stopped and looked back, casting an appraising eye over him.

"How is your rejuvenation elixir holding up?"

Alex chuckled. Not much got past Dr. Kellin. He opened the middle drawer of his desk and pulled out the silver flask.

"I am running a bit low," he said, shaking it.

Dr. Kellin took the flask, weighing it in her hand.

"That should have lasted longer," she observed. "I'll make up some more, but it will take a few days. Come by the house once this is empty," she said, handing the flask back. "I know Jessica would love to see you."

Alex returned the flask to the drawer and closed it.

"Say hi for me," he said, then walked Dr. Kellin out.

The address Dr. Kellin gave him led Alex to a row of neat shops on a fairly busy street. Nestled between an upscale haberdasher and a millinery shop, he found Grier's shop, *The Philosopher's Stone*. As Doc had said, the closed sign was in the window, and the front door was locked.

Peering through the window, Alex saw an orderly-looking shop with shelves lining the back wall behind a long counter. A display case along the side wall held bins full of colored powders, along with pre-packaged tins. Nothing looked out of place or unusual.

Undaunted, Alex visited the neighboring shop. Mr. Kensington, who ran the haberdasher, had noticed that Grier's shop had been closed, but knew nothing about the man or his habits. The millinery shop was owned by Mrs. Osbourne, a plump woman of middle years with an affable disposition. She told Alex about Charles Grier in great detail, including his habits and how he only closed his shop if he were ill or out of town.

"Did he go out of town regularly?" Alex asked.

"No," Mrs. Osbourne answered. "He went to Europe last year to speak at an alchemy conference, and the year before that, he was looking for some rare mineral in South America. Something to do with a potion he'd been working on."

"So is it possible Mr. Grier went on one of his trips?"

"Oh, no," Mrs. Osbourne said, shaking her head emphatically. "He always puts up a notice in his window the week before he leaves, explaining how long he'll be gone."

"Does Grier have an assistant or someone that helps him out around the shop?"

"Not that I know of."

Mrs. Osbourne looked like she was going to continue when the bell over her door rang and two ladies came in.

"I must be going," she said with a warm smile.

Alex thanked her and returned to the street. He didn't know much more than he had before, but he was convinced that Dr. Kellin had been right to be worried. Neither of Grier's neighbors knew where he might be or where he lived, so Alex would have to take more drastic measures to find him.

Walking down to the end of the block, Alex turned the corner and made his way along the alley behind the shops until he reached Grier's. *The Philosopher's Stone* had a single door set into the brick wall with no windows or other means of entry.

"Why is nothing ever simple?" he asked, glancing up and down the alley. With the fog still thick in the city, he was relatively sure no one could see him.

Pulling a piece of chalk from his pocket, Alex drew a doorway on the plain wall that made up the back of *The Philosopher's Stone*. Pulling a vault rune from his red book, he stuck it to the wall, inside the chalk outline, and lit it with his cigarette lighter. A moment later, a heavy steel door appeared inside the chalk outline. Alex fished a large brass key from his pocket and inserted it into the keyhole in the center of the door, then pulled it open.

Rather than going through to the shop beyond the wall, this door led to Alex's vault, an extra-dimensional workspace all his own. He entered quickly, moving to a secretary cabinet just inside the door and opening the top part. Inside were several leather doctor's valises, but he chose the battered one on the right. This was his kit, the bag that held his investigative tools for examining crime scenes. It also held the ornate pencil box where he kept the various rune writing pens and pencils he might need in the field.

Stepping back outside, Alex closed the steel door and let it vanish back into the brick wall from whence it had come. Setting the kit bag down, he pulled out the pencil case and, after turning it upside down, pushed the flat bottom sideways to reveal a hidden space. Inside were his lock picks, and he selected two before setting the pencil case down and turning to the back door of Grier's shop.

It took Alex almost two minutes to get the lock open. Iggy would have been appalled by such a showing. Clearly he needed to practice more.

Returning his tools and the pencil box to his kit, Alex took one more look up and down the alley, then opened the door and quickly stepped inside. Fortunately the lock didn't have a keyhole on the back, just a mechanical knob, so Alex gave it a twist once he had the door shut.

It was still early afternoon, but the interior of *The Philosopher's Stone* was dark nonetheless. With the fog outside, and the magelights turned off, the shop had an almost ghostly quality to it. Rather than turning the lights on, Alex waited for his eyes to adjust before moving.

When at last he could see, Alex found the shop just as orderly and neat as he had seen it from outside. Nothing seemed out of place and even the floor had been swept. A thick apron hung on a peg by the door that connected the back room to the storefront and the waste baskets were all empty.

Clearly whatever had happened to Charles Grier, it hadn't happened here. It looked to Alex like he tidied and cleaned the shop before heading home...and just never came back.

Alex thought about using the apron to cast a finding rune, but it looked relatively new. He'd need something with a definite connection to Grier, something he would be much more likely to find in the man's home.

As he inspected the room, something bothered Alex.

"Where is he brewing his potions?" he asked aloud.

A quick check of the back room revealed a sturdy door that must lead down to a basement. Remembering Jessica and the booby-trapped door to Dr. Kellin's lab, Alex turned the knob with the tips of his fingers until the door popped open. An acrid, chemical odor assaulted him and Alex gagged, stepping back.

Retreating to his kit, Alex opened it and pulled out a small gas mask from under the left lid. Fixing it firmly over his face, he returned to the door and found a stairwell leading down into blackness. Even with the mask on, Alex could taste a chemical tang in the air.

Moving carefully, he descended the stairs, turning the corner at the bottom. The room below the store was laid out almost exactly like the one at Dr. Kellin's house, with rows of tables containing impressive arrays of glasswork. Beakers and jars were hooked up to distillers, evaporators, and condensers, each with multiple inputs for chemicals and solutions to be added. Several of the tables had burners on them that were still lit, but the jars above them were empty. Clearly these potions hadn't been attended in several days and whatever they'd been heating had boiled away.

Alex moved through the room, checking under the benches and turning off burners. Other than the neglected burners, there was no sign that anything was amiss. Nothing had been disturbed or knocked over. At the back of the room there was a vent pipe with an electric fan to push air. Alex turned it on and, after a few minutes, the fumes in the basement lab dissipated.

Pulling off his mask, Alex went over the lab again, looking for anything that might be out of place. He was tempted to go get his oculus and multi-lamp, but the lab would be full of the residue of hundreds of chemicals. He would be lucky to find anything among all that.

Shutting off the vent fan, Alex went back upstairs to the little office in the back room. It was just a desk, a filing cabinet, and a worn chair. On the back wall were pictures of a tall, slightly plump man Alex took to be Charles Grier, standing with various groups of smiling people. Each picture was labeled with a place and a date, and Alex saw images of Grier in France, Brazil, the Congo, Nepal, and even Japan. Souvenirs of his travels hung beneath each picture, ranging from a carved lion head to a beautiful watercolor painting. The most interesting to Alex was a big, wicked-looking, bent dagger in a glass-covered frame. According to the label, it was a kukri knife he'd received from someone named Gurkha, in Nepal in 1922.

Alex turned back to the desk, switched on the lamp, and sat down. A stack of thin, leather-bound accounting books sat neatly on the back edge of the desk. Picking up the one on top, Alex turned to the first page and read a neat list of materials ordered, amounts paid, and to whom. Two hours later he set the last book aside and rubbed his eyes. According to the books, Grier had enough orders for rare and expensive concoctions to keep him working through the rest of the decade, and his accounts showed a thriving business.

"So you're not on the run from creditors," he said with a sigh. "You're just gone."

Alex stood up and went to the filing cabinet. Clearly there wasn't anything here in the shop relating to Charles Grier's whereabouts. All that was left was his home, and unfortunately Alex had no idea where that was. Unlike Dr. Kellin's shop, there was no place to live above *The Philosopher's Stone*.

The first drawer was filled with invoices from Grier's various chemical suppliers, and Alex pulled them out, checking them one by one, then dropped them on the desk. All of them had the shop address on them. Picking up the stack of folders, Alex began returning them to the drawer. He was about to move on to the next drawer, but stopped, his eyes resting on the telephone on the desk. He'd seen it before, no doubt where Grier placed and took orders, but if there was a phone...

"There we go," Alex said, picking up the phone. Underneath it was a slim address book bound in green leather. He flipped it open and read the first entry, *Abernathy Glassware*, followed by a phone number. There were no actual addresses in the book, but Alex hadn't expected any. Most people knew where the people they called regularly lived.

Paging through the book he scanned through the A's, B's, M's, and eventually the S's. He stopped when he found an entry marked, *Superintendent*. Alex didn't know if this was the owner of the shop or the building where Grier lived, but either one would know Grier's home address.

"Hello," a gruff voice came at Alex when he dialed the number.

"Yes, I'm Bartholomew Franklin with Manhattan Gas," Alex said, putting on his best Jersey accent. "We got a report of a gas leak from this number, was it you that called it in?"

There was a brief stunned pause, then the voice came on again.

"No, but it might have been someone in my building, I'm the superintendent," there was a note of panic in the man's voice and Alex smirked. People were always more willing to tell you things they shouldn't when they were under stress.

"What's the address of the building?" Alex asked.

The superintendent rattled off an address only a few blocks away.

"Oh, well then it's not you," Alex said. "The guy who called said he lived over on the East Side. Sorry to bother you."

"Are you sure?" the super pressed.

"Well," Alex said, drawing the word out. "We could send one of our investigators over to take a look if you want."

"Thank you, I do."

"What's your name," Alex said. "I'll tell him to ask for you."

"Henry Travis," the man said.

"Ok, Mr. Travis, we'll send somebody over just to check things out. Sit tight."

Alex chuckled as he hung up the phone. He returned Charles Grier's desk to the way he'd found it, then let himself out through the back. He hadn't found any keys inside, so he had to re-lock the door with his picks, but he needed to give himself some time before he showed up at Grier's building anyway.

Alex's watch told him it was just before four in the afternoon, but the fog had gotten so thick that the city had turned the streetlights on. Since he was walking, the fog didn't slow Alex down much, and ten minutes later he found himself outside a well-kept apartment building with a covered entrance. It looked like it might have had a doorman during better times, but that kind of luxury was only found in the inner-ring and the core these days.

A short, broad-shouldered man in a button-up shirt and tie stood waiting in the foyer when Alex entered. A bank of mailboxes lined the wall to his left and he spotted the name Charles Grier on a box marked 404.

"You Mr. Travis?" Alex said, sticking out his hand. "I'm Charlie Miller from Manhattan Gas."

Travis looked up at him and smiled. Alarm bells went off in Alex's head. People worried that their building was about to explode didn't smile. Before Alex could react, Travis balled up a fist and slugged him in the gut.

Air whooshed out of Alex's lungs while Travis followed up with a left hook across the side of Alex's face. Stumbling back, away from the unexpected assault, Alex struggled to catch his breath.

"I don't know what game you're playing," Travis growled, advancing on Alex. "But I called the gas company and they didn't send you."

He took another swing at Alex, but this time Alex caught the blow on his arm.

"I also called the police." Travis swung again, driving Alex back. "It'll take them time to get here on account of the fog, so that means I get first crack at you."

Alex held up his left hand, pressing his thumb against the plain bronze ring he wore on his middle finger. Last year a bad guy gave him a concussion with a force rune tattooed on the palm of his hand. Alex stole the idea and improved it. The ring had a series of five runes engraved around the outside. It had taken him weeks to make with a stylus and a magnifier, but he'd finally managed it. As his thumb touched the ring, he willed one of the runes to activate.

Frustrated that Alex's much longer legs kept him out of his reach, Travis chose that moment to bull rush his opponent. Alex closed his eyes and turned his head as a blinding white light flared up from his palm. The flash rune pulsed twice and then died.

Henry Travis bellowed as he came on. The light had blinded him, but being only light, it had no effect on his mad rush forward. He slammed into Alex, trying to bowl him over. Alex twisted with the blow, grabbing a handful of Travis' shirt and using the man's own momentum to throw him forward into the wall of mailboxes. He hit hard, sliding down to the floor in a daze.

"Good news, Mr. Travis," Alex said as he made his way to the door. "Looks like your building is safe from gas leaks."

A police siren was wailing in the distance as Alex left the apartment building. He buttoned his coat, turned in the opposite direction, and began walking slowly, as if nothing were happening. He now knew where Charles Grier lived, but he'd need a way to get inside that didn't involve tangling with the manager. Since Travis had seen his face, that was going to be tricky.

Alex lit a cigarette as he headed for the nearest crawler station. With everything moving at a snail's pace on account of the fog, he'd have plenty of time on the way back to his office to figure it out.

6

COLD RECEPTION

By the time Alex got back to his office it was after four. He probably shouldn't have bothered, but he wanted to call Dr. Kellin and update her on his progress. If he'd been thinking, he'd have just stopped by her place on his way home, but it had been hours since he'd had a swig of the rejuvenator and he was a bit fuzzy. Not to mention the superintendent's fairly solid left hook.

When he reached the third floor, he was surprised to see light shining out through the frosted glass panel of his office door. It had been lunchtime when he left, with plenty of light despite the fog so the lights had been off.

He reached into his pocket and felt the lump of chalk he always carried. He hadn't bothered to strap on his 1911 when he went out. Looking for a missing alchemist didn't seem that dangerous, his fight with the superintendent of Charles Grier's building notwithstanding. It would have been simple to go back down to the second-floor landing and open his vault. His pistol and shoulder holster hung in a gun cabinet just inside the door, along with his enchanted brass knuckles and a few new toys. He could have them in less than a minute.

Alex hesitated. Whoever had turned on his office light hadn't broken the door getting in; maybe he'd simply left it unlocked. Also, with the light on, they weren't exactly lying in wait for him.

Making up his mind, Alex hefted his kit bag and walked quietly to the door. With a quick motion, he turned the handle and pushed it open. The office was as he had left it with two exceptions. Now a man and a woman, both wearing suits, sat on the couch opposite the door. The man was older than Alex, probably in his late forties with jet black hair and a thin, clean-shaven face. He wore spectacles that made his blue eyes look larger than normal and he sat easily, with his legs crossed and his hat in his lap. His suit was clean and pressed and of sturdy quality, though not too expensive. Everything about the man screamed, "Cop."

The woman was a strange sight. She was much younger than the man, maybe mid-twenties, with smooth olive skin, dark eyes, and brown hair that erupted from her head in a mass of tight curls. Her suit looked like it had been made by the same tailor as the man's, though she wore a long pencil skirt with it instead of trousers. She too had a man's hat, sitting beside her on the couch, and the square bulge of a semi-automatic pistol under her left arm.

If she was armed, it was a cinch the man was too, but his weapon fit perfectly and showed no outward sign of its presence. To be fair, the woman's weapon only showed because her rather generous bust pushed it to the side.

"Okay," Alex said, affecting a gruff voice. "Which one of you mugs is Lockerby?"

The man and woman exchanged glances and the man moved his head almost imperceptibly in Alex's direction. The woman stood and Alex touched his thumb to his flash ring just in case. Rather than reaching for her weapon, however, the woman reached into the outside pocket of her jacket and produced a heavy leather wallet. Holding it up, she allowed it to fall open, revealing a brass shield with the letters FBI clearly visible across the front.

"Mr. Lockerby isn't here," she said in a confident voice. "And we have some questions for him when he gets back, so why don't you just run along?"

Alex glanced at the man who hadn't moved during the conversation. He just sat, watching with his legs crossed and his hat in his lap, but Alex got the impression he was coiled, like a snake ready to strike.

Having no idea why the FBI would be looking for him, Alex decided he didn't want to bother with them. He'd go home and let Leslie find out what they wanted when she came in on Monday.

"Fine," Alex said, holding up his free hand in a gesture of acquiescence. "I'll go."

"Will you now?" a familiar voice came from the open door to his private office. The voice was full of sly amusement and it sent a shiver up his spine. A moment later, the Ice Queen, Sorsha Kincaid, stepped out of his office. She wore a form-fitting dress of a dark color, somewhere between blue and black, with a beige vest over it. A gold watch fob hung from the left vest pocket and she carried a long cigarette holder in one hand.

Alex took all that in at once, then his eyes sought her face. Her lips were raised on one side in a mocking smile and her pale blue eyes twinkled. She wasn't wearing her typical bright lipstick, but rather a more subtle shade of burgundy. Her platinum blonde hair was still cut in a shoulder-length bob that framed her lovely face. And she was perfect, flawless, as if she had been carved of marble.

Alex stared just a moment too long and the half-mocking smile rose up into a full grin. Recovering quickly, he pasted a smile on his face and forced himself to relax. The last time Sorsha had been in his office with her FBI lackeys, she'd threatened to freeze him solid.

"Sorceress," he said, in his most nonchalant voice, the one she hated. "I didn't realize you were here." He jerked his thumb at the man and the still-standing woman. "That explains the federal welcome wagon over here." The man just sat there with the same neutral expression on his face, but the woman scowled at him. "What brings you to my neck of the woods? You're not still looking for that Archimedes thing, are you?"

Sorsha's mocking smile vanished, replaced by a look of irritation.

"The government has decided that my skills are better employed elsewhere," she said, walking toward him slowly. "But if you'd like to discuss what happened to the Archimedean Monograph, I'm sure I can find the time."

She stopped just a few feet away, her eyes boring into him. Alex grinned wider at that.

"If it was anything like the last time we talked, I suspect it would be very pleasant," he said, his grin growing wider. "But we might want to go into my office, away from any...witnesses."

Sorsha had suspected that Alex knew more about the Monograph than he'd admitted, so she'd used an illegal truth spell on him. Before she did it, however, she'd sent her former FBI agents Davis and Warner out of the room. Alex had managed to tell her what she wanted to hear without actually lying, a little-known weakness of the spell.

Sorsha's face blanched for an instant and the female agent smirked. Anyone who didn't know about Sorsha's illegal spell would assume Alex's comment about witnesses meant something else entirely. If the male agent was shocked by the implication, he gave no sign.

"I see you still like to play dangerous games," she growled at him. "What happened to you anyway? You look like hell."

Alex shrugged with all the false modesty he could muster.

"Oh, you know, just saved the city."

Her brows dropped down over her eyes in an unamused look and she reached out to touch his cheek.

"This, you idiot."

Alex winced as her touch made his cheek ache. He'd forgotten about how Henry Travis had punched him in the face earlier. It was probably bruising up nicely.

"Just making new friends," he said, probing the sore spot with his fingers.

"With your usual charm, no doubt," Sorsha said. "Give me your handkerchief."

Alex did as she asked, and she pressed it gently to his face. When it touched him, it was icy cold, and he jumped.

"Stop that," Sorsha said, pressing it against his cheek again. "Hold it there and follow me."

"Do you want us, Ma'am?" the man on the couch asked.

Sorsha looked at Alex and sighed.

"No," she said. "Mr. Lockerby may look like a mile of bad road, but he's harmless."

"Aren't you going to introduce me to your friends?" Alex said, pressing the cold handkerchief to his face.

"This is senior agent Buddy Redhorn," she said, indicating the man. Agent Redhorn nodded at Alex but didn't otherwise move. "And this is his trainee, Agent Aissa Mendes."

"I didn't know the FBI had any female agents," Alex said to Agent Mendes. "Nice to meet you."

"Present company excepted, I suppose you mean," Sorsha said. Her face and voice didn't change, but there was a sudden fire in her pale eyes.

"It's a pilot program," Agent Mendes said, a little defensively.

"Which she earned her way into," Agent Redhorn added. His voice was smooth and even, like a radio announcer's, but like the man himself, it carried a subtle note of threat within it.

Alex held up his hands in a gesture of surrender.

"No judgement," he said and meant it. "Just an observation."

Alex had worked with Sorsha and he knew the FBI wouldn't use her as a consultant if she weren't good at the job. If they wanted some female agents for whatever reason, it was nothing to him.

"Now that you've met my team," Sorsha said, turning back to his office. She entered, leaving the door open, and sat down in one of the chairs in front of his desk. Alex went around to his side and pulled open the middle drawer, removing the silver flask. If he was going to be sparring with the Ice Queen, he needed his mind to be sharp.

"Excuse me," he said, uncapping the flask. "It's past time for my medicine."

He took a swig and put the cap back on.

"Not going to offer me any?" Sorsha said. Her voice held a tone of mockery, but Alex couldn't be sure she wasn't serious. He opened the top again and held the flask out to her.

"I doubt you'd enjoy it," he said as she took the flask and held it under her nose.

After a moment, she handed it back with a strange look on her face.

"Well, that explains a lot," she said, no doubt meaning that she'd expected Alex's condition to be much worse by now.

Alex didn't know what those pale eyes saw when they looked at him. Sorcerers had all kinds of strange and esoteric powers. Could she see how much life he actually had left?

He pushed that thought from his mind, hoping she couldn't. He might spar with Sorsha and get on her nerves, but he wouldn't wish that knowledge on anyone.

"So what can I do for you, Sorceress?" he asked, returning the flask and sitting down.

Sorsha crossed her legs, sitting back in the chair. She just regarded him for a long moment, her expression neutral.

"How much do you know about the weather we've been having?" she asked.

It was a strange question and it caught Alex off guard.

"I know it's slowing down crawlers and taxis all over the city," he said. "It took me over an hour to get here from the South Side mid-ring."

"It's causing problems all over town," she said. "The problem is that we don't know what's causing it."

"I always thought it had something to do with warm air and the sea," Alex suggested, helpfully.

"Under normal circumstances that's exactly how fog forms," Sorsha said. "But this fog is different." She pointed out the window at the glowing haze created when the yellow light of the street lamp below lit up the fog. "The FBI has spoken to the best weather experts in the country and they all assure us that the conditions are all wrong for fog."

Alex remembered his conversation with Iggy. He'd mentioned that the fog had baffled the meteorologist at the Times.

"It doesn't matter if they can't account for it," he said with a shrug. "It's here just the same."

"But it shouldn't be," Sorsha said, tapping out the stub of her cigarette in Alex's ashtray. She opened her hand as if to drop the cigarette holder and it just vanished into thin air.

"You think the fog is magical," Alex guessed.

She nodded.

"I didn't do it," Alex insisted.

She raised an eyebrow at that.

"Could you have done it?" she asked.

Alex thought about that for a moment. There were some powerful runes in the Archimedean Monograph, but nothing that made fog. Still, there were more ways than a direct rune to get the job done.

"Maybe," he said at last. "Some rune that produces the right temperature or maybe just an illusion. You're sure the fog isn't natural?"

"I tried simply blowing it away," she said. "I got a wind up to hurricane force and all it did was clear a little patch that came back as soon as I stopped the gale."

"If it's magical, can't you just," he shrugged then wiggled his fingers at her, "magic it away?"

"No," she said. "Though not for lack of trying. I've been to all my brothers and they can't do anything about it either. It must be some kind of magic we don't understand."

"Which led you to me."

She nodded again.

"We have to find out where this fog is coming from, Alex," she said, sounding tired. "Is this some magical accident or is someone doing this on purpose?"

Alex thought about that. Just last year he'd met a group of South American runewrights who used Mayan glyphs for their magic. The form was different than he was used to, but the magic wasn't actually different from what he did. He hadn't heard of any new or different magics, but Iggy taught him never to assume.

You can't draw accurate conclusions without evidence, the old doctor's voice echoed in his head. Alex stood and picked up his kit, placing it on his desk.

"Let's take a look and see what we're dealing with," he said, opening his bag. He took out his oculus and his multi-lamp, then clipped the ghostlight burner into the bottom of the lamp.

The burner was just a round oil reservoir with a wick inserted in it and runes all around the outside. Inside was an alchemical solution that Alex had modified with rune ingredients. The resulting flame burned with a ghostly greenish light that would reveal magical residue when viewed through the oculus.

Alex went to the window and pulled it open, letting little wisps of fog drift inside. He lit the ghostlight burner with the touch tip on his desk, then strapped the oculus over his right eye. The light from the multi-lamp radiated out in a greenish beam that seemed dim to the naked eye, but lit up the fog brightly through the oculus.

As Alex played the light over the room, several things jumped out immediately, phosphorescing in the glow of the light. He could see the permanent strip of paint on the back wall where he regularly opened his vault, along with the faint glow of the focusing circle he'd drawn on the floor, showing through the rug. The cold box over his door glowed, even though he'd removed the enchanted stones that kept the room cool once the fall weather turned.

What did not glow, not even a little bit, however, was the fog. Alex moved to the window and shone the light outside. The magelight in the streetlight below glowed back at him, but the fog showed nothing.

"Huh?" he grunted, pulling the lamp back inside.

"What?" Sorsha asked. She had remained quiet and let him work, sitting in the client chair with her legs crossed demurely.

"As far as I can tell, the fog itself isn't magical," Alex said, setting his lamp back on the desk. "Let me try something else."

He blew out the ghostlight burner and replaced it with the silverlight one. Silverlight would reveal biological residue like fingerprints and blood. He doubted the fog would show him anything like that, but it was worth a try. Three minutes later he was back at his desk with the window closed.

"Nothing?" Sorsha demanded.

Alex shook his head. He took out his cigarette case and offered one to the sorceress, giving himself time to think.

"Maybe the fog is just fog, but whatever's creating it is magical," Alex suggested as Sorsha selected a cigarette. As she raised her hand, her long, black cigarette holder reappeared from nowhere.

"I hadn't thought of that," she said, fixing the cigarette into the end of the holder. "But that doesn't explain why the fog isn't dissipating."

Alex ignited his lighter and offered the flame to Sorsha before lighting his own cigarette.

"Maybe it is," he said with a shrug. "Maybe whatever magic is creating it is just too powerful, or maybe this fog is more dense than regular fog."

Sorsha puffed on her cigarette for a long moment, then finally shook her head.

"I hate to say it, but the why doesn't matter. The fog has already cost the city thousands of dollars with traffic accidents, the need for increased police presence, and turning on the streetlights early. Not to mention how it's affecting business. We have to find out what's causing this and stop it."

Alex put away his lamp, oculus, and burners, returning his kit to the floor by his desk.

"I disagree. If someone is doing this on purpose, the real question is why?" he observed. "Are they trying to start a panic, maybe blackmail the city?"

"We thought of that," Sorsha said, irritation marring her features. "But so far no one has made any statements or demands."

"What about using the fog to cover a crime?" Alex said. "It would make escaping a bank job much easier."

Sorsha smirked at that.

"It's always a bank job with you," she said. Just last year Alex had sent the police on a wild goose chase checking every bank in the city for tunneling thieves. Even though he'd ultimately been proven right, the police hadn't let him forget his initial mistake.

Alex shrugged.

"What else might conveniently go missing in the fog?" he wondered. "Have you checked to make sure Lady Liberty is still in the harbor?"

"Yes," Sorsha said with no trace of humor.

"Could this be another weapon?" he asked. "Like that alchemical plague?" The thought chilled him.

Sorsha looked up and met his eyes. He could see the doubt there, warring with her innate desire to be in control.

"It's possible," she said. "Though after the plague incident, the war department is keeping tabs on potential threats. As far as they know, no foreign agents are in New York." She chuckled, mirthlessly. "Well, no new ones at any rate."

"Is it some kind of accident?" Alex wondered. "Maybe one of your brother sorcerers tried something new and it got out of hand?"

"Don't be absurd," she said, giving Alex a scolding look. "Sorcerers have complete control over their magic. If a sorcerer did this, they would have been able to stop it easily."

"Well, then I'm out of ideas."

"It doesn't matter why it's happening at this point," Sorsha said, though she sounded more like she was trying to convince herself than Alex. "What matters is finding what's causing it, and stopping it." She locked eyes with him again. "And I believe that finding things is your specialty."

"Absolutely." Alex nodded, picking up his kit bag again. This time he ignored his oculus and multi-lamp, withdrawing his city map and the cigar box with the jade weights and brass compass inside.

Laying the map out on his desk, he secured it with the jade figurines, then placed the compass in the center.

"I'm going to need some of the fog," he said, moving to open the window. "Enough to be in contact with the compass."

Sorsha raised an eyebrow at that, but rose and moved to the window as well. She opened her hand and mumbled something. As she spoke, her voice dropped several octaves and the sound echoed. Wisps of fog began to move sluggishly through the window until they coalesced above Sorsha's open palm. She walked back to the desk and turned her hand over, allowing the ball of fog to drift down until it rested exactly on the compass.

"You could have just taken the map outside," she said, giving him an amused look as she sat back down.

"And miss the show? Never."

In truth there was a very good reason Alex didn't want to try this outside — the focusing circle under his desk. He'd painted it on the hardwood floor, then rolled the rug back over it. Any rune cast on his desk would have the added benefit of the circle. Eventually the runes he painted into it would fade and he'd have to redo it, but that was only time consuming.

Pulling out his rune book, Alex tore out another of the finding runes he'd prepared yesterday. Folding it, he set it on the compass, inside the bubble of fog, then lit it with his cigarette. The rune burned into existence as the flash paper vanished, hovering above the bubble. It drifted around in a lazy circle, then stopped and began turning the other way.

"What's it doing?" Sorsha asked in a hushed voice.

Alex shook his head. He could see the compass below the rune and the needle was spinning with the rune. The two were connected, but they didn't seem to have locked on to any specific location.

"Well, it's linked to the fog," Alex said, looking up at Sorsha. "Unfortunately all it's telling me is that the fog is all around us."

Sorsha sighed and tamped out her cigarette.

"It was worth a try," she said, rising. She pulled a small clutch bag from the air, opened it, and deposited a crisp, new twenty on Alex's desk.

"For the rune," she said.

"I charge twenty-five these days," Alex said with a grin. "But I only charge ten if the rune doesn't work."

"Is there something more you can do to get it to work?" she asked, holding his gaze.

Alex thought about that. Maybe if there was some way to find the thickest concentration of fog, it might work. That was bound to be wherever it was originating.

"Maybe," he hedged. "Let me think about it."

She reached back into her clutch.

"Keep the change," she said, depositing one of her white business cards on top of the twenty. "And call me when you figure it out." She turned and headed for the door, casting him a sidelong glance over her shoulder as she went. Once back in his waiting area, he heard her call for her new federal lackeys to follow, and together they left the office.

7

FINDING RUNES

Alex stood at the window of his office and watched as the Ice Queen and her FBI escorts exited the building. They crossed the street and got into a nondescript black car parked across the street. Alex chided himself for not noticing it when he came in, but law enforcement tended to favor drab cars for just that reason. He would have noticed if Sorsha had used her own car, a long, sleek floater, but that would draw more eyes than just his.

"Probably why she left it at home," he muttered as they drove away.

He closed the curtain over the window and returned to his desk. He didn't know what to do about the fog or making a better finding rune, but Iggy would probably have a suggestion or two, so Alex ignored that for the moment.

Taking his address book from the top, left drawer of his desk, he flipped to the K's and dialed Dr. Kellin's number. The phone rang for a long time and he was about to hang up when the call connected.

"Hello," Dr. Kellin's voice answered. It was thick and garbled as if she'd only just woken up. Alex knew she usually slept in the evening while Jessica tended the lab, but it was barely five, so he hadn't expected the doc to be resting. Still, he felt like a heel for waking her.

"Hey, Doc," he said. "Sorry to bother you, but I thought I'd give you an update on your friend, Grier."

"Oh, Alex," she said, her tired voice brightening. "I'm sorry; I've been working long hours these past few months and I'm afraid it's been catching up with me. Did you find him?"

"No," he admitted. "And I think you were right to be worried about him. I went by his shop and had a look around."

"How did you get in?" She asked, still sounding a bit groggy. "Wasn't it locked?"

Alex chuckled.

"It was," he admitted. "But I try not to let little things like locks stop me."

"Oh," Dr. Kellin said, catching his meaning.

"Anyway, everything inside looked to be right where it was supposed to be. The floor was clean, and the garbage can was empty, like he cleaned up on his way out."

"Was there *anything* suspicious?" Kellin asked. "Or did he go out of town unexpectedly?"

"Well, I can't be sure," Alex said. "But I talked to the owners of the shops on either side of Grier's place and they said that when he went out of town in the past, he put a sign in the shop window. There was one thing that was curious though," he went on. Alex explained about the basement lab and how some of the burners had been left on. "The chemicals in the air were so thick, I had to use my gas mask to get down there."

"You have a gas mask?"

Alex chuckled. He'd never really thought about it; the mask was just something Iggy told him to carry in his kit. Now that Alex did think on it, Iggy had seen the big war, so maybe the idea of carrying a gas mask wasn't that far-fetched.

"I do try to be prepared," Alex admitted.

"Well I'm sure Charles would never go off and leave any of his potions brewing," Dr. Kellin said. "After the liquids boiled away, anything volatile could ignite and burn the shop down."

"So if your friend went out of town suddenly, he would at least stop by the shop to turn off the gas, right?"

The Long Chain

"Not necessarily," Kellin said. "Most likely he would hire another alchemist to come by and babysit his potions. Plenty of apprentices will do it to earn extra income. I even did it for him once as a favor when he couldn't get anyone else."

Alex was going to ask if maybe Grier had gone out of town so suddenly that he couldn't find someone to help him, but clearly if he'd needed to, he would have called Dr. Kellin.

"I'm really very worried," she went on when Alex didn't speak. "Is there anything else you can do?"

"Of course," Alex said easily. "I found out where he lives, but the super in his building is on to me. I'll have to come up with a way to get in and see Grier's apartment, and hopefully that will tell me more. I've got an idea about that, but it might take a day or two."

"Please hurry, Alex," Dr. Kellin said, sounding a little bit afraid beneath the tired voice. "Charles Grier is a dear friend and I can't stand the idea that anything has happened to him."

"I'll do my best, Doc," Alex promised. "Is — uh — is Jessica there?"

Now it was Dr. Kellin's turn to chuckle.

"I'm sorry, Alex," she said. "Jessica left for Albany right after we closed the shop today."

Albany was where Dr. Kellin's daughter Linda was being treated for polio. Of course 'treated' might be too strong a word. According to Jessica, Linda spent her days being kept alive in an iron lung. To Alex that seemed like spending your life in your very own coffin. The idea made his skin crawl. He understood why Jessica would take the time to be with her childhood friend as much as she could, but he didn't have to like it.

"How is Linda doing?" he asked, trying to push the image of giant metal coffins out of his mind.

"Not well," Dr. Kellin said in a small voice. "Dr. Phillips doesn't think she has much time left."

Alex felt like a heel for judging Jessica and her frequent trips upstate.

"How are you doing?" he asked. He didn't know why he did it, it just sort of slipped out. He knew even as he was saying it that there wasn't a good answer to that question. How would he be doing if his child lay dying and the cure you were working on remained tantalizingly out of reach?

"My formula is almost ready," she said wearily. "So I'd better get back to it. Thank you for looking in on Charles. Please let me know as soon as you find anything else."

Alex promised that he would and hung up.

He stood and paced around his office, suddenly needing to burn off some energy. He'd been upset with Jessica the last time they talked, angry that she never had time for him. He understood that she was helping the doc to create a cure for polio, but up to this point, Linda Kellin's illness had just been a fact of life, something that existed but didn't change. The idea that Linda was dying, and Dr. Kellin and Jessica were spending almost every waking moment trying to stop it, felt like a new revelation.

Alex slammed his fist into his open hand. He would have to apologize to Jessica when she got back and admit to being a heel. Maybe if he found Charles Grier, he'd have an excuse to go by the shop.

With that in mind, Alex circled back around his desk and sat down. Picking up the phone, he dialed a number he knew by heart.

"Central Office of Police," a woman's voice greeted him.

"Transfer me to Detective Pak, please," Alex said.

A moment later the phone rang again, and Danny picked it up.

"What do you want?" he growled when he heard Alex's voice.

"Now is that any way to treat the man who saved your life?" Alex said with a grin. He looked at the back of his left hand, at the round scar that marked where a tommy gun bullet had passed right through it. That had happened when Alex jumped in front of Danny to keep him from being gunned down.

"You need to lay off that life-saving routine," Danny said, though his tone had softened quite a bit. "You milked that dry a long time ago."

"Still," Alex protested. "What did I do to deserve so much hostility?"

"You introduced me to Mary," he said. Alex could tell that Danny regretted saying it almost instantly, but by then it was far too late.

"That bad?"

Danny sighed.

"Yeah. I don't want to talk about it, so I might as well hear what you want."

"I'm looking for an alchemist, name of Charles Grier," Alex explained. "A friend of his thinks something happened to him and I need to get into his place for a look-see."

Alex had used Danny's police badge to get him into places before.

"What? You can't charm your way in?"

Alex explained about the gas company routine and his run-in with Grier's super, Henry Travis.

"So how am I supposed to get you in?" Danny asked when Alex finished. "The super knows you; if you show up with me, he'll just think it's another put-up job."

"I'll think of something," Alex said. "Mostly I just need to see if it looks like someone grabbed him out of his apartment and you can do that just as easy as I can."

There was a long pause.

"All right," he said at last. "I'm on during the day tomorrow, but I can meet you there after my shift; say six o'clock?"

Alex said that would be fine, then gave Danny the address and hung up.

"Well that takes care of that," he said to the empty room. "At least for now."

Leaning down, Alex picked up his kit, then he stood and turned off the magelight in his office. Shutting the door, he repeated the process with the waiting area, making sure to lock the door behind him. Exiting his building, Alex headed across the street to the five-and-dime to buy a newspaper for his sure-to-be-long ride home.

It took Alex almost two hours to get home. By the time he paid the cabbie and stepped out onto the sidewalk in front of the brownstone, he could barely see the building right in front of him.

Sorsha had been right, something had to be done. If this kept up, he'd have to sleep in his office tomorrow, because nothing would be moving in the city.

Taking his time, Alex groped his way across the sidewalk to the brick pillar that marked the beginning of the stairs up to the brownstone's stoop. The runes in his watch lit up the fog in a multi-colored halo as they peeled back the building's protective wards, then he stepped inside.

"I was considering sending out a search party," Iggy called from the kitchen as Alex hung up his hat by the vestibule door. "Is it as bad as this everywhere else?"

"As far as I can tell," Alex said, crossing the library to the kitchen door. The aroma of food assaulted him as he arrived, and Alex almost felt as good as he did with a slug of the rejuvenator.

Iggy stood at the stove stirring a pot of something. He wore a dark green tweed suit with the jacket removed and an apron added to cover his shirt and vest. Two more pots sat on top of the stove, and Alex could tell that the oven below was also in use.

"It's pork roast tonight," Iggy said, in response to Alex's probing looks. "I've also got new potatoes cooked in butter, and broccoli in cream sauce."

Alex's mouth began to water overtime and he remembered that the last thing he'd had to eat was an undercooked hamburger at the lunch counter across the street from his office. Their usual cook had quit last month and they hadn't had any luck replacing him. Iggy, on the other hand, had picked up cooking when he was in the Royal Navy. He'd made a serious hobby of it ever since, and his skills were considerable.

Alex made his way to the cupboards next to the sink. Retrieving the tableware, he set the table as Iggy finished up.

"There was a story in the paper about the fog," Iggy said as he pulled a roasting pan from the oven. "The weather forecasters are all baffled."

"The FBI is looking into it too," Alex said.

"I don't remember seeing that in the paper," Iggy said with a raised eyebrow. "How do you know that?"

"They came to see me today," he explained. "Apparently they think it's magical in nature." He recounted his visit from Sorsha and her federal pals.

"Well that would explain a lot," Iggy said, once Alex was done. "What do you think?"

Alex shrugged as he carried the plate of pork roast to the table.

"I don't know," he said. "The fog is just fog, but I don't have any idea how to find where it's coming from."

"You're assuming it's coming from one place," Iggy said as they sat. He waited expectantly for Alex to say grace, then he went on. "Covering a city the size of New York can't be easy. If it really is being done by some rogue sorcerer, he—"

"Or she," Alex interjected with a grin.

Iggy shot him an irritated look.

"Your sorceress is not involved," he said.

"Don't be so sure," Alex said, ribbing him for the fun of it now. "Fog takes heated or cooled air and water of the opposite temperature. She's got exactly the skill set to make as much fog as she wants."

"I know for a fact she's not behind this," Iggy said, grinning himself.

"How?"

Iggy speared a bit of potato on his plate and used it to point at Alex.

"Because if she were the one wrapping the city in fog, you, dear boy, would be the last person she'd bring the problem to."

"You don't think she'd jump at the chance to make a chump out of me?"

Iggy scoffed.

"She knows how good a detective you are. If she did this, she'd make sure to keep you as far away from it as she could." He wiped his mustache with his napkin. "If it were me, I'd have arranged for a lucrative, out-of-town case to come your way to keep you occupied. Sorsha's no fool, she'd have done the same." He shrugged and winked at him. "Or just saved herself the trouble and had you killed."

"Thanks," Alex said, his voice dripping with sarcasm.

Iggy grinned back at him, and Alex had to admit that he had a point. Sorsha was not a fool, and the fact that she had brought this case to Alex, after working it herself, spoke volumes.

"So what if a sorcerer is behind it?" Alex asked.

"It would take a tremendous amount of energy to do it all at once," Iggy said. "I'd imagine other sorcerers would be able to sense that, so they'd have to run all over the city casting a bunch of small spells instead of one large one."

"Possible," Alex admitted. "But not very practical. And if some sorcerer is doing it, what's his game?"

"Maybe he's got stock in zeppelins."

Alex hadn't thought about that, but the fog must have grounded all conventional airplanes. As it stood, only a big, slow-moving zeppelin would be able to land at the Aerodrome. It must have been playing hell with people's travel plans.

"Maybe it's about keeping someone from leaving the city," Alex suggested, then he shook his head. "Nah. Too much trouble to go through just for that."

"I've been thinking," Iggy said after a few minutes of silence. "What if whoever is doing this is using the sewers?"

Alex considered that.

"You mean generating the fog somewhere central and then pumping it out along the tunnels?"

"Think about it. The tunnels and sewer line run under every street in the city. With enough air pressure to move it, the fog would pour out everywhere and then push all the way out to the rivers."

Alex nodded, chewing absently.

"It could work," he said. "But if the fog had been seen coming up from the sewer inlets, someone would have called the Times." After a long minute, he put down his fork and sat back from the table. "This isn't getting me anywhere," he said. "Sorsha was right; it doesn't matter why whoever's behind this is doing it, not yet anyway. The only thing I've got to go on is where the fog is coming from. Is it in one central place or lots of little ones?"

"I think that's a sound starting point," Iggy said.

"So how do I find the source with just the fog to go on?" Alex asked. "Is there some way to use a finding rune to trace the fog back to its source?"

"Nothing leaps to mind," Iggy said, rising from the table. "But I am by no means the font of all runic wisdom. I suggest that you consult the textbook."

Alex glanced back at the library. The textbook was the less obvious name they used to refer to the Archimedean Monograph. Alex had been largely forbidden from consulting it by Iggy, who had so far not considered him ready.

He looked back at Iggy and the old man nodded.

"Okay," Alex said, not bothering to hide the smile that sprang to his lips.

"After you do the dishes, of course," Iggy added with an amused chuckle.

Half an hour later, Alex entered his third-floor room. He laid the thin red leather book on his bed, then took off his coat and vest. His comfortable reading chair beckoned to him, but this wasn't pleasure reading, and he'd need a table and space to make notes.

Opening his own red rune book, Alex tore out a vault rune and licked the back of it. He'd followed Iggy's example in the kitchen and painted a thin line on his wall in the shape of a door frame. Sticking the rune to the center of that imaginary door, he pulled out his cigarette lighter and ignited the paper. A moment later the heavy steel door to his vault appeared, melting out of the wallpaper and into existence. Alex pulled out the heavy brass key that would unlock the door and opened it.

Since Iggy's brownstone was squarely in the middle ring, the magelights inside the vault flared to life even before he'd finished opening the door. Last year Alex had finally gotten a look inside Iggy's personal vault. His mentor had everything in there; it was like an entire spare house with a bedroom, kitchen, library, and a surgery, in addition to the standard runewright's workroom.

It had amazed Alex, whose own vault had consisted of a single workspace, up until that point. More than that, it had inspired him. Now Alex's vault was at least as big as Iggy's, and he'd moved his workroom to one side and put in a comfortable sitting room complete with a bearskin rug he'd received as payment for clearing a big game hunter of murder. It even had a fireplace that could produce heat by means of a boiler stone.

His workroom was much larger as well, with an enormous drafting table for rune writing and shelves and shelves of the various inks, powders, pigments, papers, and pens needed for the work. Along the wall behind the door were his secretary cabinet where he kept his kit bag, and a new cabinet that held his 1911, his brass knuckles, and a twelve-gauge shotgun with runes running up the grip beneath the barrel.

A short hallway at the back of the sitting room led to a small kitchen and bedroom that he'd managed to furnish piece by piece. It wasn't as lavish or impressive as Iggy's, but Alex was still working on it.

Moving to a large desk in his workroom, Alex laid the Monograph reverently on top. Opening one of the drawers, he extracted a bound notebook and a pencil box, then switched on the desk's lamp and sat down.

He fidgeted a moment, making sure his pencil was sharp, and turning to a blank page in the notebook. Then he took a deep breath and opened the Archimedean Monograph.

The cover opened on a blank page, so Alex turned to the next. The first few pages were filled with DaVinci's writing, explaining how he'd learned of Archimedes' notes and then collected them. Alex's Latin wasn't great, but he could make it out. He wanted to press on, but out of respect, and a fair amount of awe, he read the forward. When at last he was done, Alex took a deep breath and, for the first time in two years, turned to the first rune and read it.

8

THE BURGLARY

Alex was so tired the next morning that even after hurriedly downing three cups of coffee so fast it left his tongue scorched, Iggy still had to elbow him twice during Mass.

"What time did you get to sleep last night?" Iggy asked on their way home.

"Don't know," Alex said, leaning against the door of the taxi. "Feels like about ten minutes before my alarm went off."

Iggy chuckled.

"Reminds me of my medical training," he said. "Did you find anything that might be useful?"

"Maybe," Alex said, stifling a yawn. "There are a few different runes that are designed to focus magic, make it more precise. I might be able to use one to limit the finding rune to a small part of the city, but if I'm reading the textbook right, I'd have to literally draw a rune around the area. So that's out."

"Two-dimensional thinking," Iggy said.

Alex knew he was tired, but he was pretty sure he hadn't gone to sleep and missed a part of their conversation.

"Come again?"

"You're thinking in only two dimensions," Iggy said again. It didn't make any more sense the second time, and Alex said so.

"Have you looked at the runes on the front door?" Iggy asked. "I mean really looked at them."

Alex shrugged, trying to remember.

"I guess," he hedged. "There's a harmonic rune linked to a couple of binding runes and an immobility rune. Maybe an absorption rune?"

"Can you make those runes?" Iggy asked, looking at him askance as their taxi plodded its way through the foggy streets.

"Yes," Alex said after thinking about it. "I'd have to study up on a couple of them, but they don't seem that involved."

"So, if you didn't have your key, could you nullify those runes? Could you break into the brownstone?"

Alex opened his mouth then shut it again. Iggy had a point, the runes on the door weren't that difficult. Any runewright of ability should be able to bypass them with a nullification rune. But Iggy would never have left the brownstone so unprotected, especially with the Archimedean Monograph just sitting on a shelf in the library.

"No," Alex guessed. "I don't think I could break in."

"And you'd be right," Iggy chuckled.

"But I don't understand why."

"That's because you're thinking in only two dimensions." Iggy's grin got wide and he leaned in, conspiratorially. "Any runewright worth his salt could nullify those runes on the door, if they were all that protected the house."

"I've seen the runes on the door," Alex said. "They're not tied to the ones on the foundation or the ones on the windows."

"Of course they are," Iggy said. "They're linked to a very powerful rune construct that covers the whole house."

"But when the front door is open, it's not even touching the house," Alex protested. "How is it part of a larger construct?"

Alex knew that runes could be connected into constructs by something as simple as a pencil line, but how could Iggy keep the runes on the door from unraveling every time the door opened?

"You're not thinking this through, lad," Iggy said. "You already know how to do this."

Alex hated when Iggy did this. Part of his teaching method was to give Alex all the pieces of a puzzle and wait for him to put it together on his own. Supposedly it helped the learner really master the subject. So far, the only thing Alex was mastering was his temper. Which, if he thought about it, was a win.

"So you want me to think in three dimensions," he said, thinking out loud. "Runes have height and width, but you want me to add depth. But paper is flat, just like the runes on the front door. So you don't mean depth...you mean distance."

He looked up and found Iggy beaming at him.

"The runes on the front door can't be nullified," Alex declared, "because they're only part of the construct. The rest is somewhere else, safe from meddling runewrights."

"The attic, to be exact," Iggy said. "Good work. Now how would you break up a complex construct?"

Alex thought about that. Iggy said he already knew how, but all the runes he used were single constructs. Some of them were complex, but none of them used remote pieces. Except—

"The escape rune," he said nodding. "It uses a linking rune to connect to an anchor rune, but the linking rune has to be touching both of the others when it's cast."

"Unless—" Iggy said, stretching the word out.

"Unless it doesn't," Alex said, not sure how that was possible, but knowing that was what Iggy meant. "If I can link runes that aren't in the same physical space, I could set up nullification runes in a circle around a few city blocks, then only use the finding rune inside that area. With a convergence rune to focus the finding rune, I might be able to see where the fog is the thickest."

Iggy nodded sagely.

"Sounds like a workable plan to me, lad. What say I show you how to link a rune back to a distant construct once we get home?"

Alex nodded. He could feel the hair on his arms standing up. He hadn't been this excited since he first found the Monograph. For a while, the only new skills he'd been learning were how to write more and more complex runes. It didn't feel like moving forward, like learning something new. If anything, it was just getting better at what he already knew. This, however, this felt like finding buried treasure or discovering an unknown island. It was new ground and Alex couldn't wait to get home.

The cab ride from the church to the brownstone usually took fifteen minutes. By the time Alex and Iggy got home, Mass had been over for almost an hour. On the way home, they'd passed two car accidents before the cab driver decided to get off the main roads and take side streets.

"You should pack it in," Iggy told the cabbie as he handed him a five spot. "This fog's dangerous. Keep the change."

The cabbie thanked them and dove off slowly into the fog. With the sun up, it was easier to see the steps, but Alex held the bannister as he went up anyway.

"I'm glad I've got some work to do here," Alex admitted as he held the door open for Iggy. "I don't want to even think about going back out into that."

Almost on cue, the phone in the kitchen rang. Alex and Iggy exchanged glances, then Alex went to answer.

"Finally," Danny's voice assaulted him over the wire. "I've been calling for an hour! Did you start going to a different church?"

"No," Alex said, "but you may have noticed the fog outside. What's so urgent? I'm not supposed to meet you until after six."

"That guy you wanted me to look into, what was his name again?"

"Charles Grier, why?"

"He's an alchemist, right?" Danny said. "Has a shop on the South Side? *The Philosopher's Stone?*"

"I take it your interest isn't academic."

"No. I'm standing in his shop right now. Someone broke in last night and tore the place up pretty good."

"Did anyone see anything?"

"No," Danny said a bit of an edge creeping into his voice. "When you said that you were looking for this guy, you tried to get into his house. Any chance you came by here yesterday?"

"I might have looked in the window," Alex said. Danny had been around him long enough to know how Alex did his job, but they had long ago agreed not to get into detail about those things. That way Alex didn't have to lie to Danny or put him in the awkward position of having to lie for him.

"Well, I need you to get down here and tell me what's missing, because all I see is a mess."

Alex looked out through the kitchen window at the fog.

"Do you really need me?"

"Well, I'd hate for the fingerprint guys to find one of yours without you being here to explain where it came from."

"Right," Alex sighed. "I'll grab my kit and be over as soon as I can."

"I thought you weren't going out," Iggy said, heading for the pantry where he kept his humidor.

"Remember that alchemist friend of Dr. Kellin's? His shop was broken into last night."

"I thought that was you," Iggy chuckled.

"I don't leave a mess," Alex said. "Danny wants me to come by and have a look. Call me a cab, will you? I'm going upstairs to get my kit."

"You look like hell," Danny said once Alex managed to get to Charles Grier's shop. He wore a brown suit with his detective badge clipped to the breast pocket of his jacket.

"Nice to see you too," Alex said. "Did you learn anything since we talked?"

"This way," Danny said, turning and leading Alex through the open front door.

As Alex entered, there weren't any signs of a break in on the front of the building. The plate glass windows and the displays behind them were undisturbed and the door showed no signs of being picked or forced. Inside, however, was another matter. The display case with the cans of colored powders had been overturned, spilling its contents across the floor in a rainbow pattern. The shelves along the back wall had been emptied, and bottles, both broken and whole, littered the floor.

Since alchemy was a volatile magic, most of the spilled potions had already evaporated, but a few puddles of colored liquids were still present.

"Tell your men to be careful of the potions," Alex said, pointing to a puddle of thick black liquid. Next to the puddle was part of a shoe print, evidence of where someone had walked through it. "I have no idea what might happen if someone tracks a random potion through all that spilled powder."

Danny checked the bottom of his shoes, one after the other, then yelled at the uniformed officer in charge of the scene to have his men pay better attention. All around the room, the various officers who were inventorying the scene got the message loud and clear.

"I take it the shop didn't look like this yesterday," Danny said once he'd led Alex into the back room. The rear door had been broken in half, as if someone had run the nose of their car into it — or hit it with a battering ram. The file cabinet that Alex had made sure to leave as he'd found it had been tipped over and its files were scattered across the floor. All the drawers in the desk had been pulled out and emptied, adding their contents to the pile, and the only thing remaining on the desk were the accounting books.

"No," Alex said quietly, looking around at the devastation. "Yesterday this place looked like it belonged in a magazine circular. Nothing was out of place. Even the wastebaskets were empty."

Danny jerked his thumb at what remained of the little office space.

"Any idea what they were looking for?"

Alex shook his head. It didn't look like whoever did this was looking for anything. From the way the folders lay, scattered across the floor, it was obvious they were all still in their drawers when the filing cabinet had been tipped over. If someone had gone through them looking for something, they would have thrown them on the floor one by one as they read them. This felt more like a distraction.

"Was there anything else on the desk when you got here?" Alex asked, pointing to the stack of Grier's account books.

"No," Danny said. "My guys picked up those after we got here.

The Long Chain

They were over there." He indicated the corner by the stairs going down.

"His lab was this way," Alex said, heading for the stairs. "Is it all torn up too?"

"You tell me," Danny said, following Alex down.

The lab was very much as Alex remembered it. The remains of the acrid chemical odor still lingered in the air, but it was tolerable, and the glassware all looked to be where Alex had left it. There was one exception, however; one of the workbenches had been moved. When Alex had been there, all the benches had been in neat rows, each exactly the same space apart. Now two of the benches had been pulled back to back and an elaborate series of glassware and tubes had been laid out on it. A dozen glass containers with various liquids and powders inside stood in a neat row on one end of the double table, next to an unlit burner.

"That was burning when we got here," Danny said as Alex examined the apparatus.

"This wasn't here yesterday," he said. "Whoever broke in did this."

"Why?"

"They must have wanted to brew a potion of some kind," Alex said.

Danny looked incredulous.

"Are you saying an alchemist broke in here just to make a potion? Then why trash the store?"

"As a distraction," Alex said, leaning close to the liquid-filled glass globes. "I'll bet you a fiver that those shelves of potions upstairs were knocked down so you wouldn't be able to tell what had been taken, and the same for the chemicals in the display case."

"How would we have known any of that?" Danny observed.

"Whoever our alchemist burglar is must have worried you'd call in an expert," Alex said with a shrug, making his way along the elaborate maze of tubes. At the far end was a small, cylindrical beaker. Being careful not to touch it, he leaned close and sniffed it.

"Did you find something?" Danny asked.

"Maybe," Alex said, putting his kit down on a neighboring table. He pulled out his ghostlight burner, clipping it into his lamp, then strapped on his oculus. Once he lit the burner, he played the greenish light over the entire apparatus on the two tables. Each jar, tube and condenser held glowing residue of the magical liquids that had been moving through them, but the last few jars did not. He shone the lamp in the little beaker positioned to catch the liquid at the end of its journey through the machine. It didn't glow at all.

Danny had remained quiet while Alex worked, but he must have seen something change in Alex's expression.

"What is it?" he asked.

"When did you get the call that there had been a break-in here?"

Danny flipped open his notebook and turned a few pages.

"Around nine o'clock this morning," he said. "From a Mrs. Osbourne."

Alex nodded.

"I met her. She owns the millinery shop next door."

"Apparently, she came to pick up something from her shop and saw the back door here broken open. Does that mean something to you?"

Alex didn't answer as he blew out the ghostlight burner and replaced it with the silverlight one. Playing the white light over the glassware, dozens of fingerprints glowed back at him. Some were big while others were small, and most were smudged. Danny might be able to get a usable set from it, but he had no way of knowing where any of them had come from.

He turned to the corner of the basement where the vent fan stood. Next to it was a large tub-style sink and a drying rack. The rack was empty, so Alex turned his light on the little beaker at the end of the brewing line. Whoever set up this new apparatus would have wanted an absolutely clean receptacle for the fruits of their labor.

"Bingo," he said as the silverlight revealed a near perfect set of prints. Alex looked up at Danny with a grin and waived him over. "Look here," he said once he'd passed over his oculus.

"You think these belong to whoever broke in?" he asked.

Alex quickly explained about how the glass at the end of the line had to be perfectly clean.

"Whoever did this would have washed the beaker," he said. "It's a cinch these are their prints."

"I don't know," Danny said, holding his thumb near the glass. "These are tiny."

Alex took the oculus back and examined the fingerprints more closely. Danny was right, they were very small.

"Maybe our burglar is a kid," Alex said. "Or a woman."

"Maybe," Danny said with a shrug. "But I've been thinking about your distraction theory." He pointed to the neat row of powders, potions, and reagents at the far end of the table. "If whoever did this didn't want us to know what they needed from upstairs, then why leave these here?"

Alex swore.

"This beaker has prints on it, but that's all," he said. "There's no potion residue inside."

"You mean they went through all this," Danny indicated the maze of glassware and tubes, "but they didn't finish?"

"Yes," Alex said, scooping up his kit and heading for the stairs. "And I think I know why."

He hurried upstairs and shined his lamp over the back door, then paused to give the little office space a look before continuing into the front of the shop.

"What is it?" Danny asked, coming up behind him.

"Find out if any of your men have had their shoes re-heeled recently," Alex said, then he walked around the spilled powders and knelt down to reach under the overturned display case.

As Danny called his men in, Alex retrieved the large tin scoop he'd seen in the display case on his previous visit. Kneeling outside the area of the strewn powder, Alex began to carefully scrape it to the side, revealing the floor underneath. After a few passes with the scoop, he uncovered a patch of clumpy powder that stuck together as he pulled the scoop through it.

"None of my men have had their shoes fixed recently," Danny said, coming up behind him.

"Well then, I think we both owe them an apology," Alex said, setting the scoop aside.

"What's that supposed to mean?"

"It means I know why our burglar wrecked the store, and why they didn't finish brewing the potion they came here to get." He pointed to the sticky lumps of chemical powder on the floor, then handed Danny his oculus and pointed his lamp at it.

"Why is it glowing like that?"

"Because it's blood," Alex said. He got up and moved to where the partial shoe print was visible on the floor. "Note the heel," he said, pointing to the sharp line. "It's new and since none of your men have new heels on their shoes…"

"You think someone walked in on our burglar," Danny said. "There was a fight and one of them was wounded. That's why the burglar didn't finish with the potion downstairs."

"That's the way I figure it," Alex said. "The second man fought with the burglar, wounded him, then overturned the display case to hide the blood. Our second man knew by the time the cops found it, he'd be long gone."

"What makes you think this is the burglar's blood?"

Alex pointed to the display case.

"Look at the size of that thing. It would take somebody big to turn it over, and we know our burglar was small."

"So the second man wounds the burglar, the burglar runs for it and the second man sticks around to clean up?" Danny asked. "Why didn't he go after the burglar?"

"He had to stick around," Alex said. "To do whatever he came here to do."

"So what was that?" Danny asked.

Alex led him to the back room and pointed to the mess that had once been Charles Grier's files. Doubtless the second man had been looking for something, or taken something, and dumped out the files to hide what was missing. He was about to point this out when his eyes caught sight of Grier's trophy wall. The glass case under the picture of Grier in Nepal, India was broken open.

"What is it?" Danny asked, reading the expression that sprung to Alex's face

"This case held a knife called a kukri," he said, pointing to the broken frame still hanging on the wall.

"Maybe the burglar grabbed it to defend themselves," Danny suggested.

Alex shook his head.

"But if the burglar stopped to get this knife..."

"The second man would have caught him...or her," Danny finished.

Alex looked down at the folders littering the floor as if seeing them for the first time.

"Here," Danny said, handing Alex the oculus before he could ask for it. "What do you see?"

Alex almost didn't need the oculus. The glass that remained in the case showed no sign of blood anywhere. If the burglar had been seriously wounded, it was unlikely he, or she, would have been able to retrieve the knife without leaving a blood trail.

He played his lamp over the floor. There were plenty of fingerprints on the folders and the desk, but no blood.

"Hang on a second," Danny said. He crouched down and shoved a big stack of the folders to one side. Immediately the floor lit up with reflected light.

"There's more blood here," Alex confirmed. He turned back to the door that led down to the lab. "But there isn't any on the door, and there was a carpet in that corner before."

"Well, that doesn't bode well for our burglar," Danny said. "You figure our big guy got to the knife first, killed the burglar, then took the burglar's body out in the missing rug?"

"Not without leaving some kind of trail," Alex said, stepping around the broken door and into the fog. Danny followed him, looking up and down the Alley.

"If you're right about that blood trail, can you find it?" Danny said, peering through the fog. "I can get my men out here to help."

"Don't bother," Alex said, catching a spot of fluorescence reflected back at him from across the alley. He and Danny crossed to the far side, where a rolled-up rug lay against the back of a laundry. A metallic tang hung in the air and Alex could smell something like rusty iron. The rug was a dark color, so Alex couldn't see any blood, but parts of it appeared to be wet. It was also much bulkier than it had been the day before.

"I don't need a lamp for that," Danny said, pointing to one of the shiny spots. "Blood."

"I guess the burglar didn't get away after all," Alex said.

Danny knelt down and took hold of the rug.

"Let's see who our small burglar was."

He pulled and the rug rolled open. Inside was a body, but it wasn't the one they expected. The man who rolled out with the rug had to be over six feet tall, or at least he would have been if his head hadn't been completely severed from his body.

9

THE OTHER MONOGRAPH

The brownstone was dark and quiet when Alex finally got home, and the grandfather clock in the foyer showed a quarter past eleven. Once he and Danny understood that *The Philosopher's Stone* wasn't just a break-in, but a murder scene, Alex had gone over every inch of the place.

The walls and ceiling of the shop had been painted with a dark green paint, probably to hide any evidence of smoke or chemical residue, things common to alchemy shops. It was also quite effective at hiding the spatter of blood cast off from a knife when it was being used to repeatedly stab someone. Whoever had dumped out the file cabinet and the display case had done a credible job of hiding the direct evidence of the crime, but once Alex knew what he was looking for, traces of a violent assault were everywhere.

The body in the alley had at least a dozen stab wounds in it, to say nothing of the missing head. Danny surmised that whoever removed it didn't want the dead man's identity known. He'd called in a dozen more beat cops to help search the alley and the surrounding area, but Alex figured that would be a waste of time. Whoever took the time and effort to remove a dead man's head wasn't about to just toss it somewhere as they fled the scene. It was probably in the East River by now, and weighted, at that.

Once he'd finished showing Danny and the cops where all the blood was, Alex had tried to get a cab, but the few daring cabbies still at work in the fog were busy serving high paying riders in the Core. Eventually, Alex had walked ten blocks to a nightclub on the edge of the Core and gotten a cab there.

He hung up his hat as he entered, but instead of going to bed, he turned into the library and sat down in his reading chair. His hands shook as he took out his cigarette case, though whether that was from fatigue, lack of rejuvenator, or the grisly scene of the headless corpse, he wasn't quite sure.

"I thought I heard you come in." Iggy's voice cut through his thoughts.

Alex jumped. He hadn't heard the old man come down the stairs from his second-floor bedroom.

"Sorry, lad," Iggy said, emerging from the darkness to clap him on the shoulder. He reached under the Tiffany lamp as he passed and switched it on, casting its multi-colored light over the bookshelves. "Well, you look terrible," he said, sitting in his own chair on the far side of the lamp.

"People keep telling me that," Alex said, taking a drag on his cigarette. "I might develop a complex or something."

"You want to talk about it?"

Alex cast Iggy a sidelong glance.

"What makes you think there's anything to talk about?"

Iggy scoffed.

"You stagger in here just before midnight, looking like ten miles of bad road, and smelling of sweat, blood, and silverlight oil. Of course there's something to talk about. If there wasn't, you'd have gone straight to bed."

Alex sighed. One of these day's he'd finally learn that he couldn't put one over on Iggy.

"Not sure I could sleep if I did," he said.

Alex had seen corpses before, of course. Iggy had dragged him to the morgue more times than he could count to teach him about wounds, bodies, decomposition, and deduction. This had been his first decapitation, however.

He took another drag on his cigarette and told Iggy about his adventures at *The Philosopher's Stone*.

"Ugh," Iggy grunted when Alex described the condition of the murdered man. "Desecration of a corpse is never a pleasant thing."

"I'm no expert," Alex said, "but based on the wounds, I'd say a lot of what was done happened after the guy was dead. Like the killer was insane."

"You may be right," Iggy said. "There's historical precedent for such an attack. In Brunei, men have been known to suddenly start attacking people, maiming, wounding, and even killing in a frenzy. They call it 'running amok.'"

"You said men," Alex observed.

Iggy nodded.

"It's a phenomenon that's never been seen in women or youth, so far as I know."

"Well I may have a case for you. Based on the fingerprints our survivor left behind, they were small, most likely a woman."

Iggy shrugged.

"I'm very progressive in my opinions on crime," he said. "Evil isn't limited to the male of the species."

"Well, Danny and the police will have to figure that part out. I'm more concerned with what happened to Charles Grier. It's unlikely that two different burglars picked the same shop to break into — they were both there looking for him."

"Could he be your headless man?"

Alex shook his head as he ground out the stub of his cigarette.

"Grier's in his sixties. Even without the head, I could tell the dead guy wasn't that old."

Iggy got up as Alex fumbled with his cigarette case again and crossed to the liquor cabinet.

"What's your next step, then?" he asked as he removed a crystal decanter with a blood-red liquid in it.

"Tomorrow Danny is going over to Grier's place to see if there's anything there," Alex said, focusing on holding his hands steady as he lit another cigarette. "He'll have to get a warrant, so it won't be till after noon. I'll meet up with him then."

"What about the body?" Iggy asked, pouring the red liquid into two glasses.

Alex shrugged.

"Down at the morgue," he said. "Danny will call me if they find anything."

"Here," Iggy said, passing him one of the glasses. "Fortify yourself with some port."

Alex accepted the glass and sipped it.

"I've got something else for you," Iggy said, sitting back in his chair. He leaned down and opened the elaborately carved wooden chest that sat under the front window. Pulp novels were Iggy's biggest weakness and he kept them in the chest rather than putting them on one of the library's shelves where he might have to explain them to a visitor.

Instead of a pulp paperback, however, Iggy pulled out a slim book bound in green leather. He hesitated, looking at the book for a long moment before he handed it to Alex.

"What's this?" Alex asked, turning the book over. Both the front and back covers were blank, though they appeared well worn.

"A little monograph of my own," Iggy said with an enigmatic grin.

Alex opened the book. The first printed page read, *On the Use of Linking Runes to Build Disconnected Constructs*. Below that was printed the name of the author, *Arthur Conan Doyle*.

"It's everything I know about writing three-dimensional runes," Iggy said. He gave Alex a somewhat sheepish look. "I was inspired by the textbook." He nodded toward the thin red volume on the shelf beside the hearth.

"I went through the textbook for at least three hours last night," Alex said, holding up Iggy's monograph. "This seems pretty important; why doesn't the textbook mention it?"

"There's quite a lot the textbook leaves out," Iggy said, sitting back in his chair. "I suspect the men who put it together wanted to make sure that if it did fall into the wrong hands, it was as difficult as possible to misuse."

Alex's tired brain chewed on that for a moment, then he nodded wearily.

"I guess that makes sense," he said. "So is that why you've spent the last two years teaching me to write more complex runes instead of digging into the textbook?"

"Just so, lad," Iggy said, sipping his port. "I know you understand a lot of what's in there, but you weren't ready to really use it."

"And now?"

"You're almost there. Once you learn the real power of linking runes, we'll move on to inverse runes, persistence runes, and finally void runes. Once you master those, you'll be ready to use the textbook to its full potential."

As he spoke, Iggy's eyes seemed to light up and his bottle-brush mustache turned up in an infectious grin. For over a year, Alex had believed his mentor had lost faith in him, that he was punishing him for sacrificing so much of his life to save the city. He felt a wave of shame, looking at Iggy's enthusiasm.

You should have known better.

"Sounds like I've got some reading to do," Alex said with a tired smile.

Iggy's face turned serious and he leveled his index finger at Alex.

"Later," he said in his best instructor's voice. "Right now you're tired and wrung out. You said yourself that Danny won't have his warrant until tomorrow afternoon, so you have plenty of time for reading in the morning."

Alex wanted to protest but he simply couldn't seem to put together a cogent response, a sure sign that Iggy was right. Finally he gave up and nodded his acquiescence.

"Good," Iggy said in a firm voice. "Now finish your port and go to bed."

The next morning, almost all traffic on the roads had stopped. Even the street-level crawlers weren't running. Alex had to walk five blocks to catch a sky bug and then walk another seven blocks to get to his office. Unsurprisingly, Leslie was there when he arrived.

Very surprisingly, she didn't look happy.

"What in heaven's name happened to you?" she said when he came in.

Alex had forgotten the black eye he'd gotten off Henry Travis, Grier's super.

"It's nothing," he said, then explained about his weekend. As he spoke, he offered her a cigarette from his brass case. When she selected one, he noticed she wasn't wearing an engagement ring.

"That's disgusting," she said when he told her about the body behind Charles Grier's shop.

"Do I dare ask how your weekend went?" he asked, offering her a light from his squeeze lighter.

"You probably shouldn't," she said, giving him a hard look. She knew Alex well enough to know he hadn't missed her bare left hand. "I've been through your notes from Saturday," she said, unambiguously changing the subject. "Your first client meeting isn't till Wednesday."

"That's okay," he said. "I've got some other work to keep me busy."

He quickly outlined his visit from Sorsha and her new feds.

"I think I might have a way to figure out where all this fog is coming from," he finished. "But I'll have to do some reading first. If anything comes up, go ahead and interrupt me. I'll be in my vault."

Leslie promised that she would, and Alex headed for his office. Once inside, he hung up his hat and pulled out his rune book. He needed to read Iggy's monograph on linking runes, but he didn't want to do that in his office. Instead, he pulled out a vault rune and opened his extra-dimensional space.

Iggy's book wasn't as secret or as dangerous as the textbook, but just the same, Alex didn't want to just be walking around with it, so he'd left it in his vault. Despite his having expanded it greatly, his vault was mostly empty space. What little furniture he had was acquired a piece at a time over several years, and at the rate he was going, Alex would need another decade or so before he'd have it decked out like Iggy's. Assuming he had that long.

Still, it did have a comfortable reading chair and a magelight lamp with a shade. It also had a security door. Alex wasn't worried that Leslie would send someone into his office without calling him on the intercom, but some clients in the past had simply barged in. To prevent anyone from entering his vault while he was inside, Alex had taken the precaution of adding a heavy door of solid oak that had been reinforced with a steel frame. The frame even had a metal stopper that stuck out, preventing anyone from shutting the vault door completely while he was inside. Only he could lock the vault door, but that wouldn't stop someone from closing it and putting something heavy against it in the hopes that Alex would suffocate or starve inside. With the security door shut and locked with two heavy steel bolts, however, no one could close him inside it.

Alex shut the inner door and locked it in place with a heavy bolt, then he moved to the comfortable reading chair in front of his fake hearth. Iggy's book was already on the side table, along with an expensive bottle of single malt scotch and a shot glass. He poured himself a slug, turned on the lamp on the table, and sat down to read.

The clock on the mantle above the hearth was an elaborate number with a carved wooden case and a glass front that covered a small pendulum. Alex glanced up at it when a knock sounded at his security door. He'd been reading for a little over two hours.

With a sigh, he set Iggy's monograph aside and went to answer the door. He knew it was Leslie because she'd knocked in the pattern he'd taught her, two quick knocks, then three slower ones. If there had been a problem, it would have been different.

"Karen Burnham is back," Leslie said when he pulled the door open. "She says she needs to talk to you."

That was surprising. She had seemed quite resolute in her dismissal of him on Friday. Alex closed his vault, but didn't lock it. He didn't want to have to use another vault rune if he didn't have to, and he was reasonably sure he could physically prevent Karen Burnham from entering his vault if the situation arose.

"Ask her to come in," he said.

Alex waited behind his desk until Karen came in. She looked tired and out of sorts, but she had managed a weak smile.

"How's your grandfather?" Alex asked, offering her a seat.

"About the same," she said. "The doctor gave me some drops to help him sleep, but he seems restless, even when he's sleeping."

"Does he remember anything?"

She shook her head.

"No. He seems more disoriented now than when he was at the soup kitchen, always muttering something about a shade tree."

"Is there a tree in your yard?" Alex asked, trying to picture Dr. Burnham's house.

"Not one big enough to cast shade," Karen said. "I have no idea what he's talking about. I'm afraid he doesn't know either. I'm very worried about him."

"What can I do to help?" Alex asked, sitting on the edge of his desk.

"I wish there was something you could do," Karen said. She opened her handbag and took out three, crisp dollar bills. "You paid for the cab when we went looking for my grandfather," she said, handing Alex the money. "I didn't reimburse you for that."

Alex had forgotten about it. It was only a couple of bucks, but Karen's integrity impressed him.

"Thanks," he said accepting the bills.

"Well, that's everything," she said, standing.

"Before you go, Miss Burnham," Alex said, standing as well. "I can't help feeling that there's something strange about the attack on your grandfather."

"You said that before," Karen returned, her voice calm and even. "I don't understand what happened to my grandfather, but now he's home where he belongs, and our neighbor Mrs. Phillips is looking in on him while I'm at work. I can't imagine he's in any danger."

Alex opened his mouth to object, but she continued.

"That said, I can't imagine him being attacked by anyone in the first place." She looked up at Alex with her plain, earnest face. "Tell me what it is that you see, Mr. Lockerby. What makes you think my grandfather is in some sort of danger?"

"I have to be honest with you, Miss Burnham, right now it's just a feeling. That said, I've been in this business a long time and I've learned to trust my gut...and my gut's telling me there's more to this affair than you and I are seeing."

"What is it you want me to do?" she asked. "Even if your gut is right, how would we know?"

"You said your grandfather spent all his time out back in his workshop, right?"

Karen nodded.

"Well, then let me go back there and have a look around," Alex said. "If what happened to your grandfather was just some random thing, he's in no danger, but if I'm right, his being attacked has something to do with that workshop."

She considered that for a long moment.

"You were right when you said my grandfather is well off," Karen said. "But he didn't get that way by being a spendthrift. I don't think there's anything to find in grandfather's workshop, and I don't want to pay you to look for ghosts."

Alex could understand that, but his gut was still telling him that Dr. Burnham, and by extension Karen, were still in danger.

"Tell you what," he said. "I've got an appointment this afternoon, but if it's okay with you, I'll come by after that and give the workshop the once over. If I don't find anything, you don't owe me."

"What if you find something you think is important, but I don't?" she asked with a raised eyebrow.

Alex laughed.

"You're very cynical for someone so young," he said. "If you don't think anything I find out is important, then the deal stands: you don't owe me. At least then we'll be reasonably sure you and Dr. Burnham are safe."

"All right," she said after a moment. She turned toward the door, but stopped. "For the record, I hope you're wrong, and not just so that I don't have to pay you."

With that, she left his office and, after a moment, he heard the outer door to his waiting area close behind her.

"What was that about?" Leslie asked as Alex stood in his office door.

"I'm going back over to Dr. Burnham's house after I meet Danny," he said. "Be a doll and run over to the library while I'm gone. See if you can dig up anything on Dr. Leonard Burnham. He used to work at Dow Chemical, and he won the Nobel Prize for Chemistry, so there's bound to be something on him."

"Is there anything specific you want to know?" Leslie said, scribbling on a note pad.

"Yeah," Alex said, looking at the outer door where Karen had gone. "I want to know who gets Dr. Burnham's money if he dies."

10

THE PURITY CONSTRUCT

Alex sat back from his drafting table and rubbed his bloodshot eyes. He'd forgotten about the bruise over his left eye, but the rubbing reminded him, and he winced in pain.

"You need to go see Jessica," he admonished himself. "She'd fix you up quick."

Absently he took out the flask of rejuvenator that he was now carrying in his back trouser pocket. Glancing at the clock over the mantle in his vault, he saw that it was almost two. He took a swig of the rejuvenator and closed his eyes as the potion eased his weariness and sharpened his foggy brain. Breathing deeply, he put the cap back on the flask and returned it to his pocket. He couldn't be sure, but it felt like the flask had two more swigs left, maybe three.

He resolved to go see Jessica once he was done with Dr. Burnham's workshop.

On the drafting table in front of him were the results of the last few hours work. Two runic constructs and three single runes all on their own sheets of paper. Four of them were on the usual flash paper, but the fifth had been drawn on a study sheet of parchment paper.

According to Iggy's monograph, separate runes and constructs could be joined by casting them in proximity to a linking construct —

a runic circle with one linking rune for every separate rune you wanted to join. Alex held up the parchment paper and reviewed it. The runic circles had three nodes, each with its own linking rune, with a fourth linking rune in the center.

Setting that aside, he picked up three of the remaining runes and examined them, one by one. These were all identical purity runes. Alex had seen these in the textbook two years ago when he'd first read it, but hadn't seen any real use for them. They originated in the past when merchants began to travel to distant lands to trade, bringing with them whatever coin they were used to. Runewrights of the day developed the purity rune to test foreign coins to see if they contained a pure sample of gold or silver. All a merchant had to do was put the trader's money in a pile alongside an impure sample of the metal, then cast the rune on a pure sample and a bit of wood floating in a bowl of water. The stick would then point to the purest sample.

Now Alex would use it to locate the densest fog inside a certain area.

Setting the purity runes aside, he picked up the last paper. This was a finding rune, but one unlike any he'd written in years. Originally, finding runes had very limited areas of effect, usually enough for a single small home or large hall. What made Alex's finding rune so effective was all the things he added to extend its range. Alex's rune could cover all of Manhattan, more if the rivers hadn't blocked the magic. For the fog, however, Alex had to think smaller. Adding a focal rune to his own finding rune would cut the area of effect in half, but that would still cover miles, and his purity runes wouldn't work at that range. What he needed was something that would only search a radius of a few blocks.

Instead of using his more powerful version, he had to go back to the original rune and find a way to increase its area only slightly. The rune would cover a radius of one hundred feet, so Alex spent most of his time trying various ways to increase that. Finally he wrote a boost rune and a doubling rune without destabilizing the construct, and that got him to roughly three thousand feet. It wasn't enough to seriously search the city, but it was big enough for a test.

Leslie had gone to the library as he'd asked, so Alex packed up his kit with the tools he'd need and headed out, putting the *Gone to Lunch* sign on the door as he left. Since New York blocks were actually rectangles, he went five blocks east from his office, then stuck one of the purity runes to the side of a random building. Before he lit it, however, he brought out the parchment paper and touched the corner to the flash paper.

The purity rune burst to life as the flash paper disintegrated, leaving the parchment paper unharmed. As the rune glowed for a moment on the brick wall, a similar rune burned itself into the parchment paper, joined to one of the three linking runes around the runic circle.

Alex repeated the process two more times to the northwest and southwest of the first building, then returned to his office. With the three purity runes spread out around his own building, he could use them to triangulate the location of the thickest fog inside the minor finding rune's range.

He bypassed his floor, pausing only to check that the sign was still on the door, a clear indication that Leslie hadn't come back. Continuing up to the roof, Alex laid out his map of Manhattan, then laid the parchment paper with its three linking and purity runes right over his location. He pulled three compasses from his bag, placing one on each of the linking runes, then adding the modified finding rune to the top.

Pulling out his lighter, he said a silent prayer that his calculations were right and that the unfamiliar construct wouldn't blow up in his face. Satisfied he'd done all he could, Alex squeezed the side of the lighter and the top flicked open, illuminating the surrounding fog with a halo of yellow light.

When he lit the finding rune, the flash paper vanished, leaving the finding rune hovering over the map as it usually did. This time, however, the parchment paper began to smoke and burn, charring at the nodes of the runic construct. After a moment, glowing runes sprang up from them as well, hovering over each compass.

Alex held his breath as the compass needles spun in time with the linking runes, then slowly stopped. He pulled out a straight ruler and drew a pencil line along the direction of the first arrow, then again for the second. When he got to the third, he cursed himself for being an idiot. The first two pencil lines already crossed inside the radius of the spell, so he didn't need the third spell at all. He'd assumed that because it was called triangulation, he needed three points.

"I'm glad no one was around to see that," he muttered as he cleared the compasses and the smoldering parchment away. His map had gotten a little singed, but he could still read it. He'd have to figure out a way to protect it in the future; maybe a rune that would resist burning?

According to the pencil lines on his map, the densest area of fog inside the spell's ten-block radius was on a ten-story apartment building just over the line in the inner ring. Alex stood and took his bearings, locating the building quickly, off to the east. It was easily the tallest building in the area, which was surprising. He'd expected the fog to be thinner up high, though now that he thought about it, he didn't really know enough about fog to make such a determination.

"Looks like it's your day for being wrong," he said to the empty roof as he rolled up his map and returned it to his kit. "Let's go see if there's anything on that building I can use to redeem myself."

The inner-ring apartment building had a doorman, but Alex avoided him easily while the fellow was hailing a cab. Since this was a nice, upscale building, it had an automatic elevator, so Alex rode up to the top floor before climbing the last flight of stairs to the roof.

The view from there would have been spectacular if the entire city hadn't been socked in fog. He thought he could make out the park, off to the south, but there just wasn't any way to be sure.

Turning away from the view, he opened his kit and pulled out his ghostlight burner. He swept the greenish light all over the roof, but found nothing, not even a trace of magic.

Undaunted, he switched to silverlight. This was much more fruitful, if Alex wanted to count finding evidence of pigeons, alcohol, vomit, and illicit encounters as success.

After almost an hour he sat down on the edge of a stone chimney and sulked. Pulling out a cigarette and lighting it, he just sat, glaring at the uncaring fog. He'd tried everything he knew and there just wasn't any evidence that the fog here was any different than any other fog anywhere in the city. He was sure of one thing, though, this fog wasn't magical in any way.

"Well that's not true," he muttered, remembering how Sorsha had said it didn't want to move, even when subjected to strong winds.

Alex stood up suddenly, startling a nearby pigeon. Flinging his cigarette away, he dug into his kit and pulled out his multi-lamp and oculus again. This time he clipped the amberlight burner into the lamp.

Amberlight would reveal what Iggy called temporal positioning. If an object was used to being in one location, it would develop a temporal bond with that place. When you shone Amberlight on the object, faint orange lines would connect it to the place where it usually was located. This was an indispensable tool for reconstructing crime scenes or following stolen vehicles back to where they were usually parked, but that was about it. Unless, of course, you had a mysterious fog that didn't seem to move. If that was true, Alex would be able to see it under the amberlight.

Lighting the burner, he closed the lamp, then swept it around the roof. Through his oculus, the fog lit up like a Macy's Christmas window. Ghostly orange lines swirled all around him, bunching and stretching as if someone had actually drawn the fog with pencil lines.

At first it was confusing, but as Alex moved around the roof, he began to see patterns. Each mass of fog seemed to be connected to the others. He followed the connecting lines until they led him to a corner of the roof where an enormous brick chimney stuck up. Lines of connection radiated out from the chimney, tying it to the surrounding masses of fog. To Alex it looked as if the masonry had grown a mass of fine orange hair.

Reaching out, he ran his hand through the faint lines, but the fog just swirled around him. There was nothing physical there to grab, at least nothing he could feel. As he moved his hand back and forth, however, the orange lines began to swirl and distort. When he stopped, they slowed and returned to their original positions. He wasn't sure how it was possible, but the fog on this roof was anchored to the big chimney. That was why it couldn't be blown away; it would move, but once the force disturbing it went away, it returned to where it had been.

If he hadn't seen it with his own eyes, Alex wouldn't have believed it. This fog clearly wasn't normal fog, but he knew for a fact that it wasn't magical.

"So far as you know," he corrected himself, remembering the glyph runewrights he'd met last year. Just because he couldn't tell it was magical, didn't mean it wasn't. Also, some kinds of alchemy stopped being magical once their initial magic was expended. Healing potions worked that way, along with some others.

Whatever this was, Alex wasn't going to figure it out standing on a rooftop in the fog. He picked up his equipment and rode the elevator down to the building's lobby. Stopping at a pay phone, he tried his office and Leslie picked up almost immediately.

"Where are you?" she asked. "Danny called, he said you can meet him over at Grier's apartment any time."

"All right," Alex said. "I'll head over. Did you have any luck with Dr. Burnham?"

"He was actually pretty easy to find," Leslie said. "He has over a dozen patents to his name, including one for making super-efficient gas mask filters. They were so good that the Army used them during the war."

"Bet that made him a pretty penny," Alex observed.

"You'd never know it, but it must have," Leslie said. "Burnham sold the process to Dow for an undisclosed sum."

"Which is the paper's way of saying a lot. What about his family?"

"He has one son, Jeremy Burnham," Leslie said. "He's the manager for a fertilizer plant in Missouri."

"Guess he's nothing like his dad."

"You wouldn't think so, but I looked him up, too. He has a degree in organic chemistry from Yale and a patent for a new kind of fertilizer."

"Well, that wouldn't be the first time today I've been wrong," Alex admitted. "Anything else?"

"As far as I can tell, Karen Burnham is Dr. Leonard Burnham's youngest heir, but I suspect her father and his wife are first in line. If you think Karen is out to bump her grandfather off, you're going to have to come up with a better motive."

Alex sighed.

"All right."

"Are you going to meet up with Danny?"

"I need to make a call first, but then I will." He glanced outside at the pea-soup fog. "Assuming I can get a cab."

"Good luck," Leslie said and hung up.

Alex pulled out his rune book and extracted the Ice Queen's business card from the pocket sewn under the back cover. She'd given him one of her cards when they first met, two years ago, but that one only had one number on it that turned out to be her home. This card had one number as well, but it was clearly marked, *Office*.

"Miss Kincaid's office," a smooth male voice answered when Alex's call connected.

"I need to talk to Miss Kincaid," he said.

"I'm sorry," the voice responded. "Miss Kincaid is out at the moment. May I take a message?"

"Yeah," Alex said. "Tell her that Alex Lockerby knows something about her mysterious fog." He chuckled at the reaction that message was sure to get, then hung up and headed out into the fog to find a cab.

11

WHAT ISN'T THERE

Alex wondered how Danny was going to get him past Charles Grier's super. By the time he arrived, however, the police were already upstairs and there was no sign of the combative Henry Travis.

"You're late," Danny said with a grin when Alex reached Grier's door.

"Blame the fog," he said. "Anything interesting?"

"There have been more accidents in the last week than in the previous six months," Danny said.

Alex shot him an unamused look.

"In the apartment."

Danny looked around at the officers who were going through Grier's home looking for anything out of the ordinary. The hall door led into a large parlor with couches that faced each other over a coffee table. Behind them was a smallish reading area with a radiator next to a comfortable chair and a bookshelf. Doors led off each side of the room and Alex could see a kitchen through the one to the left.

"The super let us in," Danny began, leading Alex into the parlor and toward the kitchen. "As far as we can tell, nothing is out of place."

They passed through into the dining room where a table big

enough for several people stood with a china hutch along one wall. The kitchen was connected through an open bar area. Alex could see a stove and oven next to a generous counter.

"Any dishes left out?"

"No," Danny said. "And none in the sink either."

Alex took a moment to look around, opening the icebox.

"It looks like he hadn't been shopping in a while, and some of the food has started to spoil," Danny observed. "It could mean Grier's been gone longer than we thought."

Alex shrugged and shut the icebox door.

"According to Dr. Kellin, Grier is a bachelor," he said, pulling open some of the cabinets. "There aren't any fancy pans or pots here. If Grier learned to cook beyond the basics, he'd have more equipment."

Danny nodded. He'd eaten at the brownstone before. More to the point, he'd helped Alex wash up before. Like any true artist, Iggy had an almost inexhaustible supply of cooking gear.

"So, you're thinking he ate out a lot?" Danny asked.

Alex gestured around at the apartment.

"Look at this place," he said. "Grier was clearly doing well for himself."

"You ain't seen nothin' yet," Danny said leading Alex back out into the parlor and across to the other door. Beyond it was a short hall with a bathroom and a linen closet, then another door opened into an enormous bedroom. A walk-in closet ran the length of the room, filled with more clothes than Alex could use in a lifetime.

"Apparently, Grier was quite the dandy," Danny observed.

Alex looked down the rows of hangers to the back where a stack of shoeboxes filled the far shelf. Since there were already at least two dozen pairs of shoes on the floor in a neat row, he wondered what might be in the boxes.

The bedroom itself consisted of a double bed with a tall dresser and a dressing stand for a suit.

"There's another bathroom through there," Danny said pointing to a small door in the wall. "And across the hall is a study."

"Let's see that," Alex said, heading for the door.

The study turned out to be a little office with a desk, a filing cabinet and a secretary cabinet that held more souvenirs of Grier's travels.

"Anything jump out at you?" Danny asked once Alex had looked around.

"No," he said, irritation plain in his voice. "Let me poke around with my lamp. Maybe there's something we can't see."

An hour later, Alex had to admit defeat. He'd been over the house meticulously and found no signs of foul play. There wasn't even anything suspicious. No signs of a betting habit, or suspicious money. No sign of a torrid affair, or even a tame one.

"Did the medical examiner have any luck with the body?" Alex asked as he packed up his kit.

"There's a tattoo on the dead man's arm," Danny said, leaning against the desk in Grier's study. "If he's been arrested before, there might be a record of it. And if the file guys can find that record, we might learn who he was, but that's about it."

"Mind if I look through Grier's papers?" Alex asked, pointing to the filing cabinet. "Maybe he really did go on a trip."

"You're welcome to look," Danny said, "but I went through those while you were doing your sweep. If he went somewhere, he didn't take money out of his bank account to buy tickets. And before you ask, there's nothing in his calendar. I checked."

Alex felt the urge to check for himself, but he knew Danny's work. If he said he'd checked, Alex knew it had been done. He moved to the filing cabinet and began going through the files inside. Most of them related to Grier's travels and his finances. There was a file of correspondence between Grier and other alchemists, but nothing that stuck out. Finally Alex shut the cabinet and turned to face Danny.

"Ready?" his friend said. "I sent the uniforms home half an hour ago. What do you say we get some dinner?"

"One more thing," Alex said, remembering the shoe boxes in Grier's enormous closet. He made his way down the wall of clothes to the boxes and began pulling them off the shelf one by one. The first contained receipts for work he'd had done on his apartment. Another held the rank insignia and decorations of an army lieutenant along with a picture of Grier during the big war. Others held bits and pieces of

Grier's life, including a collection of stamps, more souvenirs he obviously didn't think were worthy to display in his glass cabinet, and a stack of old letters.

Alex thumbed through the letters, scanning the names. When he got to the back , he found several that were signed simply, Andrea. There were five of them, and Alex set them aside, returning the rest to their box.

"Find something?" Danny asked.

"I think these letters are from Dr. Kellin," he said, scanning through them. The first letter dealt with a project they were working on, presumably in college. From the text, Alex gathered that Dr. Kellin had gone out of town to secure some rare ingredient and she had written to inform him of her success.

The second letter had obviously been written during the war. There weren't any declarations of affection in it, but Alex felt like the subtext was there.

The third letter was the longest of the five. In it, Dr. Kellin explained that she was leaving their graduate school to go to medical school. She regretted leaving and wished Grier luck with something he was working on called Leon's Libation. There was no mention of a relationship in this letter either, but it was clear, Andrea was leaving more than just school.

The last letters were written while Grier was overseas on his travels. They were mundane to the point of being boring.

"Do you think Dr. Kellin knows more about Grier's disappearance than she's letting on?" Danny asked, once Alex brought him up to speed.

"No," Alex admitted. "This last letter was written almost ten years ago."

"What about that potion he was developing, Leon's something-or-other?"

"Libation," Alex supplied. "I've never heard of a potion called that, but I'm no alchemist."

"But he would have it written down somewhere, wouldn't he?" Danny asked. "We didn't find a book or file of his alchemy formulas. Not here or at his shop."

Alex nodded, seeing where Danny was headed.

"You're thinking he's got some kind of secret safe?"

"No, actually," Danny said. "I was thinking he's got a deposit box at his bank."

Alex felt a bit sheepish.

"That would make sense," he admitted. "How long will it take to track that down?"

"Well, since there are deposit stubs in his office for Manhattan Central Bank, I'm guessing not long," Danny said with a grin. "Getting a warrant for Grier's box? That will take some time."

Alex sighed.

"Let me know when you find it," he said. "Maybe that's what our burglars were looking for."

"If either of them grabbed Grier, they already know where it is," Danny said.

He was right, of course.

"So where is Grier in all of this?" he wondered. "Maybe he knows someone's after his recipe book, so he took the book and went on the lam?"

Danny shrugged.

"Your guess is as good as mine," he said. "Now what about dinner? It's been a long time since we had the chance to talk about something other than work. On top of that, I'm starved, and I brought my car so we won't need to find a cab."

Alex hadn't eaten since breakfast and his gut growled at him.

"I can't," he said. "But we can meet up at the Lunch Box tomorrow."

"How about somewhere else?" Danny said.

Alex had forgotten about his falling out with Mary.

"Sure," he said. "Call me when you get free. Also, would you mind dropping me over on the South Side? I've got to look in on a client."

When Alex arrived, the home of Dr. Leonard Burnham was dark, with the exception of a single light on the second floor where Burnham's room was located. Alex assumed that Karen wasn't home from her job yet, so he avoided the house and made straight for the workshop.

He did pause to take stock of the back yard before he went in. Karen had been right; there were only two trees in Burnham's back yard, and both of them were saplings, far too small to give any meaningful shade.

So much for that idea.

He tugged open the workshop's carriage door and stepped inside, flicking on the light switch. It still looked like there had been a protracted fight in the workshop, but nothing appeared out of place from the last time he'd been there.

Alex moved to the workbench with the chemistry set on it and put down his kit bag. He tried using his silverlight to examine the room, but the glow in his oculus almost blinded him. Every surface was covered in chemical residue from whatever Burnham had been doing. He'd find no clues that way.

With a sigh, he put away his lamp and oculus. He would have to do this the old-fashioned way. Looking around, he decided to start with the papers that were all over the work surfaces and the floor. An hour later, he'd made three stacks on one of the workbenches he'd cleaned off. The first stack were ordinary papers he'd found on the floor, the second were papers that had been scribbled out, and the third were the more important-looking ones.

One by one, Alex read through the papers until he finally gave up. Most of them were inscribed with chemical formulas that might as well have been written in Sanskrit for all the sense they made. The rest were covered with notes in the form of unintelligible sentence fragments.

"You'd think a Nobel Prize winning chemist would keep better notes," he said, finally. Even as he said it, Alex realized that Burnham would have had to keep better notes. The papers that littered his workshop were just convenient places to jot ideas, a literal written record of his own stream of consciousness. A man who'd worked for a big chemical company for decades and had developed a gas mask filter before that would have to keep detailed notes.

"The question is, where?"

Alex turned around, looking over the workshop with a more critical eye than before. He didn't see any obvious hiding places, but something still bothered him about Burnham's home lab. Something wasn't right.

He walked back to the door and turned, looking in. Everywhere he looked, the lab was a sea of chaos...except for one place. Right inside the door was a large, open space where there just wasn't anything. A table nearby was piled with strange metal parts and an overflowing tool box, but none of that encroached the empty space.

"Something's missing," he said at last.

Alex cursed himself for not seeing it sooner. Karen said her grandfather spent all his spare time out here, so what was he working on? Whatever it was should be the central focus of the workshop, but all he'd seen when he came in was the chaos.

He'd been right from the beginning. This was a robbery. Whatever Dr. Burnham had been working on, it had been stolen. Burnham had probably walked in on the thief or thieves and gotten brained for his trouble.

Alex went to his kit and pulled out his lamp and oculus again. This time he clipped the amberlight burner inside the lamp and pointed it at the empty space. The ghostly outline of a machine appeared, occupying the space where its real counterpart had been. It looked like some kind of motor on a small, wheeled trailer. A large tank of some kind sat on top of everything, but Alex couldn't tell if it was for the engine's fuel or some kind of pressure vessel.

Almost invisible orange lines showed where the whatever-it-was had been pulled out of the workshop. He could try following them with the lamp, but that only worked when following something back to where it had been for a long time. Since Alex was starting where the missing motor had been stored, he knew the trace lines would vanish after he'd gone a few dozen feet.

He was about to put his lamp away when another set of lines caught his eye. These surrounded one of the pictures on the workshop wall. They appeared to trace around the frame, as if it had been repeatedly moved and then replaced. Setting his lamp down, Alex lifted the frame and found a hollow space behind it. Inside was a plain folder and

The Long Chain

a few sheets of writing paper. Alex removed them, then picked up his lamp. Shining it inside revealed that the cubby used to hold several rectangular objects. No doubt these were Dr. Burnham's missing notebooks.

Alex put away his tools and then turned his attention to the folder. It was labeled rather neatly along the protruding tab: Shade Tree. The inside of the folder was empty except for several handwritten receipts. Each of them was for a cash draft of several hundred dollars out of an account that was labeled SEI. There was a name on the stub, but it was poorly written. It looked like Adam Tennon.

"Stand your ground," a rough voice boomed from the door and Alex whirled around.

A uniformed policeman stood in the carriage door, his .38 drawn but not raised.

"Who are you and what are you doing in here?" the policeman asked.

Alex put his hands up where the cop could see them. He was older than Alex, on the job long enough not to get spooked and shoot Alex by mistake. Provided, of course, Alex didn't give him any reason to.

"My name's Lockerby," Alex said. "I'm a private investigator hired by Karen Burnham, she lives here."

"Why'd she hire a private dick?"

"Do you know the Burnhams?" Alex asked.

"I see the old man sometimes," he said. "Just to speak to."

"Well, he was assaulted on Thursday and went missing. We found him and got him home, but now Miss Burnham wants me to find out who did this and why."

The cop seemed to mull this over.

"I have Miss Burnham's permission to be in here," Alex continued. "She should be home by now if you'd like to check."

"You got a P.I. license?"

Alex nodded and opened his coat so the officer could see that he wasn't armed. He then pulled out his rune book and handed it over.

"My license is in the back."

"You're a runewright," the cop said, paging through the book toward the back. "Are you friends with Detective Pak?"

"Danny and I go way back," Alex acknowledged.

The cop seemed to relax at this, holstering his weapon. He still checked Alex's license before handing the rune book back, though.

"Sorry about the gun," the cop said. "Neighbor lady saw the lights on and called us." He looked around as if seeing the workshop for the first time. "Wow, that must have been some fight. The old man must have a few left in him. What did they want?"

Alex explained about the missing motor and the strange pay stub.

"You ever hear of something called the SEI?" he asked.

The cop shrugged.

"Sounds like the government," he said.

That actually made sense. Government was a veritable alphabet soup of acronyms from the FBI to the OSS to the WPA.

"You ever hear of an Adam Tennon?" Alex asked, showing the cop the name on the pay stub.

"No," he admitted. "But that doesn't look like Adam. It's just A D M. That's Navy for Admiral."

"How do you know that?" Alex asked, staring at the signature. It was very messy...but the cop might be right.

"I used to walk a beat down by the Navy Yard," he said. "They print that on the side of the big cars."

"Thanks," Alex said.

"If you want to find out who this Admiral Tennon is, you should go by the central office and ask for Detective Hawkins. He was an officer during the war and he still has a lot of Navy pals."

"I don't know Hawkins," Alex said, more thinking out loud than talking to the policeman.

"He's in Lieutenant Detweiler's division," the cop said. He turned and headed for the door. "I've got to get back to my beat," he said. "You have a good night."

"Thanks," Alex said as the man left. He held up the pay stub and examined it again. He still didn't know where Leonard Burnham's motor was, but thanks to the meddling neighbor, he now knew where to start looking.

12

BROWNING'S THUNDER

Alex took a sky bug from the South Side, past Empire Tower, then along Central Park West to 111th. From there he walked east until he came to the neat little house with the Alchemist sign in the yard. The neon light in the sign that proclaimed the shop 'Open' had been switched off hours ago, and now the only light to be seen was a magelight on the porch that cast a yellow halo in the fog.

It was after seven, and Dr. Kellin would have already gone to bed. Jessica worked the evening shift, until early morning, then they'd trade off.

The entire yard of the house was encircled by a high fence, mostly to keep the neighborhood dogs out of Dr. Kellin's herb garden. Many of the ingredients used in alchemy were best when they were fresh. Alex moved to the right side of the house and opened the hidden gate there. Slipping into the back yard, he closed it behind him, then headed down the hill at the back of the house to the walk-out basement.

Enormous windows ran along the entire back of the house and the alchemy lab was plainly visible inside. Alex expected to find Jessica hard at work inside, but instead she was outside. The back yard had a small greenhouse and an underground root cellar. Between them stood a tall chimney leading down to a brick firebox. Spoiled or failed potions could be dangerous and, as Jessica had pointed out to him on multiple occasions, you couldn't just dump them down the drain, so Dr. Kellin had a small incinerator to handle such things.

Jessica stood with her back to Alex, picking up glass bottles from a box at her feet and pouring them, one by one, into a round chute that led to the incinerator's interior. She had on a white blouse, the dark pair of heavy slacks she wore when working, and a thick, green apron.

He waited until she stooped down to extract another bottle from the box before calling out to her. She squeaked in alarm and dropped the bottle. Her hand went into the front pocket of her apron, but she stopped when she saw Alex.

"For the love of God, Alex," she gasped. "You scared me."

"It's the fog," he said, stepping closer so she could see him better. "You didn't hear me coming."

She put a hand to her chest and tried to slow her rapid breathing.

"Don't do that."

"Didn't the doc tell you I was coming?" he wondered. "I'm out of the rejuvenator." He held up the now empty flask and shook it.

"I remember," she said. "Give me a minute to finish here and I'll get you fixed up."

"Sure," Alex said. She looked at him for half a moment before she turned back to the box of waste potions. It was a look he'd seen often of late. Regret and anger mixed with something he couldn't define. He wasn't sure what had come between them, but something had. Maybe it was the ever-present specter of his own mortality, but he didn't think that was likely. She knew he was dying when they met, though maybe she regretted their relationship now that she knew him better. Then there was Linda Kellin, her best friend. According to her mother, Linda had taken a turn for the worse that was bound to weigh heavily on Jessica.

"All right," she said as she put the last empty bottle away and shut off the gas to the incinerator. "Come inside."

Alex picked up the box of empty bottles and followed Jessica in through the storage room on the left of the lab.

"Just put that down by the sink," she said, indicating the area where she and Dr. Kellin cleaned their equipment.

Alex did as he was told, then followed her into the lab. She held out her hand and he passed the empty flask over to her. She weighed it in her hand, then gave him a sardonic look. He hadn't seen that fire in her eyes in a long time, and it made him smile.

"You're not just dumping this out a little bit each day as an excuse to come see me, are you?"

Alex chuckled.

"Would that work?"

She laughed as well, then fixed him with a stern but playful stare.

"No," she said, then her face turned serious. "You're using this faster than we thought."

Alex shrugged. If he were honest, he was going longer than he should between uses.

"I guess you need to make it a bit stronger," he said.

"Any stronger and it would send you into cardiac arrest and kill you," Jessica said, moving to the table where she brewed the rejuvenator. As she picked up the collection beaker at the end of the brew line, she shot him another sly smile. "I guess I'll just have to put up with seeing you more often."

"You sure?" Alex asked. He'd have been lying if he'd said he didn't want to see her more. He'd see her every day if he could, even with her weird schedule, but that had to be her choice.

"Yes," she said, pouring some of the clear liquid in the beaker into a large, round container.

"Because lately I got the impression you didn't want me around." Alex pressed.

She closed her eyes and took a deep breath.

"I know," she said, her voice low. "You've been great, letting me work and not pushing me. I'm sorry I put you through that."

"The doc said that Linda isn't doing well," Alex said. "I'm not going to make you choose between me and her."

"And I love you for that," she said, adding powder from a jar to the container. "I expect...I expect that I'll have more time for us soon."

Her hands were shaking, so Alex took the container and set it aside.

"Is it that bad?"

She didn't look at him, but nodded.

"Dr. Kellin thinks our serum will be ready in time," she said. "But one way or another, it will be over by next week." She drew a shuddering breath and let it out slowly. "Now give me back the Florence flask.

"Is that what this is?" Alex asked, handing the round-bottomed container back to her.

"Finish this up then, and I'll get out of here and let you work."

Jessica wiped her green eyes and accepted the container. She swirled the liquid around, then held it over a burner for a few minutes and repeated the process. The potion began to turn cloudy and the color shifted to a muddy brown. She swirled it some more, then added a few drops of something from a tiny bottle.

"Almost done," she said, setting the container on the table. She reached to the top of her apron where several tiny pockets had been sewn. Each had a round metal handle protruding from it, and Jessica ran her finger along them until she reached the one she wanted. Grasping the handle, she pulled out a tuning fork and struck it smartly on the edge of the table. A clear note rang out and she held the vibrating fork next to the Florence flask.

Inside the glass, the cloudy brown potion shimmered at the point where Jessica held the fork. The shimmering grew, almost like the liquid inside was boiling, then the brown changed to a golden color that spread out in a pulse of light until it affected the entire potion.

"Done," Jessica said, replacing the tuning fork in her apron. "Harmonic resonance," she answered Alex's unanswered question. "It unifies the solution."

She ducked under the bench and pulled a copper funnel from a bin, then opened the silver flask and carefully inserted the funnel.

"It has to be copper," she explained as she put the round container in a wire holder above the funnel. "Ferrous metal will sour the potion."

She tipped the round container in the holder until the sludgy potion began to slide out into the funnel.

"Thanks," Alex said, watching the potion gurgle.

An awkward silence stretched out between them as the thick liquid seemed to just sit in the funnel.

"Are you working on anything interesting?" she finally asked.

Alex told her about finding Dr. Burnham and then searching his workshop.

"That reminds me," he said, when he got to the part about Burnham's missing notebooks. He opened the back of his rune book and pulled out one of the pages he'd found during his search. It wasn't any more comprehensible than the others, but there was a circle drawn around the complex formula instead of an X so Alex reasoned it might be important. "Does any of this make sense to you?" he asked, handing the paper to Jessica.

She looked it over for a long time, then finally handed it back, shaking her head.

"It's a chemical formula, but I have no idea what it's for," she said. "It's much more complex than anything I saw when I was in school." She pointed to a spot below the formula where Burnham had written several words, though most of them were illegible. "I don't know what this word means either," she pointed to the paper. "Maybe if you can find someone who does, they can tell you what the formula is for."

Alex squinted at the word she indicated, *Polymer*.

"Thanks for taking a look," he said, tucking the paper back into his rune book. He glanced at the flask. The liquid had gone down in the funnel a bit, but it was still at least half full. "I can keep an eye on it if you need to get back to work."

He looked up and found Jessica looking at him. There was a hesitant look in her green eyes, like she was suddenly unsure of herself.

"I don't want you to go," she said, looking down. "I'm pretty much done here until midnight." She looked up at him. He expected the usual mischief in her eyes, but she was still unsure. "I'm sorry things have been so crazy."

Alex shrugged.

"I know it wasn't your idea," he said. "I can stay if that's what you want."

"What I want is to get out of here," Jessica said, looking around at the lab equipment and the brewing potions. "I can't remember the last time I was out of the house."

"We saw a picture over at the plaza last month," Alex said. "I hear Errol Flynn is in some pirate movie right now, if you want to do that again."

She smiled at him. It was the first real smile he'd seen on her face in six months, and he remembered why he'd fallen for her.

"I'd like that," she said. "Let me get my coat and we'll go."

Alex felt the weariness leaving his body, and he hadn't even had a shot of the rejuvenator.

The Plaza theater was eight blocks from the alchemy shop and after the movie, Alex had no chance to hail a cab, so he just walked Jessica home. That old spark she'd had when they first met had come back with a vengeance and she seemed like her old self again. Alex knew he was only helping her forget her troubles, not erasing them, but he could live with that. When he was with her, he forgot his own problems as well. Even the fog seemed romantic instead of some magical blight on the city.

"You know," Jessica said as Alex opened the gate to the back yard for her. "There's still half an hour till midnight."

This time when she looked at him, her green eyes smoldered.

Alex offered her his arm and walked her down the hill to the back yard. As they reached the corner of the house, she turned and kissed him. It felt good to hold her again, to feel what he'd felt for her. He was so distracted, he almost missed the movement behind her.

He lunged backward, pulling Jessica with him. Something solid caught him in the shoulder and rebounded into the side of his head. Stunned, Alex found himself face down on the ground. Jessica screamed but before he could rise, two shots thundered in the darkness and he felt the bullets as they impacted his shoulder and lower back.

It took Alex a few moments to recover his senses. The shield runes drawn in the lining of his jacket had stopped the bullets from killing him, but they still hurt like hell. Stifling a groan, he pushed himself to his feet. There was no sign of Jessica or whoever had jumped him, but they hadn't passed him after he fell, so they must be inside.

Alex wobbled as he stood and put his hand on the wall of the house to steady himself as he shook off the effects of being brained. From inside he heard a man's voice yelling, followed by a woman crying out. He had an almost overwhelming urge to run to the back door, but he strangled it. All that would accomplish was to give his trigger-happy assailant another shot at him, and he was running out of shield runes.

Reaching into his pocket, Alex pulled out his chalk and quickly drew a vault door. A few moments later, he lit the rune paper, then unlocked and pulled open the heavy door. Ducking inside, he opened the gun cabinet and grabbed his 1911. It was an effective gun, one most people didn't want to tangle with if it were pointed at them, but Alex didn't know how many people might be in the lab with Jessica. He needed something more intimidating.

Dropping the pistol into his jacket pocket, Alex took down the shotgun. It was a Browning Auto-5 with 12-gauge rounds, and it was plenty intimidating all by itself. Alex checked the magazine and switched off the safety, then slung the weapon over his shoulder and dashed back outside.

Peeking around the corner, he saw that the back yard was empty. Moving to the store-room door, he leaned to the side enough to see through the lab's big windows. Inside, three men were searching the lab, while a fourth stood watch over Jessica. She had her hand over her cheek, and Alex could see a bruise forming there.

Moving quietly, Alex opened the back door and let himself in. The needle trap in the knob still worked, and he wondered how the men inside had avoided it.

If they avoided it, he reminded himself. If one of them had opened the door normally, the tiny needle would have pricked them and exposed them to a deadly nerve toxin.

"You'd better wise up," someone with a Bronx drawl said. "Tell us where Dr. Kellin is, and we'll go easy on you."

"I already told you," Jessica protested. "She's not here, she went to Albany."

"And I say you're lying," the man said. "We had Julie watching this house all day and he saw her come in, but she never left."

"Well, Julie must have missed her in the fog," Jessica said. "You've looked everywhere already and she's not here."

Jessica suddenly cried out and Alex heard the sound of a slap. Bronx accent started to say something, but Alex was done waiting. He shouldered the lab door aside, leveling the A-5 as he rounded the corner. As soon as he brought the weapon up, his thumb touched one of the runes on the stock. Ghostly green light began to pulsate along the length of the weapon.

The man that could only be Bronx accent stood looking down at Jessica, who had fallen off her stool and was clutching her face. Two of the other men were farther into the lab, one facing Alex and the other with his back to him. The fourth man had disappeared, probably through the open door to Jessica's bedroom.

He knew instantly that they were too spread out for him to cover with the shotgun. The only chance he had to control the situation would be to thin out his opponent's numbers.

With the decision made, Alex didn't hesitate. He pulled the trigger and the shotgun roared. The runes on the stock enhanced the sound and added fire to the pellets. Flaming slugs the size of .38 rounds slammed into Bronx accent, catching him in the arm and side and sending him to the floor in a heap.

Alex turned, pointing the shotgun at the thug facing him.

"Don't," he said as the man started to reach inside his coat. "Let me see your hands. Get 'em up. You too," he said, turning the A-5 toward the man in the back.

They both complied, holding their hands up.

"Now where's your friend?" Alex asked.

Before either of them could speak two shots rang out from inside Jessica's bedroom. One hit Alex in the arm, but the other went wide.

He felt his third shield rune activate, stopping the bullet. That only left two of the shield runes remaining.

Alex grunted as the bullet stung his arm. Thinking he'd been shot, the two men in the room leapt to action, reaching into their coats. Alex couldn't be sure they both had heaters but with only two shield runes left, he wasn't about to take chances.

The shotgun roared, catching the closest thug square in the chest. He cried out and collapsed onto one of the benches, knocking the brewing equipment to the floor in a shower of multi-colored liquids and glass. Another shot rang out from the bedroom, but Alex was moving, and it went wide as well, shattering a glass beaker behind him.

Tracking to the left, Alex jumped over the body of Bronx accent, drawing a bead on the thug he could see. The man had a 1911 like Alex's, and he started shooting as fast as he could pull the trigger. Bullets and equipment exploded around Alex, pelting him with foul-smelling liquids and shards of glass.

Alex squeezed the trigger and the third thug went down as the buckshot caught him in the face, nearly decapitating him.

The remaining thug dashed out of the bedroom, firing wildly as he ran, and jumped through the window at the front of the lab. Alex was forced to take cover, and by the time he regained his footing, the last man had fled.

The silence in the lab following the enhanced roar of the shotgun was deafening. Alex could hear his own heartbeat.

"Alex!" Jessica screamed.

In the wake of the unearthly silence, the sound hurt his ears.

Jessica pulled herself to her feet on one of the lab tables and looked around until she caught sight of him.

"Oh, God," she said, rushing into his arms. "I thought you were dead. I saw him shoot you. Are you all right?"

"I have shield runes on my jacket," he said, wincing as she squeezed him. The runes might keep the bullets from killing him, but he'd be bruised up pretty good by morning. "Sorry about the mess," he said, looking around at the destruction the fight had caused. His eyes rested on the door to the back room, which stood open. Inside was the brewing apparatus for Dr. Kellin's polio cure. Alex felt the air squeezed out of his lungs when he saw a stream of bluish liquid pouring down from the distiller onto the table.

"Uh, Jessica?" he said, pointing to the leak.

She followed his finger and when she saw the spilling liquid, she screamed.

13

GROWTH MEDIUM

"Help me," Jessica screamed as she rushed to the brewing table in the little back room. "Get me a clean rag, something to stop the leak."

Her voice was high pitched and desperate, but her words were calm. Alex looked around, then pulled his handkerchief from his pocket and passed it over.

"It's clean," he explained as she eyed it suspiciously.

If she wanted to argue, she shoved the urge aside, grabbed the handkerchief instead and jammed it against the crack in the glass body of the distiller. Above the apparatus a chunk had been torn out of the brick wall, though whether it was the result of a ricochet or a stray bit of buckshot from Alex's shotgun, he couldn't tell. What was obvious was that the chunk of wall had hit the distiller.

"This isn't going to hold," she said, looking around, desperate.

Alex pulled out his rune book and began turning pages.

"I've got a mending rune," he said, tearing out the page. "It'll repair the crack, good as new."

"No," Jessica said. "I can't let any foreign magic near the potion."

Alex dropped the lesser mending rune and darted back out into the lab. Finding a brew line that wasn't damaged, he grabbed the empty beaker at the end of the line.

"Here," he said as he ran back. "Catch the liquid in this."

He stuck it under the steady stream of drips falling from the bottom of the rapidly saturating handkerchief.

"That won't work," she said. "This is growth medium, the enzymes in the potion need it to mature. Once it leaks out, anything could contaminate it, the potion will be useless. Think." This last she directed at herself.

Alex watched the liquid in the distiller drop, slowly. It was almost half gone and showed no signs of slowing.

"Alex!" Jessica shouted even though he was standing right there. "Do you remember the day we met?"

Alex nodded and she went on.

"I took some blood from you. Do you remember the case where I kept my syringes and collection bottles?"

Alex thought back.

"Brown leather case," he said, picturing it in his mind. "Thin, with a zipper."

"That's it," she gasped, obviously relieved that he remembered. "Do you remember where it is?"

Alex closed his eyes and cast his mind back to when he first met Jessica. The image of her in her white shirt and green scarf, mocking him from the back gate, flowed over him, but he resisted the urge to linger.

"Fourth table from the end against the windows," he said. "in the little cabinet underneath."

"That's it," she confirmed. "Get it for me. Hurry."

Alex ran. The blood kit was exactly where he remembered it and he paused only long enough to unzip it and make sure it was what he sought. Inside were four glass syringes, each fitted with a needle. Several small bottles with screw on tops were held in place by elastic loops and there was a container of alcohol and a box of cotton.

"I got it," Alex called, running back across the wreckage of the lab. He didn't even register that he was having to jump over the corpse of one of the thugs as he went.

"Hold this," Jessica said as Alex put down the blood kit on the workbench. She stepped away from the distiller to make room so Alex could move in and take over pressing the sopping handkerchief to the cracked glass.

Jessica opened the blood kit and poured alcohol from the little bottle all over the needle of one of the syringes. She jerked a handful of cotton from the box, wet it with the alcohol and used it to wipe the rubber tube that connected to the bottom of the cracked distiller.

"Pinch this," she said, pointing to the rubber tube a few inches down the line from where she had wiped it. "Hold it as tight as you can."

Alex did as he was told, gripping the rubber tube between his thumb and forefinger.

When Jessica was sure he had a good grip, she turned a valve on the bottom of the distiller and the liquid inside began to flow into the tube. Taking the syringe, she pressed it into the tube, through the rubber, and then began drawing out the liquid within. It was a strange teal color with mottled bits of yellow and red swirling inside. When she'd pulled the plunger all the way back, Jessica withdrew the needle, leaving a small dripping wound in the rubber.

"Don't let go," she said to Alex.

He hadn't intended to, but he nodded in agreement anyway.

Jessica picked up the wad of cotton she'd used to clean the rubber hose and rubbed it on the inside of her left arm.

"Hey," Alex protested as she took the syringe in her right hand. "What are you doing?"

She pressed the needle against the crook of her arm and casually pressed the needle through her flesh.

"Growth medium," she said, grimacing as she wiggled the needle a bit. After a second she pressed it all the way in. She looked up at Alex, took three quick, deep breaths, then slowly and deliberately pressed the plunger down. The bluish liquid disappeared as it rushed up the needle and into her arm.

"You can let go, now," she told Alex.

"You kept me busy," Alex protested as he let go of the rubber tube and set the soaked handkerchief on the workbench.

She simply raised an eyebrow at him, daring him to object.

"You want to tell me what that was all about?" he pressed, pointing to the syringe.

"During the final phase of this potion it has to rest in a growth medium."

"So you said."

"Don't interrupt," she chided. "The medium is prepared along with the potion. It would have taken weeks to brew up a new batch and the potion might go bad in the meantime."

"So you decided to use your own body as a growth medium?" Alex said. "Didn't you just say the growth medium had to be some special mix?"

She smirked and nodded.

"You always were too smart for your own good," she said. "This potion has needed infusions of human blood. It started with Laura's, so she would be able to handle the finished potion. Along the way, however, both Dr. Kellin and myself have...donated to the cause."

Alex felt a little queasy at that, wondering which of the potions he'd consumed over his life had been made with things he'd rather not know about.

"That's disgusting," he said.

Jessica laughed and put her arms around his neck.

"We all like sausage," she said, "but no one wants to know how it's made."

She kissed him and he let her.

"Speaking of sausage," he said, nodding in the direction of the ruined lab.

The intensity of the last few minutes had obviously driven the memory of her attack from Jessica's mind, and her face soured as it came back to her.

"I'd better go call the cops," he said. "Someone's bound to have heard the shots, so they're probably already on their way."

Alex turned and started to make his way across the lab. He knew from experience that there was a phone in the storage room on the far side.

"Alex?" Jessica said from behind him.

Her voice sounded strange. He turned to find her standing next to the workbench in the back room, swaying unsteadily.

"Alex, I think...I think I might have..."

She never finished whatever she had been about to say. Alex had seen it coming but as he rushed forward, he was almost too late to catch her before she collapsed. Staggering under the unbalanced load, Alex hefted her up into his arms. Her head lolled to the side, and he tipped her unconscious form backward so her cheek pressed against his shoulder. He didn't know if this was the realization of what had happened catching up with her, or an effect of the unfinished potion she'd just injected herself with, but since there wasn't anything he could do either way, he carried her out into the lab.

Alex's first thought was to put Jessica down in her own bed, but the police would want to search her room for any evidence left by the remaining thug. Instead, Alex lifted her up onto an empty workbench. Once he was sure she wouldn't roll off, he pulled out his rune book and opened his vault. Carrying Jessica inside, he moved to the back room and deposited her on the bed. He covered her with a blanket, then went to the little dresser in the room and pulled a bottle of scotch and a glass from one of the drawers. Pouring himself a shot, he downed it, then left the bottle and the glass on the bedside table along with a note explaining that this was his vault, in case she woke before he returned.

Satisfied that Jessica was as safe as he could make her, Alex left the vault, pulling the security door closed behind him. When he'd first put it in, Alex hadn't bothered to make a way to lock the door from the outside; after all, the whole reason for a security door was to keep people out. Fortunately he'd thought about it and realized that there might come a time when he needed to keep a client somewhere safe while he investigated. He could lock the vault door, of course, but if he was injured or killed with someone inside, there would be no way for them to escape. He decided an external lock he could control was probably a good idea.

"Lock up," he said, leaning close to the door. The same purple rune he used to secure his cashbox glowed briefly and he heard a metallic click.

Alex made his way across the wreckage of the lab, where he called the police to give them the address of the alchemy shop, along with instructions to come around to the back. That done, he went and picked up his shotgun and unloaded it, laying it and the shells out on one of the workbenches in full view. His 1911 hadn't been involved in the gunfight, so he returned it to the gun cabinet in his vault.

Since he had no idea how long it would take the police to arrive, Alex went back to the phone and called Iggy. It was after midnight, so it took him a few minutes to get to the phone.

"I don't like that," the old man said when Alex explained about Jessica injecting herself. "I've never heard of anyone trying to mature a potion in their own body."

"Is there anything I can do for her?"

"I don't know," he said. "If this is just her nerves, give her some spirits when she comes to. For now, I think the best thing you can do is let her sleep."

Alex explained about putting her in his vault to keep her away from the parade of police who were about to descend on the alchemy shop.

"Good idea," Iggy said. "Just let her sleep as long as possible before you let the police talk to her."

Alex promised that he would, then hung up.

It was almost an hour later when the first police officers arrived. When they saw all the dead men, they drew their guns and searched Alex before continuing. Unlike the nice officer he'd met in Dr. Burnham's workshop, these cops weren't swayed by his P.I. license and winning smile. They handcuffed him and left him sitting on a stool while they took stock of the scene.

"What's this?" asked one of the cops, a blocky man with bushy hair and eyebrows that looked like two caterpillars trying to mate. He gestured to the locked door leading to Alex's safe. Caterpillar brows had thus far proved to be a man of little imagination and Alex was regretting not simply closing his vault door to avoid such questions. Of course if he spent the night in jail, it would be hours before Iggy or Danny could get him out, and he didn't know what Jessica would do if she woke up and couldn't leave the vault.

"I'm a runewright," Alex explained for what felt like the tenth time. "That's my vault. It's a magical room where I keep my supplies."

"Open it."

"No," Alex said.

The cop got an ugly look on his face and walked over to where Alex sat.

"I said open it," he growled.

"Not until somebody with authority gets here," Alex said. "I'm sure you can busy yourself until then; there's lots to do."

"For a guy who admitted to three murders, you're not making it easy on yourself," the cop said in a dangerous voice.

"I didn't admit to murder," Alex said. "I found these men assaulting my girl, and she lives here."

"So you just decided to shoot them? You're going to need all the help you can get to stay outta the chair."

Alex gave the cop a bored look.

"You pulled handguns off all of them and at least two of them have been fired recently. I'll take my chances."

"You coulda staged all that before we got here," he said, leaning close and dropping his voice. "Those guns are probably yours."

Alex grinned at that.

"You wound me, officer," he said with as much mock sincerity as he could muster. "I'd never lie to the police."

"Well we both know that's not true," a familiar voice cut in.

Alex turned to find Danny's boss, Lieutenant Frank Callahan, striding through the door. Alex hadn't seen Callahan for months, but the man seemed impervious to change. He still looked like a recruitment poster for the Police Academy, square jaw, big shoulders, and at six foot four he towered over everyone.

"You know this mug, Lieutenant?" Caterpillar brows asked, pointing to Alex.

"I do," Callahan said with a sigh. "Uncuff him."

"But Lieutenant, he already confessed to killing the three guys we hauled out of here," the cop protested.

"I don't doubt it," Callahan said, picking up the shotgun. "This yours?"

Alex nodded.

"See," Caterpillar brows said. "He don't deny it."

"Did you look at those guys, Gibbons?" Callahan asked the man. When he didn't respond, the Lieutenant went on. "Well, I did. One of them is James Monaghan, a.k.a Jimmy the Weasel." He looked at Alex. "He's a small-time hood with delusions of grandeur. He'll do anything if you pay him enough." Callahan looked back to Officer Gibbons. "Not the kind of company an upstanding citizen like Dr. Kellin would be keeping at this hour."

"We, ah, we still haven't found Dr. Kellin," Gibbons said.

"She's in Albany," Alex supplied. "Like I told you before."

"Then what are you doing here, Lockerby?" Callahan demanded.

"Her assistant, Jessica O'Neil, is my girl. We were coming home from the Plaza when one of them jumped me and grabbed Jessica. When I came to, they were slapping her around, demanding to know where the doc was."

Gibbons opened his mouth, but Callahan waved him quiet.

"Where is Miss O'Neil now?"

Alex nodded toward his vault.

"As you can imagine, she was a bit overwrought," he said, not bothering to mention her having injected herself with the polio potion. "She's sleeping in my vault."

"He said he wouldn't open it," Gibbons added, helpfully.

Callahan smiled at Alex the same way a shark might smile at a sea lion.

"I'm sure he'll open it for me, won't you Lockerby?"

Alex held up his cuffed hands and after a long moment, Gibbons unlocked them. Alex led them over to the open vault door and the security door behind it.

"Open sesame," he said, knocking on the hidden rune. It flared and glowed purple for a moment, followed by a metallic ringing sound. Alex took hold of the handle and pushed the door open. He started to go in, but Callahan grabbed him.

"I'll go first," he said, giving Alex a sideways look. "You stay here," he told Gibbons.

Callahan stepped inside and looked around. Alex saw him noticing the gun cabinet, but he didn't say anything about it.

"Jesus, Lockerby," he said at last. "This place is bigger than my first apartment."

"The fruits of clean living," Alex said without even the hint of a smile.

"All right, Gibbons," Callahan said, beckoning Alex inside. "I'm going to interview Miss O'Neil. Go make yourself useful."

Gibbons nodded, then scurried off. Once he was gone, Callahan turned back to Alex.

"You could have gotten into a lot of trouble with this stunt," he said, pointing around at the vault.

"I guess I'm lucky you showed up."

"Where's the girl?" Callahan said. He was only three inches taller than Alex, but he still managed to look down at him.

Alex pointed toward the back room.

"Luck had nothing to do with it," the lieutenant said as he followed Alex across the sitting room to the little hallway at the back. "When three bodies drop a block from Central Park, in the home of a private citizen, you're lucky they didn't send Captain Rooney."

"So how did you get the call?"

"There's a list of names," Callahan said. "When dispatch gets a call about someone on the list, they know who to call."

"And I'm on yours," Alex said, positively beaming. "Why Lieutenant, I'm flattered."

"Shut up, Lockerby," Callahan growled. "The way I hear it, you're also on Detweiler's list."

"Then I guess I really am lucky," he said, knocking softly on the door that led to his bedroom.

"I'm up," Jessica's voice came from inside.

"I have the police with me," Alex said, opening the door.

Jessica sat on his bed with the blanket over her legs. She had retrieved a book from the shelf in his sitting room and the glass next to the scotch bottle was half full. There wasn't any sign of the dizziness she'd experienced earlier, though that didn't mean she was all right.

"This is Lieutenant Callahan of the New York Central Office," Alex said by way of introduction. "As you might imagine, he's very curious about what happened."

"That's enough," Callahan said to Alex. "Go wait in your workshop while I talk with Miss O'Neil." He looked at Jessica. "If that's all right with you."

"It's all right, Lieutenant," she said.

Alex winked at Jessica and went back out into the main room. While he was waiting for the cops to arrive, he tried to avoid doing anything that would disturb the scene, but his instincts as a detective were just too hard to overcome. He'd assumed that the man asking the questions was the one in charge, so he'd gone through the man's pockets.

Sitting at his drafting table, Alex pulled a rumpled piece of paper from the pocket of his coat. Smoothing it out, he laid it on the table, then pulled an ordinary sheet of paper from a set of drawers to his left.

The paper had been in the leader's pocket. At the top was the name, Andrea Kellin, and the address of the alchemy shop. Below it was a list of potions and what Alex assumed to be alchemy ingredients.

Being careful to match the style of the writing, Alex duplicated the list, then he used a blotter to dry his copy. It took him about ten minutes and as he was finishing up, he could hear Callahan thanking Jessica for her cooperation.

Alex stuffed the rumpled original back into his pocket and folded the copy he made in half.

"All right, Lockerby," Callahan said, emerging from the back. "I've got what I need. Unless you have anything to add, I suggest you get that young woman somewhere safe. I'll probably have some more questions for you tomorrow, so don't leave town or anything."

"Just call my office, Lieutenant," he said. "My secretary will know where to find me. By the way," he went on, pulling the folded paper from his jacket pocket. "That guy you called Jimmy the Weasel dropped this."

He handed over the note and Callahan read it.

"So this slipped your mind until now?" he said, giving Alex a penetrating look.

"Well," Alex said as innocently as he could. "I was just so distraught and worried about Jessica."

"Uh-huh," Callahan muttered in a tone that clearly conveyed his disbelief in Alex's explanation. "Well, if you suddenly remember any other details that might have slipped your mind, I'd better be your first call."

"My word of honor, Lieutenant," Alex lied. "My word of honor."

14

SIDE EFFECTS

Alex shut the security door after Callahan, and pushed the upper bolt into place. He wasn't worried about being in danger with all the police just on the other side, but he didn't want anyone just waltzing in, either.

Secure against surprise, he made his way back to his room and knocked respectfully on the door.

"Come in," Jessica called.

He pushed the door open and found her reading again. The overhead light was off, and she had turned on the little lamp on the bedside table. As he came in, she set the book aside and Alex saw the spine: *Treasure Island*.

"Didn't you get enough pirates at the movie?" he asked with a grin.

"I'm a sucker for Robert Louis Stevenson," she admitted. "How soon until we can go back to the lab?"

"I suspect the police will be busy most of the night," he said, sitting on the edge of the bed. "I'll call a cab and we can go over to the brownstone. You'll be safe there, and we can come back in the morning."

She shook her head at that, and put her hand on Alex's.

"If it's okay with you, I'd rather stay here," she said. "I...I don't want to be a burden."

The Long Chain

Alex was quite sure she meant to say something else. He tried to hold her gaze, but she looked away.

"It's the potion," he said at last. "Isn't it? You need to be here, close to your lab in case something bad happens."

She smiled humorlessly, and looked back up at him.

"Always too smart for your own good," she said.

"What aren't you telling me, Jess?"

Sighing, she took his hand, holding it between both of hers.

"As you might imagine, maturing a potion inside your own body isn't a common practice," she said.

"So it's dangerous," Alex guessed. "Otherwise people would do it more."

"There can be..." she hesitated. "Side effects. Most of them are harmless, but..."

"But some aren't," Alex finished. "How bad?"

"I could die," she said. There was no hesitation or prevarication this time. "It's not likely, but it's possible."

Alex pulled his hand back, making a fist. He wanted to punch the wall, but his extra-dimensional stone was too far away.

"Then why did you do it?" he demanded.

When she didn't answer, he looked back at her and found her watching him with shining eyes and a soft smile.

"You know why," she said. "For the same reason a brave hero would sacrifice his own life to save a whole city — except my city is just one person."

Alex closed his eyes, rolled back his head, and sighed. He did understand, and that just made it harder. Now he reckoned he understood what Iggy had felt when he found out what Alex had done. He couldn't fault Alex any more than Alex could fault Jessica, but that didn't mean either of them had to like it.

"You know," Jessica said, putting her hand back on top of his. "If we went back to the brownstone, Iggy would make you sleep on the couch in the sitting room."

Alex looked at her hand on his, then up to her face.

"But this is Dr. Kellin's house, and she isn't here." As she spoke, she leaned in until her lips were mere inches from his.

127

Every synapse in Alex's brain screamed at him to move, to close that tiny gap that separated them and kiss her. Instead he moved back. As he moved, he saw confusion and then disappointment in Jessica's pale eyes.

"When was the last time you slept?" he wondered. "Before you passed out earlier."

"I'm a grown woman, Alex," she said, giving him a hard, challenging look. "I don't have to eat my vegetables, and I don't have a bedtime."

"You've got dark circles under your eyes."

"No worse than yours," she countered.

Alex hated to do it, but he played his trump card. Reaching beside her head, he took several strands of her hair between his fingers and drew it up where she could see.

"You're starting to get gray in your hair."

He was braced for her anger, but instead she laughed.

"Side effects," she said. "One of the most common side effects of live culturing is loss of pigmentation in the hair. It will pass in a few days." Her amused look grew to a wide grin that showed her perfect teeth. "Now, I just had a harrowing experience. Are you really going to let me sleep in here, by myself? All alone?"

Her voice started in a serious tone, but it drifted into playful mockery by the end. Her eyes were locked on him and they smoldered in the dim light of the lamp. Alex wavered with a moment's indecision, then he leaned forward and kissed her for a long moment.

"What kind of a man would I be, leaving you alone at a time like this?" he said when they finally broke apart.

Jessica's grin grew into a wide smile.

"My hero," she said in her best, damsel-in-distress voice as she wrapped her arms around his neck and pulled him down toward her.

Alex was late getting up the next morning. He wanted to stay until the glazier came to fix the broken back window, but Jessica finally had enough of his hovering and shoo'ed him away. He walked back to the sky crawler station and rode it south and east until he arrived in front of the ten-story building that housed the Manhattan Central Office of Police.

"You Hawkins?" he asked a gray-haired man in a dark, pinstriped suit who was typing up a report at his desk. The placard clearly read, Det. Phillip Hawkins, but Alex tried not to make assumptions.

"That's me," the man said, not looking up. He was solidly built with big shoulders, a barrel chest, and thick fingers that, despite their size, worked the typewriter efficiently. His hair and mustache were streaked with gray, but he had a youthful look in his eyes. "What do you want?"

Alex introduced himself and then gave Hawkins a quick rundown on his encounter with the beat cop in Leonard Burnham's workshop.

"He said you might have some friends who were still in the Navy," Alex finished.

All the while Alex had been talking, Hawkins continued typing. As Alex finished, he paused and looked Alex up and down.

"You're that private dick who helped Lieutenant Detweiler catch the Ghost Killer, right?"

Alex nodded.

"I might have had something to do with that case," Alex said, a bit evasively. Billy Tasker, the reporter for the *Midnight Sun* tabloid, had made a big deal about Alex's involvement in that case. It was great for Alex's business, but cast a shadow over Detweiler's victory. The way Alex heard it, Detweiler hadn't been happy about that.

Hawkins turned away from his typewriter and leaned forward, putting his elbows on his desk.

"You're also pals with that Japanese kid, Park?"

"Pak. Danny Pak."

"Word around here is that you helped him out on a couple of his cases," Hawkins said in a shrewd voice. "Now suddenly he's Callahan's golden boy."

"What's your point, Detective?"

Hawkins smiled and shrugged innocently.

"I've got a lot of years in the department," he said. "I've got a good record, too. A lot of cases closed."

"And you'd like to retire on a lieutenant's pension?" Alex guessed.

Hawkins' smile turned predatory.

"I heard you were smart," he said. "I also heard you've got a nose for the kind of cases that can make a cop's career."

"How can I help you, Detective Hawkins?"

"This case," he said, holding up his hand with his fingers spread apart. "A Nobel Prize winning chemist," he ticked off a finger. "Who developed new gas masks for the army." Another finger down. "He retires from a place he's worked for thirty years. Now he's working on something in his shed, something somebody almost killed him to steal, *and* he's getting mysterious payments from the Navy?"

Alex nodded.

"That's about it," he confirmed.

"I'd be happy to call my friends in the service for you, Mr. Lockerby," Hawkins said. "I've never heard of the SEI, but if it's Navy, I'll find it for you. All I want is in. If this case is as big as it sounds, it might just be the career maker I've been waiting for."

Alex thought about that. It wouldn't cost him anything to have Hawkins on board, and having the actual police involved could grease certain wheels. On the other hand, having an official nursemaid looking over his shoulder the whole way could cause more problems than it solved. Then there was Detective Hawkins himself. He looked presentable and he knew how to type, but Alex knew nothing about the man's work.

"All right," he said, making up his mind. "You call your friends and if this case goes anywhere, you'll be the first to know."

Hawkins looked up from his desk, holding Alex with his brown eyes for a long moment. Clearly he was sizing Alex up as well.

"Where can I reach you?" he said at last.

Alex left one of his business cards and told Hawkins to call Leslie as soon as he knew anything.

"Say," Alex said as he turned to leave. "You ever hear of a small-time loser named Jimmy the Weasel?"

Hawkins looked back up from his typewriter, his brows knitting together.

"Monaghan," he said, nodding. "James Monaghan. He's a bouncer over at the Blue Room. It's a swanky club off Broadway, just outside the core."

Alex thanked him and headed for the elevators.

It was well after noon when Alex finally trudged up the stairs to his office. He'd grabbed a sandwich from an automat on his way from the Central Office, but what he really needed was the rejuvenator. He'd worried that he'd left it at the alchemy shop, but remembered seeing it in the tiny kitchen in his vault. Jessica must have brought it in for him before he left.

He was far more tired than he wanted to admit, but at least he'd be able to get some of the potion once he reached his office and opened his vault.

"There you are," Leslie yelled at him when he opened the door. She seemed much more irritable since she returned from her weekend with Randall. "Your Sorceress has been calling all morning, demanding to know where you've been, and I'm out of excuses. She threatened to have the police put out a bulletin on you."

"Sorry, doll," Alex said. "I was out with Jessica last night and something came up."

Leslie raised an eyebrow at him and her stern look softened. Her amusement turned to horror, however, when he recounted the events of the evening.

"So Lieutenant Callahan might call or send someone by," he said when he was done answering all of Leslie's questions. "I'm sure they'll have more questions at some point."

Leslie shook her head.

"What is this city coming to?" she said. "I'm sorry your evening got ruined, but I'm glad you and Jessica are all right."

"And what about your evening?" Alex pressed. She still hadn't told him what happened over the weekend.

Leslie sighed and her hazel eyes met his.

"I thought Randall was going to propose." Alex prompted.

"He was," she sighed, breaking eye contact. She strode around the desk and opened the middle drawer, pulling out a half-empty cigarette pack. "He had a ring and everything, just like in the movies."

She pulled out a cigarette and then offered Alex one. He accepted it, then offered her a light from his lighter.

"What happened?" he asked once Leslie had taken a long drag.

"His daughter didn't want him to get married."

"His daughter?" Alex asked; it was the first he'd heard of a daughter.

"She lives with her mother after the divorce," Leslie said. "And she's eight."

Alex wasn't sure why that mattered.

"So?" he said. "She doesn't live with him, she'll get over it."

Leslie fixed him with an exasperated stare.

"Randall's not going to break his little girl's heart just because he couldn't make it work with her mother," she said. "If he was the kind of man that would do that, I wouldn't want him."

She turned to the window behind her desk and looked out on a solid wall of fog.

"I guess I just don't get it," Alex admitted.

Leslie laughed, but it was a sad sound. She turned to look at him, her eyes full of compassion.

"Someday you'll have a kid of your own, boss. When that happens, you'll understand. There's nothing in this world a parent wouldn't do for their kid."

Alex still didn't understand, but the look of pain and resolution on Leslie's face told him that she knew what she was talking about. He'd take her at her word.

"So...you don't need me to go out to Suffolk County and rough up Randall for you?"

She laughed at that, almost dropping her cigarette.

"Don't you dare," she said, but her eyes sparkled. She knew he was only half kidding, that if Randall had really hurt her, he'd be willing to do exactly that, and she was grateful for the support. "Now go in your office and call the Ice Queen before she cuts off our supply of cold disks. I don't want to be sweaty next summer."

Alex promised that he would and left Leslie to her work. Once in his office, he hung up his hat on the stand beside the door and pulled a vault rune from his book. After opening it, he went to the little kitchen. On his way past, he looked into the bedroom. Sometime in the morning, Jessica had made the bed. The only evidence of last night was the book on the bedside table, *Treasure Island*.

Alex picked it up and smiled. It was the only book by Robert Louis Stevenson in his library, but there was a little book shop around the corner from the Central Office. He'd stop by next time he was out that way, and pick up something else by Stevenson as a surprise for Jessica.

Taking the book with him, Alex went to the kitchen. It was small, just a sink, counter, icebox, a few cupboards, and a round table with two chairs. A cistern held the water for the sink and the waste water drained into a collection tank. He had to fill and empty them, respectively, but that was a once-a-month job at worst.

The flask with his rejuvenator sat on the counter next to a short juice glass. Alex picked up the flask and took a swig before dropping it into his jacket pocket. Picking up the juice glass, he moved to the sink. He'd thought he'd washed all the dishes from breakfast, but he must have missed that one — either that, or Jessica had used it before she left.

He turned the valve that would let the water flow through from the cistern, but before he put the cup under the stream, he held it up. The inside was coated with a thick, slightly bluish liquid. He sniffed it and then poked it with his finger.

"Rejuvenator," he said, sure of it.

He knew he hadn't had any this morning, or last night, which meant that Jessica had used the glass. The rejuvenator she'd filled his flask with was a canary yellow color, though, so she must have added something to it.

"Which is why she used the glass instead of just taking a swig," he decided.

He wasn't surprised. Both Jessica and the doc had been burning the candle at both ends for as long as he'd known them. They probably needed the potion worse than he did. Alex did wonder why she had added something that turned the potion blue, but that could have been as simple as the fact that she was a woman, and it had been made for him.

Pushing the little mystery out of his mind, he washed the glass and set it in the rack to dry.

When he got back to his office, he sat down at his desk and called Sorsha.

"Where have you been, Alex?" she demanded when her secretary finally put his call through. "I've been calling you since yesterday."

"Sorry, Sorceress," he said, too tired to be annoying despite the rejuvenator. "I was a little busy yesterday. I do have something that will make your day today, though."

There was a long silence and Alex could tell that Sorsha's basic desire to reprimand him was warring with her need to solve the case of the magical fog.

"All right," she said at last. "What is it?"

"You were right about the fog, it's definitely not natural." He launched into a detailed description of locating the fog cluster on the apartment rooftop and how the fog seemed to be attached to the big chimney.

"That doesn't make any sense, Alex," Sorsha said. "Although it would explain why my efforts to move the fog failed."

"It also means that someone is doing this on purpose," Alex said.

"And what is it they want?" Sorsha picked up on his train of thought and finished it. "Can you try your experiment in some other places around the city?" she asked.

"Sure," Alex said. He probably wouldn't hear back from Detective Hawkins for a few days anyway, and he didn't have any client meetings until tomorrow.

"Do that," she said. "And call me if you learn anything new."

Alex promised that he would and hung up. He wasn't terribly excited about running all over the city, but at least he now knew he only needed two purity runes for the modified finding construct instead of three. It would take him an hour or so to write up the runes and then he could get started.

He stood and made his way around the desk toward his still open vault but the buzzer on the intercom stopped him.

"What is it?" he asked once he'd pushed the talk button.

"Can you come out here?" Leslie asked. "There are some gentlemen here to see you."

That was code for possible trouble.

"I'll be right out," he said.

Moving quickly, Alex closed his vault and picked up his hat, leaving the flask of rejuvenator on his writing table. He checked to make sure his flash ring was in place. He'd used one of its charges but that still left three, more than enough.

He opened the door to his office and walked out into his reception area. Two large men in blue Navy uniforms stood by Leslie's desk. They both had flat faces and small, piggish eyes. A white band ran around each man's left arm with the letters S.P. on it. They reminded Alex of the bouncers he'd seen in low rent bars, the kind that would just as soon start a fight as break one up.

"You Alex Lockerby?" the one on the left asked.

Alex plastered a smile on his face.

"How can I help you gentlemen?" he said in his most genial voice.

"Admiral Walter Tennon would like to have chat with you," the other one said. They were so alike, Alex was having trouble telling them apart.

"Now," the first one added.

15

INTERROGATION

The Navy men each grabbed one of Alex's arms when they reached the street, as if they feared he would suddenly bolt into the fog. They had a car waiting and while the tall one opened the door and moved the seat-back forward, the second man searched Alex for weapons. Satisfied that Alex wasn't carrying anything more dangerous than his lighter, the shorter man shoved him into the back seat. As soon as he was in, the tall man put the seat-back down and climbed into the driver's seat.

Since the car was a coupe, the Navy men had no fear that Alex would be able to flee the car, not that he had any intention to do so. These Navy escorts had said that Admiral Tennon wanted to see him. Tennon was the name of the man who had been paying Leonard Burnham and there was no way that was a coincidence.

Word had reached the Admiral about Alex's inquiry very quickly. Either Detective Hawkins had called exactly the right person at the Navy Yard or whatever the SEI was, it was a big deal. Either way, Admiral Tennon was smack in the middle of it and Alex was about to meet him.

"So, what does SP stand for?" Alex asked after ten minutes of riding in silence.

"Shore Patrol," the shorter of the two said.

"So, what?" Alex went on. "You guys are Navy cops?"

"Shut up," the taller man said.

Alex shrugged.

"Just making conversation, boys," Alex said, sitting back in his seat and pulling out his cigarette case. "It's likely to be a long ride with all this fog."

Neither of the men answered, so Alex just smoked in silence. The Navy Yard was quite a bit north of his office, but with a car it should only have taken twenty minutes or so. An hour later, the shore patrol car pulled up to the gate. Two armed sailors stood blocking the road and they stayed where they were while a third man came out of a guard house to speak to the Shore Patrol men. Alex expected it to be a short conversation; after all, who would hassle Navy cops?

As it turned out, the gate guard grilled the driver on who he was, where he'd gone in the city, who Alex was, and why they were bringing him on base. The Navy cops even had to show their identification cards and the gate guard wrote their names down on his clipboard. After a full ten-minutes of interrogation, the guard waved them through and the armed men at the gate stepped aside.

"You boys always this formal?" Alex asked. He was sure they wouldn't answer, but he wanted to see how they'd react. The Navy cops looked at each other, somewhat pointedly, but said nothing.

Alex had never been to the Navy Yard before. Several of his cases had involved Navy personnel, but he'd always managed to do his surveillance or interviews out in the city. He knew that the Navy built ships here, but that was about it. The military life wasn't one that appealed to him. If nothing else, he had a hard time getting up at six in the morning.

The tall sailor stopped the car in front of a low building that had been constructed out of corrugated metal and painted some shade of tan. It didn't look very solidly constructed considering the whole purpose of this installation was to build things.

"Out," the tall sailor ordered, once he'd pulled the seat up for Alex.

The sign on the building said, *Brig*. Alex knew that was the Navy word for jail, but it didn't look like this place could hold a stiff breeze.

His escorts took Alex by the arms again and led him inside, past a desk with a bored-looking sailor with a matching SP armband. They deposited him in a tiny room with a plain table and a chair on either side. There was no label on the door, but Alex knew an interrogation room when he saw one.

"Sit," the short sailor said. "Someone will be here in a minute."

Alex knew that for the lie it always was. Word of Detective Hawkins' call had somebody rattled. They'd pushed back and found out where Hawkins heard of the SEI and that led them to Alex. Right now he was the last link in that chain and whoever had the other end of it would want to make sure he was nervous and disoriented before asking any questions.

The Navy cop closed the door and Alex heard a latch being secured on the other side. The room was a plain box with no other openings. Recently the interrogation rooms in the Central Office had been outfitted with one-way mirrors so that suspects could be observed before and even during questioning. This room, however, had nothing.

Alex chuckled. He had a momentary thought of pulling out his chalk and waiting for the inevitable questioning in the comfort of his vault, but if he did that, he'd almost have to let whoever came through the door inside. He did not want the Navy poking around his rune books and supplies, or his gun cabinet. What he needed was a special vault with a comfy chair, a few books, and a bottle of cheap liquor, nothing he'd miss if it were stripped bare. It was a great idea, but unfortunately runewrights could only have one vault at a time, so if he wanted his own, portable waiting room, he'd have to give up the vault he had — and he wasn't about to do that.

Lighting a cigarette, Alex sat down on the far side of the table so he could see the door and put his feet up. He'd smoked through three of his cigarettes by the time the door opened. A fat man in a Navy officer's coat came in, reading something in an open file folder he held. He had blond hair, cut short, with large, watery eyes and a round face.

"Alexander Lockerby," he read. "Get your feet off my table."

Alex pulled his feet down and sat up as the man sat down.

"Thirty-three years old," he continued reading. "Became a private investigator in twenty-eight, you frequently work with the New York Police, and you've become quite the darling of the tabloids."

"I'm also a Sagittarius," Alex said. "In case you were wondering."

The man finally looked up at Alex. He seemed soft, probably because of his weight, but his eyes had steel in them.

"You're a funny guy, Mr. Lockerby," he said. "But as you might notice, I'm not laughing. You see, you're in a lot of trouble right now, and whether or not you get thrown in a holding cell as a guest of the Navy is entirely up to me."

Alex had no interest in spending time in a Navy jail, but he wasn't about to let this uniformed marshmallow intimidate him.

"And just who might you be?" he asked, cradling his chin in his hand, his face a mask of mock interest.

"I'm Lieutenant Commander Vaughn," he said.

Alex wasn't sure what that meant, but it sounded important.

"I'm one of three people on Earth who's ever heard of the SEI," he continued. "Imagine my surprise when I got a call today from one of my officers telling me that a New York detective wanted to know what the SEI was. Then I learn that the detective heard about the SEI from you."

"Oh, I wouldn't be too surprised," Alex said, not bothering to suppress a grin. "I'm the kind of guy who knows lots of things he shouldn't."

Vaughn glared at him and Alex worried he might have pushed the man too hard. He wanted answers, which meant he'd keep Alex here until he got them, unless he believed Alex was a dead end. If that happened, he'd either throw Alex out or into a cell. Either way, Alex would lose the only lead he had on what Dr. Burnham was working on. If he could push Vaughn a bit, though, keep him talking, he might let something slip, but Alex needed him off his game for that to work.

"What do you know about Shade Tree?" Vaughn asked.

The question caught Alex by surprise. He hadn't expected the Lieutenant Commander to be direct with any of his questions. Apparently he was playing the same game with Alex.

"I know someone named Admiral Tennon is paying Dr. Leonard Burnham to work on it," Alex said.

Vaughn sat perfectly still as Alex spoke, but his eyes widened ever so slightly. He was surprised to hear that.

"Shade Tree is a top secret Navy project," he said. "Just knowing about it is a crime. I could have you arrested right now as a spy."

Alex laughed.

"No, you couldn't," he said. Vaughn's face hardened, but Alex held up his hand before the man could speak. "First," he said. "Whatever Shade Tree is, it isn't an official Navy project." Vaughn's expression grew hard, but Alex rushed on. "Because if it was, Burnham wouldn't be working on it in his garage, it would be here under heavy guard."

"Even if you're right, I can still have you arrested."

Alex gave him a steady look.

"If you could have me charged with anything, you'd have arrested me before we met, and you'd be using those potential charges to bludgeon answers out of me."

That shut Vaughn up. He closed the open folder and glared at Alex. The look was pure venom.

Time to stop being an ass and turn on the charm.

"Now that we all know where we stand, Lieutenant Commander, how about you ask me your questions and then I have a few for you."

Vaughn's look didn't soften, and he held Alex's gaze for a long moment.

"Where is Seaman Tyler McCormick?" he said at last.

Alex shook his head.

"Never heard of him."

"Where is Dr. Burnham?"

"At home."

"Then why can't I reach him on the phone?"

"He was attacked four days ago," Alex explained. "Whoever did it hit him over the head."

"Is he alive?"

Alex nodded and explained about Karen hiring him and finding Dr. Burnham in the soup kitchen.

"If he's lost his memory," Vaughn said, giving Alex a very skeptical look, "then how do you know about the SEI?"

"Because I found a receipt in Burnham's workshop," Alex said. "A bank draft from Admiral Tennon out of an account labeled SEI. Since only the Navy has admirals, it was a cinch to trace it back here."

Vaughn stared at Alex hard as if trying to read the truth by staring through him. Finally he nodded and stood and picked up the folder from the desk.

"Wait here," he said.

"Hey," Alex protested. "Don't you want to know about Burnham's motor?"

Vaughn looked up a little too quickly.

"What about a motor?"

"You first," Alex said. "What's the SEI?"

"It's classified," Vaughn said. Then he turned and walked out, shutting the door behind him.

Alex sighed. It had been worth a try, but he still wasn't any further along than he had been. Worse, now that the Navy knew about Burnham, they'd be throwing up roadblocks to keep Alex away. He didn't really care what Burnham had been doing for the Navy, but he did want to find out who had bludgeoned the old man. He wanted to find them and bring them to justice for Karen, and for Leonard.

He still had a few clues. The paper with the word polymer on it might mean something to Burnham's former colleagues at Dow. Burnham had lived in that house of his for years, so his old office must be in the city somewhere. Alex resolved to find it as soon as Vaughn and his flunkies let him out.

Alex smoked another cigarette, but there was no sign of Vaughn returning. He might be trying to sweat Alex some more, but Alex doubted it. They'd both shown that they knew how the game was played. Vaughn wouldn't believe that Alex would be intimidated like that. Still, there was the Admiral. Since he signed Dr. Burnham's bank draft, he was probably the one in charge of whatever SEI was. Vaughn would likely have to report to him before he could do anything with Alex. If the Admiral was anything like the president of a company, it might be hours before Vaughn could get in to see him.

Alex folded his arms on the desk and put his head down. It had been too long since he had any of the rejuvenator and he was starting to feel a bit fuzzy. Within a minute he was asleep.

The door to the interrogation room opened with a boom, startling Alex awake. Normally he would have leapt to his feet at such a noise, but he was woozy and slow to respond.

He really needed a shot of the rejuvenator, which was still in his vault.

"All right, you," the tall Shore Patrolman growled. "On your feet."

Alex had no idea how much time had passed, but he had managed to drool on his shirt cuff, so it had been a while. He stood up and picked up his hat.

"Where to now?" he asked, finally managing to get his brain in gear.

The man didn't answer, but when Alex left the little room, he didn't grab his arm like before.

"This way," he said, marching off down the hall.

Alex followed without much caring where they were going. At the door to the brig, they were met by the tall sailor's shorter companion, who took up a position behind Alex as they went through the door. Together they crossed the parking lot and went down past a row of round-topped quonset huts to a wooden building that looked just as shoddily constructed as the brig had been.

Once inside, Alex was conducted to a small waiting area where a thin, handsome man in an officer's uniform sat behind a desk. He had sharp features, blue eyes, and dark hair that he kept slicked back. His mouth curled up in a perpetual half smile as if he were trying to be charming and amused all at the same time.

"This is him, Lieutenant," the short one said.

"Take a seat," the lieutenant said as the shore patrol twins left.

The waiting room had a row of metal chairs, but Alex worried if he sat down, he might fall asleep again. The handsome lieutenant picked up the phone and dialed a single number.

"He's here," he said after a moment. "Yes, sir."

The lieutenant put the receiver down and looked up at Alex.

"It'll be just a minute," he said.

"What will?" Alex asked, still not sure what he was doing here. Was this Vaughn's office?

"Until they're ready for you," the man said as if that explanation made all the sense in the world.

Alex stuck out his hand.

"I'm Alex," he said.

The lieutenant looked confused for a moment, then shook Alex's hand.

"Lieutenant Randall Leavitt," he said. "Aide to Admiral Tennon."

So, this was the Admiral's office. He must really have made an impression on Vaughn.

"What does an Admiral's Aide do?" Alex asked, trying to keep his weary brain in motion.

Lieutenant Leavitt shrugged.

"I keep the Admiral's appointment book, arrange his communication and travel, lock things in the safe," he said. "It's mostly just logistics."

Alex nodded sagely at that as if it were remotely interesting.

"Do you travel with him?"

The lieutenant looked confused but nodded.

"Yes," he said. "I handle his bags and papers when he travels and such. Why did you ask?"

Alex pointed at the floor by the Lieutenant's desk. A small duffle bag was sticking out from underneath with the cuff of a shirt sticking out of it.

"Oh," Leavitt said, bending down to stuff the errant sleeve back into the bag. "That's my emergency travel bag. Sometimes the Admiral has to go to Washington on short notice."

Alex had lived out of a suitcase for most of his childhood, so he understood being ready to move. Leavitt sat down at his desk and began going through a stack of papers, so Alex started to wander around the room.

"Hey," he said on a sudden impulse, turning back to the lieutenant. "Who is Seaman McCormick?"

If Lieutenant Leavitt thought that was a strange question, he didn't let it bother him.

"A sailor missing off the *Chicago*," he said. "She was supposed to sail yesterday, but Seaman McCormick didn't show up for duty."

"So what?" Alex asked. "Have you never had a sailor skip town before?"

"Sure," Leavitt said. "But nobody remembered ever seeing Seaman McCormick. When the Captain pulled his service record, they found out he didn't exist."

"How does a guy who doesn't exist get duty aboard a Navy ship?" Alex asked.

"That's why the base is under lockdown," Leavitt said. "This McCormick guy might be a spy, and he might be hiding on base. The Admiral is going to keep the base on lockdown until he's found or we're certain he's gone."

No wonder the Navy cops seemed so irritable. Alex didn't envy them the task of hunting someone through the shipyards in a thick fog.

The phone buzzed and Leavitt beckoned to Alex.

"Follow me," he said.

They crossed to the back of the room and the lieutenant opened the door. Inside was an office almost the same size as the waiting area. A simple desk stood between two posted flags; one was the stars and stripes and another Alex assumed represented the Navy. Behind the desk sat an athletic-looking man with iron-gray hair and steely eyes. He wore an officer's coat that looked very much like the one Lieutenant Commander Vaughn had worn, just with a few more decorations.

Vaughn, himself, stood beside the admiral's desk with the folder on Alex open in his hands. On the other side stood a woman in a green jacket with a close-fitting pencil skirt. Her back was to him, but Alex knew her immediately.

"So here's where I find you," Sorsha Kincaid said, turning to face him. Her imperious features were colder than usual and something around her eyes told him that she was very irritated.

Alex was pretty sure the Ice Queen's presence was the reason he'd been let out of the brig. He was also sure, from the look on her face, that she would make him repay that debt in full, probably in the most uncomfortable way possible.

16

CALL THE WIZARD

"Come in, Mr. Lockerby," Admiral Tennon said. At least Alex assumed the gray-haired man behind the desk was the Admiral.

"Thanks," Alex said, moving to stand in front of the desk, next to Sorsha. He put on an easy smile, as if he'd just been invited to a steak dinner by the Governor. Sorsha rolled her eyes at him.

Lieutenant Leavitt moved to a small writing table in the corner of the room and sat down with a pencil and a notepad.

"Don't be so glib," Tennon growled. "If I had my way you'd be rotting in the brig until you told Vaughn here everything you know." He jerked his thumb at the Lieutenant Commander. "But," he continued, "since I've been advised by Miss Kincaid that you are absolutely essential to a current investigation by the FBI, I've decided to give you a chance to play straight with me."

"What is it you want to know, Admiral?" Alex asked. There wasn't any point in posturing. Tennon wouldn't have threatened to lock him up and throw away the key if he couldn't make good on that threat. Alex had ways to get out of whatever jail the Navy might put him in, but he had no desire to become a federal fugitive over the Burnham case.

"How did you learn about the SEI?" Tennon demanded.

Alex recounted the story he'd told to Lieutenant Commander Vaughn. In the corner, Leavitt diligently made notes as Alex spoke.

"Have we been able to verify that Dr. Burnham is, in fact, convalescing at home?" Tennon asked.

Vaughn looked pointedly at Leavitt.

"Yes, Admiral," he said. "I spoke with his granddaughter Karen Burnham a few minutes ago. She confirmed Mr. Lockerby's story and admitted to hiring him."

Tennon nodded and smiled appreciatively at the young man. When he looked back up at Alex, however, his face was stern and implacable.

"All right, Lockerby," he growled. "It seems you've told us the truth so far. Now what's this you told Lieutenant Commander Vaughn about a motor that Dr. Burnham was working on?"

Alex looked thoughtful, mostly to give himself time to think. Explaining amberlight was something he'd learned not to attempt long ago. Most people just couldn't wrap their heads around it.

"I can't be sure it was a motor," Alex said, choosing to explain his knowledge of the motor more simply. "But it was clear Dr. Burnham was working on something big and mechanical. There were machine parts all around the area where it had been. When I investigated, I found tire tracks leaving the workshop where the thief or thieves pulled it out. Apparently it was mounted on some kind of trailer."

Tennon and Vaughn exchanged a meaningful look.

"Anything else?" the Admiral demanded.

Alex shook his head and shrugged, trying to look as innocent and truthful as he could.

"That's all I know."

Tennon shot Vaughn another look, and this time the Lieutenant Commander shrugged almost imperceptibly.

"All right," Tennon said. "I can see you're not a spy, just some busybody sticking his nose in where it doesn't belong. That said, I do appreciate your finding Dr. Burnham and getting him home; that was a good piece of work."

Alex was surprised. That sounded suspiciously like a compliment.

"I also appreciate your bringing the matter of Dr. Burnham's missing work to our attention. That said, this is a Navy matter now, Lockerby. If myself or Lieutenant Commander Vaughn hear that you're investigating on your own, I'll have you locked up indefinitely. Am I clear?"

"Crystal," Alex said.

"Now," Tennon said, turning to Sorsha. When he did, his expression softened a bit. Sorsha wasn't just powerful, respected, and dangerous — she was also quite a looker, and the Admiral seemed taken with her.

That's a mistake, Alex thought. He'd seen Sorsha use her considerable feminine wiles to manipulate men before. She was good at it. Alex wouldn't be surprised to learn that she'd done exactly that to get him out of this jam.

"Miss Kincaid has personally vouched for you and she's assured us that she'll be keeping you busy. With that in mind, Lockerby, I'm authorizing your release. Don't make me regret that decision," he added, giving Alex a hard stare. "If I see you back here, I'll make you regret it. Now get out."

Alex didn't have to be told twice, but Sorsha lingered for a moment to thank the Admiral and assure him that Alex would be far too busy helping her to be a bother.

"So what do you think happened to Burnham's project?" Lieutenant Leavitt asked as he followed Alex back into the waiting area. He'd spoken in a low tone so that Vaughn and the Admiral wouldn't overhear, but his voice was full of curiosity.

"No idea," Alex said, truthfully. "I was hoping you guys could tell me what it was, then maybe I could use a finding rune to locate it."

"Sorry," Leavitt said, shrugging his shoulders with a grin. "Shade Tree is top secret and I'm just a lowly lieutenant."

He went back to his desk and sat while Alex waited for Sorsha. She emerged from the office a moment later and swept toward the door, pulling Alex along in her wake.

"What were you thinking?" she demanded once they were out in the hall, headed for the front door. "Having someone call the Navy about a top secret project? How did you think that would end?"

"That's not what happened," he protested. "And whatever Shade

Tree is, it's not a government secret. Burnham was building it in his garage."

Sorsha opened her mouth to protest, but shut it again as she processed what Alex had said.

"It might be a secret," Alex continued. "But Tennon is paying for it out of some off-the-books account."

"Well, whatever he and his lackeys are doing, it's no longer your concern," she said in a dead-on impression of a scolding schoolmarm.

"Don't be so sure," he interrupted before she could go on. "Did you see how nervous Tennon and Vaughn got when I mentioned Burnham's missing motor? Whatever was in that garage, it's dangerous."

"So is this," Sorsha said, waving her hand at the fog. "The city has already lost over a million dollars from work slowdowns, traffic problems, and accidents."

"I left a message with your secretary," Alex protested.

Sorsha rounded on him and fixed him with a penetrating stare.

"Yes," she admitted. "A message that told me nothing. And then you disappeared for almost forty-eight hours. Your secretary kept giving me excuse after excuse, each one flimsier than the last, until she finally admitted you were here. And what are you doing here? Are you investigating the fog? No, you're sticking your nose into the Navy's business over a missing man that you've already found."

"His daughter asked me to find out why he was attacked," Alex said with a shrug. "I think mysterious Navy secrets is a pretty good explanation."

"Well you can tell her you don't know and leave it alone," Sorsha said, a note of finality in her voice.

Frankly Alex didn't care what Tennon or Vaughn or even Sorsha thought, something was rotten about the whole business with Dr. Burnham.

"I mean it," she said, sticking her finger in his face. Apparently, Alex's intention to continue investigating the curious matter of Dr. Burnham was obvious. "Drop it."

"Fine," Alex lied, being careful to keep his expression neutral.

"Now," Sorsha said as they reached her long black floater. "Open the door for me, and then you can tell me all about this mysterious discovery you made."

Alex tugged the door open and held it while the Sorceress got in, then he went around to the far side of the car and climbed in himself.

"Is your office still in the Chrysler building?" he asked.

She nodded.

"Well then, let's go there and I'll show you."

She eyed him for a moment, then turned to the driver in the front of the flying car.

"Back to the office, Rodger. And stick to the streets until we're out of the Navy Yard."

Rodger did as he was instructed but as soon as they passed through the main gate, he pulled a large lever on the car's dashboard and it lifted gently off the street. Alex had never ridden in a floater before and he held on tight to the armrest until the car broke through the fog into the late evening sky. It had been a while since he'd seen the clouds and he spent a few minutes just looking through the window.

"Here," Sorsha said as he craned his neck to look up at the moon. She waved her hand as if she were shooing a troublesome fly, and the roof above them became as transparent as glass.

Sorcerers had all the good tricks.

Sorsha Kincaid maintained an office on the sixty-fifth floor of the Chrysler building. It was the headquarters of Cold Disk, Limited, her rather unimaginatively named company that sold her refrigeration disks.

Alex had looked into her business after their first encounter two years ago. The office employed a secretary and several salesmen who processed orders through to a warehouse down by the aerodrome. There was a large office that Sorsha almost never used, and a conference room that mostly served as a meeting place for her FBI team.

What Alex didn't know was that there was also a garage for her floater. As the driver approached the building, Sorsha said something in her deep, echoing magic voice and a smooth piece of the building's side dropped down like a drawbridge.

The floater drifted left and right in the constant wind that always blew at the top of tall buildings, but Rodger maneuvered the vehicle slowly and expertly, bringing it into the sky garage and setting down gently.

Alex reached for the door, but Sorsha put a hand on his arm.

"Wait till I close the door," she said.

"Actually, it would be better if you didn't." He pulled the handle and pushed the door open against the stiff wind that now blew inside the garage. Sorsha glared at him with her short hair whipping around her face. She waved her hand and the hair instantly returned to normal, as if she felt no wind at all.

"Show off," Alex said with a grin.

He climbed out of the floater and made his way to the wall farthest from the open drawbridge. Using his chalk and a vault rune he had to hold against the wall, he managed to get his vault open. Sorsha exited the floater, no doubt curious about his vault, but Alex ducked inside and was back in a flash with his investigation kit before she could make her way around the far side of the car.

"Why didn't you just do that inside?" she shouted at him over the wind.

Alex finished locking his vault and the polished steel door melted back into the wall of the garage.

"You need to see what the fog really is," Alex yelled back, opening his kit. During their conversation, Sorsha's driver exited the car and sensibly went inside the office to wait.

Alex took out his lamp and lit it, being sure to close the back to keep the wind out, then he slipped his oculus on, settling it over his right eye. He pointed the yellowish amberlight out along the drawbridge. All along the edges of the door, he could see bundles of the hair-like clumps, clinging to the outside of the building.

"Here," he said, slipping off the oculus and passing it over.

Sorsha put it on and Alex had to swallow a chuckle when she looked like some kind of Hollywood pirate.

"Out there," he said, pointing to the edge of the opening.

Sorsha's mouth dropped open when she turned.

"What is all that?" she called over the noise of the wind. "And why isn't it blowing away?"

"It's anchored to the building somehow," Alex said.

Sorsha moved before he could stop her, walking purposely out, past the car and onto the open section of wall.

"What are you doing?" he yelled after her. "Get back here."

She had started to lean down, to examine one of the bundles on the very end of the drawbridge door, but when Alex called, she stood up. She gave him an exasperated look which was made comical by the oculus covering half her face.

"Really, Alex?" she said, her voice dripping with sarcasm. "And what do you think will happen if I somehow manage to fall?"

It was a rhetorical question. Sorsha was a sorceress; if she fell off, she could just teleport herself back up again. It was an unnerving and uncomfortable way to travel, but she'd done it before and had even carried Alex along with her. As fast a method of getting around as teleportation was, Alex had no desire to experience it again.

"Right," Alex said, managing not to look sheepish. "Sorry."

Sorsha squatted down, perching precariously on her moderate heels, and ran her hand back and forth a few inches over the door. Alex knew she was running her fingers through the ethereal, hair-like strands that anchored the fog. After a minute, she rose and came back to where Alex stood, taking off the oculus and handing it to him.

"Let's go inside," she said. She pulled a lever on the wall and the drawbridge door moved upward until it sealed the garage. Once that was done, Sorsha led Alex through a door in the side wall that exited into a small room with pegs for hats and coats.

Sorsha passed through this room and out into a hallway that ran past several offices. It was after six and they were quiet and dark. At the end of the hall, Sorsha entered a large conference room with a long, polished table and comfortable chairs.

The sorceress passed by the table, heading for the back of the room and the standing liquor cabinet there. As she poured herself something from a crystal decanter of dark liquid, Alex pulled the flask of rejuvenator out of his kit and took a swig. He immediately felt better.

"Do you want some?" Sorsha said, holding up the decanter with her back toward him. "It's Napoleon brandy."

"No thanks," Alex said. He'd learned the hard way that alcohol and the rejuvenator didn't go well together.

Sorsha shrugged and poured herself another glass, downing it as well. She closed the cabinet and turned back to Alex, pulling her long, black cigarette holder out of thin air.

"Do you have a light?" she asked, sauntering over to where Alex stood by the table.

Alex knew the sorceress could light the cigarette herself without even thinking, but he pulled out his lighter and squeezed the side, popping open the spring cap and igniting it.

"So," she said, blowing smoke as she talked. "What did I just see?"

Alex shook his head and shrugged.

"It's some kind of binding between the fog and the building," he said. "It has to be some kind of magic, but I've never seen anything like it."

"Neither have I," Sorsha said.

"All I can really tell you is that it isn't natural," Alex admitted.

She fixed him with an annoyed look.

"That's it?" she said. "All you can tell me is that the fog doesn't blow away because it's somehow attached to buildings with magical bonds that break apart when you try to grab them but form up again afterward?"

She was frustrated, mad at the situation and not really at Alex, but he was the only target for her rage in the room.

"It's more than you knew before," he said, keeping his voice neutral and friendly. Even though her problems weren't his fault, she could still freeze him solid if she felt peevish, so it was in his best interest to placate her.

"That doesn't tell me anything," she growled.

"What do your FBI monkeys think?"

She glared at him.

"The bureau came to me because they had nowhere else to go," she said, puffing on her cigarette.

Now Alex understood. He'd assumed working with the Feds was something she did for fun, but apparently it was much more than that. Her professional reputation was on the line, not to mention her mystique as a sorceress. Alex could practically feel the frustration rolling off her.

"Maybe it's time you talked to the Wizard," he offered. It was a suggestion he hadn't wanted to make, but in that moment, he felt for Sorsha. He'd been in her current situation many times and it was never fun.

She glared at him and the temperature in the room dropped precipitously.

"If it isn't some new kind of magic, maybe it's one of his creations," Alex suggested.

Sorsha looked like she wanted to argue, but after a moment she sighed.

"Thomas Edison may hate sorcerers, but he is not flooding New York with clingy fog," she said.

"Well, then I'm out of ideas," Alex said.

"What about trying to find the source?" Sorsha said. "You said you might have an idea about that."

"I did," Alex confirmed. "I tried narrowing my finding rune, but there was just too much fog to find any place where it was concentrated. I ended up using a rune that can detect the strongest example of a sample material and expanding it as far as I could. That's how I discovered the fog clumps."

"Can you use that to find the source of the fog?" she pressed.

"The maximum range of this construct is a five-block radius," he explained. "It would take me a year to find anything like that."

She glared at him, her teeth clamped on her cigarette holder.

"Then I suggest you stop looking for secret government projects and get to it."

"Are you going to pay for the runes?" he asked. "It cost me almost five bucks to cast the one I did."

"Fine," she growled, stalking over to glower at him from close range. "Now get busy. And if I find out you're doing anything other than this..." She left the sentence hanging, giving him a hard stare.

"There's something else I need to do first," he said.

"No," she said, holding his gaze. "Nothing is more important than this."

"Four men broke into the alchemy shop of Dr. Andrea Kellin last night," Alex said, anger creeping into his voice despite his resolution to remain calm. "They roughed up her assistant, demanding to know where the doc was."

Sorsha's face blanched at that.

"Her assistant?" she said in a soft voice. "Isn't she the woman you're seeing?"

Alex was a bit surprised at that. Because of Jessica's schedule, there weren't many people who knew he'd been seeing her. Had the sorceress been keeping tabs on him, or maybe the FBI was watching? He wasn't sure he liked either option.

"Yes," he said, some of his anger bleeding away. "Fortunately I was there. I got three of them, but the last one got away."

"Why did they want Dr. Kellin?"

"She asked me to find a missing friend of hers, an alchemist."

"And now someone's looking for her?" Sorsha said.

"That's the way I figure it," Alex said. "Whoever grabbed him either knows she hired me to find him or they didn't get what they wanted from him and now they're looking for another alchemist."

Sorsha strode over to the writing desk along the inside wall of the conference room that held a typewriter and a telephone. She picked up the phone and used the end of her cigarette holder to dial.

Alex suddenly realized that he hadn't spoken to Jessica since this morning. It wasn't likely that the remaining thug would return during the day, but it had been dark for over an hour.

I should have left Jessica my .38.

"Agent Redhorn," Sorsha said, breaking Alex's train of thought. "I want you to put a detail on the shop of Dr. Andrea Kellin, she's an alchemist."

Alex felt the knot forming in his gut loosen. The FBI might not be much in the actual investigation department, but they were aces when it came to gunning down bad guys.

"Yes, that's the one," Sorsha went on. "Dr. Kellin lives there with her assistant—" She looked up at Alex.

"Jessica O'Neil," he supplied.

Sorsha repeated the name to Agent Redhorn.

"Make sure you send at least two teams," she went on. "Someone tried to grab the good Doctor last night." She paused, listening then looked back at Alex. "Do the police know about the attack?"

Alex nodded.

"Lieutenant Callahan has the case."

"Yes," she said into the phone, passing on the bit about the Lieutenant. "Be sure to coordinate with them; I don't want any errors on this. Thank you, Buddy."

It took Alex a moment to remember that she'd introduced Agent Redhorn by that nickname.

"There," she said, hanging up. "Now that your paramour and the good Doctor are safe, I'll expect you to spend your time tracking down the source of this infernal fog."

As she spoke, she stalked across the floor toward him and her pale eyes seemed to glow from within.

"I'll still need to check on them," Alex said.

"That's what phones are for," she growled. "Now get out of my office and get to work."

17

GENESIS WATER

Alex had no intention of spending his days scanning the city block by block. Someone had attacked Jessica and tried to kidnap the doc, and there was no way he was letting that stand, sorceress or no sorceress. Still, he would have to do something about the fog, or risk having Sorsha follow him everywhere personally. He could try stopping off at the Blue Room and asking about Jimmy the Weasel, but if Detective Hawkins knew Jimmy used to bounce there, it was a cinch Callahan did, too. He had probably already been there. He'd call the lieutenant in the morning and find out what he'd learned.

It was only six when Alex mounted the steps to the brownstone. It had been over a day since he'd been there, but it felt longer. A lot longer.

He pulled out his pocket watch and flipped it open, then took hold of the door handle — and walked straight into the unyielding door.

At first, he thought he'd gotten lost in the fog and got the wrong house, but the oval stained-glass window in the center of the door was the right one.

"Damn it," he swore.

He'd forgotten to call Iggy after the attack on Jessica. That meant

The Long Chain

that Iggy had worried about him all night and now the old man wanted his pound of flesh for such a breach of decorum. He'd enabled the bars that wouldn't let the door open until Alex knocked.

Alex really hated the Brits and their elaborate social rules.

Putting his pocket watch away, he knocked on the door. Almost three minutes passed before he heard the door to the vestibule open, then saw Iggy's silhouette through the stained-glass panel.

"The face is familiar," the old man smirked as he opened the door. "But I can't remember the name."

Alex had expected Iggy to be relieved to see him. On the rare occasions when he'd forgotten to call that he'd be late or out, it seemed to weigh on his mentor. When Alex searched his face this time, there was no sign of that.

"Callahan called you," Alex said.

Iggy grinned.

"It sounds like you had an interesting evening last night," he said, stepping back to let Alex in out of the foggy night air. "I assume Jessica is okay."

"She was this morning," Alex said, heading for the kitchen. "I need to give her a call, though."

"Meet me in the library when you're done," Iggy called after him as he closed the outer door.

Alex tossed his hat on the kitchen table, then moved to the phone on the wall.

"Hello," Dr. Kellin answered.

"Doc," he said, relief flooding through him. "It's good to hear your voice."

"Yours too," she said. "I'm very grateful to you for saving Jessica and…and my life's work."

Alex's smile evaporated at that. He'd forgotten about Jessica using her own body to finish their polio cure.

"Can I talk to Jessica?"

There was an uncomfortable silence on the line, then Dr. Kellin answered.

"I gave her something to help her sleep," she said. "Her decision to save our cure by injecting herself was…"

She struggled for the right word.

"Dangerous," Alex supplied.

"I was going to say risky," Dr. Kellin replied. "It's very unlikely that it will have any permanent effect on Jessica, but it will make her tired as her body's natural defenses try to fight it off."

"Isn't that a bad thing?" Alex asked, not entirely sure what the doc meant, which was usual when talking to her.

"In this case it's a very good thing, Alex," she said. "As her body reacts to the potion, the potion will change. When it no longer reacts, we'll know it's ready."

Dr. Kellin seemed very excited about all this, but that didn't take the edge off Alex's worry.

"Will you tell her I called when she wakes up?" he asked.

"Of course, Alex," she said in a gentle voice. "And thank you again. I don't know what I would have done if she'd been hurt."

Alex hung up and shook his head. Doc was brilliant, of course, but she was a very odd duck.

"Everything okay?" Iggy asked as Alex entered the library.

"You got me," Alex said, dropping heavily into his reading chair. He'd told Iggy the high points of last night's adventure during their hurried phone call, but he took his time and filled in the rest of the details, ending with Jessica's decision to inject her unfinished potion into her body.

"That's actually less worrying than the rest of it," Iggy said when Alex finished. "I gave it some thought and I remembered that the idea of using the body to create vaccines and cures isn't new." He then explained in graphic detail how doctors used to push a needle through the boils of people infected with smallpox, then use them to deliberately infect healthy people with a mild case of the disease. "It was called variolation," he finished.

"Yuck," Alex said, pulling a cigarette from his case and lighting it. "Do you think she'll be okay?"

He considered that for a moment, then nodded.

The Long Chain

"Most likely," he said. "But then alchemy isn't my strong suit. What do you plan to do about the missing ruffian?"

Alex thought about that for a moment. His only lead was that Jimmy the Weasel worked at the Blue Room.

"I'll call Callahan in the morning," he said, not really able to think of a better plan. "See what he knows."

"I'm surprised at you, lad," Iggy said, using his penknife to cut the tip off a cigar. "You said that last fellow went through the lab window."

Alex raised an eyebrow, not sure where the old man was going with this.

"I'd say it's quite likely he cut himself jumping through a window that size," he went on, puffing on his cigar to light it. "Wouldn't you say?"

Alex shot to his feet. If Iggy was right, and he usually was, there was a good chance some of the glass in Dr. Kellin's back yard had the thug's dried blood on it. Blood Alex could trace right to the man.

"Sit down, lad," Iggy said, sitting back in his chair and blowing out a cloud of scented smoke. "You'll never find anything in the dark. Besides, Lieutenant Callahan said he's got a couple of uniforms parked out in front of Dr. Kellin's house. You wouldn't want to get shot if they thought you were an intruder."

Alex sat down, chuckling at the thought of the police and the FBI minders all trying to be inconspicuous.

"I'm sure they'll play nice," Iggy said when Alex explained his mirth. "And the better to keep Andrea and Jessica safe."

"Well, if the cops don't like it, they can take it up with the Ice Queen," Alex said.

"So how did she come to know about last night's festivities?"

Alex related the rest of the events of his day, including his visit to the Navy Yard and subsequent rescue by the sorceress.

"I'm intrigued," he said when Alex finished. "Just imagine what a man of Dr. Burnham's intellect was working on. You said he made gas mask filters for the Army, right? What if he's come up with a machine to make breathable air on submersibles? The possibilities fire the imagination."

"Well I'm going to be far too busy to have my imagination fired,"

Alex grumbled. "Unless I get lucky, it will take a year to scan the city looking for the source of all this fog."

"I've been thinking about your rune construct," Iggy said after a short silence. "It was very clever of you to use purity runes to triangulate the position of the densest fog." He studiously avoided mentioning Alex's mistake of using three purity runes when he only needed two. "The problem you have is that you're trying to scale up a rune that was never meant to have much range. You did it beautifully," he added with a wink. "But what you really need is a way to triangulate over a wide area."

"If you've got any suggestions," Alex said, tapping his cigarette in the ash tray on the little table between them, "I'm all ears."

Iggy gave Alex an enigmatic look as he puffed his cigar.

"What are you up to, old man?" Alex asked, recognizing that look.

"I'll have to do some reading in the morning," he said. "Give me half a day to figure it out."

"You're assuming Sorsha won't be here in the morning bright and early to conduct me around the city."

Iggy waved his hand as if brushing away a troublesome fly.

"If she does, tell her you'll need a day to write all the runes for your searching. She'll buy that. And then you'll have time to chase down the men who attacked Dr. Burnham."

Alex laughed somewhat mirthlessly at that.

"I don't have any way to trace what he was working on," he said. "The only clue I've got is a piece of paper with an unintelligible formula on it and the word *polymer*. I figured I could go over to Dow, where Burnham used to work, and ask around. Somebody over there can probably read the formula."

"I'd say the game is afoot, then," Iggy said, tapping out his cigar. "You go see Burnham's old cohorts and I'll figure out how to refine the rune for you."

"I've got to go to the alchemy shop in the morning and look for that glass," Alex said. "Whatever Dr. Burnham was working on can wait."

"I expect that those FBI men the sorceress sent over to watch the shop have orders to hold on to you if you show up there," Iggy said. "Let me figure the rune out, then you can find the source of the fog magic and the Ice Queen won't have any reason to bother you."

Alex didn't like it, but Iggy was probably right — as usual.

"All right," he said. He wasn't excited about chasing down chemical formulas, but staying here and waiting for Iggy would just be torture.

"It's settled, then," Iggy said, standing up and giving Alex an expectant look.

"And?" Alex asked.

"And I'm famished," Iggy said. "I think after making me worry about you last night, the least you can do is buy me dinner."

Alex grinned and nodded, crushing out his cigarette.

"Well, never let it be said that I didn't do the least I could do."

The next morning's fog seemed a little better, and Alex hoped that meant that whatever strange spell had been cast on the city was wearing off. He'd taken the precaution of calling a cab ahead of time, so he had a ride ready when he left the brownstone. Much of the usual traffic was gone thanks to the fog, so the trip across town to the laboratory where Dr. Burnham used to work only took fifteen minutes longer than it otherwise would have.

"Can I help you?" a perky young woman with dark hair and a pretty face asked. She sat behind a simple wooden desk in an unremarkable lobby. Clearly this was not where Dow Chemical brought its investors, or anyone else they might consider important.

"Actually, I think you can," Alex said, turning on the charm. "Did a Dr. Leonard Burnham used to work here?"

The woman's cheerful smile slipped for just a second, but she recovered admirably.

"Yes," she said, keeping the confusion off her face. "But he retired last year."

"I was wondering if I could speak with one of Dr. Burnham's former associates?" Alex said, as if such a request were the most normal thing in the world.

The woman thought about it for a moment, then her smile returned full force.

"Let me make a call," she said.

Alex stepped away from the desk for a moment while the perky receptionist spoke on the phone. The little lobby of the laboratory was empty except for the receptionist's desk and a worn couch on the opposite wall. A few pictures of people in white coats standing beside men in business suits hung on the walls, but they seemed more of an afterthought than intentional decoration.

"Someone will be out in a minute," the woman said, hanging up the phone.

Alex thanked her and turned back to the pictures on the wall. Dr. Burnham appeared in two of them, along with several other people Alex recognized from the pictures in Burnham's workshop.

"Can I help you?" an annoyed voice assaulted him.

Alex turned and found a balding man with a wiry build, a bushy mustache, and thick spectacles facing him. He wore a shirt and slacks with a white coat over the top, and he had his hands on his hips.

"I hope so," Alex said. "I'm Alex Lockerby, a private detective, and I'm looking for someone who knew Dr. Leonard Burnham when he worked here."

At the mention of Alex's status as a private detective, the man blanched.

"Is Leonard in some sort of trouble?" he demanded.

"Well, yes and no," Alex said. He explained about Dr. Burnham's disappearance and his memory loss.

"That's terrible," the man gasped. "Did the police catch whoever was responsible?"

"Not yet," Alex said. "That's why I'm here, Mr.—?"

"Doctor," the man corrected. "Doctor Harlan Taylor. I worked with Leonard for years. I'm shocked to hear this news."

"Dr. Burnham's granddaughter hired me to find out who did this to him," Alex continued. "Right now the only thing I have to go on is that he was working on something in his garage and whoever attacked him stole it."

Harlan's face grew angry.

"I can assure you, Mr. Lockerby, that no one here would stoop to violence and theft to get Leonard's designs," he said.

"Easy, Doc," Alex said, holding up his hands in a placating gesture. "I don't think anyone here hurt Dr. Burnham." He pulled the paper with the formula on it from his pocket and handed it over. "I just want to know if this means anything to you?"

Harlan put his glasses up on top of his head and squinted at the paper. Alex watched him closely as he read. Clearly Harlan didn't like what he was reading.

"You recognize that," Alex said. It was a statement rather than a question.

Harlan sighed and handed the paper back.

"I was hoping it was something else," he said. "Something new." He took his glasses off and rubbed the bridge of his nose.

"I take it you know what he was working on?"

"No," Harlan said, putting his glasses back on. "You can never tell with Leonard. But if that paper is part of it, I can tell you where it all started. Come with me."

He turned and headed through a plain, white door behind the receptionist's desk. Alex followed into a long, stark hallway with doors on either side. The doors on the left all had frosted windows in them and Alex could see the vague appearance of offices beyond. On the right, the doors were plain with only a number stenciled in the center.

The last door on the left had *Dr. Harlan Taylor* printed on it in white lettering, but Alex's guide went past it without a pause, entering a set of double doors at the end of the hallway. Following, Alex found himself in a large workroom that reminded him of Dr. Kellin's lab. Beakers, tubes, burners, and graduated cylinders were everywhere, along with rows and rows of glass jars containing various liquids and powders.

Harlan led Alex past all these and through another door in the back of the room. This time the door led to a smaller space with many glass enclosures. Most had holes with rubber gloves mounted in them to allow someone to work on whatever was inside without being exposed to it.

"Over here," Harlan said, indicating one of the gloveboxes.

Inside was a shallow dish of liquid with a lid on it and a metal ring connected to a wire. Dr. Taylor took a plug from underneath the enclosure and inserted it into a socket on the wall.

"So what am I looking at, Doc?"

"This is Leonard Burnham's obsession," he said. "It's a special kind of polymer, one Leonard invented himself."

"So what is a polymer, Dr. Taylor?" Alex asked. "I've never heard of that."

"Few people have," he admitted. "A polymer is a special kind of molecule. While molecules make up everything, they usually bond together to form other compounds. A polymer is a molecule that bonds to itself in an organized structure, like a long chain."

"Okay, so what?" Alex said, not understanding why that mattered.

"It means that instead of taking something in nature and shaping it to be what we want, we can just build what we want in the first place. Just imagine if we could make cables that were thinner and lighter than steel but just as strong. Or silk stockings that would never wear out."

Alex nodded as if he understood. He wasn't really sure he did, but he knew what Leslie and Jessica would think of stockings that never needed replacing. If Burnham or Taylor cracked that, they'd make millions upon millions.

Harlan flipped a switch on the base of the container and something inside began to hum.

"Normal polymers have to be created under very specific conditions in a lab." He shoved his hands into the rubber gloves and then removed the lid covering the dish of liquid. "What Leonard did was to figure out a way to literally grow polymers in any shape you need. Watch."

Harlan picked up the metal ring connected to the wire and dropped it into the liquid in the dish. Almost immediately a cloudy substance began to form on the surface.

"What's that?" Alex asked.

Harlan didn't answer but instead picked up a small screwdriver next to the dish. He dipped it into the cloudy liquid and then lifted it free. As it came up, a thin fabric clung to it, rising up out of what had once been pure liquid.

"That is fabric made of a polymer," Harlan said. "Leonard dreamed that up. Just imagine the possibilities." His voice was reverent and awed. "Instead of wearing bulky parachutes, pilots could carry a tiny vial of the liquid and a battery. If they had to jump out of their plane, they could literally grow a parachute on the way down."

As he spoke, Harlan lifted the fabric higher and higher out of the liquid. It was at least a foot long already and showed no signs of weakening or tearing. Alex wasn't sure he wanted to trust his life to a parachute made of this stuff, but it was impressive.

"So why aren't you making socks that never get holes out of this stuff, or instant handkerchiefs, or something?" Alex asked.

Dr. Taylor's smile of excitement turned melancholy and he set the fabric down across the bottom of the container.

"It's the electricity that keeps the molecules together," he said, withdrawing his hands from the gloves.

"So if you turn off the juice, it goes back to being a liquid?" Alex guessed.

"Worse, I'm afraid," Harlan said, reaching for the switch on the bottom of the container. He flipped it with a clack and the box stopped humming. Alex watched the fabric, expecting it to melt back to the sludge from whence it had come, but nothing happened.

"I thought you said—" he began, but at that moment the fabric exploded into flame. The box was completely enclosed in glass, but Alex could feel the heat from the conflagration. As quickly as it had happened, the fire burned away, only a bit slower than Alex's flash paper.

"What just happened?" he asked.

"This particular polymer is unstable in solid form," Harlan explained. "As long as it's exposed to an electrical current, it stays together, but as soon as that current is cut off," he motioned upward with his fingers. "Whoosh," he said. "The fire burns so hot that it would set anything flammable on fire. You can see why we don't make things out of this."

"And this is what Dr. Burnham was working on in his garage?" Alex said, stunned by the thought of it. He'd felt the heat through the thick glass, and there wasn't any safety container like this one at Burnham's workshop. "It's a miracle he didn't burn it to the ground."

"I'm afraid you're right," Harlan said, running his hand over the glass of the cabinet. "Leonard was always bothered by this. He wanted to solve it so badly, to make it work. In truth, we all did."

"Can you think of any reason he'd want to sell this idea to the Navy?"

"I can think of a dozen," Harlan said. "but he'd have to solve the instability issue first."

"What if he's using it as some new kind of explosive?" Alex asked.

"No." Harlan shook his head. "This burns very hot, but there are much more efficient ways to blow something up. If Leonard was going to use this, he'd have to start by making it stable."

Alex looked at the empty case as if willing it to reveal its secrets, to tell him what Dr. Burnham was doing with exploding fabric and why the Navy would care.

"I remember the first time Leonard showed this to me," Harlan went on, oblivious to Alex's consternation. "He'd used a conductive mesh over a hot plate that vaporized the Genesis Water—"

"The what?"

Harlan looked irritated at having his story interrupted, then realized why Alex had asked the question.

"Leonard always had a flair for the dramatic," he said. "He called his liquid Genesis Water, since anything could be created from it. Anyway, when the vaporized water hit the mesh, it made tiny strands. They sprung up like a moving picture of hair growing. Leonard claimed that once we braided them together, they would replace rope, maybe even steel. Of course right after that, he almost burned down the lab."

Alex looked at the glass container again. The metal probe that had conveyed the current was blackened and scorched where the conflagration had burned it. Chills ran down his spine as he realized the very real danger of Dr. Burnham's invention.

"Can I use your phone?" he asked.

18

THE BAD NEWS

A lex dialed Sorsha's number from the phone in Harlan's office without having to look at her card. He expected her secretary, but got the woman herself.

"Where are you?" she demanded, her voice going frosty when she heard his voice. "I called your house this morning and that duplicitous doctor told me you'd gone to your office. When I called your office, your useless secretary told me you were still at home."

Alex chuckled.

"Sounds like she's not so useless after all," he said.

"You'd better be calling me to report that you've found whatever magic is crippling my city," she said in a voice that hinted at what would happen to him if he wasn't.

"Nope," he said in the most innocently cheerful voice he could muster.

"Where are you?" she breathed, her voice barely audible.

"The midtown office of Dow Chemical," he said without hesitation.

There was a short pause, during which Alex would have sworn he heard the sound of glass breaking.

"So," she said at last, her voice tight and even. "After my bailing you out with the Navy and giving you strict instructions to find out where this damned fog is coming from, you decided to keep investigating the no-longer-missing chemist?"

"Well," Alex hedged. "Not exactly."

"You stay right there," she said. "I'm coming over to break your fingers. Remind me which hand you write with."

"Before you do anything rash," Alex said, grinning at the thought of how angry she sounded, "you might want to hear what I found out."

She made a noise that sounded somewhere between a growl and a curse. Alex knew he really shouldn't antagonize her, but he just couldn't help himself. She made it so easy.

"I know who's making the fog and I may have a way to find where it's coming from," he said, deciding he'd better speak before the sorceress regained her voice.

"How," she growled. "How do you know who but not know where?"

"That's a long story. You'd better get over here quick and I'll show you."

Alex hung up before she could respond and then dialed Iggy.

"Any luck figuring out how to boost the purity rune?" he asked.

"No," Iggy admitted. "But I think I can make the finding rune function like a purity rune. It turned out to be much simpler than I thought. Once I—"

"Great," Alex cut him off. "So if I had a sample of some unique material, could the rune find out where more of it might be located?"

"That's exactly how it would work," Iggy said.

"Perfect. How fast can you get to the Dow Chemical building in Midtown?"

Iggy laughed at that.

"I'd have to write the rune first," he said. "Right now, it's just an idea, and if you want to use it today, I'd better get started figuring out how to make the construct. I'm sorry, lad, but you'll have to come by here and pick it up later."

Alex wasn't thrilled to hear that, especially since he'd antagonized Sorsha so much. He'd hoped to be able to lead her right to the source of the fog without any additional delay.

"All right," he said. "You get busy, I'll get everything else ready."

Iggy promised to hurry and hung up. Alex checked his watch. He guessed it would take Sorsha a good half hour to arrive, even with her floater, longer if she took the time to round up her FBI lackeys. He picked up the receiver and dialed the phone again, this time to the Central Office of Police.

"Callahan," the Lieutenant's voice greeted him once the police operator had transferred Alex's call.

"It's Alex," he replied. "Did you have any luck chasing down Jimmy the Weasel at the Blue Room?"

To his credit, Callahan didn't ask how Alex knew about Jimmy working there.

"Only that he didn't show up for work last night," he answered. "No surprise there. What have you found?"

"Nothing yet," he said. "The FBI's got me running errands for them, but with any luck I should have something for you this afternoon."

"Listen to me, Lockerby," the Lieutenant growled. "I know better than to tell you to drop this, but three people are already dead. If you find anything, and I mean anything, you bring it to me, understand?"

Alex understood and he said so. This case was way too personal for him and when things got personal, people made mistakes.

"Nobody thinks you were out of line, killing those men," Callahan went on. "'But if bodies start piling up, the Chief is going to want someone to blame. You got me?"

"I get it, Lieutenant," Alex said. "You'll be my first call."

Callahan hung up and Alex sat on Harlan's desk, looking at the phone receiver. He wanted to put it down and head straight over to Dr. Kellin's shop, Sorsha and her fog be damned. With a sigh, he put the receiver back in its cradle. The Ice Queen was already mad at him; if he left her hanging, she might just decide to make an example out of him. A warning to other presumptuous PIs.

"All right, Mr. Lockerby," Harlan Taylor said, coming into his office from the hall. "I got the equipment together like you asked, but I'm a bit concerned. You saw what happened to the fabric."

"Trust me, Doc," Alex said. "It'll be fine."

Harlan looked uncertain.

"I don't like doing things in the lab that I know to be unsafe."

"Lockerby!" Sorsha's voice rang out from the front of the building. "Where are you?"

The only way she could have arrived already was if she had teleported, something Alex knew she didn't like. He must have seriously underestimated how angry she was with him.

"What on earth?" Harlan said, shock giving way to anger in his face.

"Easy, Doc," Alex said, putting a restraining hand on the wiry man's arm. "It's about to get a lot more dangerous in here, so just smile and play along."

The door at the end of the hallway burst open, and Sorsha stormed through. Her short, platinum hair bounced with the rhythm of her steps and the heels of her pumps clacked on the concrete floor. Behind her came Agent Redhorn and Agent Mendes, both looking a bit green around the gills.

Alex smiled at that. The effects of teleportation were funny when he wasn't the one suffering them.

"Who are they?" Harlan muttered as Sorsha approached with all the energy of a runaway train.

"There you are," Sorsha snapped before Alex could respond. She seemed about to give Alex a piece of her mind, but with Dr. Taylor there, she thought better of it. "Explain yourself," she managed, clenching her fists so tightly her knuckles went white.

"Doctor Harlan Taylor," he said, pointing to Sorsha. "This is Miss Sorsha Kincaid, sorceress and a consultant to the FBI. Those two," he indicated Redhorn and Mendes, "are Agents with the Bureau. Miss Kincaid, this is Doctor Taylor, head of research and development at this facility."

A shocked look played across Harlan's face, but he recovered quickly and stuck out his hand.

"A great pleasure, Miss Kincaid," he said.

Sorsha almost didn't take his hand, but she seemed to remember at whom she was actually mad. After a long second of hesitation, she shook the man's hand.

"Now," she said, turning to Alex. "Why, exactly am I here?"

"Until about a year ago, this is where Dr. Burnham worked," Alex explained.

Sorsha's eyes narrowed dangerously.

"I know that," she said through clenched teeth.

"Yes, but you don't know what he was working on in the days leading up to his retirement."

"How is that relevant?"

Alex indicated Harlan.

"Dr. Taylor showed me Dr. Burnham's pet project," he said. "It was very enlightening."

Sorsha shifted her gaze to Harlan and raised one of her eyebrows.

"Uh," he stammered. "I'm not sure what Mr. Lockerby is talking about. Dr. Burnham's polymer experiments were a failure."

The sorceress looked back to Alex and he smiled easily.

"Trust me, Doc," he said to Harlan. "Miss Kincaid will be very excited to see what Dr. Burnham was working on."

Harlan shrugged and pointed toward the back room.

"If you say so. It's right through here."

He turned and started forward, but Alex didn't follow. He suddenly couldn't move at all.

"You seem to take a perverse delight in annoying me, Alex," Sorsha said under her breath. She moved in front of him and he could see her pale blue eyes literally glowing. "If you're wasting my time here, I assure you that I will take great pleasure in making you suffer for your attitude."

She waved her hand and her eyes stopped glowing. A moment later Alex staggered forward, gasping for breath. He hadn't realized that the magic she'd used on him had stopped his breathing as well. Sorsha had done this to him once before, and he shivered at the memory.

Sorsha swept past him as Alex took a few deep breaths. Redhorn passed him with an amused look on his face, followed by Mendes, who ignored him. Once Alex was sure his heart rate had returned to normal and his face wasn't flushed, he went through the double doors into the large workroom.

Harlan had some of his people clear out a space in the center of the room and had placed a metal pan on top of a metal lab stool there. A heavy electric wire ran to a heating element in the bottom of the pan, and a second wire connected to a metal plate that was held over the pan by a wire stand.

"I just need to add the Genesis Water," Harlan said, picking up a heavy jar full of a pinkish liquid. He tipped it up and poured some into the bottom of the pan, then set the rest aside.

"What is this?" Sorsha muttered from his left.

"Just watch," Alex whispered back.

Harlan plugged in the heating element, and a moment later, the liquid in the tray began to steam. He explained about how Dr. Burnham was trying to make polymers that could be shaped using electricity, going into detail on chemical reactions that gave Alex a headache.

Once a steady stream of vapor rose from the tray up to where the metal plate was suspended, Harlan plugged in the wire leading to the plate. Almost instantly, long, thin strands of something sprang up through the tiny holes in the metal plate. They looked like a woman's long hair flowing in some invisible wind.

Alex leaned close to Sorsha.

"Look familiar?" he said under his breath.

She gasped as she recognized the way the fog strands had looked through Alex's oculus.

"I think now we know what Dr. Burnham was building for the Navy," Alex continued. "A smokescreen generator."

Sorsha tried not to look impressed.

"Does this mean you can find it?" she wondered, giving him a cold look.

"I think so," he said. "Iggy's working on modifying my finding rune as we speak."

"That's very good news."

Alex shrugged and turned to Harlan.

"Okay, Doc, you can shut it down."

"You'd all better take a step back," Dr. Taylor said as he gripped the plug that powered the metal plate.

"Why?" Sorsha asked as she and Alex took two steps back.

"That's the bad news," Alex said.

Before Sorsha could demand what he meant, the elaborate, hairlike strands erupted in a truly impressive fireball. Alex was ready for it this time, but it still made him jump. To his right, Agent Redhorn threw up his hand in front of his face, and Agent Mendes stumbled, falling on her backside.

The only one who hadn't moved was Sorsha. She raised her hands palm out and then rolled her fingers closed, starting with the little finger and working inward. As she did the flames flickered and died until all that was left was the charred remains of the experiment.

She turned to Alex, shaking her hands as if the effort stung them.

"What was that?" she demanded.

"The compound is unstable," Harlan volunteered. "Once I cut off the electric current, it ignited."

Sorsha took a moment to absorb that information, then she grabbed Alex's arm in a surprisingly strong grip and pulled him over to the side of the room.

"Is he saying that turning off Burnham's missing machine will cause the fog to—"

"Combust," Alex said with a nod. "Yes. I'm betting that's why whoever turned it on hasn't turned it off yet."

Sorsha gave him a patronizing look.

"If whoever stole Burnham's device knew about the burning fog, why would they turn it on in the first place?"

"I don't think they knew that when they turned it on," Alex said. "Remember, Burnham's notebooks are also missing. The thief might have turned it on to make sure it was working, then gone through the notebook while it warmed up. By the time he realized his mistake, it was too late."

"So you're saying that even if we find the machine making the fog, we won't be able to turn it off?"

Alex shook his head and shrugged.

"Not without Dr. Burnham's memory or his notebooks," he said.

Sorsha crossed her arms and chewed on her lower lip.

"What if we wait until it rains?" she pondered. "That flash was hot, but it didn't last long."

Alex pointed to where Harlan was putting away the wires from the experiment.

"Dr. Taylor says that the size of the fireball will depend on how much of Dr. Burnham's unstable polymer is available to burn," he said.

Sorsha's eyes widened.

"How big a fireball will an entire city full of it make?"

"I don't know," Alex admitted, "but think about this. Most of the houses in the city are made of wood. Half the city still has wooden sidewalks and every building except a few of the skyscrapers have wooden roofs. If the fog combusts, it will burn the whole city down."

Sorsha shivered and nodded.

"It would be worse than Chicago." She looked up at Alex with no trace of her former irritation; it had all been replaced by worry. "So what do we do now?"

"We go back to the Navy Yard and have another chat with that Admiral," Alex said.

"What if he's involved?"

Alex shook his head at that.

"Tennon was paying for everything, he wouldn't need to send someone to knock Dr. Burnham over the head and steal the machine."

"Unless he ran out of money," Sorsha suggested.

"No," Alex said, rejecting that idea out of hand. "The admiral in in charge of a giant government construction site, if he needed money, he could easily find some in his budget."

Sorsha raised an eyebrow at the idea but after a moment, she shrugged and nodded.

"So why talk to Tennon if he's not involved?" She asked.

"It's a long shot, but they might have copies of Burnham's notes, or even know how to shut down the machine."

"And if they don't?"

Alex shrugged.

"By then Iggy should be done modifying my finding rune," Alex said. "If the Navy is a dead end, I'll use some of the Genesis Water to locate Burnham's machine and we'll see if Dr. Taylor or one of the other eggheads they've got here can figure out how to safely shut it down."

"Assuming they can, what will happen to the fog?" Sorsha asked.

"According to Dr. Taylor, once the electric current from Burnham's machine stops, the fog should just break down and dissolve," Alex said.

"Unless it burns the city down."

"Or that," he agreed.

"All right," Sorsha said, her take charge attitude returning. "Let's go see if Admiral Tennon wants to talk about his secret project now."

Alex snorted.

"I want to know why they didn't say anything before," he said. "They must have known that the unnatural fog covering the city was from Dr. Burnham's generator."

"I was thinking the same thing," Sorsha said. With that, she turned on her heel and stalked out through the door, her FBI agents trailing in her wake.

19

SMOKESCREEN

The last time Alex had been to the Navy Yard, the gate guard had grilled the Shore Patrol sailors he was with for almost ten minutes before letting them in. When Sorsha arrived, unannounced, the wait was almost half an hour. Clearly the Navy hadn't found their missing man, Seaman McCormick, or whoever was pretending to be him.

Alex leaned on a metal railing that ran around the cement pad where the guard hut stood, smoking a cigarette while Sorsha glared imperiously at the sailors who were currently searching her floater. During their wait, the sailors at the gate had called in a stream of higher-ranking men as they each tried to explain to the sorceress why she was being delayed. The final one was a man named Williams with thick rough hands, a perpetual scowl, and no discernible neck.

"All right, Miss Kincaid," Chief Petty Officer Williams said, with as much of a smile as his gruff face could manage. "Admiral Tennon has agreed to see you and you've been cleared through the gate." He turned and pointed off through the fog. "Just follow this road and—"

"I know the way," Sorsha cut him off, peevishly. "Thank you."

"Sorry again for the delay, ma'am," Williams said, though whether he meant it or not wasn't evident from either his face or his tone.

Sorsha shot Alex a dark look and he tossed away his cigarette as he headed for the floater.

"Do you think the Admiral is burning any evidence of his link to Burnham?" Agent Redhorn asked, as Sorsha's driver got the vehicle moving through the now-open gate.

Sorsha seemed to consider it, but Alex shook his head.

"He doesn't think he's in any danger," Alex said. "Even if we had proof that Dr. Burnham's missing machine is what's causing the fog, it's not his fault that someone stole it from Burnham."

"That's exactly what he'll say," Sorsha agreed, disgust in her voice.

"What I can't figure is why he doesn't seem to be worried about the fog," Alex said.

"He must not know that it can burst into flames at any moment," Agent Mendes said.

Alex hadn't thought of that. This project was off the books for some reason; that was why Burnham was working from his home instead of here at the Navy Yard. Maybe that meant that the Admiral didn't know about the problems with the device. He looked back at Agent Mendes. Women weren't common in federal agencies and he'd never heard of a female FBI agent. Clearly she wasn't there just as a pretty face, though. She noticed him looking at her and cocked an eyebrow, daring him to say something.

"If Agent Mendes here is right," Alex said, giving her a nod, "then it's likely the Navy doesn't have any of Burnham's notes on his device."

"So we're back to square one," Sorsha said, her brows knitting together in frustration.

"Not necessarily," Alex said. "Let's hear what the Admiral has to say first. He might have notes from Burnham but just didn't read them. From what I saw in Burnham's workshop, his notes weren't very well organized."

"And if he doesn't?" Mendes asked.

Alex reached into his jacket pocket and pulled out the glass bottle with the rubber stopper that Harlan had given him. Inside was a small amount of Dr. Burnham's Genesis Water.

"Then I'll try to use this to find out where the smokescreen machine is," he said. "Whoever stole it also stole Dr. Burnham's notes, so it's likely that if we find one, we'll find the other."

"Why aren't we doing that first?" Agent Redhorn asked.

"I'm told the rune isn't ready yet," Sorsha said, giving Alex a cold look.

"Iggy will get it done," he said, slipping the bottle of Genesis Water back into his pocket. "But you can't rush that kind of work. I'll call him once we're done with Tennon."

"Speaking of which," Agent Mendes said. The floater had just pulled up in front of the shoddy wooden building that housed the Admiral's office.

Lieutenant Leavitt stood from behind his desk in the reception area as Sorsha swept into the room. Unlike Chief Petty Officer Williams, Leavitt was all smiles, though Alex detected a hint of tension in his face.

"Miss Kincaid," he said with an ingratiating look. "I'm sorry you had to wait at the gate for so long."

"Am I to assume my waiting is at an end?" she demanded, eyeing him with a raised eyebrow of disapproval.

His smile somehow managed to become even more charming and he swept his hand forward, indicating the closed door with the Admiral's name on it.

"He's expecting you," Leavitt said. He moved to the door, knocked quickly, and pushed it open for the sorceress.

"Miss Kincaid," Tennon said, standing as she came in.

Alex noticed that the portly Lieutenant Commander Vaughn was also present, and he rose as well.

"Thank you for seeing me, Admiral," Sorsha said, no trace of the harshness in her voice that she'd used with Williams or Leavitt.

"I'm a very busy man, Miss Kincaid," Tennon said, his own annoyance clear. "I hope this is important."

Sorsha's eyes hardened at that. The Admiral was trying to get a rise out of her, and not just to annoy her like Alex would have. He wanted her off balance. It was a tactic Alex used frequently. People who were flustered tended to say things they shouldn't. From the look on Sorsha's face, Tennon's play was working. She drew in a breath to reply, but Alex spoke first.

"Why didn't you tell us that Dr. Burnham was making a smokescreen generator for you the last time we talked?" he asked.

The question caught Tennon flat-footed and his mouth opened and closed like a fish in a bowl. The Admiral's attention had been focused on Sorsha, and he hadn't seen Alex.

"I thought I told you to stay out of the Navy's business," he snarled when he recognized him.

"Since I'm not one of your sailors, I don't much care what you told me," Alex said. He kept his face serious, but there was a certain flippant tone in his voice.

Tennon's face turned red.

"Arrest this wharf-rat," he shouted at Vaughn.

"Enough," Sorsha said. She spoke in her normal voice, but the sound rolled through the room like thunder, amplified by her magic. Tennon's attention returned to her and she held his gaze for a long moment before she spoke again. "Mr. Lockerby has a frequent bad habit of speaking out of turn, but he isn't wrong. You must have known that the fog currently blanketing the city wasn't natural and yet you didn't mention that you were paying Burnham to develop a device to generate just such a fog."

Tennon held Sorsha's gaze without blinking. Clearly he was not the kind of man to be intimidated in his own office, which was probably how he became an admiral in the first place.

"Of course I knew," he said, his voice firm and defiant. "We figured it was Burnham showing off or trying to hold us up for more money."

"So you decided to just take his machine?" Agent Redhorn asked.

Tennon's eyes shifted to Redhorn and a snarl turned his lip.

"He doesn't have it," Alex said before Tennon could explode. "The fog started the same day Dr. Burnham was assaulted."

Tennon gave Alex a stern glance, then looked back to Sorsha and nodded.

"We didn't learn about the theft of the device until this private dick started poking around. So, if that's all?"

"Did you know that the fog is unstable?" Alex asked. "That if someone turns off Dr. Burnham's machine it could cause a fireball that might burn the whole city down?"

For the first time since they arrived, uncertainty flashed across the admiral's face. He glanced quickly at Vaughn, but the Lieutenant Commander shook his head.

"Are you sure about that?" Tennon barked at Alex.

"We are," Sorsha said, her voice losing its hard edge. "I've seen the effect with my own eyes." She briefly outlined what Dr. Taylor had shown her at Dow Chemical. "So you can understand our eagerness to find Dr. Burnham's machine," she concluded. "And to learn as much as we can about it. More importantly, how to safely turn it off."

Tennon stood there for a moment, as if weighing his options. Finally he nodded and waved toward the chair in front of his desk.

"Sit down, Miss Kincaid," he said, then added, "please."

He waited until she'd seated herself, then sat behind his desk.

"None of us knew that Burnham's machine had any dangers associated with it," he began. "In truth we didn't know his machine was actually finished. As far as we knew he was still working on it."

"He probably was," Alex said. "His colleague at Dow said that he'd have to solve the instability problem before he could use his formula."

Tennon gave Alex an irritated look, then continued.

"We do have his original proposal, but that just details what the device would do, not how it would work."

"Doesn't the Navy already have smoke machines?" Agent Redhorn asked.

Unlike his irritation at being interrupted by Alex, Tennon actually smiled at that.

"Not like Burnham's," he said. "The smoke generators we have now can block an enemy ship from targeting our vessels, but it can be blown away."

"Of course," Alex said, snapping his fingers. "Burnham's smoke clings to brickwork. All the Navy would have to do is put a stack of bricks on the deck of a ship and the cloud would move with the ship."

Tennon nodded.

"Why would that matter?" Agent Mendes asked. "The ships inside the fog wouldn't be able to see where they were going. How could they fight like that?"

It was a good point, but Tennon's smile only grew wider.

"You're assuming we want if for warships," he said, then he turned to where Lieutenant Leavitt was sitting at the little table taking notes. "Get the thing," he told him.

"Yes, sir," Leavitt said, rising. He crossed the room and pulled open a cabinet revealing a heavy safe. As he turned the dial on the front, Admiral Tennon went on.

"The last time there was a war in Europe, we sent hundreds of cargo ships across the Atlantic loaded with men, munitions, equipment, and supplies," he said, "even before the US got into the war. With things heating up on the continent, the Navy plans to be ready if we have to do that again."

"Why do you want to hide our convoys?" Sorsha asked.

At that moment, Leavitt pulled the lever on the front of the safe and swung the door open. It was thicker than usual, which meant it was probably fireproof, a sensible precaution for something that held military documents. Inside, Alex could see stacks of papers, folders, ledgers, several guns and boxes of ammunition, and a thick leather folio, no doubt used to transport the Admiral's important papers.

The lieutenant reached into the safe and pulled out what looked like a yellow lava rock with a long string wound around it.

"You'll find this interesting, Miss Kincaid," Tennon said, accepting the stone from Leavitt. He took a moment and unwrapped the string until only the end was tied around the strange rock. That done, he held it out to Sorsha. She hesitated a moment, then put out her hand, palm up.

Tennon placed the rock into Sorsha's palm, but the second he let it go, the yellow rock shot upward, out of her hand, and bounced off the ceiling with a clack. Sorsha gasped, staring up at the floating rock on the ceiling. She reached out and took hold of the dangling string and pulled it down like a child with a balloon.

"What magic is this?" she said, her voice full of wonder.

"That's something the Nazis have cooked up," Tennon said. "The rock is coke, the kind of coal you use in a forge, but it's been treated with some kind of alchemy. This is the result."

"Why do floating stones make the Navy want sticky fog?" Alex asked.

"Because," Tennon said, his gruff voice back. "The Germans are making these things by the ton and stuffing them into their zeppelins instead of using hydrogen."

"According to our engineers," Lt. Commander Vaughn said, "if this rock is an example of the lifting capacity of the process, existing zeppelins will be able to carry twice what they could before at the same volume."

"Which means the Nazis could load them up with guns or bombs and use them as stable offensive platforms," Tennon explained. "They could cut off the Atlantic supply route."

"Unless they can't see the convoys because they're covered in fog that moves with them," Alex said, finally understanding what Project: Shade Tree really was.

Tennon flashed an evil grin.

"They could shoot and bomb all day and not hit anything," he said.

"But the Navy didn't see it that way," Alex guessed.

"What do you mean?" Sorsha asked.

Alex nodded at Tennon.

"Remember, he was paying Dr. Burnham out of some private account," Alex said. "And Burnham was doing his work at home."

Tennon sneered and sat back down behind his desk.

"The next time you come see me, Sorceress," he growled, jerking his thumb at Alex, "leave this guy at home."

"The admiralty didn't think that zeppelins would be an effective fighting platform," Vaughn said. "And as long as they're filled with hydrogen, they aren't. But with this," he pointed at the floating yellow rock, "zeppelins would be much more difficult to shoot down. If they flew high enough, it's possible our aircraft couldn't even reach them."

"So Vaughn and I created the SEI," Tennon said. "The *Strategic Engineering Initiative*, and I've been paying Dr. Burnham out of my own pocket. If he was successful, we'd sell his invention to the Navy."

"And retire?" Alex guessed.

Tennon shot him a look that was pure venom.

"I am not doing this for money!" he shouted. "Do you know how many ships will set sail from here if there's another war? Hundreds. Those brave men are my responsibility and I'll be damned if I send them out without the best protection I can get my hands on!"

Alex held up his hands in a gesture of peace, and Tennon got a hold on his temper.

"Now you know what we were doing," he growled, turning back to Sorsha. "We don't have Dr. Burnham's device, and we didn't know the fog was dangerous until you told us. Now if that's all, I've got a dozen ships I need to send out of port before this fog, how did you put it? Combusts?"

Sorsha nodded.

"Thank you, Admiral," she said, handing him one of her cards. "If you think of anything that might be helpful, please call me."

Tennon looked at the card for a moment, then he took it.

"If you find Dr. Burnham's machine and you manage to get it turned off," he said, "we'd appreciate getting it back."

"That's certainly fair," she said in a neutral voice. She passed Tennon the floating rock on its string, then turned and strode gracefully from the room.

Alex admired her as she went, walking like a movie starlet at a premier. The sorceress was a strange mix of things. She had a way of being soft and hard at the same time. Her power made her intimidating, and she used that to the fullest. At other times, she dropped the pretense, and simply let her feminine grace and beauty speak for her.

He followed her out into the reception room, past Lieutenant Leavitt's desk and out into the foggy afternoon.

"Do you think he's telling the truth?" Agent Redhorn asked, once they had all piled into the floater.

"Yes," Sorsha said. "I could make a lot of trouble for him if he isn't, and he knows it."

"I bet the city would still sue him if the fog burns anything," Alex added. "Even though he didn't know that was possible."

"So what do we do now?" Agent Redhorn asked.

"Shouldn't we evacuate the city?" Mendes said.

"No," Sorsha replied, shaking her head. "It would cause a city-wide panic."

"But if the fog combusts, isn't that worse?" Mendes looked around the back of the floater and saw only grim faces.

"That might not happen," Sorsha explained. "But if we tell the public that the city might burn down, everyone will rush into the streets and across the bridges. Thousands could be killed in the chaos."

"Besides, over a million people live in this city," Alex said. "We'd never be able to get even a fraction of them out — it would take weeks."

Mendes clearly didn't like that answer, but she didn't argue.

"Then what do we do?" she repeated Agent Redhorn's question.

"Now we go to my place," Alex said, mustering a smile. "If Iggy has the modified finding rune done, I'll use it and hopefully we'll find the Navy's missing fog machine."

"And if the rune doesn't work?" Sorsha asked.

"Then I'll let you buy me lunch," Alex said with a grin. "I'm starving."

20

IGGY'S RUNE

The trip from the front gate of the Navy Yard to the street in front of the brownstone took twenty minutes, and Alex couldn't help but be impressed. He didn't have a high opinion of floaters; they were both expensive and slow, but he did have to admit they were an efficient way to get around.

"This looks a bit uptown for you, Lockerby," Agent Redhorn said, once they were far enough up the front stair to see the town home.

"I just live here," Alex said mildly. Agent Redhorn seemed to be going out of his way to get a rise out of him, so Alex decided not to play the game.

"The building belongs to Alex's mentor, Doctor Ignatius Bell," Sorsha said. "Late of His Majesty's Navy. I expect you to conduct yourselves with the utmost respect."

Alex hid a smile as he flipped open his pocket watch. He felt the runes inside activate and mesh with the ones in the door. This time when he pushed, the door swung open, and he ushered the sorceress and the agents inside.

"Just a minute," he said, as Sorsha tried to open the inner door to the vestibule and found it shut tight. Alex closed the outer door without closing his watch and the inner door popped open.

"Interesting security you have here," Agent Mendes observed as Alex tucked his watch back into the pocket of his vest. "Just out of curiosity, would I be able to open the door if I had your watch?"

Alex gave her an enigmatic smile. She was much more observant than he'd given her credit for being. Iggy would like her.

"No," he said, then hung up his hat on the usual peg in the hall. "This way," he went on, leading them through the library.

The kitchen was large, serving as both a place to prepare food and a dining room. A long, heavy oak table occupied the bulk of the room with ten chairs set around it. To the left was the back door that led out into the green house, where Iggy grew orchids, and the brownstone's tiny back yard. To the right was the oven and range next to the icebox and a large sink. Beside the icebox a door led into the pantry.

A third door stood beside a wall-mounted telephone, only this door wasn't always there. Iggy had long ago painted a line from the floor up, over, and back down again in the shape of a door. Whenever he wanted to use his vault, he simply stuck the rune inside the painted doorway and opened it there.

Iggy considered his vault a personal sanctuary and almost never invited anyone inside. Alex was Iggy's apprentice and he had been in the vault exactly once, last year. Since that time, his mentor had hung a fancy beaded curtain with an oriental design inside the door to his vault, making it impossible to see inside when the door was open.

Alex knocked respectfully on the wall next to the open vault door.

"I'm back," he called out. "And I've brought guests."

A moment later the curtain parted, and Doctor Ignatius Bell emerged from inside. He was dressed in a plain shirt and trousers, the clothes he used to tend his beloved orchids, and his face lit up when he saw the sorceress.

"Sorsha," he said throwing his arms wide. "How are you?"

Alex expected the Ice Queen to rebuke the old man for such a gesture of intimacy, but she smiled fondly and embraced Iggy.

"I'm sorry I haven't visited," she said, as if they were old friends.

"How's your hip?"

"Fully healed," she said. "Thanks to you."

Alex was taken aback. As far as he knew, the only time Sorsha and

Iggy had met was when the old man had pulled a bullet out of her when one of her former FBI men had shot her.

"These—" Alex was about to say *gentlemen* but figured Mendes wouldn't appreciate that. "Agents," he substituted, "are from the FBI."

Sorsha introduced her team and Iggy shook their hands as if having the feds in the brownstone were all part of a perfectly normal day. Never mind that the infamous Archimedean Monograph, the most dangerous book of rune lore in history, was sitting on a bookshelf in the library, not fifteen feet away. Alex wondered what Sorsha and the Agents would do if they knew that.

"Alex says you might have a way to find Dr. Burnham's fog machine," Sorsha said.

Iggy gasped at that and turned to Alex.

"It's a machine?" he asked, his voice full of wonder.

Alex gave him the short version of Dr. Burnham's project for the Navy.

"Fascinating," Iggy said once Alex had finished. "Did the Germans really come up with a floating rock? That's amazing."

"Why is that amazing?" Agent Mendes asked. "New York has six floating castles."

"True," Sorsha said. "But a sorcerer can only maintain one flying construct at a time. If the Germans can mass produce their yellow rocks, they could put a fleet of airships into the field."

"So," Alex said, getting back to the subject at hand. "Do you have it?"

Iggy pulled his green-backed rune book from his shirt pocket with a theatrical flair and tore out a page, passing it to Alex. The construct on the paper was delicate and complicated. Alex recognized the foundations of his finding rune, but instead of the nodes that would trace a person's essence, there was a rune he didn't know.

"This is a transmutation rune," Iggy said, indicating the new part.

Alex shook his head.

"I don't know that one."

"It's based on ancient alchemy," Iggy said, dropping into his lecture voice. "Years ago, alchemists wanted to turn lead into gold, so they used a bit of real gold as a sort of catalyst. The rune operates on the same principle."

"So it will turn lead into gold?" Mendes asked.

Iggy chortled at that.

"No," he said. "Mostly this rune is used in developing countries to purify tainted drinking water. The idea is that you use a small sample of pure water and make the polluted water change to match it."

"So how does that help Alex find the fog machine?" Sorsha asked.

"The original rune uses the symbol for change," Iggy said. "I substituted the one for *duplicate*, or *exact match* in this case. The finding rune will use a small sample of something and find the best example of that thing inside its radius."

"And since no one else is going to be using Dr. Burnham's Genesis Water," Alex pulled the stoppered bottle from his pocket and set it on the table, "the only thing the rune should lock on to is the fog machine itself."

"Let's get started, then," Sorsha said, sounding tired.

Alex went to the wall where Iggy's vault door stood open.

"Do you mind?" he asked his mentor.

Iggy nodded, and Alex shut the door. Iggy pulled the ornate key out of the lock on the outside. Immediately the door melted into the wall, leaving no trace that it had been there. As Iggy stepped back, Alex pulled out his red rune book. He tore out a page with a vault rune on it, licked the page, stuck it to the wall, and then ignited it. A moment later his own heavy vault door appeared.

Using his own ornate key, Alex pulled the door open and stepped inside to retrieve his kit bag and his maps and compass. Leaving the door open, he went to the massive kitchen table and rolled out his map of Manhattan.

"What if the machine isn't on the island?" Sorsha asked.

Alex opened the cigar box where he kept his jade figurines and the brass compass he used with finding runes.

"We know it's in the city," he said, using the figurines to weigh down the ends of his map. "If it's not in Manhattan, I'll make more of these runes and we'll use them around the city until we find the machine."

Sorsha looked as if she wasn't happy with that answer, but she didn't say anything. Alex put the battered brass compass down on top of the map, then folded the modified finding rune and set it on top. To that, he added the bottle of Genesis Water, placing it on top of the folded rune.

Taking out his lighter, Alex cleared his mind. He thought about what he knew of the fog machine and the man who had created it. When he was satisfied that he had it firmly in his mind, he squeezed his lighter and ignited the flash paper.

Usually when Alex ignited a finding rune, it burst into a glowing orange symbol that hovered over the compass. This time the rune was a sickly shade of yellowish-green, and it didn't spin so much as wobbled like a wounded bird. Eventually the needle in the battered compass began to spin with it until the rune popped and fizzled out of existence.

"Did it work?" Sorsha asked.

Alex put his finger and thumb gently on the edges of the compass and moved it slowly across the map. As he did so, the needled stayed pointing squarely at a spot near the South Side docks.

"Here," he said, sliding the compass across the map until the needle began to spin. He lifted the compass off the map, which broke its connection, and pointed to the spot directly under it.

Sorsha took a minute to study the area, then put out her hand to Alex.

"Take my hand," she said.

Alex knew what she had in mind, and he held his hands up and away from her offered one.

"Just like that?" he said, incredulous.

"We don't have time to waste," she said, giving him an exasperated look.

"Do you mind if I get a few things first?"

Sorsha rolled her eyes but acquiesced. Alex packed up his crime scene kit, then headed back to his vault.

"Follow me," he said to Redhorn and Mendes. The pair of them exchanged looks but followed Alex into the extra-dimensional room. Alex took off his jacket and hung it on the standing coat rack inside the door before heading to his gun cabinet. First, he took down his shoulder holster and put it on, then he shoved his 1911 into it after checking that it had a full magazine. He pulled two other magazines from a shelf in the cabinet and slipped them into the elastic holders on the opposite side from his gun. One of them had a white stripe painted on the bottom, indicating that it held special rounds, the ones Alex had inscribed with a spell-breaker rune.

Satisfied that he was as prepared as he could be, Alex took down his Browning A-5 and offered it to Redhorn.

"No thanks," he said, opening his jacket to reveal his own 1911. "I prefer this."

Alex shrugged and offered the shotgun to Mendes. She thought about it for a second, then accepted the weapon, checking the magazine expertly.

"One more thing," Alex said, opening the cupboard door below the gun cabinet. He withdrew a heavy bag, much like his kit, and passed it to Redhorn. "There's a trench coat in there," Alex said. "When we get where we're going, open the bag and put it on, just make sure I'm at least twenty feet away when you do it."

Redhorn looked confused as Alex pulled on his suit jacket.

"Why?" he asked.

"The coat has five shield runes on it," Alex explained. "They'll stop bullets from killing you, at least until they run out."

"How many bullets can they stop?" he asked.

"One per rune."

"Then why don't you put a hundred on there?" Mendes asked.

"Shield runes don't work well in large groups," Alex explained. "The most you can have at one time is five."

"Why do I have to wait to put it on?" Redhorn asked.

"Because I have two of them left on my jacket," Alex said. "If more than five get too close together, they start to lose their effectiveness. Just leave it in the shielded bag until we get there."

Redhorn nodded, hefting the heavy bag.

"You're all right, Lockerby," he said. "But if you tell anyone I said that, I'll deny it." His voice was gruff, but he wore a half-smile.

"If you're quite finished in there," Sorsha's impatient voice drifted in from the kitchen. "We should be going."

Redhorn and Mendes exchanged worried looks, and Alex didn't blame them. Teleportation might be fast, but it was a horrible way to get around.

Alex followed the feds back into the kitchen and shut his vault door.

"It was very thoughtful of you to provide Agent Mendes with a cannon," Sorsha said with a raised eyebrow.

"We're going to confront people who stole a secret project," Alex said with a shrug. "They might be jealous chemists...but they could just as easily be dangerous mobsters, so I figured we'd better be prepared."

Sorsha gave him a hard look.

"You'll be with me," she said as if that explained everything. "You won't have anything to fear."

Alex stepped close to her and dropped his voice so that only she could hear him.

"The last time that happened, I lost several decades of my life and you almost died."

She looked as if she wanted to be angry, then changed her mind.

"Do you have your special bullets?" she asked. Alex wasn't sure until that moment that she'd forgiven him for having spell-breakers, and he nodded.

"Of course," he replied.

"All right then," she said, taking his hand. "Let's go."

Alex felt as if his body had been pressed flat under some enormous weight, then rolled up and passed through a tube. It made him queasy, and bile rose in this throat. Just before he was sure he'd lose his breakfast, the feeling vanished, and he found himself kneeling on the sidewalk on a foggy street corner. Beside him, Agent Redhorn was struggling to stand and Agent Mendes was curled into a ball on the ground. Sorsha put a hand on his arm, and he turned to find her sitting beside him with her head bowed. All of them were breathing hard.

Pushing himself up, Alex got to his feet. Taking Sorsha's hand, he pulled the sorceress to her feet and held on while she steadied herself.

"Are we in the right place?" Agent Mendes asked as Redhorn helped her rise.

Alex let go of Sorsha's hand and pulled his battered compass from his pocket. The needle pointed steadily to a small, run-down building across the street. It looked like it might have been a warehouse or a garage in the city's former days, but it was much too small to fill that role in the era of modern trucks.

"I think this is the right place," Redhorn said. When Alex looked at him, he pointed up at the roof of the building. One look and Alex could see that the fog above the decrepit structure was definitely thicker than anywhere else.

"All right," Sorsha said. "Agent Redhorn, take Mendes and go around to the back. Alex, you're with me."

"Don't forget to put on the coat," Alex said as Redhorn and Mendes headed out across the street.

"What coat?" Sorsha asked as the FBI agents vanished into the fog.

As they crossed the street to the front of the little stone building, Alex explained about the trench coat and his shield runes.

"If you've only got two runes left on your jacket," Sorsha asked, "why didn't you keep the coat and just give him your jacket?"

"I'm planning to stand behind you," Alex whispered, letting her go up to the front door first.

"And they say chivalry is dead," she said with a smirk.

"I'm not the one that can freeze bad guys solid," Alex pointed out. He drew his 1911 and held it ready.

Sorsha put her hand on the door of the storage building and closed her eyes. Alex had no idea what magic she might be using or what it would tell her, so he just stood ready. After a moment, she looked back at him and nodded.

"Cover your eyes," she whispered, then raised her hand and touched the door with her outstretched finger.

The door exploded, bursting as if it had been stuffed with gunpowder. Alex had seen her do this particular trick before and he waited until the sawdust and splinters stopped raining down on him before uncovering his face.

Sorsha strode boldly through the opening where the door had stood. At the same time, Alex could hear a door being kicked open from somewhere inside. He hurried after Sorsha, but ran right into the back of her when she stopped suddenly.

"What's the idea?" Alex hissed, grabbing her to keep her from being knocked down.

Sorsha didn't answer, but she didn't have to. The room was blackened and charred as if a roaring blaze had swept every surface. In the center of the space stood a large device mounted on a trailer with two rubber wheels. It had a large tank on top and a brass funnel in the front. Undoubtedly this was Dr. Burnham's machine.

As welcome a sight as the fog generator was, it was not what Alex noticed first. His eye was drawn to the two charred, motionless bodies on the floor.

21

THE MACHINE

"Stay here," Alex said, finally releasing Sorsha. "Have Redhorn and Mendes clear the building, then tell Redhorn to put my trench coat back in the bag."

"Check the machine first," she said as he stepped past her. "Specifically, find out how much fluid is left in the tank."

Alex put down his kit while Sorsha moved around the edge of the charred room to where Redhorn and Mendes had just entered. He suppressed a grin at Redhorn, whose broad shoulders barely fit in a coat made for Alex.

Turning his attention to the room, Alex looked at the machine. A long, black wire ran from it to an electrical box mounted on a wooden support beam. The rubber coating on the wire was melted, and he could see shiny copper peeking through. Black soot clung to the beam and there were scorch marks on the wood lattice that held up the tile roof. Fortunately they were at least ten feet higher up or they'd have burned as well, sending the ceiling crashing down. There was a small hole in the roof with a pile of broken tile on the ground below it, but Alex couldn't tell if it was recent or not without getting closer.

Returning his gaze to the machine, Alex observed that it wasn't moving or making any noise. He supposed there must be a heating element of some kind inside and that it wouldn't make noise, but the brass funnel on the end looked like it was where the fog was supposed to emerge, and that should need an electric fan to push the fog.

"Find anything?" Redhorn called. He had taken off Alex's coat but still held his pistol.

"Not yet," Alex said. "Look first, then move," he continued, quoting an old maxim of Iggy's.

Redhorn raised an eyebrow, but didn't comment further.

From his current angle, Alex couldn't see anything more, so he began to slowly circle the machine until he came to one of the bodies on the floor. The rough boards that made up the floor of the building were scorched and black, obscuring any evidence of a struggle or even footprints. All that Alex could see was that the man had fallen face down when he died.

Moving on, Alex came to the second man. He was lying face up and his face and hands were burned beyond recognition. He was dressed in a standard business suit, though most of what Alex could see had been burned too badly to tell its quality.

"I don't see any signs of physical injury on these two," he said as Sorsha moved around the scene, toward him. She was walking just beyond the marks Alex's shoes made in the soot covering the floor.

"What do you think happened?" she asked.

Alex looked around at the evidence of fire.

"I'd say the machine flared up right after they turned it on," Alex guessed. He pointed to the second man. "This one caught the blast right in the face, while that one was done in by the smoke."

"Why didn't the fire spread?" Redhorn asked, looking up at the charred beams still holding up the roof.

" The walls are brick and the roof is tile," Alex said. "The only wood in here are the beams and the planks on the floor, and they're all really thick."

"So?" Mendes said.

"You ever try to catch a thick piece of wood on fire?" Redhorn asked her. "It takes a while."

Sorsha folded her arms, watching Alex as he made his way toward the fog machine. Her posture was relaxed, but he got the impression she wanted him to hurry.

"Give me a minute to look this over, then I'll check it with my lamp," he said before she could ask. "You might want to have Agent Mendes call this in to the police. Ask for a detective named Hawkins and tell him to alert the coroner."

Mendes looked to Sorsha, who simply nodded.

As she hurried out to find a phone, Alex turned his attention to the machine. Its metal surfaces were covered in the same soot as the rest of the room, but it seemed largely unharmed. He reached out and carefully knocked on the large metal tank that occupied the top of the machine, and it answered with a hollow ring.

There wasn't much of the Genesis Water left.

He was about to continue circling the machine, stepping carefully over the melted wire, when he stopped.

"Uh, oh," he said, looking down.

"What is it?" Sorsha and Redhorn said together.

"I know what happened," he said, putting his foot down. "Whoever these guys were, they turned the machine off."

"How do you know that?" Sorsha asked.

"Because," Alex said, bending down to pick up the melted wire with his thumb and forefinger. "It's still off."

He held it up so that the others could see that while one end was plugged in to the outlet box, the other end wasn't connected to anything.

Sorsha looked up at the fog hovering over the dilapidated building, clearly visible through the hole in the roof.

"Then what's causing that?" she asked.

"I'm pretty sure it's this," Alex said, rapping on the nearly empty tank again.

"How?" Redhorn asked. "I may not be the brightest guy in the world, but even I know that things that need electricity to work, don't work so well when they're unplugged."

Alex looked up at the hole in the roof, then, stepping carefully, made his way over to the pile of broken tiles beneath it. Crouching down, he moved one of the tile fragments.

"The floor under these tiles is scorched," he reported.

"What does that mean?" Sorsha asked.

"It means the ceiling broke after the fire started," Redhorn supplied.

"I get that," Sorsha said with exaggerated patience. "But why does that matter?"

Alex didn't answer, moving instead to the spot where he left his kit. He took out a silverlight burner, clipped it into the bottom of the multi-lamp, and lit it. Strapping on his oculus, he moved to the pile of tiles and went over them meticulously with the silverlight.

Small spots lit up on two of the tiles along with another tiny one, glowing faintly beneath the soot between the debris and the face-down man.

Moving on, Alex swept the lamp over the two bodies and then the machine. As he expected, there wasn't much to be seen. A few smudged prints remained, but most had been obliterated by the fire.

"Well?" Sorsha said as Alex took off his oculus.

"Help me roll this one over," he said to Redhorn.

Together they rolled over the face down corpse, revealing an Asian man of middle years. A long gash was open on his forehead, caked with sludgy dried blood.

"Can I go through his pockets?" Redhorn asked.

Alex nodded, then stood.

"Okay," he said, walking over to where Sorsha was tapping her foot impatiently. "Do you want the good news or the bad news?"

She eyed him warily.

"What's the good news?"

"I'm pretty sure I know what happened," Alex said.

"And the bad news?"

"I'm pretty sure I know what happened," Alex repeated.

Sorsha's eyes narrowed and Alex hurried on.

"Whoever stole the machine brought it here, presumably to sell it to these two," he indicated the bodies. "He turned it on to demonstrate that it worked."

"Why can't these men be the thieves?" Sorsha asked.

"Because of what's missing," Alex said. "If these were the thieves and they just wanted to test the machine, then Dr. Burnham's notebooks would be here somewhere, and they're not. There's no way they'd try to test the machine without those notes."

"That doesn't rule out one of these men being the thief," Sorsha said. "He might have left the notebooks at his house while he met with the buyer."

"A buyer who came here without any money?" Alex asked. "Nobody uses a check to buy a stolen fog machine, they need cash. So where's the bag full of cash or gold or precious stones or whatever?"

Sorsha thought about that for a moment, then nodded.

"Go on."

Alex pointed at the face up man. "Once they paid off the thief, that one tried to turn the machine off using the switch on the machine. When the reaction didn't stop right away, he panicked and pulled the wires out."

"Then the fog started burning," Sorsha said, following the narrative.

"The flash catches him in the face, and he falls down," Alex went on, "The pressure from the blast knocks those tiles off the roof and they hit our second man in the face on their way down. He manages to stagger away but everything is on fire by now and he's overcome and collapses there." Alex pointed to the second body.

Sorsha looked up at the ceiling, then around at the room.

"Your story fits," she said. "But it doesn't explain how the fog spread if the hole in the roof happened after the machine was shut off."

"That's the bad news," Alex said. "We know from experience that the flash from the fog is extremely hot. I think it vaporized the top layer of Genesis Water in that tank." He pointed to the big metal tank on top of the machine.

"Okay, but where did the electricity come from?"

"This building is less than a mile from Empire Tower," Alex pointed out. "Normally this would be in the outer ring, but Andrew Barton has been testing his new generators. They're much more powerful than the previous ones. I'd be willing to bet that this spot now has as much power in the air as the inner ring."

The Long Chain

Sorsha flicked her wrist and her cigarette holder appeared.

"So the vaporized chemical became fog from the electricity in the air," she said, pulling a silver cigarette case out of thin air. "But why did the reaction keep going after the vaporized fuel became fog?"

Alex motioned for Sorsha to follow him and he crossed the floor to Burnham's machine, taking out his handkerchief as he went. When he reached it, Alex wiped the soot off of a section of the tank, then pressed his palm against it.

"Feel that," he said, moving back so Sorsha could touch the tank.

"It's hot," she said.

"I don't know why," Alex said. "Maybe something inside is made out of the same metal as Barton's power receivers, or maybe it has something to do with the contents of the Genesis Water, maybe both. But whatever it is, something is heating up the tank, and that's caused the liquid to vaporize."

"How much is left?" she asked, tapping the tank and eliciting the same hollow note Alex had.

"The real question is, what happens when it runs out," Alex said. "The only person who knows that is Burnham."

"What about his notebooks?" Sorsha asked. "Is there any way for you to find them?"

Alex shrugged.

"Only if we get lucky." He turned to where Redhorn had just finished examining the second man. "Find anything interesting, Agent Redhorn?"

"Keys, cash, a folding knife, and this," he said, holding up a black booklet. "They each had one." He stood as Alex and Sorsha came over.

"What are they?" the Sorceress asked.

"Identity cards," Redhorn said, opening them to reveal an official-looking paper with a picture on it. "Both these men are foreign nationals. They're required to carry their identity cards at all times."

"Li Yang Zin and Bao Bin Cheng," Sorsha read. "Both Chinese."

"This one worked at the consulate," Redhorn said, turning the page in the booklet to reveal another official-looking photograph.

"Why would two Chinese men want to buy a fog machine?" Alex asked.

"China is at war with the Empire of Japan," Sorsha said, as if that explained it.

"A war they're currently losing," Redhorn added.

"I know," Alex said, "but this machine isn't a new weapon, it's designed to hide convoy ships from armed zeppelins. How does that help the Chinese?"

Sorsha shrugged.

"I suppose they could use it to make the Sea of Japan unnavigable," she said. "It doesn't matter though. If you're right, and I think you are, these men came here to buy Burnham's machine from our missing thief. A thief we absolutely must find."

"Don't we need to figure out a way to stop this thing from burning the city to the ground?" Redhorn asked, nodding at the fog generator.

"The thief has Burnham's notebooks," Sorsha said. "With Burnham's memory still gone, that might be our only chance of preventing disaster." She turned to Alex as police sirens began to wail in the distance. "So how do we find the thief?"

Alex shook his head. There wasn't an obvious answer. The fire had obliterated any trace of him, and there weren't any other real clues.

"I don't think whoever did this was a pro," Alex said, rubbing his chin. "If he steals government secrets for a living, he would have sold it to some other country, one who could pay more."

"You're thinking he picked the Chinese because he knew them?" Redhorn said.

"How does that help?" Sorsha asked.

"How many consulate workers do you know?" Alex said.

"A few," she replied. "But I see your point. We need to find out who knew these men. They aren't diplomats, so they probably don't have a lot of American contacts. Who would know that kind of thing?"

"The American Ambassador to China," Alex said.

"You want me to call over to China?" Sorsha said.

Alex shook his head.

"America's Ambassador to China is a man named William Henderson and he's here, in New York," Alex said. "The President recalled him because of the war. It was in the papers."

Sorsha raised an eyebrow at that.

The Long Chain

"So our Ambassador returns from China during a war that they're losing, and suddenly American military secrets are stolen and sold to the Chinese," she observed, exchanging a knowing look with Redhorn. "Does that sound like a coincidence to you?"

Redhorn shook his head.

"No, ma'am, it does not."

At that moment the back door opened, and Agent Mendes came in.

"The police are here," she said.

"Good," Alex said, putting away his gear.

"Where do you think you're going?" Sorsha asked.

"You needed me to find the source of the fog," he said, picking up his kit. "I did that, and now I have a two-bit thug to find."

"What if I need your deductive skills when I talk to William Henderson?"

Alex laughed.

"You don't really want me around while you're sweating an important political figure," he said.

Sorsha looked as though she wanted to argue, but after a moment to think, she nodded.

"You're right," she said. "Get your cannon back from Mendes and get out of here."

Alex collected his A-5 and the bag with his trench coat, stopping long enough to drop them off in his vault. He had just shut the heavy door when Detective Hawkins came sweeping into the building with a dozen officers in tow.

"Jeez, Lockerby," he said, coming over to stand beside Alex. "What did you get me into?"

"Glad you could make it, Detective," Alex said. He took a minute and explained the scene.

"So let me get this straight," Hawkins said, rolling his eyes. "That thing is a smoke machine a retired chemist was making for the Navy," he said, pointing at the device. "Someone stole it and tried to sell it to these gentlemen, who just happen to be Chinese nationals."

"That's pretty much it," Alex said with a completely straight face.

"You realize that even if the scary FBI lady catches the thief, none of this is going to make the papers, right?"

"I promised I'd call you, Detective," Alex said, clapping him on the shoulder. "I never promised I'd make you famous. Still, the Navy will probably thank the chief for the return of their property, and that'll reflect well on you."

"Except *you* found it," Hawkins grumbled.

Alex put his finger in front of his lips in a gesture of silence.

"I was never here," he whispered, then he winked at the detective and strode out of the ramshackle building.

22

THE GIRL

A black police car was parked next to the curb in front of Dr. Kellin's home, making no attempt to be inconspicuous at all. As Alex approached from the direction of the sky crawler station, he could see a bored-looking cop sitting behind the wheel. He had his window down and was alternating between puffing on a cigarette and watching the little brick house. His partner in the passenger seat was asleep with his head on his chest and his arms folded.

Alex walked a bit heavier than normal as he approached the car, until the cop leaned out of the window to get a look at him. He was blond with a blocky face broken up by a bulbous nose.

"Officer Johansson," Alex said, recognizing the man.

The big man looked confused for a moment, then grinned.

"You're the scribbler, right?" he recalled. "Detective Pak's friend."

"That's me," Alex acknowledged. "Whose doghouse are you in to be pulling this detail?"

Johansson chuckled at that.

"This here is a prime job," he said. "All I have to do is sit and keep an eye on Dr. Kellin. No walking my shoe leather off or chasing after pickpockets, just sit here, relax, and get paid."

He leaned back in his seat and put his hands behind his head to emphasize his point.

"Well, I'm glad it's working out for you," Alex said.

"What are you doing here?" Johansson asked. He almost managed to make it sound like idle curiosity instead of him being a cop.

"I was here for the festivities the other night," Alex said. "I think I dropped my key ring out back and I just want to take a look, if that's okay."

Johansson thought about it a minute and then shrugged.

"It's okay by me," he said.

Alex looked back over his shoulder at the house. The 'Open' light on Dr. Kellin's sign was out and the windows were dark.

"Is Dr. Kellin home?" he asked.

"Yeah, but I think she went to bed. The girl left about an hour ago and she hasn't come back yet."

Alex's stomach soured. He'd wanted to see Jessica, to find out if she was really okay after the events of the other night. Though, if she'd gone out, she must be feeling all right. It wasn't much, but it wasn't nothing.

"Thanks," he told Johansson. "I shouldn't be more than a couple of minutes."

Officer Johansson waved at him and went back to smoking his cigarette. Alex looked around as he made his way through the front yard to the hidden gate. He saw one of the FBI cars half a block down, but there was no sign of the second detail. Maybe Agent Redhorn had recalled it as being redundant.

Once in the back yard, Alex hurried to the spot where the missing thug had crashed through the window. The hole in the wall had been boarded up and much of the broken glass had been swept into a pile. Alex was grateful no one had picked it up yet as he set down his kit.

Finding blood on fragments of broken glass would have been difficult at noon on a clear day, and it was already getting dark and still foggy. Alex, however, had other options. He shone his silverlight lamp over the glass pile and the ground behind the house. The bits with blood on them glowed back at him with a purplish light and he easily picked them out from their fellows.

Once he had four, he put away his lamp and oculus, switching them for his rolled-up map and cigar box. Moving quickly, he laid out the map and weighed it down to keep it from rolling up again. He placed the battered brass compass on the map, then added a folded finding rune and finally the bloodstained glass shards.

Since he didn't want the spell to find glass, but rather the owner of the shed blood, Alex also took out a bottle with a dropper from his kit. Being careful, he added a drop of the liquid to the dried blood, which turned the liquid red. After a few moments, he tipped the shard up so that the liquid ran down onto the flash paper that contained the rune. This would link the blood to the rune, allowing it to ignore the broken glass.

His preparations finished, Alex took out a cigarette and lit it. Being back at the lab was grating on his nerves and he half-expected the missing man to loom out of the fog and take another shot at him.

Pushing that thought from his mind, Alex touched the burning end of the cigarette to the flash paper and the rune flared to life. Casting an orange glow into the persistent fog, the rune spun around, slower and slower, until it drew the compass needle along with it.

"Gotcha," Alex growled as the rune shuddered, then vanished in a shower of sparks.

According to the compass, the missing thug was in a rural block on the West Side of the mid-ring. Fortunately it wasn't too far from a sky bug station. If Alex hurried, he could be there in half an hour.

The compass led Alex to a quaint little house with a neatly-mown lawn and rosebushes, right up against the outer ring. It was full dark when he arrived, and the fog obscured most of the street, so he wasn't too worried about being observed. A single light was visible through the front window by the door, but it was dim, probably from a back room rather than the parlor.

Patting his side, Alex felt the mass of his 1911 hanging just below his left arm. Reassured by its weight, he crossed the front lawn to the side of the house. All the windows had the curtains drawn, so he continued around to the back. A small wooden porch connected the back of the house to the yard through a door in the center of the rear wall. There was a socket for a magelight, but it was empty, and the yard was in darkness. Alex could barely make out the shape of a dog house but no growls or barks greeted him as he stalked toward the porch.

Moving slowly, he mounted the porch, which creaked a little under his weight. From inside he heard the muffled sound of a radio playing band music, which would cover any noise he made crossing the porch. As he reached the door, Alex slipped his hand inside his jacket and pulled his 1911 free of the holster, then slowly cocked the weapon. He didn't want trouble, just information, but it paid to be prepared for both.

Gripping the pistol tightly, Alex took a quick breath, then put his hand on the doorknob. Before he turned it, though, a smell like rust hit him and he could suddenly taste iron. The only thing that did that was blood, and only when it was fresh and there was a lot of it.

Alex turned the door knob but his hand slipped and when he pulled it away it was wet.

He swore.

Grabbing the knob again, he squeezed it tight and turned it. As he expected, the door wasn't locked and opened into a little kitchen. A single bulb burned over a round table strewn with playing cards, cash, and blood. Four chairs were around the table, three of them lying overturned and two bodies lay on the floor in sludgy pools of red. Streaks of blood covered the walls and reached up to the ceiling.

The nearest body was a big man with massive shoulders and arms; a .38 that looked like a toy was still clutched in his massive hand. The other man was smaller, with a bushy mustache and a snipe nose. He lay against the wall with a look of shock frozen on his rat-like face. Alex could see at least a dozen knife wounds on his arms and torso.

Being careful not to step in any of the blood, Alex moved to the opening that led from the kitchen to the front room. A quick look inside showed him another man lying dead on the floor just inside the front door. His throat had been cut with what looked like one long stroke, and there weren't any other wounds he could see on the body.

"So our boys are playing poker," Alex said, thinking out loud. He looked back to the lone chair that was still standing upright. "Someone knocks at the door, and that one gets up to see who it is and gets his throat cut for his trouble. His friends jump up from their card game, but the attacker is on them quick."

Alex sniffed the air. Underneath the smell of blood and offal was the faint hint of gunpowder.

"The big guy gets off a shot but either misses or only wings the attacker. He goes down next, followed by rat-face...so where's our fourth player?"

Alex would have expected the man who answered the door to be the homeowner, but he definitely wasn't the man who had fled the workshop. Neither were the two dead men in the kitchen.

"So, let's say this house belongs to the guy from the lab; what does he do while his friends are being cut up by a knife-wielding maniac?" Alex looked down the hall toward the bedroom at the back of the house. "He goes for a weapon."

Alex had to hop over the big man to stay out of the blood and even then, he managed to get a little on his shoe. Not wanting to confuse the evidence, Alex dropped his pistol into his jacket pocket and pulled out his handkerchief. He wiped the blood from the bottom of his shoe, then cleaned off the blood he'd picked up from the knob of the back door.

Satisfied he'd gotten off all he could, Alex carefully folded up his handkerchief with the blood on the inside, and tucked it into his trouser pocket. Then he pulled out his pistol and continued carefully down the hall. He passed an empty bathroom and a linen closet, then reached the bedroom. Gripping his 1911 tightly, he ducked his head out around the door and just as quickly back. The bedroom was dark, but he could make out a dresser, an overturned chair, and a bed with a bloody body sitting against it.

He stepped around the door, sweeping the room with his gun but nothing moved. A sawed-off, double-barreled shotgun sat on the floor by the body, just out of the dead man's reach.

Alex fumbled for the light switch and finally got it on. When the bulb on the ceiling bloomed into light, the dead man gasped. Alex brought the gun to bear but he needn't have bothered. The man was still alive, but he was bleeding from multiple stab wounds.

Alex swore and the man looked up at him with a glassy-eyed stare. He had several scabs on his cheek from where he'd previously jumped through Dr. Kellin's window.

"C-come to...to finish the job...you son-of-a-bitch," he slurred. "I should have...put a bullet in your head...when I had the chance."

"Shut up," Alex said, slipping his gun back into its holster. He took off his jacket and pulled out his handkerchief, moving to the man to try to stop the bleeding. The worst wound was in the man's abdomen, so Alex pressed the handkerchief into it, eliciting a groan from the man. Blood oozed out over Alex's hand. His handkerchief wasn't going to be enough. Without a major healing potion, nothing would be enough.

"Who did this?" Alex asked, keeping any urgency out of his voice.

The man started to chuckle but coughed instead, spewing out blood as he did so.

"Girl," he gasped. "Said her name...was Lilith."

"A woman did this?" Alex asked, remembering the small footprint at Charles Grier's alchemy shop. The man there had been beheaded by a knife, probably taken from the scene.

"N-no," he coughed. "A...a kid. Couldn't have...have been more than twelve."

The idea that an adolescent girl could have cut down four grown men with a knife was absurd, but Alex could tell the man absolutely believed what he was saying.

"What did she look like?" he asked. "What did she want?"

"White hair," he gasped. "Gray...eyes. Old eyes. Asked me abo...about Charles Grier. Who took him. Why they went after...after that other bitch...Kellin."

His breath was coming in rasping wheezes now and he couldn't seem to hold his head up.

"And what did you tell her?" Alex demanded. "Who has Grier? Who's after Dr. Kellin?"

Alex grabbed the man's hair and pulled his head back, but when he did, the man's eyes had already gone glassy and distant. A long, shuddering breath escaped his lungs and his body slumped down. Dead.

Alex released the man and swore again.

The man had been his best lead on whoever was targeting alchemists, and Alex didn't even know his name, much less who he worked for. All he'd really discovered was that the men who came for Dr. Kellin were the ones who had grabbed Grier, and he'd already suspected that. Worse, there was some crazed, knife-wielding killer who looked like a child involved somehow, but he had no idea who she was or what she wanted.

He put his hand on the carpet, intent on pushing himself to his feet, when a wave of exhaustion passed over him and his vision went dim for a moment. Shaking his head to clear it, Alex leaned on the side of the bed and pulled his jacket over to him. He extracted the flask of rejuvenator from the pocket and took a swig. Instantly he felt better, but it wasn't the usual shot of energy he got from the potion. That was worrying. He'd been using more than usual of late and now it didn't seem to be working as well. Either he was getting used to it or he simply didn't have enough life energy left.

Pushing that cheerful thought to the back of his mind, Alex used the bed to pull himself to his feet. He had to be careful, since his right hand and shirt cuff were covered in the dead man's blood. For a moment, he considered retrieving his handkerchief, but he decided against it. By the time the coroner found it, there wouldn't be any way to link it back to him.

Alex left the bedroom and the dead man and went to the bathroom in the hall. Unbuttoning his sleeve, he rinsed the blood from his hand and did his best to scrub it from his shirt cuff. The red stain persisted, but he could remove it later with a restoration rune. Right now he needed to get out of this house. Whoever the knife-wielding girl was, she'd tried to brew some kind of potion at Grier's shop. She seemed to be fixated on him, but she might just as easily break into Dr. Kellin's lab and try to use her equipment. He didn't even want to think about what might happen if Jessica or the doc walked in on her.

Satisfied that he'd removed all the blood he could, Alex dried off his hand and rebuttoned his cuff. He was just heading back to the bedroom to pick up his jacket when he heard the creak of a floorboard.

"Hold it, you!" a rough voice boomed. "I mean it," he continued when Alex started to turn around. "Get those hands up, and don't you move a muscle."

Since his jacket and its two remaining shield runes were still in the bedroom, Alex did as he was told. He had no idea who would be in the dead man's house, but most likely it would be one of his friends. Not someone late for the poker game, since all the available seats had been taken. Who did that leave?

He heard quick steps behind him and then the muzzle of a pistol was jammed into his ribs. A man pressed up against his back, reaching around his body from the left, then across his chest to grab the 1911. As soon as he had it, the man jumped back.

"All right," the man behind him said. "You turn around, real slow."

Pressing his thumb against his flash ring, Alex complied. Once he'd turned, he found himself facing a blue-uniformed policeman with dark hair, a pug nose, and a scar on his cheek. Alex recognized the man; they'd met two years ago at the apartment building of one Jerry Pemberton. The cop hadn't liked Alex then, and there was no reason to think time would have softened his opinion.

He wondered how the police had ended up here. He was certain no nosy neighbor had seen him this time. A memory of gunpowder tickled his mind and he remembered, the big man had gotten a shot or two off before the girl had cut him down. You didn't need nosy neighbors when people were shooting next door. The cops probably got half a dozen calls.

"Now just who are you?" the cop asked.

"I'm Alex Lockerby. I'm a licensed private investigator and I came here to get information from the dead guy in the bedroom. Of course, I didn't know he was dead until I got here."

At the words 'Private Investigator,' the cop's look, which was already sour, turned positively grim.

"What happened here?" the cop demanded.

Alex shrugged and ran the man through his reconstruction of the crime based on the clues at the scene. He left out the bit about the assailant being an adolescent girl named Lilith and just left it at 'a knife-wielding-maniac.'

"Well that's a very pretty story," the cop growled in a voice that indicated he found it neither pretty nor credible. "But I've got a better one. A crummy private dick tortured some answers out of a bum he'd been following, and then shot him." He held up Alex's 1911 with his free hand. "With this gun."

It took all of Alex's willpower not to sigh.

"I think you'll find that these men were killed with a blade, not a gun," Alex said.

The cop smiled, showing a jagged row of yellow teeth.

"I don't think the Captain will see it that way," the policeman said. "He's going to point the finger at the man standing over all these bodies." His grin managed to get even wider. "I'll make sergeant for bringing you in."

He tossed Alex's gun onto the kitchen table among the cards and cash, then pulled out a set of handcuffs.

"Put these on," he growled, his expression letting Alex know that he would prefer it if Alex were to resist.

Letting the sigh through this time, Alex snapped the cuffs around his wrists.

"When you call this in," he said, "tell them to alert Detective Danny Pak. He's already looking for a knife killer."

"Don't tell me how to do my job," the cop yelled, then motioned for Alex to move into the parlor with his gun.

As Alex sat on the dead man's couch waiting for Danny or some other responsible policeman to show up and rescue him, his mind kept drifting back to the dying words of the man in the bedroom. He'd said a girl had done this. His mind was still foggy and he longed for another swig from the rejuvenator, but it was in the bedroom with his jacket.

Someone else had said something about a girl, he was sure of it, but for the life of him, Alex couldn't remember who, or where he'd heard it. Sitting back on the couch, Alex closed his eyes and tried to focus his thoughts. Surely if he thought about it, the answer would come to him.

23

JOHANSSON

Someone was yelling. Well, not really yelling, but speaking very loudly. It was making it hard for Alex to sleep.

"-Don't care who you are, that's my suspect and you'll just have to wait your turn."

Alex tried to pry his eyes open, but they seemed to be stuck shut. Through the fog that seemed wrapped around his brain, he recognized the voice. It belonged to the pug-nosed policeman. The one who had arrested him for the massacre at the little house. Where the girl had...had—

"Johansson," he gasped, sitting up.

Immediately, his head started throbbing like he'd been coshed. He tried to grab the back of his neck but only succeeded in hitting himself in the face due to his hands still being cuffed together.

"Ow," he muttered, finally managing to force his eyes open. For a moment he had no idea what he was seeing. He sat in a strange parlor with policemen standing everywhere. When he saw the sheet-covered body on the floor, it all came rushing back to him. He must have fallen asleep.

"Do you mind?" Alex said, focusing his barely working eyes on the pug-nosed policeman who stood talking to a man with his back to Alex. "How's a fellow to get any sleep with all this yelling?"

The policeman's face, which was already the color of steamed beets, shifted toward purple and he took a breath, most likely to continue yelling.

"That's enough," a familiar voice cut him off. "I don't care what you or your captain want with Lockerby, I get him first and I get him right now."

Alex recognized Agent Redhorn's voice. He'd expected Danny, but it was quite likely that no one had told his friend about this yet.

"Agent Redhorn," Alex said, not even trying to stand. "You do care."

Redhorn turned, shooting Alex a stern look.

"About time you woke up," he said. "Did this flatfoot brain you or something?"

Alex shook his head and shrugged.

"No," he said. "I was just waiting for something interesting to happen. It was a long wait."

Redhorn looked around at the body on the floor and the blood in the kitchen.

"You and I have different ideas of what's interesting," he said. "Get your things. Miss Kincaid wants a word."

Alex held up his hands, showing the handcuffs.

"Keys," Agent Redhorn demanded, turning back to the cop.

The pug-nosed cop set his jaw and stuck out his chest.

"I don't care who you are or where you're from," he growled. "I ain't turning over a suspect to anybody without authorization."

"Who wants our suspect?" Danny said, stepping around the covered body as he entered. Alex breathed a sigh of relief. He didn't know how Redhorn had found him; as far as he knew sorcerers couldn't trace people like one of his finding runes, so that ruled out Sorsha. However he'd managed it, he was clearly involved in a jurisdictional pissing match with the policeman. It was a contest Redhorn could win, but without Danny there to cut through posturing and the egos, it was likely Alex would be handcuffed for the rest of the night.

"Are you in charge here?" Redhorn said, shouldering his way past the officer.

Danny produced his gold detective shield and held it up.

"Detective Pak," he said, keeping his voice calm but firm. "Now just who are you?"

Redhorn flashed his FBI badge.

"Now I'm taking that man with me and I'm leaving," Redhorn said through clenched teeth as he jerked his thumb over his shoulder in Alex's general direction. "If you still want him, I'll bring him down to your office in the morning."

Danny looked around Redhorn, and Alex gave him a big smile and a wave with his cuffed hand.

"Oh for the love of..." Danny muttered, rolling his eyes. "Unlock him, Wilkins," he said to the cop.

Wilkins looked like they'd just canceled Christmas, New Years, and his birthday, but to his credit, he wiped the outraged expression off his face and stood straight.

"Yes, sir," he said, then marched over to Alex and unlocked him.

"Thanks, officer," Alex said, standing. He almost expected Wilkins to take a poke at him, but the short cop just stalked away, muttering.

"That's better," Redhorn said, motioning for Alex to join him. "I've already wasted too much time here; let's go."

"Just a minute," Danny said, moving to intercept Alex. "I need a word with our suspect before you take him."

Alex could see the muscles in Redhorn's jaw tighten but before he could explode, Alex spoke up.

"My jacket is in the back bedroom and my pistol is on the kitchen table," he said. "A Colt 1911, you can't miss it. Why don't you grab those while I talk to the Detective?"

"Fine," the FBI man grumbled, then headed for the kitchen.

"What happened here?" Danny asked, glancing at the body on the floor. "Did you kill someone?"

"Not me," Alex said. He quickly ran through what had happened, and what he guessed had happened before he arrived. Unlike with officer Wilkins, he didn't leave anything out.

"He said it was a child?" Danny asked incredulously.

Alex could only shrug. He knew how it sounded.

"That would explain the footprint at *The Philosopher's Stone*," Danny continued. "It has to be the same killer. It also means that the disappearance of Charles Grier and the attack on you and Miss O'Neil are connected."

"That's what I figure," Alex said.

"Anything else?"

Alex shook his head in frustration.

"I could swear I'm missing something, though," he said.

Danny raised an eyebrow, expectantly, but said nothing. Alex tried to remember what he was thinking about when Redhorn's yelling had pulled him from sleep, but nothing came.

"Okay, Lockerby," Redhorn said, stepping over the pool of drying blood and back into the parlor. He carried Alex's jacket and had removed the clip from the 1911. "Let's go."

"I'll walk you out," Danny said, as Redhorn passed Alex his coat and the clip, then handed Alex's pistol to Danny.

"It hasn't been fired recently," Redhorn said. "But you should check it anyway."

"I'll get it back to you as soon as I can," Danny told Alex as he escorted them to the lawn in front of the house. A half-dozen police cars were parked along the curb, including Danny's green sedan. Sorsha's sleek, black floater hovered over the grass at the edge of the lawn with Roger, her chauffeur, leaning against it, smoking.

"Make sure your people keep a close eye on Jessica and the doc," Alex said over his shoulder as he followed Redhorn to the floater.

"I will," Danny promised.

Redhorn didn't say much during the short trip in the flying car, and Alex wasn't in a talkative mood. He kept going over the crime scene and the words of the dying man. It still bothered him, but he simply couldn't put his finger on why.

When the floater came to a stop and Alex got out, he found himself in front of the neat home of Dr. Leonard Burnham.

"What's all this?" Alex asked. "Did you find something new?"

"That's what you're here for," Redhorn said.

Alex followed him inside and found Karen Burnham sitting at the kitchen table with Sorsha and Agent Mendes. The former was wringing her hands nervously, while Sorsha drank tea from a china cup.

"Sorceress," Alex said, acknowledging her as he entered.

"It's about time," she said, slipping a sidelong glance at Agent Redhorn, who moved to the kitchen and stood by the stove. Clearly she was in a mood. It must not have gone well with William Henderson, the Chinese Ambassador.

"How did things go with the Ambassador?" Alex asked with an absolutely straight face.

Sorsha glared at him, and then sipped from her steaming cup of tea.

"He has an airtight alibi," she said after carefully replacing the cup on its saucer. "From the moment he landed in New York, he's been a guest of the Governor."

Alex shrugged at that.

"Doesn't mean he didn't have the fog machine stolen," he said. "I'm sure he knows people."

"He was convincing," Sorsha said.

Alex gave her a penetrating look. Sorsha knew how to use illegal truth spells, and he knew from experience that she wasn't above using them, but her face was an unreadable mask.

"What about his family?"

Sorsha shook her head.

"His wife doesn't have the mind for this kind of game," she said. "And their only son passed three years ago."

"So why am I here?" Alex asked. "How did you even find me?"

Sorsha actually smiled at that, but said nothing. Alex worried if she put some kind of sorcerer's mark on him that let her know where he was. He used enchanted pebbles or coins to track cheating husbands, so he assumed a sorcerer could do something like that. But Sorsha hadn't come after him herself, she'd sent Agent Redhorn, and that meant that she didn't just know the direction and distance to him, she'd known exactly where he was.

"You're on my call list," Alex guessed. He knew the police operator had a list of people to alert if certain names were mentioned in a police call. Both Danny and Lt. Callahan were on his list, and so, apparently, was Sorsha.

Her pale eyes slid up from her cup of tea to challenge him.

"I find that you are often nearby when trouble occurs," she explained, with no trace of embarrassment or deception. "And as I told you when we first met, the FBI pays me to know things."

"So what do you know that brings me here?" Alex asked.

There was the sound of someone on the stair and Sorsha's gaze darted past Alex to the front room. Alex turned and found a tall, gaunt man with a sunken face and long, almost skeletal fingers helping Dr. Burnham down the stairs.

Sorsha rose and Karen rushed from the table to take her grandfather's other hand.

"Thank you, dear," Dr. Burnham said, giving her a smile. "But I'm all right, really."

Karen beamed at the tall man.

"Thank you so much," she said, tears springing to her eyes.

"He looks much better," Alex muttered to Sorsha.

As Karen continued to help her grandfather to the kitchen table to sit, the tall man approached Sorsha.

"There was swelling in his brain," he said in a soft voice. "I've reduced it as much as I can, but only time can heal the rest. There are certain alchemical curatives that might help, but they would have been more effective if administered right after Dr. Burnham sustained his injuries. I can give you the names of a few excellent doctors with alchemy knowledge."

"I know one as well," Alex interjected.

The tall man's brown eyes shifted to Alex. At just over six feet, Alex was used to looking down at most people, but this man had him by at least six inches. He looked to be of middle years, with a pleasant face and dark, slicked-back hair. Alex hadn't recognized him initially, but now he knew the man. His name was Malcom Henderson, one of the New York Six.

Alex had researched all the sorcerers who lived in the city, which turned out to be fairly easy, since the tabloids followed virtually everything they did. Henderson had been a surgeon when he came into his powers. He'd spent his time as one of the most powerful men on Earth learning to use those powers to enhance his former profession. To his credit, he'd become one of the most effective and sought-after doctors in the world. The downside of that was that his skills were unique to him. None of his knowledge or skill could be passed on since they also required his talent.

"You must be the detective," he said with a slight smile. Clearly he'd been sizing up Alex while Alex had been doing the same. He held out his bony hand. "I hear good things about you from Andrew and Sorsha."

Alex took the man's hand and found it cold but strong.

"Alex Lockerby," he said. "It's a pleasure to meet you, Mr. Henderson." He was surprised how used to sorcerers he was becoming. Sorsha had been the first one he'd encountered, and she'd been just short of terrifying. Anyone with the kind of power sorcerers wielded should be respected in the same way as an unexploded bomb.

And yet you provoke her every chance you get, Alex reminded himself.

Maybe he wasn't actually as smart as he thought he was.

"I must be going," Henderson said, turning to Sorsha. "But I'll look in on Dr. Burnham in a few days to check on his progress."

"Thank you, Mal," Sorsha said with a beaming smile. She stepped forward, and Henderson leaned down so she could kiss him on the cheek.

Straightening, Henderson took his hat from the credenza in the parlor and, putting it on his head, vanished from the room with a soft pop. Alex had been teleported several times now, and the thought still made him shudder.

"He actually likes traveling that way," Sorsha said, reading his expression. "Now, to work."

"If Dr. Burnham's okay now, what do you need me for?" Alex asked.

Sorsha didn't answer, but motioned for him to follow as she moved back to the kitchen table. Karen and Dr. Burnham were talking quietly while Agent Mendes sat drinking tea, politely pretending not to hear them.

"How are you feeling, Dr. Burnham?" Sorsha asked, sitting back down by her half-empty cup.

"Much better," he said. His voice was much stronger than when Alex and Karen had found him at the soup kitchen. "I still don't remember who attacked me, though," he added.

Alex looked at Sorsha, but her attention was focused on Burnham.

"What about your formula," she prodded. "For the artificial fog. How did you stop it from combusting when the power was turned off?"

Burnham thought about that for a long moment, then shook his head.

"I know I must have," he said. "You say the machine is in a working state, and I never would have finished building it if I didn't know how to control the reaction, but I'll be darned if I can remember how I did it."

Alex opened his mouth to speak, but Sorsha held up her hand.

"Would you have written it down?" she pressed.

Burnham nodded vigorously.

"Of course," he said. "That's the first rule of science — when you discover something, always write it down."

"So it would be in your notebook," Alex said, seeing where Sorsha was going with her questioning.

Burnham nodded.

"But you said that's missing too?" he asked Sorsha.

"Unfortunately," she said. "But now that Mr. Lockerby is here, we hope to be able to find it."

"Right," Alex said, pulling out a vault rune and his ornate key. He retrieved his kit and returned to the kitchen table.

"I'll never get used to that," Agent Redhorn said from the kitchen, where he stood leaning on the counter.

Alex ignored him and set out the equipment for his finding rune.

"Do you remember your notebooks, Dr. Burnham?" Alex asked as he worked. "I mean, can you see them in your mind?"

"Of course," Burnham said. I kept my theorizing and my various attempts in the black ones and my discoveries were in the yellow one."

"Good, then since the notebooks belong to you, I'm going to use you to find them. Give me your hand."

Burnham put out his hand and Alex guided it on top of the brass compass. He folded up the finding rune and placed it in Burnham's palm.

"This is going to burn," he said, pointing to the flash paper, "but it will be so fast you'll just feel a little heat. Whatever you do, don't move your hand or stop touching the compass until I tell you."

Burnham nodded and Alex squeezed the side of his lighter, operating the mechanism that flipped open the cap and struck the spark. The flash paper erupted just as he'd promised it would, and a moment later the pulsating orange rune hovered over Burnham's hand.

Alex moved the doctor's hand out of the way and watched the compass. Normally, the needle would spin in time with the rotating rune, but this time it just stayed where it was, obstinately pointing north.

"What's wrong?" Agent Mendes said, reading the look on Alex's face.

"It's not working," he responded. "The rune doesn't have anything to grab on to."

"What does that mean?" Redhorn asked.

"It could mean one of several things," Alex said. "The notebooks could be too far away, maybe off Manhattan island. Water also blocks the magic, so if they're across the river in Jersey or out to sea, that could make it impossible to trace them."

"So they're gone," Sorsha said. It was a statement rather than a question.

"Not necessarily," Alex said. "They might be underground, or under water, or magically shielded."

"So we're back to square one," she said, boiling anger beneath her voice.

"Sorry." This last came from Dr. Burnham rather than Alex. "I wish I could tell you how to neutralize the fog, but I just...can't remember."

"It's not your fault, Grandfather," Karen said, putting her hand on his.

"I know, my girl," he said.

His voice went on speaking, something about wanting to get Karen out of the city to her Aunts in Connecticut, but Alex wasn't really listening.

Girl.

Something about that word resonated in his head, like the last peal of a distant echo.

He stood up so fast he sent his chair flying.

"Johansson!" he shouted, finally making the connection.

"Who?" Mendes asked, looking at Alex as if he were insane.

Alex ignored her and turned to Burnham.

"I need to use your phone."

24

CHARLIE

"Detective Pak," Danny's voice came down the wire almost half an hour later. Alex had called the Central Office and finally managed to talk the operator into getting the number of the house where Danny was leading the investigation into the murder of four lowlifes. Just his luck, Officer Wilkins answered the phone and Alex had to get Sorsha on the line to threaten him before he agreed to put Danny on the call.

"It's Alex," he blurted out. "You remember Officer Johansson."

"Yeah, I know him," Danny said. "He was with me when we found those trucks last year."

"Right," Alex said. "I saw him earlier; he was staking out Dr. Kellin's house. Would he still be there?"

"I don't know," Danny admitted. "It's not my stakeout so I didn't make the shift assignments."

"Is he using a radio car?"

"Of course," Danny said. "All stake outs and protection details use radio cars in case there's trouble."

"Call him," Alex said. "Right now."

"Are you all right?"

"Please," Alex said. "I think the doc and Jessica might be in trouble. I called over there, but no one's answering. I need you to talk to Johansson for me right now."

"Okay, Alex," Danny said. "What do you need to know?"

"When I talked to him, he said that Dr. Kellin was still in the house," Alex said. "But he also said that 'the girl' left. Ask him what the girl looked like."

"You know what Jessica looks like," Danny said.

"Just do it, Danny," Alex said.

"All right," Danny said. "Stand by, I've got to go to my car to use the radio."

Alex heard the unmistakable sound of a telephone receiver being put down and Danny was gone. He pulled out his watch and flipped open the top; it was just after one in the morning.

"What is it?" Sorsha's voice intruded on his thoughts. She had left the table and crossed to the front room where Alex stood at the telephone.

"I might need you to give me a ride," he said.

Sorsha looked back at the table where Redhorn and Mendes were talking with Dr. Burnham.

"We should be finished here soon," she said. "We can drop you wherever you need to go."

"Dr. Kellin's place."

She nodded.

"You had me put an FBI detail on her house," Sorsha said. "Just north of the park."

Alex nodded.

"It shouldn't take more than a half an hour to get there," Sorsha said. She gave him a penetrating look, then reached into thin air and produced her silver cigarette case. "Here," she said, opening it and offering the contents to Alex.

"Thanks," he said, only just realizing how badly he needed a smoke right now.

"Are you thinking that the missing burglar might return?"

"No," Alex said, lighting the cigarette.

He explained his visit to the thug's house while Sorsha magic'ed up her long, black cigarette holder and lit a cigarette of her own.

"And you believe him?" she asked. "About the girl, Lilith?"

"All I know is that it fits with the murder at Charles Grier's shop," Alex said, still pressing the phone receiver to his ear. "That guy was as big as I am and twice as broad, and somebody removed his head from his body. Somebody who would need thick socks to wear your shoes."

"So what does Lilith have to do with Dr. Kellen?"

"The cop watching the house told me that he saw a girl leaving the house," Alex said. "I assumed he meant Jessica."

"But what if he saw Lilith?" Sorsha finished.

"Alex, you there?" Danny's voice came back through the receiver.

"Yeah," Alex said, focusing his attention back on the receiver. "Go ahead."

"Get over to Dr. Kellin's as soon as you can. I'm leaving here as soon as I hang up and Wilkins will call it in to dispatch."

"What did Johansson say?"

"The girl he saw leaving Dr. Kellin's was a teenager with platinum blond hair wearing a black skirt with a white shirt."

Alex swore.

"I told Johansson to go in and sweep the house with his partner right now," Danny said.

"Call him back," Alex said. "The doc booby traps some of her doors."

"Johansson knows about that," Danny said. "Dr. Kellin removed those when we started watching the house. Now shut up and meet me over there."

"Right," Alex said, hanging up.

"Well?" Sorsha said. Her face was a mask of calm, but Alex could see worry in her eyes.

"It was Lilith the cop saw. I need to get over to Dr. Kellin's right away."

Sorsha nodded, then turned to where Karen and her grandfather were still talking with Redhorn and Mendes. She motioned Redhorn over and he excused himself from the table.

"You know the alchemy shop we put the watch on?" she asked quietly when he approached.

"Sure," he nodded, pulling his notebook out of his inside jacket pocket. He flipped a few pages, then read off the address.

"I want you and Mendes to take my car and meet me there," she said. Then she grabbed Alex by the arm and they both vanished.

All the lights were on in Dr. Kellin's home when Alex and Sorsha appeared on the sidewalk out front. After the nausea and the dizziness wore off, Alex got to his feet and then helped Sorsha up.

"I really hate when you do that," he said, supporting her as she swayed on her feet.

"You said you were in a hurry," she said, leaning against his arm and breathing heavily. "How does Malcom do this all the time?"

Alex had no answer for that, and his mind was elsewhere. He could see shadows moving around inside Dr. Kellin's house as Johansson and his partner searched the place. Once he was sure Sorsha could stand on her own, he released her arm and headed for the still-open front door.

The jamb had been broken where one of the policemen had kicked it in, and the deadbolt was still set, sticking out of the side of the open door. Beyond the front door, in what would have been the parlor, was Dr. Kellin's shop. Alex had seen it once or twice, but he usually spent his time downstairs in the lab with Jessica.

The walls of the shop were lined with neat shelves, each with racks of heavy bottles and slender vials. Some were brown glass, others clear, and many had their cork stoppers sealed with lead. Beside the prepared potions were small bags and cans of various dry ingredients and restoratives designed to be diluted with water or alcohol. Along the back of the shop was a low counter with a cash register atop it, standing in front of a curtain that, no doubt, led to the rest of the house.

A fancy screen with an Oriental design stood against the right wall, with a doorway behind it. Next to the screen was a comfortable-looking couch and an end table piled with periodicals. Alex knew from experience that the room beyond the screen was the examination room where Dr. Kellin saw patients.

Along the back wall, next to the curtain, were rows of pictures, news clippings, and certificates that told the story of Dr. Kellin's career. Alex noted her medical and alchemical licenses as well as her diploma among them.

Alex swept the room, his eyes moving slowly from left to right, but nothing looked out of place. There were no signs of violence, or even a struggle. Everything appeared to be as it should be.

"Hello," Alex called, knocking on the frame of the open front door. "Officer Johansson, are you in here? It's Alex Lockerby." He had no desire to surprise a couple of cops looking for a potential killer.

The sound of someone big coming down a flight of stairs echoed through the house and a moment later, Johansson's blond head peeked out through the curtain at the back of the shop.

"Mr. Lockerby?" he said, stepping through the curtain. "What are you doing here?" He lowered his service revolver but didn't holster it, holding it loosely in his hand. "Detective Pak assured me you were on the other side of town."

"That would be my doing," Sorsha said, stepping around Alex and into the room.

Johansson looked stunned, but Sorsha tended to have that effect on men. Today she wore a white, pinstriped shirt and high-waisted slacks with a man's necktie and a pair of white suspenders over her shoulders. They were an affectation, of course; even with the sorceress' narrow hips, she wouldn't need anything extra to hold her slacks in place. Despite the progressive clothing, Sorsha was a looker.

"I'm Sorsha Kincaid," she said. "I'm a consultant for the FBI."

At the name, Johansson went pale. Beautiful women were common enough, but being in the same room with a sorcerer was a new experience for most people. Rather like wading in the Atlantic and suddenly turning around to see a large shark fin gliding by.

"How do you do, ma'am," Johansson said after he managed to wrangle his tongue. He quickly jammed his pistol into the holster on his hip and stood at attention.

"Have you finished searching the house?" Sorsha asked, walking along the shelves of potions, idly reading the paper labels.

"Yes, ma'am," he said. "There isn't anyone here."

Alex felt his shoulders relax. He wasn't happy that Doc and Jessica were gone, and the policemen assigned to watch them had somehow missed it, but at least the shop wasn't a murder scene.

"But you told me Dr. Kellin was here earlier," Alex said, managing to hide both his relief and his irritation.

"Honest, Mr. Lockerby, that's what I was told when I got here," Johansson said. "I saw the blonde girl leaving, but nobody else came or went all night."

"The blonde girl," Sorsha said, leaning casually against the counter. "Are you certain it wasn't Dr. Kellin? She has gray hair and it's quite foggy outside."

"No ma'am," he said. "This girl walked right by the car and I got a real good look at her. She was pretty young to look at, but not so young I wondered about her being Dr. Kellin's assistant."

"Like a teenager?" Alex asked.

"Maybe," he said with a shrug. "I guess."

Alex and Sorsha exchanged glances while Johansson looked chagrined. Before anyone could speak again, the cop Alex had seen sleeping in the car earlier came in through the curtain. He had an olive complexion with dark hair and thick eyebrows that seemed to slump down over his eyes in a perpetual scowl.

"There's a bedroom downstairs," he said to Johansson, "but nobody's there."

"Mind if I have a look around?" Alex asked.

The second cop looked like he wanted to tell Alex just what he could do with his request, but a glance at Sorsha made him hesitate, and he looked at Johansson.

"This is Miss Kincaid," the blond cop said. "She's with the Feds."

"I understand that Detective Pak is on his way here to take over," Sorsha said. "Why don't you boys head out front and secure the building until he arrives?"

The second cop got that barely-controlled outrage look on his face again, but before he could speak, Johansson snapped a salute to Sorsha.

"Yes, ma'am," he said, then nodded toward the open door. "Come on, Gibson."

Sorsha watched them go with a rather self-satisfied smirk, then turned to Alex.

"Where do you want to start?" she asked.

He didn't have to think about that one. If something was wrong, there was one place that would tell the tale.

"Downstairs," he said. "In Dr. Kellin's lab."

The lab looked different from the last time Alex had been in it. The broken glass from the shattered equipment had been swept up and the floor had obviously been scrubbed. Several of the empty tables had been pushed against the wall in a double row and the working brew lines were set up in the center.

Alex knew something was amiss immediately. The equipment on the central tables had clearly been set up and looked to have been working recently, but none of the burners were lit. He checked the alarm clocks on each table and while they were wound and ticking, the lever on the back that activated the alarm had been set to the 'off' position.

"You almost wouldn't know there was a gun battle here a few days ago," Sorsha said, sauntering around the room. While her posture looked relaxed, Alex saw her eyes darting around, taking in the details. "Except for the bullet holes."

She reached up to touch the large clock on the back wall. It was an ornate wooden number with a weight and pulley system to keep it wound. Just above the clock's face were two holes in the decoratively carved frame.

"Buckshot," Alex corrected.

Sorsha ran her finger around the neat hole, brushing a few splinters away, then turned back to the lab tables.

"What is Dr. Kellin working on here?"

"Nothing," Alex said. He pointed to the inactive burners. "She's shut everything down."

"I take it that's not normal?"

Alex shook his head.

"Jessica told me that the only time an alchemist shuts down their brewing lines is if they're going to be away for some time."

"You think they got spooked?" Sorsha said. "Took what they needed and set up somewhere secret?"

Alex hadn't thought of that, but it made sense.

"Just a minute," he said, then headed into the little bedroom off the lab that belonged to Jessica. Alex had seen it many times and it looked exactly as he remembered it. Nothing obvious looked out of place. Jessica's hairbrush and makeup were on her dressing table and a quick check of the closet revealed that her clothes were still there. It didn't look like the room of someone who'd left in a hurry.

Unless she left so quickly, she didn't have time to grab anything.

Alex left the bedroom and climbed up two flights of stairs to the floor where Dr. Kellin lived. He'd never been up here before, but he found the doc's bedroom easily enough. Just like Jessica's, it showed no signs of having been ransacked by someone packing in a hurry; in fact, two small suitcases still occupied the shelf in the top of her closet.

"What are you thinking?" Sorsha asked. She'd followed him, watching quietly as he'd made his search.

"They left of their own free will," Alex said.

Sorsha nodded.

"If they'd been abducted or forced to go, they wouldn't have bothered to shut down the lab," she said. "What else?"

"They were in enough of a hurry that they didn't stop to pack anything."

Or did they?

Alex pushed past Sorsha and headed back down to the shop on the main level. He wasn't terribly familiar with the alchemy shop, but he'd been in shops before. He walked slowly along the shelves until he found a row of vials with a decent coat of dust on the ones in the back. Normally when shopkeepers sold something off a rack, they would move the others forward at closing. The first two holes in this rack were empty, and there was a space beside one of the empty holes where the dust had been wiped away by whoever removed it.

Fuller's Oil, the label read.

Since the price on the label was only thirty cents, Alex assumed it must be an unusual ingredient to be so dusty. He'd seen that name before, and recently. Pulling out his black notebook from his shirt pocket, he flipped through it until he came to the page with the notes on the lab break in. The note in Jimmy the Weasel's pocket had a list of potions and ingredients on it and Alex ran his finger down the list until he found Fuller's Oil. Next to the name was the number two.

Moving quickly, Alex checked the shelves and found gaps in all of the rows that held ingredients on Jimmy's list. That might be a coincidence, but Alex had stopped believing in coincidence after his second murder case.

"I don't like that look," Sorsha said as Alex chewed his lip in thought.

Alex ignored her and opened his kit bag, pulling out his amberlight burner, lamp, and oculus. He swept the shop and the little examination room beside it. As he expected, there were hundreds of objects that had been moved all over the shop and in the examination room. When Alex pointed the light at the shelves he'd identified, ghostly brown images of the missing materials appeared. If they'd been gone for more than a day, their images would have degraded to nothing.

He was about to put the lamp away when its amber light played over the back wall, behind the counter and the cash register. As expected, the pictures and certificates mounted on the wall showed no outlines at all, they'd been put up years ago and were probably only taken down and cleaned once a year or so. One of the pictures, however, lit up brightly. It had been taken down recently.

Remembering Dr. Burnham's hidden compartment, Alex put away his equipment and then gently lifted the picture off the wall. Disappointingly, there was nothing behind it. Turning the frame over, Alex saw a picture of three people standing in front of a building. One of them looked a little like Jessica must have looked when she was in her late teens or early twenties. She stood next to a shorter young man with thick spectacles and unkempt hair that looked about the same age.

On young Jessica's other side there was an older man, though probably only mid-thirties. He was dressed in an old-fashioned suit with shiny shoes and a silk hat on his head. A sign in the foreground was partially visible and read *Sciences Building*.

"Let me see," Sorsha said, leaning in close to get a look at the picture. "This must be Dr. Kellin," she said, pointing to the woman.

"That's Kellin's assistant, Jessica O'Neil," Alex corrected her.

"No," Sorsha said, pointing to the man in the suit. "Look at that hat. Those have been out of style since the turn of the century. This picture is at least thirty years old."

Alex looked at the picture again. The girl did look like Jessica, but could just as easily have been the doc. He flipped the picture over and moved the tabs that kept the frame together. Opening it up, he set the frame and the glass on the counter and turned the picture over. On the back was a single line of hand-written text.

Connie, Charlie, and Me. - 1892

"I guess you're right," Alex said. "This must be Dr. Kellin when she was in college."

"She went to Harvard," Sorsha said, looking at the medical degree on the wall.

"No," Alex said, staring intently at the picture.

"I'm looking right at her diploma," Sorsha said in an exasperated voice.

"Look at this guy right here," Alex said, ignoring her comment. He pointed at the short man with the glasses. "That's Charlie, right next to the doc."

Sorsha leaned close to the picture for a moment, then looked up at Alex.

"How do you know? It could just as easily be Connie."

"Because I've seen this guy before," Alex said. "In the pictures on the wall in the back of Charles Grier's shop. He's Charlie."

Sorsha shrugged.

"Okay," she said. "But it's probably still Harvard."

"No," Alex said again, "Charles and the doc were an item when they were at school studying alchemy, but something happened, and she left. She told him she was going to go to medical school."

Alex turned to the wall and moved along until he found a bachelor's degree in Alchemical Science.

"This is it," he said, pointing to the name of the school. "This picture was taken when Dr. Kellin and Charles Grier were attending Columbia."

"Okay," Sorsha said again. "I suspect that you're right, but why is it important?"

"Because," Alex said, putting the picture down on the counter. "Before Jessica and the doc left, they took the exact potions and ingredients that the burglars were looking for the other night. And somewhere along the line, somebody took this picture down and looked at it."

Sorsha moved the picture aside, and picked up the glass, holding it up to the light.

"I think you're wrong about one thing, Alex," she said, moving the glass so that Alex could see the magelight on the ceiling shining off its surface. Right where Charles Grier would have appeared behind it was a lip-shaped smudge. "I don't think Dr. Kellin left here of her own volition. I'll bet whoever has Charles Grier called her and they threatened to harm him if she didn't come."

25

LEON'S LIBATION

The pale light of dawn had already begun to light up the fog by the time Alex staggered up the steps to the brownstone. He pulled the flask of rejuvenator from his pocket before he remembered it was empty again and he just held it in his limp arm, not bothering to put it away. He'd drunk its entire contents over the last hours, trying desperately to do something that would reveal where Dr. Kellin or Jessica had gone. Efforts that had all been in vain.

Leaning his head against the stained-glass window of the front door, he swore. He had used everything he could think of as a catalyst for his finding runes — Dr. Kellin's hairbrush, Jessica's makeup, even unmentionables from both women, all to no avail. The finding rune had more success with Dr. Kellin, and seemed to indicate that she was somewhere in the inner-ring, maybe even in the core, but that was as good as he could get. The rune simply failed to find Jessica at all, and he hoped that meant that Dr. Kellin had sent her to Albany for safekeeping.

What it really meant was that despite his best efforts, he wasn't any closer to finding any of them — Grier, Jessica, or Doc — and he couldn't help feeling that he was running out of time.

A click sounded in front of him, and suddenly the window Alex was leaning on vanished as the door was pulled open. He staggered forward, nearly running into Iggy, who stepped back quickly.

"Good heavens, lad," he said, seizing Alex by the hand. "You look a fright, and why do you smell like blood and Miss Kincaid's brand of perfume?"

"Sorry I didn't call," Alex said, struggling to make his eyes focus. "Been a...a really long night."

"You look dead on your feet," Iggy said, grabbing his arm and half-leading, half-pulling Alex inside. "Let's get you to bed and you can tell me about it later."

Alex shook his head.

"No time," he said. "Put on a pot of the strongest coffee you've got. I'll tell you about it now."

"Nonsense," Iggy said, guiding Alex toward the stairs. "You're barely able to speak in complete sentences."

Alex focused his mind and pulled back against Iggy's guiding hand, breaking the old man's grip. He took a deep breath and did his best to sweep the cobwebs from his brain.

"No," he insisted. "Two lives are at stake. Jessica's life might be at stake, too. They're depending on me. I need your help."

Iggy considered him for a long moment, then nodded, taking Alex by the arm again. He led Alex into the kitchen and put him in one of the heavy oak chairs. A few minutes later, the smell of percolating coffee roused Alex enough to talk.

He told Iggy about the events of the night before, starting with the men Lilith had cut down and ending with his failure to locate Dr. Kellin. Somewhere in the middle of the story, Iggy had pressed a cup of coffee into his hands. When he finished the tale and the coffee, Alex felt more awake.

"Do you believe the Sorceress is right?" Iggy said, refilling Alex's mug.

Alex nodded.

"Kellin and Grier were dating when they were in college," he said. "And when the doc left her house, she took the exact things that were on the list in Jimmy the Weasel's pocket. It's a cinch that whoever took Grier used him to get the doc to go along."

"Why?" Iggy asked. "Why not just send someone to her shop to buy that stuff?"

Alex's brain might have still been a bit foggy, but he knew that tone in his mentor's voice. Iggy had spotted something that Alex had missed.

"Well, they're both alchemists," he said, "Maybe he needed a potion and Grier wasn't up to it, so he brought in the doc."

Iggy scowled and shook his head.

"Oh, I don't think so," he said. "Alchemists are like runewrights, they don't share their recipe books with the competition. Andrea first noticed Grier was missing when she went to buy a potion she needed, so clearly there were things he could do that she couldn't. If whoever took Grier needed him to brew a potion, then it stands to reason that he already knew how to do it. Why involve Andrea?"

Alex hadn't thought of that.

"Whoever it is must be desperate," Alex said. "Or they think all alchemists know the same recipes."

Iggy stroked his bottle-brush mustache as he considered that.

"That's possible, I suppose," he admitted at last. "But most people know that potions vary greatly from alchemist to alchemist. There must be some reason, something that connects them, other than dating a long time ago."

"Leon's Libation," Alex said.

Iggy looked at him expectantly.

"It's something they were working on when they were at school," Alex explained. "In the letter where Dr. Kellin told Grier that she was leaving for medical school, she mentioned it. It kind of sounded like she thought it was dangerous, but she didn't say anything about what it was supposed to do."

Iggy went back to stroking his mustache and Alex went to take another sip of his coffee, but found his mug mysteriously empty.

"You need to find out what Leon's Libation is," Iggy said, refilling Alex's mug from the coffee pot.

Alex drank deeply, enjoying the scalding heat of the liquid that was pulling his mind out of the fog of exhaustion.

"How am I supposed to do that?" he asked.

"You said they were in college when they worked on this?" Iggy asked.

Alex nodded, taking another swig from the mug.

"It was right before the doc went to Harvard for her medical degree."

"But she does have a Bachelor's Degree in Alchemy from Columbia?"

Again, Alex nodded, not sure what Iggy was driving at.

"That would mean that she left after she graduated," Iggy said.

"Why is that important?"

Having never been to college, Alex had no idea how such things worked.

"Because it probably means that Leon's Libation was Kellin and Grier's senior project."

Alex took another swig of coffee, but that didn't help.

"So?" he asked.

"Research projects done at a college are carefully controlled," Iggy said. "Andrea and her partner would have had to get their project approved by the dean of the alchemy school. They would have had to document everything they were doing and submit a report at the end."

"Reports that the college would still have, forty years later?"

Iggy gave him an amused look.

"Academics never throw anything away," he said. "I'll wager that if you go see the current dean, he can get the file on Leon's Libation in less than an hour."

Alex drained his coffee cup and pushed himself to his feet.

"Thank God for paperwork," he said. "Columbia's not too far, even with the fog. I'll go see the dean and get a look at the file and then ..." He faded off as he tried to figure out what he would do once he knew what Dr. Kellin and Grier had been working on in college in 1892.

"Then," Iggy said, giving Alex a penetrating look. "You ask who knew about Leon's Libation other than Andrea and Grier? Whoever has them must have known about that connection — unless this is all one big coincidence," he added.

Alex chuckled at that.

"No such thing," he said. "Now where was I going?"

"To bed," Iggy said. "You can barely stand, and the dean won't be in his office for at least another five hours."

Alex pulled out his flask of rejuvenator before he remembered that it was empty.

"I'll be all right," he said, putting the flask back in his jacket pocket. "But the doc might not be if I take too long."

"Are you out of that?" Iggy said, ignoring Alex's declaration and pointing to his pocket.

"I've been going through it faster than I used to," Alex admitted. "It doesn't have the same kick as before."

"I thought you got that refilled a few days ago," Iggy said quietly, his voice subdued.

Alex met his eyes and nodded.

"I don't figure the doc changed her recipe," he said, his voice just as quiet. "I guess it means I'm running out of time."

It had been two years since Alex spent a significant portion of his life energy to power the spell that moved Sorsha's falling castle out over the Atlantic. If he were honest with himself, he hadn't expected to last this long.

When Iggy didn't respond, Alex went on.

"I need to do this," he said. "I've got to find Jessica and the doc. I have to make sure they're safe, then...then I can rest."

Iggy held his gaze for a long moment, then sighed.

"I'll call the Dean's office as soon as the college opens," he said. "Which won't be till nine and that's over four hours away. So you go up to your room and sleep, and I'll come get you once I've talked to the dean."

Alex wanted to object, but couldn't seem to figure out how to do that. Instead, he let Iggy lead him up two flights of stairs to his room, where he passed out on his bed, still fully dressed.

Alex felt like he hadn't slept at all when Iggy shook him awake five and a half hours later. He wanted to be angry, but Iggy had pushed a full flask of rejuvenator into his hand on the way to the front door.

"Andrea brought this by the other day," he'd said in response to Alex's questioning glance. "For emergencies. I figure this qualifies."

"Thanks," Alex said, taking a swig from the flask. It was still weak, but Alex could feel his mind coming slowly into focus as he slipped the flask into his pocket.

"There's a cab waiting for you out front, and Dean Richardson is expecting you," Iggy said as they reached the front door. "He said he'd have someone pull the file so it should be waiting for you when you get there."

Alex thanked him and headed out into the fog to the waiting cab.

Wesley Richardson, Dean of the Alchemy Department at Columbia University, was a pudgy man with a serious face, a receding hairline, and spectacles that made his eyes look comically large. When Alex was shown into his sumptuous office on the top floor of the Alchemical Sciences building, he was sitting behind his desk, just staring at a yellowed folder that looked to be an inch-and-a-half thick.

"Sit down, Mr. Lockerby," he said, once his secretary had announced Alex.

"Thanks for seeing me on such short notice," Alex said.

Richardson took off his thick spectacles and wiped his face with a handkerchief he pulled from his pocket. Alex hadn't noticed before, but the little man was sweating even though it was quite cool in the office.

"I agreed to see you under duress, Mr. Lockerby," Richardson said, putting his handkerchief away. "When Dr. Bell called me, I told him I didn't have time for wild goose chases. Then the President of the University called. He informed me in no uncertain terms that Dr. Bell has been a great help to the University and that I was to give him whatever he needed."

Alex resisted the urge to smirk. Iggy did his share of private consulting work in his retirement, and it didn't surprise Alex that some of it had been done here.

"I did as Dr. Bell asked," Richardson went on, picking up the thick folder. "Had one of my grad students pull this file from the archives." He plopped it back down on his desk, but with the underside facing up this time. Across the front of the folder, the word *Restricted* had been printed in large, red block letters.

"There's a reason I'd never heard of Leon's Libation," he said, stabbing down on the folder with his index finger. "There's a cover letter on this file from a Dean Bennett stating that this file is never to be released. According to him, this potion and the incident it spawned are scandalous." He stared daggers at Alex. "I don't care what the University President says," he went on. "I'm not showing this file to anyone. Now get out of my office."

Alex just sat there for a long minute, daring Richardson to say more.

"Dean Richardson," he began. "Eight people are already dead because of what's in that folder," Alex said in a neutral voice. "And the two students who cooked up Leon's Libation are missing. One of them is a personal friend of mine. Now I could threaten you with a visit from the police, the FBI, and the Ice Queen herself, but I don't have time for that. So here's what's going to happen. Either you're going to give me that file, or I'm going to take it — your choice."

Richardson grabbed the file protectively, and Alex thought for a moment that he might try to run. After reconsidering, however, he released the file and sat back in his chair.

"I can't let you read this file," he said. "I'm the only one allowed to see it."

Alex glared at him and he hurried on.

"But...but I can tell you what's in it."

Alex smiled and relaxed.

"What's Leon's Libation?" he asked.

Richardson put his thick spectacles back on and opened the front cover of the folder.

"According to the summary, Leon's Libation was supposed to be a restorative. It would produce mental and physical recovery from fatigue without the cellular degradation that is usually associated with lack of rest."

"What does that mean?" Alex asked.

Dean Richardson looked up from the folder and pursed his lips.

"In layman's terms, this potion would make it possible for someone to work or study for extended periods without rest and without the effects of fatigue," he said.

"How extended?"

"Days," Richardson said. "Maybe even weeks without rest."

Alex whistled, thinking of the possibilities. He could follow leads day and night until a case was done; he could see Jessica at night, and work during the day. Of course if Leon's Libation existed, Jessica would have used it to work on the polio cure around the clock, and he still wouldn't be able to see her often.

"It would have been an amazing rejuvenator," Richardson said with a sigh.

"What did you say?" Alex asked, his attention snapping back to the Dean.

"Well if it had worked, it would have rejuvenated the body of anyone imbibing it," he said.

A shiver ran up Alex's back and his hand dropped to the pocket of his jacket. He could feel the silver flask inside that held Dr. Kellin's rejuvenator, the potion that wiped away the fatigue brought on by Alex's diminished life energy.

"So what was so bad about Leon's Libation?" he asked, his throat suddenly dry.

Richardson looked back down at the folder.

"According to this, the research would have used quite a few rare and expensive ingredients, as well as being quite volatile to brew," he said. "The Dean at the time had to sign off on the project." He turned a page in the folder, then flipped a few more in rapid succession. "The students who proposed the project, Andrea Flynn and Charles Grier, must have been exceptional students. There are a dozen glowing letters of recommendation in here from various faculty members."

Alex was caught off guard by Andrea's last name. He'd always known her as Kellin, but she had a daughter, so it stood to reason that she must have had a husband at some point.

"Here it is," Richardson said. "During Flynn and Grier's senior year, they had been given permission to test the formula on student volunteers."

That shiver up Alex's spine returned with a vengeance.

"According to this, the trials were going well until the end of the term. During the lead-up to final examinations, four of the students in the test group broke into the lab and stole some of the potion to help them study. Rather than the standard potion they had been receiving, they stole a concentrated solution."

"What happened?" Alex asked, positive he didn't want to know.

"During the examinations, all four of the students became agitated," Richardson read. "One picked up a teacher's desk and threw it out a third story window. According to eyewitnesses, she then jumped out the window and ran off." He skimmed the report for a moment, then looked up at Alex. "The other three were involved in similar incidents and had to be physically subdued."

"What about the girl who ran off?"

"Her body was found in the park the next day," Richardson read. "The four students exposed to the concentrated potion, William Billingsley, Jessica Davis, Lilly Hanson, and Andrew O'Neil, all died of heart failure. After that, the project was canceled." Richardson took off his glasses and rubbed his eyes. "Dear God," he said, shaking his head. "Those poor youths."

"It sounds like they just got too much of the potion at once," Alex said. "So how come they canceled the project?"

Dean Richardson put his spectacles back on and scanned through the next few pages.

"It looks like the Dean had all the evidence reviewed by the campus doctor and the Professor overseeing the project," he said. "They determined that the potion built up in the student's bodies over time until it became toxic. Drinking the concentrated potion just made it happen faster. The whole line of research was discontinued."

"And that's it?" Alex asked.

Dean Richardson flipped more pages until he reached the end.

"It looks like Charles Grier did try to submit another project based on this one," he said. "Even got his professor to buy off on it, but Dean Bennett rejected it." He traced his finger along a line of text, then shook his head. "It seems Mr. Grier had a flair for bad alliteration; he called this one Ponce's Poultice."

Richardson chuckled, but Alex didn't hear. He suddenly felt that familiar adrenaline rush that would temporarily wipe away his need for Dr. Kellin's rejuvenator, or, if he was guessing correctly, Leon's Libation.

"The professor," Alex said. "The one who oversaw the research, is he the same professor who supported Grier's second project?"

Richardson flipped back and forth between the pages of the folder, then nodded.

"Yes," he confirmed. "A Professor Constantine Torres." He looked back up at Alex. "Does that mean something?"

"Yes," Alex said, getting to his feet and putting his hat on. "It means I know what Ponce's Poultice is. It also means I know who kidnapped Charles Grier, and I'm pretty sure I know why."

26

CONNIE

Alex took a slug of the rejuvenator as he waited for the operator to connect his call. The rush of energy washed over him and he took a deep breath, enjoying what there was of it.

"Tasker," came the response when the line connected.

"This is Alex Lockerby," Alex said. "I need a line on a guy you might know; do you have a minute?"

"Sure," Billy Tasker replied. Billy was a talented reporter, but he worked for *The Midnight Sun*, a tabloid of the most sensational variety. He was also the reporter who had given Alex the moniker, *The Runewright Detective*. "Anything I might make into a story?" he pressed. Billy was always in search of a story, and Alex had given him a few good ones in the past. "I heard a rumor that the cops have got a headless body over at the morgue. You wouldn't know anything about that, would you?"

"Sorry," Alex lied. "I am working on a kidnapping case, though. I'll tell you about it once I wrap it up. How's that?"

"Kidnapping's good," Billy said eagerly. "What is it you need to know?"

"Ever hear of a guy named Constantine Torres? He's an alchemist and I'm pretty sure he's got money."

Based on the number of goons he was capable of hiring, Alex guessed Constantine Torres had a lot of money.

"You mean Connie Torres," Billy answered after a few moments. "He came up with some miracle face cream, you know the kind ladies wear at night. Made a fortune."

"Where can I find him?"

"I'd have to ask around about that," Billy said. "He's not the kind of guy who does the social circuit."

Alex pulled out his pocket watch and checked the time.

"If he lives in the city, he'll have a place in the core," he said. "I'm at Columbia University right now so I figure it'll take me half an hour or so to reach Empire Station. Do you think you could find out by then?"

"Sure," Billy said. "Should only take a few minutes."

Alex thanked him and was about to hang up when something occurred to him.

"Hey, what do you know about a guy named William Henderson?"

"The Ambassador? I know he comes from the best kind of money. Old money."

"Does he still have it?" Alex asked.

"Oh, yeah," Billy said. "Rumor has it his old man was an original investor in Standard Oil. Henderson's loaded."

"What's he like?"

"Pretty boring, really," Billy said. "Sure he flies all over the world and he married a gorgeous actress, but the guy just doesn't make my kind of headlines. He only goes to the highbrow parties, you know, the ones where no one gets thrown out for being three-sheets-to-the-wind. He avoids press and scandal like the plague. The last time we wrote about him was five years ago or so, and that was mostly his son David."

"Why him?"

"Oh, the usual," Billy said. "David was a real libertine, drove fast cars and wrecked them, dated faster women and got them in trouble, that sort of thing."

"And daddy didn't like it."

"Nope, he cut the kid off without a penny."

"What happened to David?" Alex asked, his interest suddenly piqued.

"Died a couple of years ago," Billy said. "There was a piece in the Times about the size of the crypt his mother built for him."

Alex sighed. He thought he was on to something with David, but it was a literal dead end. He thanked Billy and hung up, heading out into the fog to try to catch a cab.

It was almost four o'clock when Alex rapped smartly on Connie Torres' door. The house was located on the part of 33rd Street near Empire Tower that had become known as Mansion Row. This was by far the smallest house of the lot, but that didn't keep it from being opulent. The entire home was done in a Greek style, with marble columns on either side of the entryway that led up to a heavy-looking plinth above. Flanking the door were alcoves with reproductions of famous statuary that faced inward, as if to judge any potential callers.

Alex had been to rich men's houses before. Usually when the door opened, it was a butler or a domestic whose job it was to send away riffraff like him. When Connie Torres' door opened, however, Alex found himself looking at a broad, squat man in a cheap suit. He had a flat face with a flat nose and eyes that were half-closed in a perpetual squint. His hands were thick-fingered and rough, and as he held the door open with his left hand, Alex could see the grip of a revolver peeking out from a shoulder holster under the man's jacket.

"Yeah?" he said in the most un-aristocratic Jersey accent Alex had ever heard.

"Tell Mr. Torres that Alex Lockerby is here to see him."

"Buzz off," the thug said, starting to close the door.

"I'd be happy to go get the cops," Alex interjected. "Tell them about how those two missing alchemists are being held here against their will."

The man hesitated, giving Alex a more scrutinizing look than before.

"Or you could just let me have a quick word with Mr. Torres," Alex finished.

The flat-faced man opened the door a bit and leaned out, as if he expected there to be a dozen armed policemen up against the front wall of the house. Finding Alex to be alone, he shrugged and opened the door.

"Inside," he growled.

Alex tried not to look nervous and stepped in. The foyer of the house was immaculate with marble floors, Persian carpets, carved art-nouveau sideboards, and padded chairs. A grand staircase ran up to the second floor with doors running off into side rooms on either side.

As opulent as the house was, Alex could see a thick layer of dust on the decorative table in the middle of the floor, and the flowers decorating the room weren't live, they were silk. Alex knew that Torres had money, more than he could ever spend, so the state of his house meant he didn't want cleaners inside.

"What's this?" a low voice said.

Alex looked to the door on the left side of the foyer and saw another thug in another cheap suit standing in the now open door. He was taller than the flat-faced man and gaunter, like a feral dog. His dirty blond hair was unkempt, and it looked like it had been some time since he'd seen a barber.

"I think the boss will want to talk to this one," the flat-faced thug said. "Cover me while I search him. Hands up, you." This last bit was directed toward Alex.

The blond thug pulled a .38 from a shoulder holster and leveled it at Alex. For his part, Alex raised his hands and allowed the flat-faced thug to pat him down. He'd taken the precaution of leaving his holster in his vault, along with his A-5, his brass knuckles, and the backup .38 pistol in his weapon cabinet. He'd even left his rune book behind, though he did have a few runes on individual papers folded up in his shirt pocket.

"He's clean," Flat-Face said once he'd finished. The blond thug looked disappointed and tucked his gun back into his holster. "This way," the first one said, heading past his companion into the room beyond.

The Long Chain

Following the man, Alex entered an elegant dining room with a table big enough for thirty people and a glass-fronted hutch loaded with fine dishware. Like the foyer, however, it was disused and covered with dust.

Alex continued to follow his guide through the kitchens and into a large room at the back of the house. It looked like it had once been a solarium, but now it was set up as an alchemy lab. Dr. Kellin stood at a table in the back, measuring some green powder out of a jar and pouring it carefully into a beaker of bubbling liquid. In the far corner of the room, a man lay on a cot with another cheap-suited thug watching him. Finally, a man in a wheelchair sat on a raised platform by a doorway that led to some other parts of the house. He was old and withered with wispy white hair and gnarled hands that gripped the arms of his chair. A look of eager avarice twisted his face as he watched Dr. Kellen work.

"What's the meaning of this?" he wheezed when he caught sight of Alex and the flat-faced thug.

Dr. Kellin gasped and dropped a vial of blue liquid she was holding, sending it shattering across the floor.

"Alex," she gasped. Her eyes were as wide as saucers and Alex saw fear in them.

"Hi-ya, Doc," Alex said, giving her a smile and a friendly wave.

Dr. Kellin recovered herself instantly, and the look of fear vanished from her face. She turned to the man in the wheelchair before anyone else could speak.

"You said you'd leave my friends out of this if I helped you," she accused him.

The man put up his hands and cocked an eyebrow.

"I assure you, Andrea, I don't know who this young man is, or how he came to be here." His gaze shifted to Alex and his eyes narrowed, scrutinizing him. "But I am most interested to find out."

Alex felt gooseflesh run up his arms as the old man looked at him. His eyes seemed to burn with the fire of passion, or madness, and Alex wasn't excited to find out which it was.

"My name's Alex Lockerby, Mr. Torres," he said. "I'm a private investigator. Dr. Kellin here," he nodded at her, "hired me to find

Charles Grier." Alex looked at the man in the cot. "Can I assume that's him?"

Torres looked surprised for a minute then he nodded.

"Is he still alive?" Alex asked.

"Of course," Torres said. "What makes you think he wouldn't be?"

Alex smiled at that.

"Well, I imagine you weren't very happy with him when you found out that you knew more about brewing Leon's Libation than he did."

Dr. Kellin's face blanched at the mention of the potion and Torres looked angry.

"How did you know that?" he demanded.

"Easy," Alex said, walking to one of the heavy lab tables and leaning against it. "Dean Bennett confiscated everything after those students died, but you were the faculty advisor to Grier and the doc. You would have had copies of everything. You used their work to make your cold cream that keeps ladies looking young."

"What of it?" Torres said, a slow smile spreading across his face.

"You tried to make the formula work, but all you got was a minor restorative," Alex said. "That must have been frustrating."

"Oh, it was," Torres said, his smile still in place. "Bennett took everything before I could make copies. I had to recreate the formula from memory, and obviously I didn't get it exactly right. Still, it did make me rich, so I'm not too upset about it."

"And it stayed that way for a long time," Alex said. "Until you got sick. How am I doing?"

"You're a very astute investigator, Lockerby," he said with a cold chuckle. "I have a degenerative nerve disease that is slowly shutting down my spinal cord."

"And when you got that diagnosis, you remembered the work you did way back in college," Alex said. "Charles Grier's rejuvenator." His eyes slid to Dr. Kellin as he said it and her cheeks pinked. "Did you know what he was really trying to do back in school, or did you figure it out later?" Alex asked, looking back to Torres.

The old man laughed at that.

"What is it you think Charles was trying to do?" he asked.

"His work wasn't some kind of energy elixir," Alex said, "like some glorified cup of coffee. Grier wanted the ultimate prize, he was trying to create a potion that would prevent the body from aging."

"How do you know that?" Dr. Kellin snapped at him.

He grinned at her and shrugged.

"It was obvious, really. Charles' flare for alliteration was the clue. Leon's Libation and Ponce's Poultice. Leon is common enough, but I've only heard the name Ponce twice before. One is a British swear word I learned when Iggy called a bureaucrat at the revenue office a ponce, and the other is the name of a famous Spaniard. His name was Ponce de Leon and he's famous for trying to find the fountain of youth."

Torres stared at Alex for a long moment, then he burst out laughing, pounding his hand on the arm of his wheelchair.

"Oh, Andrea, where did you find this boy?" he wheezed. "He's priceless." Torres stopped to wipe away a tear of mirth. "You're right, of course," he said. "Grier loved to talk about his project. He told me what he envisioned and where he wanted to go with it."

"Too bad it wasn't his idea," Alex said. "If it had been, he might have been able to make it work."

Torres mirth dried up, and he sneered, but didn't respond.

"Did you have to torture him before he told you the truth?" Alex asked. "That the whole thing had been Andrea's idea from the start?"

"I did have to have my boys lean on him a bit," Torres admitted.

"So, you see why I asked if he was still alive?"

"Yes, I see," Torres sneered. "And yes, Grier is still with us, just to insure Dr. Kellin's cooperation. For my own curiosity, how did you know that Leon's Libation was Andrea's idea?"

"Simple," Alex said. "If it had been Grier's idea, he wouldn't have just let it drop after the accident at Columbia. He'd have kept working on it until he cracked it. But he didn't, did he? He became a regular alchemist. Nothing in his work indicated that he'd even thought about Leon's Libation after college. Even you knew more about it than he did."

Torres sour face split into a grin and he clapped his hands together in applause.

"Bravo, Mr. Lockerby," he said. "I must confess to being excessively entertained by your mental gymnastics. But, as you said, I'm an old and sick man. I don't have a great deal of time left to me." He looked at Dr. Kellin. "Andrea has been working diligently to recreate her old formula, but the work hasn't exactly been going quickly."

Torres looked back to Alex, then his eyes shifted to the side and he nodded. Suddenly, Alex was seized from behind and strong arms pressed his head down on the lab table.

"With you here, I suspect we can prevail upon dear Andrea to work faster."

"I told you I'm going as fast as I can," Dr. Kellin snapped. She was calm but Alex could detect a note of panic underlying her voice. "The potion base takes a week to brew and no amount of cajoling or threats can make it any faster."

One of the thugs pulled Alex's arm up behind his back, hard, and he grunted in pain.

"I think you are stalling, Andrea," Torres said. "Now you get me results or I'll have the boys cut apart your detective friend piece by piece."

Dr. Kellin ground her teeth and cast Alex a worried look.

"If I may," Alex said, keeping his voice calm. "I believe I can help speed things along."

All eyes turned to Torres.

"How?" he asked.

"You don't want to wait for the doc to brew the foundations of her potion," Alex said. "So what you need is a supply that's already been brewed."

A long moment passed and then Torres nodded at the man holding Alex. The pressure on his arm vanished and Alex pushed himself up from the table.

"And you know where to get some?" he asked.

Alex nodded.

"I should warn you," he said. "Dr. Kellin never solved the toxicity problem. If you drink her rejuvenator it will slowly build up in your system until it kills you. The only reason I can imagine why anyone would drink it is if they're dying anyway." He shrugged and cast a side-

The Long Chain

long glance at Dr. Kellin. "Or if maybe they had something real important to do and they didn't care if they lived or died afterward."

Dr. Kellin couldn't meet Alex's gaze, looking down at the measuring spoon she still held in her hands.

"Well, I don't see as I have much choice," Torres said, "now do I? So if you have access to what Andrea needs, you'll be doing her, and yourself, a favor by getting it for me." His voice was mild, pleasant even, but the implicit threat was obvious. "Tommy here," he nodded at the flat-faced thug, "will take you wherever you need to go. And if you give him any trouble, he'll put a bullet in you."

Tommy grabbed Alex's arm.

"No need for that," Alex said, pulling the silver flask out of his jacket pocket. "I have it right here."

The look of naked avarice was back on Torres' face, but it was mixed with caution.

"Alex!" Dr. Kellin gasped.

"So he's telling the truth," Torres said, smiling at Dr. Kellin's reaction. He looked back at Alex and beckoned him forward. "Bring that here."

"This is just the base," Alex said, wiggling the flask. "Doc has to add something to it before it will work for you. The good news is that, unless I'm very much mistaken, she carries it on her person all the time."

Alex watched Dr. Kellin as he spoke. The expression on her face was one of horror that bled away like water out of a sink, leaving only shame behind. He turned back to Torres and mimed giving the flask to Kellin. After a moment's consideration, the old man nodded.

Holding the flask up so everyone could see it, Alex walked around the table and up to where Kellin stood. When he reached her, she looked up at him but didn't accept the offered flask.

"Go ahead," he said. "It's okay."

Reaching inside her collar, Dr. Kellin pulled out a small chain with a little phial hanging from it. Inside, Alex could see a small amount of blue liquid.

Opening the flask, Dr. Kellin poured the contents of the phial inside, then closed it and shook it up.

"This is what you want, Connie," she said, turning to him.

He reached out eagerly, motioning for her to bring it to him. Alex forced a sly smile onto his face, making sure Torres saw it.

"Wait," the old man said, suddenly suspicious. "You try it first."

Dr. Kellin went pale and cast a furtive look at Alex, but he just nodded.

Her hands were shaking as she opened the flask and she hesitated.

"Do it, Doctor," Torres said, and the flat-faced thug pulled out his pistol.

Dr. Kellin put the flask to her lips and tipped it up, taking a long drink.

"There," she said, screwing the cap back on. "It's as I promised."

"Boss, look," Flat-Face said, pointing at Dr. Kellin.

As Alex watched, Dr. Kellin shivered as if she were cold, then she gasped. A smile of pure pleasure came over her face, and she leaned her head back as her body trembled. Her arms grew thinner and more toned, and her skin lost the wrinkles of age. From the top of her head, her gray hair disappeared, flowing red down to the tips. When she lowered her head, Dr. Kellin was gone, and Jessica stared back at him.

27

LILITH

"Oh, dear Andrea," Connie Torres said, practically giggling with glee. "That is most impressive."

As Alex watched, Jessica looked down at her hands and smiled. Her face glowed with a delighted radiance, and she drew in a long, satisfied breath.

The look vanished almost instantly as she seemed to become aware of her surroundings. The events of the last day, in particular the last few minutes, seemed to pour into her, as if the part of her mind that was Kellin and the part that was Jessica were inherently separate — though obviously still connected.

A look of both shame and chagrin clouded her beautiful face, and she turned to face Alex.

"I ..." she began, the words catching in her throat. "I'm so sorry."

Alex gave a slight shrug. He'd hoped he'd been wrong about the real relationship between Jessica and Dr. Kellin, but he'd been prepared to be right.

Jessica's eyes hardened and her face fell. She'd obviously expected a different reaction from Alex.

"How long have you known?" she asked.

"I wasn't sure till a minute ago," Alex admitted. "Your hazel eyes really had me fooled. I didn't pick up on how you always wore green and Doc always wore blue. Some detective I am."

"I hate to break up this tender moment," Torres said. "But I'll have that flask now."

He nodded at the thug with the unkempt hair and the man took the flask from Jessica.

"I'm so sorry," she whispered again, as the man carried the flask to Torres. "The potion...it lowers inhibitions. I knew I shouldn't have pursued a relationship with you, but..." She looked at him with shining eyes. "I just couldn't help it."

"If it helps, you didn't have to pursue all that hard," Alex said.

On the raised platform, Torres eagerly took the flask and unscrewed the cap. His face was pulled up in a rictus grin and his eyes were alight with the same avarice Alex had seen before. Without hesitation, he put the flask to his lips and drank.

"How did you figure it out?" Jessica asked, ignoring Torres.

"The students who died," Alex said. "One was named Jessica Davis. One was named Andrew O'Neil. I knew that couldn't be a coincidence."

She looked down, then nodded.

"They were my friends."

"So you started making your special rejuvenator when Linda got sick," Alex said. "Sooner or later someone saw you like this, and you needed to make up a fictitious lab assistant to explain how you looked."

"How long is this supposed to take?" Torres said, holding up the flask so that he could observe his gnarled, liver-spotted hands.

"Your body isn't used to the formula," Jessica said in her sultry contralto voice.

Torres raised the flask to his lips again, but Jessica put up a warning hand.

"Alex was telling the truth," she said. "The formula is toxic; if you take too much at once, it will kill you."

Torres hesitated, then lowered the flask, looking back at his hands.

Jessica leaned close to Alex.

"I appreciate your gallantry, coming here to rescue me, but do you actually have some sort of plan? Once the formula affects Connie, things might get dicey."

"Of course I have a plan," Alex hissed back in his best indignant voice. "What do you think all that storytelling was for?"

"Knowing you?" she asked. "I'd say you were showing off how clever you are."

"That was just a bonus," he said. "I've been stalling."

"You brought the police with you?"

"Well," Alex equivocated. "Danny's on his way with a few dozen cops. They'd already be here if it wasn't for Leo Burnham's cursed fog."

"What?"

"Never mind," Alex said. Torres' frown had just vanished, replaced on his wizened face by a look of pure wonder. A moment after that, the wonder turned to triumph.

"Yes!" he shouted, turning his hands over and back again. Even at this distance, Alex could see the skin smoothing, the signs of age vanishing.

"I hope they get here soon," Jessica said, inexplicable urgency in her voice.

"Why?" Alex asked nodding at Torres who was tentatively feeling his face. "I expect he'll be looking at himself in a mirror for at least the next ten minutes."

Jessica turned to him and gripped his hand in a death grip.

"The potion lowers inhibitions," she said again, as if that explained everything. "Now that he has what he wants, he doesn't need us."

"What about the formula?" Alex said.

She looked down and Alex's heart sank.

"He threatened to kill Charles if I didn't write it out for him," she confirmed his guess. "Now that he knows that it works, and he has the formula to keep him young for long enough, he can make it himself."

A creaking noise pulled Alex's attention back up to the platform. Torres stood up from his wheelchair. He looked only a bit older than Alex now, with coal-black hair and handsome features. His face wore an expression of ecstasy, and he laughed with an almost childlike delight.

"Oh, Andrea," he said spreading his arms wide as if to embrace a whole new life. "Why didn't you market this? You'd have made a fortune."

"You know why," she said. "It's far too dangerous."

Torres laughed again.

"Then just sell it to rich people who want to be young again and charge a fortune," he said. He put his hand to his chin in a thoughtful gesture. "Yes, I like that idea. That's just what I'll do." That cold, hungry light was back in his eyes. "Just imagine how much money I'll make."

He held out his hands again and admired them.

"How long does the effect last?"

"About twelve hours," Jessica said. "Then you'll revert back to yourself."

"This is who I am now," he shouted at her, leaning on the railing that ran around the raised platform. "I'll never go back."

He held up the flask as if it were his child, something to be loved and protected, and Alex felt a shiver run down his back. Jessica had said the formula lowered a person's inhibitions, but Torres was ranting like a loon.

"Then you'll need more of that," Jessica said. "A lot more."

Torres' face hardened, going from elation to anger in an instant.

"And you mean to say that I'll need you for that," he accused her. "You're saying that you didn't write everything in that formula you gave me. Take him."

This last was addressed to the flat-faced thug and he pulled out his .38 and pointed it at Alex. The blond thug grabbed Alex from behind and they led him away from Jessica.

"Well?" Torres said to Jessica.

"Don't be foolish, Connie," she said, sounding more like Dr. Kellin than Jessica. "Of course I wrote the formula down correctly, but it is fairly complex. You're going to want someone who's done it before helping you."

Alex wondered how much Jessica shared with the doc's personality; were they the same person, or two different ones that shared a body? He reasoned the answer was probably somewhere in between.

Torres sneered.

"I don't need your help to read a recipe. But..." He scrutinized her thoughtfully. "I do want to be sure you haven't lied to me, Andrea dear." He looked to the men holding Alex. "Start breaking his bones until I'm satisfied she's telling me the truth."

Alex pressed his thumb against his flash ring as the flat-faced thug grabbed his wrist. If he timed it right, he'd be able to blind them long enough to escape. He still had two shield runes on his jacket so flat-face's gun shouldn't be a problem.

"Stop!" Jessica shouted in a manner that again reminded Alex of Doc. Her voice was both loud and commanding, and all eyes in the room turned to her.

Alex knew instantly that something was wrong. Very wrong. Jessica was leaning heavily against the lab table and her breathing was shallow. She was looking right at Alex, but he didn't see fear in her eyes, only a deep and abiding regret.

"You didn't believe me," she gasped. "About the formula being dangerous." She collapsed to the top of the workbench, leaning on her elbow.

Torres watched her with a look of disdain. Clearly he thought she was acting. Jessica's feet went out from under her and she dropped to the floor with a noise that sounded like someone had punched her in the gut.

"You're boring me, Andrea," Torres said, stifling a yawn.

Alex could feel his own breathing coming faster and his heart racing. Dr. Kellin had said that the potion was toxic over time; she'd told him so the very first time she'd made it for him. Jessica had said that the potion lowered inhibitions. He'd seen how maniacal Torres had become with just one sip. What would happen to someone who had been exposed for years?

The sound of laughter brought Alex's galloping thoughts to heel. It wasn't Torres this time, it was coming from the spot where Jessica had vanished beneath the table, but it wasn't her voice.

"I think your day is about to get more exciting than you bargained for," Alex said to Torres.

The young, old man looked at him with a sneer, but it vanished when he read the look on Alex's face. Before he could call a warning to his men, a hand rose up and grabbed the edge of the workbench. It wasn't Jessica's feminine hand, but a rather smaller, younger one.

"Boys," Alex said, trying very hard not to be terrified. "Meet Lilith."

The girl who rose up from behind the table couldn't have been more than thirteen. She was slender and small, with the delicate features of a youth. Now that Alex knew what, or rather who, she was, he could see the ghosts of Jessica and Dr. Kellin in that young face. Her hair wasn't platinum blonde, like Johansson had said, nor gray like Doc's, rather it was utterly white, like Alex's. Lilith's eyes were hazel, just like the others, and because she wore no colored clothing, they looked iron gray.

Those eyes swept the room, as if she didn't know where she was for a moment. When they locked on Alex, her brows dropped down over her eyes and her angelic young face twisted into a snarl that would set a feral dog running. He felt his blood run cold as he looked into those eyes. They were the exact opposite of Jessica's, cold and utterly devoid of human feeling.

"Shoot her," Torres yelled, perceiving the danger before his men could react.

Everything seemed to happen at once. Flat-Face released Alex's wrist and went for his gun. Lilith reached into Dr. Kellin's medical bag and came out with Charles Grier's missing kukri dagger. Torres turned from the platform and ran out of the lab through the side door.

Alex activated his flash ring.

Blinding light bloomed up into the room, pulsing and blazing as the rune expelled its suspended magical energy. Alex had been so focused on Lilith that he'd forgotten to close his eyes and he swore as the flash temporarily burned away his vision. The blond thug cried out and let go. Alex jabbed an elbow behind him as hard as he could but missed, causing him to fall blindly into a heap on the floor.

From the direction where he'd last seen Lilith came the sound of a lab table being turned over. Glass and liquid hit the floor with a cacophony of sound and two shots rang out in quick succession. Someone screamed and Alex was sprayed with a hot liquid he felt sure was not spilled potion.

Hoping not to cut himself on shards of broken glass, Alex pushed himself up, blinking in rapid succession, hoping to clear his vision. He bumped into the blond thug and the man grabbed at him. Alex pushed the groping arm away and punched where he assumed the man would be. He hit something solid but yielding, and heard the man's breath whoosh out.

Gut punch.

Alex's vision cleared enough to see the blond thug whirl around and point the muzzle of his pistol at him. Alex leapt forward, but the blond man was faster. The gun barked and Alex grunted as the slug hit him in the left side of his chest. His shield rune stopped the bullet, but it still felt like getting hit in the ribs with a Louisville Slugger.

As painful as the shot was, bullets didn't have much mass. Alex continued forward without stopping, driving his fist right into blondie's jaw. He felt the bone shift under his hand and the thug collapsed into a heap.

Alex grunted, shaking his stinging hand and trying to stand up straight with the pain in his side. Behind him, he could hear the sound of liquid dripping onto the hardwood floor. He turned as quickly as he could and found a scene out of a nightmare.

Lilith stood facing him, just a few feet away. Her white shirt was stained with blood and her face was spattered with drops of red. The wicked kukri knife hung down from her hand, dripping slowly on the floor with heavy, wet splats. Behind her, Flat-Face's body lay on the floor, flayed open from hip to shoulder across his torso. Alex could see the man's guts spilling out of the horrific wound and it turned his stomach.

Looking away, he found Lilith just staring at him. Her eyes weren't dark and cold, like they had been before. Instead they burned with a manic fire and energy. He thought her unhinged...until she smiled at him. It was a wide, eager, hungry smile that stretched across her young face.

Lilith wasn't unhinged, she was fully insane.

"Hello, Alex," she said in a voice that sounded excited and perky. "I was so hoping to meet you."

Alex had no idea what to say to that, so he forced an easy smile on his face.

"Nice to meet you too," he said, not really knowing what else to say.

Apparently, that wasn't it. Lilith's cherubic face hardened into a mask of fury and she jerked the Kukri up, splattering the front of Alex's suit with cast-off blood. Before Alex could move, or even object, she hurled the bent dagger right at him.

It passed so close to his ear that he felt the wind from it. He turned as it hit behind him with a solid-sounding thunk.

The blond thug lay, staring at the kukri's handle that was now sticking out of his chest. A rattling wheeze came out of his mouth as he tried to keep breathing. His eyes started to glaze over, but he raised his pistol toward Lilith with dogged determination.

Alex moved.

Launching himself off the workbench he was using as a support, he tackled Lilith just as the gun went off. He anticipated the slug hitting him in the back, but it missed entirely. What Alex didn't miss was the broken glass that littered the floor.

He landed hard, sliding across the floor as the shards tore holes in his suit and his flesh.

"Ow," he grunted, unable to move with Lilith still on top of him.

"Are you all right?" he asked as Lilith looked down at him from where he held her. The murderous light was gone from her eyes and she gave him a look that reminded him so much of Jessica that he shivered.

"You didn't have to do that," she said. "He couldn't have hurt me."

Alex raised an eyebrow at that and opened his arms so she could stand up.

'What? Do bullets bounce off you?"

She smiled and Alex saw some of the madness return.

"No, silly," she said. "But I heal really fast."

She got up and her face went from smiling to cross.

"Unlike you," she added.

Alex looked down and found himself bleeding from a number of small wounds. Most of it was minor and he'd have a devil of a time fixing his suit, even with mending runes. The problem was the large chunk of glass sticking out of his leg.

He reached for it, but Lilith slapped his hand away.

"Don't touch it," she said. "You'll only make it worse."

She picked her way carefully over to where the blond thug lay dead, and tore a strip off the front of his suit. The fabric was cheap; still, Alex doubted he could have torn it, yet Lilith made it look easy. He remembered the story about the girl at Columbia who had thrown a desk out of a window. Whatever Dr. Kellin's potion was doing to her, it had given Lilith enough strength to take a burly man's head off, then roll up the body in a rug and hide it.

Once she was done, Lilith yanked the kukri free of the dead man and came back to Alex. He was very grateful when she set the knife down on the floor before turning to him.

"Give me your handkerchief and hold still," she said, wrapping the torn strip of suit around his leg. She packed the area around the shard with the handkerchief and held it in place with the strip of suit. "Now don't go walking on that until you see Iggy."

She grinned at him and wrinkled her nose. It would have been adorable except for the flecks of blood still clinging to her cheeks.

"Aren't you a doctor?" he asked, trying to sit up against the overturned table without cutting himself further.

Lilith cocked her head and laughed.

"That's Andy," she said.

From somewhere above, Alex heard a door slam. In the confusion of the fight, he'd forgotten about Connie Torres. Lilith looked up at the ceiling, then down at the bloody knife on the floor.

"The police are on their way," Alex said. "Do you know how many more people are in the house?"

She smiled at him, half-warm, half-crazy, then looked around at the dead men.

"These are his day minions," she said. "He's got a night crew too. Three more." Her hand dropped to the hilt of the kukri and Alex reached out, taking her arm.

"We need to stay put," he said. "Let the police have Torres and his men when they get here."

Lilith's eyes softened and her smile turned down.

"Aww," she said, patting him on the cheek. "You don't want me to get any more blood on my hands...or is it Jessica's hands?"

She gave him a look that was both hungry and extremely disconcerting, coming from a thirteen-year-old.

"Let the police do their jobs," he said. "They get irritable when someone else takes care of the bad guys. Besides," he said, nodding toward the cot where Charles Grier was still lying. "Someone needs to make sure he's okay."

Lilith smiled her sweet smile again.

"He's fine," she said. "Andy gave him something to make him sleep. He'll be out for hours."

"You don't have to kill Torres," Alex said.

She pinched his cheek in the manner of a proud grandmother to a toddler.

"You're so sweet," she said. "I know I don't have to kill Connie." She smiled and the madness returned to her face. "I just really, really want to."

She leaned forward and kissed him on the cheek, then she picked up the knife and headed for the door where Connie Torres had disappeared.

28

THE COST OF VICTORY

Alex gritted his teeth and pulled himself up onto one of the heavy lab tables. Bits of glass stung his hip and leg as they bit into his flesh. Eventually, he got his good leg under him, grinding the glass shards into tiny fragments with his shoe.

He stayed there for a moment, collecting himself as blood oozed from a dozen minor wounds on his legs and back. Tentatively, he put weight on his injured leg. It hurt, but it would hold him well enough.

Alex knew the flat-faced thug had a gun, but he didn't want to look at the bloody mess that remained of his body, so he turned to the blond man instead. His .38 was still in his hand, and Alex limped over and pulled it from his dead grasp. He hefted it, feeling a small measure of comfort in its weight.

Turning toward the door where Torres — and more recently Lilith — had vanished, he walked unsteadily across the room. It took him a minute to climb the wooden steps to the little platform that had been put in to accommodate old Torres' wheelchair, and his leg ached with every step. He could feel the wet blood running down his leg, but he'd have to deal with that later.

Beyond the door at the back of the platform was a long hallway paneled with dark wood and hung with pictures. As Alex limped along, he saw images of Torres with all manner of famous people, actors, athletes, singers, and senators. There were even a few with presidents in them. Unlike the pictures kept by Burnham or Dr. Kellin, none of the pictures seemed to be of friends, just the kind of people a wealthy, ambitious man might use to advance himself.

Alex paused to look at one particular picture with Torres standing next to the King of England. The sight distracted him, but he still managed to catch sight of movement in the reflective glass covering the picture.

The floor creaked behind him and Alex knew there wasn't time to turn. He lunged sideways, gasping as he was forced to put weight on his bad leg. A pudgy, colored man stepped forward with a short club in his hand, swinging right for Alex's skull. He hadn't expected Alex to move, so his aim was off, but he still managed to rap Alex on his back.

Grunting in pain, Alex turned, and bringing his borrowed .38 to bear, he fired twice at point blank range. The man staggered back but kept his grip on the club. Shock and then anger played across his dark face, and he drew back the club again.

"Stop," Alex said, aiming the pistol at the man's heart.

He didn't stop, and Alex put two more rounds into him. This time he fell forward, slamming into Alex and driving him into the wall. Pictures rained down as Alex's head bounced painfully off the paneling and before he knew what was happening, he found himself sitting on the floor with the colored man staring up at him from lifeless eyes.

Beyond the dead man, Alex could make out an opening in the wall. It was a concealed door he'd missed, being too preoccupied with the pictures.

The mistake that had nearly cost him his life.

Stupid.

Alex was still looking at the opening when a second shadow appeared. Alex raised the gun and pulled the trigger, but the cylinder clicked empty.

"I told you to stay put," Lilith said, emerging from the dark beyond the opening with a half-smile. "What would you have done if I was one of Connie's men?"

"I'd have thought of something," Alex said, still a bit groggy from hitting his head.

Lilith stepped over the dead man.

"Try to stay out of trouble till I get back," she said, moving past Alex. As she went, she reached out and began dragging the tip of the kukri along the paneling, gouging a long line in the wood.

"Where are you, Connie?" she called as she went. "Don't you want to play with me?"

She'd pitched her voice higher than normal, making her sound even more like a little girl. It sent shivers up Alex's spine.

He had more than half a mind to leave Torres and his men to their fate. His leg was still bleeding, and his head hurt from slamming into the wall, but he knew that somewhere under Lilith's murderous exterior was Jessica. The image of her came, unbidden, to his mind, standing by the gate to the back yard of the shop in her green scarf, just as she'd been when he first met her. He had to keep Lilith from destroying herself and Jessica in the process.

Pushing the broken picture frames and shattered glass away from him, Alex rolled onto his good leg. Using the wall for support, he pushed up into a standing position.

Or he tried to.

No sooner had he gotten up than a wave of dizziness washed over him and he slid back down the wall and into a sitting position. His vision went in and out for a few minutes and he was vaguely aware of gunshots coming from somewhere above him.

"Come on," he said through clenched teeth. "Pull yourself together."

After another minute, his vision finally stopped swimming around and focused. A picture lay on the floor and he forced himself to look at it, to see the people in it and the background. It was Torres standing next to a stunningly beautiful blonde woman. She reminded Alex of Carole Lombard. They stood in a theater, up on the stage with the house in the background. Torres was clearly taken with her, but she seemed to be posing for the picture on suffrage.

As the picture finally moved into focus and his mind cleared, Alex took a deep breath and leaned against the wall. Gathering himself, he began to push himself upward again.

"Stop that at once," Dr. Kellin's voice interrupted.

Alex slid back down, turning to look at the end of the hall. Dr. Kellin stood there, leaning against the wall. She was breathing heavily, and she struggled to pull on a man's button-up shirt. Alex could see her brassiere and her torso, including what appeared to be several bullet wounds. As he watched, the wounds rippled and shrank, closing until they spat out the expended slugs, sending them clattering to the floor. Alex had seen that kind of magic repair before, but only with powerful, and expensive, healing potions.

"Hi-ya Doc," Alex said, forcing a smile to his lips. "Just the person I wanted to see. I've got this little problem with my leg."

"Shut up," she snapped at him, moving slowly down the hall as she fumbled with the shirt buttons. When she reached Alex, she squatted down to look at his leg. She prodded the makeshift bandage and Alex grunted, trying to ignore the pain by focusing on Kellin's mis-buttoned shirt. "Stupid girl," she muttered.

"Isn't she...you?"

Kellin's face twisted into a mask of disgust, but only for a second before she looked down, unable to meet his gaze.

"You shouldn't have come," she insisted.

Alex chuckled at that.

"Yeah," he scoffed. "You were doing just fine when I showed up."

"I didn't..." She took a deep breath then looked back up at him. "I didn't want you to know the truth," she said. "About Jessica. About me."

"You figured with my dwindling life energy we wouldn't have to have this conversation?" Alex guessed.

"Something like that," she admitted.

"What about *your* life energy?"

Her eyes grew sad as she looked at him, but she didn't answer.

"You've been sacrificing your own life to power your transformation," he said. "Buying time to finish your polio cure. How much of your life do you have left?"

"You always were too smart for your own good," she said with half a smile. "How did you know?"

"Jessica has red hair," Alex said. "Just like you did when you were young. But Lilith's hair is white, like mine. It's a symptom of spending your life energy. I bet you only burn a little when you're Jessica, but Lilith has all that power, all that strength." He nodded to Dr. Kellin's shirt and the wounds behind it. "The ability to heal. You must really burn through it when you're her. So how much is left?"

"Almost none at all," she said without hesitation.

Alex thought he was prepared for that answer, but it still hit him hard. It wasn't just the doc who had been condemned with that statement, it was Jessica too.

"This will have to come out," she said, pointing to the shard of glass that still stuck out of Alex's leg. Her usual brusque professional manner had returned. It was almost as if she hadn't just told him she was dying. "Come on," she said, standing and offering him a hand up.

She helped Alex limp back to the lab and had him sit on one of the worktables.

"I don't have my usual potions," she said, producing a sealed vial from her bag. "But this will close the wound and keep it from bleeding."

Being careful not to disturb the glass shard, Dr. Kellin unwound the bandage and removed the handkerchief. Immediately the wound began seeping blood, so she gently pulled out the glass and poured a stinging powder into the hole from the little vial.

Alex grunted in pain, clamping his jaw shut. After a few minutes, the pain began to subside, and he could breathe normally again.

"Thanks," he said, swinging his legs off the side of the table so he could sit properly.

Dr. Kellin had moved to the back of the room where Charles Grier was still sleeping peacefully in his cot. She bent down and retrieved a green medical bag like the kind Alex kept his kit in, then returned.

"I'm going to need your help, Alex," she said, digging around in the kit until she found a white leather case. She opened it, taking a large syringe from it and laying it on the table.

"I wouldn't be any good with that," he said.

"That isn't what I'll need help with," she said. Picking up the needle, she held it facing toward her and in an almost casual manner, pressed it into the crook of her left arm.

Alex winced but Dr. Kellin didn't even flinch. She pulled out the plunger until the syringe was full of dark red blood, then she withdrew it.

"I need you to take this to Dr. Miles Phillips," she said, squirting the blood into a glass vial. "You'll find him at the Chadwick Sanatorium in Albany." She jammed a rubber stopper into the top of the vial, then repeated the process with a second one. "This one is for my daughter, Linda," she said, pressing the first vial into Alex's hand. "Dr. Philips will know what to do."

Alex dropped the vial into his shirt pocket.

"All right," he said. "Now take it easy. As soon as Danny gets here, we'll head up to Albany together."

Dr. Kellin picked up the second vial.

"Put this one in your icebox," she said, ignoring him. "Keep it cold. If the cure works on Linda, Dr. Phillips can use this one to try to synthesize a general cure."

"And if the cure doesn't work on Linda?"

"Then this is a second chance," she said.

Alex took the second vial and added it to his pocket with the first.

"Is Torres..." he began without thinking.

"Dead," Dr. Kellin said. She leaned heavily against the table and Alex felt like a heel. "As I told you, the potion lowers inhibitions."

"You'll get no judgement from me," Alex said, sliding off the table to stand beside her, his injured leg stinging. "But if he's gone, we don't really have to wait for the cops. Let's get going, right now. I'll smooth it over with Danny later."

She turned and suddenly sagged against him. Alex stumbled back as her weight suddenly came down on his injured leg, and he was forced to lay her on the floor or risk falling.

"Come on, Doc," he said, cradling her against him. "Don't do this now."

She opened her eyes and looked up at him.

"You were right about Lilith," she said. "She drained my life energy. I don't have any left."

Alex thought desperately.

"The rejuvenator," he said.

"It won't help," she said, reaching up to touch his face. "At this point it wouldn't even give me five minutes. I fought the good fight, Alex, but my time is up."

Alex wanted to say something, but what was there to say?

"I don't regret it," she said, then locked eyes with him. "Any of it."

Alex nodded, not sure what else to do.

"A parent would do anything for their kid," he said, remembering Leslie's words.

"That's not what I meant. Well, not all of it, anyway. The potion, it—"

"Lowers inhibitions," he finished.

"No," she said, her voice gentle. "It gave me a gift. We...I...got to love again. I got to love you."

Alex took her hand in his and squeezed it.

"I do, you know," she said, her voice getting frail. "I love you."

"I love you too, Andrea," he said, and meant it.

"It wasn't supposed to be like this," she said, her eyes getting a far-away look. "You were supposed to go first. Then you'd never know what...what a horrible person I am."

She was smiling, as if she spoke in jest, but Alex could tell the smile was an attempt to hide the truth of those words from herself.

"You spent your own life to save your daughter," he said softly. "And you came here to try to save Charles Grier. You are a good person, Andrea."

"Thank you, Alex," she said, slurring her words slightly. "Would it be okay if I waited for you? You know, on the other side?"

"Of course," Alex said with a mirthless chuckle. "I have a feeling you won't be waiting long."

Andrea smiled as if she'd heard him, but she was past hearing. After a long moment, he gently closed her eyes, then leaned down to plant a kiss on her forehead.

Alex lifted Andrea as gently as he could with his injured leg, and laid her on one of the workbenches. He wanted to cover her, but he would have to go upstairs to get a sheet, and he simply didn't have time for that. He did take the time to re-button her borrowed shirt, so it was straight, then he took off his suit coat and laid it over her, covering her face.

Grunting with every step, Alex limped back toward the foyer until he reached the kitchen and found a phone mounted on the wall.

"Mr. Lockerby," Sorsha Kincaid's secretary answered. "I've been trying to reach you. Miss Kincaid wanted you to know that she hasn't had any luck locating Dr. Burnham's notebook and she recommends you get your secretary, Dr. Bell, and Miss O'Neil out of town right away."

Alex gripped the receiver and took a deep breath to cover the raw emotion boiling up inside him.

"I need you to get a message to your boss," he said once he found his voice. "Tell her I know where the notebook is, and I know who took it. She needs to come get me and I'll explain everything." He gave the young man Connie Torres' address and then hung up.

Next he called Iggy and told him to pick up Leslie and get out of the city. To his credit, Iggy didn't argue and promised to be on the move within the hour. Alex thanked him and hung up.

Outside, he could hear the sound of cars pulling up in a hurry, their brakes squeaking. He ignored the locked front door and headed through the back hallway to the lab and onward to the far hall with the pictures and the dead man. Bending carefully, he retrieved the empty .38 and the picture from the broken frame, carrying them back to the lab and laying them on the workbench next to Dr. Kellin's body.

From the front of the house came the sound of the police breaking down the front door. Alex looked down at Andrea and sighed.

"Sorry Doc," he said. "I'm going to have to keep you waiting, just a bit longer."

29

THE PRODIGAL

By the time Sorsha arrived at Connie Torres' house there were no less than two dozen police officers going over every inch of the place. Alex had given his statement to Danny when he'd arrived with the cavalry. He mostly told the truth, though he left out the part about Andrea and Lilith being the same person. Danny knew Alex well enough to know he was covering up something, but he didn't press.

"All right, I'm here," Sorsha said, sweeping into the lab. She sounded both eager and irritable, and she looked as tired as Alex felt. She'd tried to cover up the dark circles under her eyes with makeup, but this late in the day it was showing through.

"Hey, Danny," Alex called, and a moment later his friend appeared from the picture hallway.

"Jesus, Alex," he said as he crossed the room. "You said it was bad, but this is worse than before. What's left of Connie Torres is barely recognizable."

Sorsha made a disgusted face, seeming to see the room for the first time. The bodies of Flat-Face and the blond thug had been covered with sheets, as had Dr. Kellin.

"Danny," Alex said, pointing at Sorsha. "You remember Miss Kincaid; she works with the FBI."

Danny put on the smile he reserved for important people.

"Delighted to see you again," he said with the smooth grace that made him a favorite of the ladies. "I wish it could be under better circumstances. What is the FBI's interest in this mess?"

"Detective Pak," she said, returning his smile, then she looked at Alex. "I need to borrow your friend for the foreseeable future."

"Actually," Alex said before Danny could respond. "I need to talk to both of you...privately."

Danny raised an eyebrow, but turned to the three policemen in the lab.

"I need the room for a minute, boys," he said. "Why don't you go have a smoke?"

The cops didn't look a gift horse in the mouth, they just nodded and filed out.

"Okay," Danny said, turning to Alex. "What didn't you tell me about all this?"

Alex sighed. He didn't want to talk about what had happened, but there was just too much that needed to be done and he could feel himself running out of time. He told them both about Andrea's college project, about Leon's Libation and how it had killed four college kids. He explained how Andrea had partially perfected it, how she'd used it to give her time to develop a potential cure for her daughter, and how Connie had sought to use it, mistakenly believing that Charles Grier knew the secret.

"So Lilith was..." Danny began but stopped, unable to finish the sentence.

"Dr. Kellin," Sorsha finished. Her face was as cold and analytical as ever, but Alex detected a softness in her voice.

"Jessica," he corrected. "Yes."

"I'm very sorry, Alex," Sorsha said, and he could tell she meant it.

"There's no time for that," Alex said, wanting to push past the awkward moment. "You've got to collect everything about Dr. Kellin's rejuvenator," he said to Danny. "Every formula, every note, and especially that flask. The cops won't know what any of it is, so they won't care if it goes missing from evidence."

Danny looked aghast. Alex had asked him to turn a blind eye to things in the past, but stealing evidence was way beyond that.

"Don't," Alex said, as his friend was about to object. "This potion grants youth, strength, and lowers inhibitions. Just imagine what an unscrupulous man could do with it." He turned to Sorsha. "Or an unscrupulous government."

Danny whistled at the thought, shaking his head.

"He's right," Sorsha said to Danny. "Word of this can't go beyond the three of us. You make sure to collect everything here and I'll go out to Columbia and get the rest."

"Can I trust you with this, Sorceress?" Alex asked, looking her right in the eye.

She drew herself up as if she was going to shout at him, but she only nodded.

"Good," Alex said. He hadn't been certain they would agree with him, but he had to make sure the rejuvenator remained a secret.

"I hate to be impertinent," Sorsha said after a brief silence descended between them. "I believe you have something else to tell me, about a certain notebook."

Alex nodded, then patted Danny on the shoulder.

"Do me a favor," he said. "Once you finish up here, go see your sister."

Danny's brows furrowed at that.

"She's in Philadelphia," he said.

Alex nodded and Danny's furrowed brows grew into a scowl.

"What else aren't you telling me?" he demanded.

"Nothing he's at liberty to tell you," Sorsha interjected.

"It's nothing you can help with," Alex assured him. "Just go see Amy."

Danny met his eyes for a long moment, then nodded.

"All right," he said. "But you and I are going to have a serious talk about your keeping me in the dark."

"Looking forward to it," Alex said, then he put out his hand. "But...if I don't get the chance...you take care of yourself."

Danny hesitated only for a moment, then shook Alex's offered hand.

"Likewise," he said. He could tell Alex meant more by the gesture than he let on, and he accepted it without comment. Alex wished he could take more time, say a proper goodbye to his best friend, but like most things in his current existence, there just wasn't time.

Danny nodded at Sorsha, then headed for the door to the picture hallway.

"I'll just go find that flask," he said, then he was gone.

"I know you wanted more time," Sorsha said. "But if there's a chance we can save New York from burning, then we need to hurry."

"I need you to promise me something first," Alex said.

Sorsha drew in a breath to argue, but something in Alex's stern look stopped her. Alex reached into his pocket and drew out the two vials of Dr. Kellin's blood.

"Can you keep these cold?" he asked, handing them to her.

She half closed her eyes in a chastising look, then held up the two glass vials. As Alex watched, they fogged up, like spectacles taken from the cold into a hot room. After a moment, she pulled her handbag out of thin air and placed them gently inside.

Alex repeated Andrea's instruction about where to take them and who to give them to.

"Next, I need you to find a place for Leslie," he said. "You've got a big company, so I'm sure you can find something for her to do. Make sure she's got a job."

Sorsha's eyes narrowed, and then her face blanched.

"Oh," she said, realizing the meaning behind his requests. "I'll see to it. Now, about that missing notebook."

"It's in Admiral Tennon's office," Alex said. "Call him and tell him we're coming to see him and have him bring Commander Vaughn along."

"You think one of them has it?" she guessed.

"I don't want to explain it twice," he said, pointing to his ripped trousers. "I've got a spare suit in my vault. "I'll change while you make the call, then you can magic us over there."

Teleportation was Alex's least favorite way to travel, and that included being shot out of a cannon. The closest thing he could imagine to the sensation was being put through a clothes wringer and squeezed flat, then being rolled up and pushed through a dark pipe. Normally the experience left him trembling with his heart racing, but after the night he'd had, he simply dropped to his knees and vomited when he and Sorsha appeared outside the little building that housed Admiral Tennon's office.

He'd managed to turn away from Sorsha, but she was having her own problems, gasping for air and unable to stand up. Finally, Alex managed to stop his trembling and force himself to stand. He wiped his mouth with his handkerchief, then helped Sorsha to her feet.

"You really know how to show a girl a good time," Sorsha said, as he pulled her up off the ground.

"Funny," he said, taking her arm and heading for the door.

The last time Alex had checked his watch it was about six, so he was sure it was after seven by now. The offices in the poorly-constructed little building were empty and dark except for the one at the end of the hall. The pudgy Commander Vaughn sat on Lt. Leavitt's desk with the receiver of the telephone pressed to his ear. He waved them forward when he saw Alex and Sorsha.

"I don't care about that," he was saying into the receiver. "He's got one good engine, tell him to get underway immediately, and that's an order."

Vaughn hung up, then stood.

"Sorry about that," he said. "We've been moving ships all day."

"I thought you did that days ago?" Alex said.

Vaughn laughed.

"Moving a big ship isn't like launching a yacht," he said. "Just getting the provisions and fuel on board can take days."

He moved to the Admiral's door and knocked, then pushed it open. Admiral Tennon sat behind his desk, also on the phone. A mountain of paperwork littered his desktop and he looked both tired and irritable.

"Just a minute," Tennon said, looking at Vaughn. "Is the *Carolina* underway?"

"Within the hour," Vaughn replied.

Tennon nodded and pressed the receiver back to his ear.

"The *Carolina*'s on her way out," he said. "Tell Captain Falwell to depart as soon as she's clear of the harbor." He hung up the phone and stood, facing Sorsha. "As you can see, Miss Kincaid, we're all quite busy, so please tell me why you're here."

Sorsha looked expectantly at Alex.

"We need Dr. Burnham's notebook," Alex said as if that were a perfectly reasonable request, like asking a librarian for a copy of the almanac.

"What are you talking about?" Tennon roared. "You know very well we don't have it."

"I hate to disagree with you, Admiral," Alex said, "but it's inside your safe."

"What utter nonsense," Tennon growled, looking at Sorsha. "I've got important work to do and you're wasting my time."

"Indulge me," she said with a winsome smile.

Tennon clenched his fists for a moment, but then he relaxed, though he did roll his eyes as he opened his desk drawer and pulled out a black, pasteboard notebook. He went to the cabinet that concealed his safe and pulled it open before consulting the book. As he began to dial the combination, Sorsha leaned close to Alex and the smell of her rose oil perfume washed over him.

"If the notebook is in that safe," she whispered, "then why couldn't your finding rune locate it?"

"That's a Chubb fireproof safe," Alex whispered back.

Tennon cranked the lever and pulled the heavy door open.

"I can see that," Sorsha said. "That's why the door is so thick, it's lined with insulation."

"And magical shielding," Alex added.

"Well?" Tennon said, motioning to the open safe. "I don't know what you're looking for, but it's not here. Care to explain yourself?"

Alex felt his blood go cold. He remembered the inside of that safe very well and now something *was* missing. The leather folio that had occupied the far side of the bottom slot was gone. Alex looked back toward the outer office, finally realizing what he'd failed to notice on their way in.

"Where is Lieutenant Leavitt?" he asked.

"In sick bay," Vaughn said. "He wasn't feeling well."

"Wait," Sorhsa said, grabbing Alex's arm. "You think Leavitt stole Burnham's machine?"

"That's absurd," Tennon barked, his face clouded with anger. "Leavitt is a fine and dutiful officer. He didn't even know about Project: Shade Tree."

"And he wouldn't know any Chinese nationals," Vaughn added.

Alex gave Admiral Tennon a flat look.

"Of course he knew about Shade Tree," Alex said. "He has access to your safe and takes notes in your meetings." He reached into his pocket and pulled out the folded-up picture he'd taken from Connie Torres' home, passing it to Sorsha. "As for Chinese nationals, the Lieutenant does know some through his connection with his father."

"Who the devil is Leavitt's father?" Tennon demanded.

"William Henderson," Alex said.

"The U.S. Ambassador to China?" Vaughn asked.

"That can't be, Alex," Sorsha said. "Henderson only has one child, David Henderson, and he died three years ago."

"No," Alex disagreed. "He didn't. Remember, David was an embarrassment to his father, so dear old dad cut him off without a penny."

"Served him right, from what I remember," Tennon said. "That boy was a lout."

"True, but he was Henderson's only son," Alex went on. "He didn't want his son living on the streets, he wanted to teach him a lesson."

"And what better way to whip a wayward child into shape than in the Navy," Sorsha guessed.

"Exactly," Alex said. "Daddy fabricates the story about David's death and then buys him a commission. Probably uses his influence to get David a nice cushy job as an admiral's aide."

"I refuse to believe any of this," Tennon said. "Lieutenant Leavitt's name isn't David, it's Randall."

Sorsha pulled her notebook out of the air and began flipping through the pages.

"David Henderson's middle name is Randall," she said.

"Now look at that picture," Alex said.

Sorsha pulled the folded picture from behind her notebook and opened it. After a moment she looked up quizzically at Alex.

"Who are these people?" she asked.

"That's Constantine Torres," Alex said, indicating the man. "He's an alchemist who made a fortune in cosmetics. And that," he pointed to the blonde woman, "is a famous Broadway star from the turn of the century. I recognized her from a picture I saw in Andrew Barton's office. He said she was in demand, with lots of suitors, but she married a swell and gave up acting."

"I know her," Sorsha said at last. "This is William Henderson's wife. She met us briefly when we interviewed him." Sorsha changed back to her notebook. "Yes. Her name is Jennifer."

"Now turn that picture over," Alex said, not bothering to hide his grin.

"Connie," Sorsha read after turning over the picture. "Best wishes, Jenny Leavitt."

"So David Randall Henderson, embarrassment to his important father, takes his mother's name and becomes Lieutenant Randall Leavitt," Alex said.

"But why would Lieutenant Leavitt steal Shade Tree?" Commander Vaughn asked.

"He did it for the money," Sorsha said. "His father cut him off because David was living it up, getting drunk at exclusive clubs, and smashing up cars. He probably hated his father for putting a stop to his fun."

"So he figured how to cash out," Alex said. "Steal a military secret and sell it to a government currently in a desperate war. A government where he already had contacts."

"But even if you're right," Vaughn said. "How does he get away? If he disappears, the Navy is going to go looking for him."

"That's the best part," Alex said. "The first time I came here, the

Lieutenant had a duffle under his desk. He said it was an emergency travel bag. The top was open, and I could see clothes in it."

"You think he ran for it?" Sorsha asked.

"No, he didn't have to run," Alex said. "He had a plan all worked out. Once he got paid, Lieutenant Randall Leavitt would mysteriously disappear, and the *Chicago* would sail with Seaman Tyler McCormick on board."

"The spy?" Tennon demanded.

Alex shook his head.

"No, McCormick was never a spy. He was Leavitt's alias, but when the fog showed up and delayed the *Chicago* from sailing, someone noticed that McCormick didn't exist."

"Why would he go from being a lieutenant to a seaman?" Tennon asked.

"Where was the *Chicago* going?" Alex said.

"Madrid," Tennon said with a nod of understanding.

"So when the *Chicago* didn't sail on time, Leavitt had to make a new plan," Sorsha said.

"He kept the money the Chinese paid him in Admiral Tennon's safe along with Dr. Burnham's notebooks," Alex said. "All he had to do was wait for the Admiral to end the lockdown and he could just walk out the front gate."

"But then he learned that the fog might combust and burn the city down," Vaughn said. "So he had to escape before that happened."

"Commander Vaughn," Tennon said, standing up straight. "Would you call over to the duty officer in the infirmary and ask him to escort Lieutenant Leavitt back here under guard."

"Don't bother," Alex said. "There was a big leather folio in your safe the last time I was here. It was the only place big enough to hide the notebooks and whatever cash Leavitt got from the Chinese...and it's gone now."

"And so is Leavitt," Sorsha guessed.

"No," Tennon said. "The base is still on lockdown. He has to be somewhere."

"He probably tried the Tyler McCormick trick again," Vaughn said. "He has access to the base clerks; he could easily have forged records for another new seaman and had him assigned to one of the outgoing ships. All he would have to do is show up at roll call."

"How many ships have you sent out in the last few days, Admiral?" Sorsha asked.

"Eighteen," he responded.

"Eleven of them are just waiting outside the fog," Vaughn said, "but the remaining seven are bound for other ports."

"It doesn't matter," Tennon said. "Now that we know his game, we'll find his forged orders and have him arrested as soon as the ships make port. He won't get away with this."

"I'm afraid that won't be good enough, Admiral," Sorsha said. "I spoke with Andrew Barton today. He informed me that his generators have been losing power ever since the fog appeared."

"It's taking more and more power to keep the fog together," Alex guessed.

Sorsha nodded at him and continued.

"If the drain on Empire Tower continues at the current rate, Andrew believes his generators will fail sometime around noon tomorrow. If we don't find Leavitt and Dr. Burnham's notebooks very soon, this city will burn."

30

THE NOTEBOOK

"We need to search those seven ships right now, Admiral," Sorsha said. "There's no telling how long it will take Dr. Burnham to formulate his counter agent to the fog."

"I'm afraid that won't help, ma'am," Commander Vaughn said. "Each of those ships have hundreds of men on board; it will take hours to search them."

"And if Leavitt's really been planning this, he will have figured out how to avoid a search," Admiral Tennon said.

Alex reflexively checked his watch. If Andrew Barton was right about his generators, then the city had less than eighteen hours of life left to it.

He knew the feeling.

Still, there were only a limited number of places Leavitt could have gone. All he needed to do was narrow the list down to a single ship.

"What about your finding rune?" Sorsha said, turning to Alex.

He shook his head.

"He would have boarded whatever ship he's on right after calling in sick this morning," he said. It was a guess, but it made sense. "There'll be too much water between him and us for the rune to work."

"Well what can we do?" she asked, looking pointedly at him. "Finding missing people is supposed to be your specialty, after all."

"I'll order those seven ships back to base," Tennon said.

"We'd still have to search them when they got here," Vaughn said. "It's the same problem."

"You said he had to fake some kind of paperwork to get on whatever ship he's on, right?" Alex asked Vaughn.

The lieutenant commander nodded.

"He'd have to have orders in whatever name he's using," Vaughn said. "He could fake those pretty easy with his access, but the ship would have to have that name on its crew list. That list comes from the base clerk's office."

"So how would he get his fake name on that list?" Alex pressed.

"He'd have to create a fake file for that sailor and slip it into the base records office," Vaughn said. "Then he'd send a letter from the Admiral's office ordering that sailor to report for the ship he wanted. The clerk would pull the record and make sure it was in order, then add the name to the ship's official list."

Sorsha gasped.

"You can use a finding rune to locate the file."

"I doubt it," Alex said. "Even if we had something that was important to Leavitt to use as a catalyst, I doubt the file was anything other than a means to an end. Finding runes require an intimate connection to be effective. That said, I think Leavitt's fake file is our best chance of finding him."

"And how do you propose to do that, Mr. Lockerby?" Admiral Tennon said. "We have over twenty-thousand records here. Searching the ships would be faster."

"But can't we narrow the search?" Sorsha asked, turning to Vaughn. "You said that the names of everyone on each of those ships was on a master list, right?"

Vaughn nodded.

"The crew manifest," he said. "But if we only pull the records for those seven ships, that still leaves us with over a thousand men."

"Then we'd better get started," Sorsha declared. "Unless anyone has a better idea."

"I'll round up the clerical staff and get them started pulling the records," Vaughn said, turning toward the outer office.

"Tell them not to start until we get there," Alex said. "I think I can narrow our search even further, but I'll need some equipment first."

Vaughn shrugged and nodded, then headed out to the telephone on Leavitt's desk.

"What are you thinking?" Sorsha wondered as Alex pulled a vault rune from his red book.

"Leavitt would have made that file himself," he said, chalking a door shape on the Admiral's wall. "He wouldn't have trusted work like that to anyone else."

"What are you doing, Lockerby?" Tennon protested.

Alex ignored him and lit the rune, stepping back as the polished steel vault door melted out of the wall. He unlocked it with his heavy skeleton key and pulled it open. Heading inside, he opened the secretary cabinet where he kept his kit bag and spare investigation equipment.

"So you're thinking that since it's the only file Leavitt handled, you'll be able to use a finding rune after all?" Sorsha asked, following him inside.

Alex grinned at her but shook his head.

"No," he said, topping off his silverlight burner from a stoppered bottle on a nearby shelf. "But we don't need fancy runes to find Leavitt's new identity."

"What is this place?" Admiral Tennon asked, his voice full of wonder. He'd followed Sorsha inside the vault and was looking around with an astonished expression on his face.

"Some runewrights can create extra-dimensional spaces for themselves," Sorsha explained.

"I didn't think runewrights had that kind of power," he admitted.

"Most don't," Alex said, pulling a box full of mismatched work gloves from a box on the bottom of a shelf.

"Do you have any idea of the size of the Captain's cabin on a warship?" he growled. "You could fit six of them in this room."

Alex chuckled.

"There's a bedroom and a kitchen down that way," he said, pointing to the hall.

Tennon gave him a hard look.

"I hate you," he said with no trace of a smile.

"I'm afraid you'll have to get in line for that one, Admiral," Sorsha said with a raised eyebrow. "Alex tends to have that effect on people. Now," she said, fixing Alex with her steely gaze. "How are we supposed to find Lieutenant Leavitt's counterfeit file among a thousand others?"

"Like I said," Alex explained, leading everyone back out of his vault. "Leavitt would have made the doctored file himself. Now a clerk might have checked it before putting that sailor's name on the manifest, but all the other records would have been handled by dozens of people."

"So you're going to use your fancy lamp to find the one folder without fingerprints all over it," Sorsha said as she figured out Alex's plan. "Very clever."

"That's why the clerks will need to wear these," he said, holding up the box of gloves. "We don't want any new prints on those files."

The clerical office and records depository for the base was in a large building a short walk from the Admiral's offices. Unlike Tennon's shoddy building, the records were housed in a very solid-looking brick structure. When they arrived, a dozen grumpy-looking sailors were already gathered in the front office.

Admiral Tennon told them what to do, and had them don gloves from Alex's box, and soon there was a steady stream of personnel records flowing out of the back room.

Alex strapped on his oculus and lit his silverlight burner, examining each of the folders and the files inside carefully. Most were obviously not new, and he put them in a pile to be returned to the long line of file cabinets where they were stored. Occasionally one would look newer than the rest and he'd set those aside, intending to review them while the clerks fetched new records.

At the end of two hours Alex had only managed to get through half of the records, and of those, only five had been set aside for review.

"How will you determine which file is Leavitt's?" Sorsha asked, as the clerks brought another stack of folders for Alex to review.

"I assumed it would be obvious," Alex said, picking up the first folder on the new stack. It was dirty and covered with prints, but he'd learned not to judge a file by its cover. Apparently the Navy reused the folders, and so he opened the file and began flipping pages. He stopped when he found one with a coffee stain in the shape of a mug bottom. Leavitt wouldn't have bothered to add an old stain to his file.

"I'll have to go back to his desk and see if I can find one of his fingerprints," Alex said, setting the first folder aside and picking up the next one. "Then I can try to match it to one of the clean files."

Sorsha looked troubled at that.

"What?" Alex said, trying not to snap at her in his irritation.

"I was talking to Vaughn while you were working," she said. "He told me that Leavitt would have known how to put together a fake file because he was responsible for pulling any file the Admiral might want to see. He's probably pulled hundreds of them in the last six months alone."

Alex groaned.

"It's still the best chance we've got," Alex said, opening the next folder. "If nothing else, we can just have the various ship captains detain all these men. Though I don't know how we'll be able to tell which one is Leavitt until they return to port."

"You won't have to," Admiral Tennon said. He'd been sitting in the corner looking through the files Alex had set aside. When Alex turned to look at him, he held up the folder he had open on his lap. "This one is Leavitt. Seaman First Class Andrew Frakes."

Alex took off his oculus.

"What makes you think that?" he asked, moving over to read over Tennon's shoulder.

"Look here," the Admiral said, pointing to the list of ships where Seaman Frakes had served. "All these ships are operating in the Pacific," he said. "According to the file, Frakes has been in for three years. Two months ago his mother got sick, so he was granted hardship leave and sent here to care for her. Once his leave was up, he was reassigned to the Atlantic Fleet."

"So Frakes is an outsider," Sorsha said. "No one he's serving with would have any reason to know him."

"Exactly," Tennon said. "It's the perfect cover."

"It could also be a coincidence," Alex pointed out. He made it a personal maxim never to believe in coincidences, but that didn't mean they didn't sometimes happen.

"No," Tennon said. "I don't think so." He pointed to the name of one of the ships on the list. "The *Minotaur* is a supply ship," he said. "She makes the run between San Diego and Pearl. She's also where the Admiralty dumps all their hard cases and their shirkers."

"Why is that significant?" Sorsha asked.

Tennon turned the pages of the file. There weren't many.

"Because," he said. "Anyone assigned to the *Minotaur* would have a disciplinary file as long as your arm. Seaman Frakes here has never even been written up for smoking on guard duty."

"Is that rare?" Alex asked.

"I have three of those in my file," Tennon said.

"So where is Seaman Frakes right now?" Sorsha wondered.

Tennon checked the front of the file.

"According to this, he's on the *Tripoli*. She's a cargo hauler bound for Liverpool."

"Where is the *Tripoli* now?" Sorsha asked.

"Looks like you were right about Leavitt leaving early, Mr. Lockerby," the Admiral said, closing the file. "The *Tripoli* sailed this morning. She's headed out across the Atlantic."

"Can you contact the *Tripoli* by radio? Sorsha asked.

"Sure," Tennon said with a nod. "Her captain and I came up together. But I doubt anyone on board will know enough about chemistry to understand Dr. Burnham's notes."

"They won't have to," she said. "If I can hear his voice, I can teleport to him. Then I'll find Leavitt, retrieve the notebook, and take it to Dr. Burnham directly."

Alex didn't know sorcerers could do that. He had a sudden flash of all the times he'd provoked her over the phone. He wanted to promise himself he wouldn't do that again, but that was a promise he knew he would break the next time he had a chance.

Captain Cross of the *Tripoli* was a no-nonsense old salt who disliked being summoned to the radio room, even by an admiral.

"What's this about, Walter?" his gravelly voice came through the radio in the harbormaster's office. "I've got a ship to run."

"Stow it, Dan," Tennon barked into the microphone. "I need to know if you have a Seaman First Class Andrew Frakes aboard."

"Everybody on my manifest checked in," Cross said.

"Check, damn it," Tennon ordered.

"All right," Cross capitulated. "Give me a minute."

"You think he might have gotten on a different ship?" Sorsha asked.

Tennon shrugged.

"I think it's good to make sure before you send yourself a hundred miles out to sea."

"You there, Walter?" Cross's voice cut through the static. "According to the list, Frakes checked in. He's on board."

"Good," Tennon said. "I want you to send two of your best men to arrest him."

Alex put up his hand and Tennon's eyes darted to him.

"What if he fights them?" he said. "If they shoot Leavitt, we might never get the notebook."

"Belay that, Dan," Tennon said into the mic. "I'm here with Sorsha Kincaid."

"Who?"

"She's a sorceress here in New York. I want you to read your logs over the radio. She's going to use your voice to travel to the *Tripoli*."

"That's the dumbest thing I've ever heard, Walter," Cross declared. "If you want Seaman Frakes, my men can get him, easy enough."

"Leave Frakes to the Sorceress," Tennon said. "That's an order, Dan. Now start reading your logs."

"Yes, sir," he grumbled. "Give me a minute."

The radio lapsed into silence and Sorsha turned to Alex.

"How many finding runes do you have on you?" she asked.

Alex consulted his rune book.

"Three," he said. "Why? You know right where Leavitt is."

"Cargo ships have lots of places to hide," she said. "I don't want to waste time searching the ship when all we need is his toothbrush and you can lead me right to him."

Alex groaned. He'd thought it would be something like that. It meant he would have to teleport again.

When Alex and Sorsha arrived on the *Tripoli* the sky was clear and dark. When Alex finally managed to shake off the effects of the teleport, he marveled at how clear the sky looked. He hadn't seen it in almost a week.

Sorsha had managed to locate the cargo ship after the Captain read his logs for the better part of fifteen minutes. She said it took so long because the ship was moving and bobbing on the ocean. Alex suspected the technique of finding a person by listening to his voice was somewhat imprecise and dangerous. As it was, the sorceress dropped them on the bow, well away from the bridge.

The reaction of the sailors who were on watch was priceless. Both of the big men had yelled in near panic and scrambled away from the place where Alex and Sorsha appeared. Alex chuckled as he helped Sorsha stand.

By the time they both had their sea legs under them, Captain Cross had come down from the bridge. He wasn't at all what Alex imagined from the radio. He'd pictured a shriveled, bent old man, probably with an eye patch. Cross turned out to be a short barrel of a man with enormous, calloused hands, a weathered face, and a jaw that looked to be carved of granite.

"So what's this fella Frakes done anyway?" he asked as he came ambling up to where Sorsha was still trying to catch her balance. She'd been wearing heels and hadn't thought to take them off before appearing on the rolling ship.

"He's stolen critical information from the government," Sorsha said. It wasn't exactly a lie and it communicated everything the short-tempered captain needed to know so Alex let it go without comment.

"He's a spy?" Cross spat. "You should have just let me arrest him."

"He has a notebook that we need to get back at all costs," Sorsha said. "Where is he now?"

Cross motioned a uniformed man with a clipboard to come forward.

"He's in the galley," Cross said after consulting the clipboard.

"Lead me there," Sorsha said. "But keep your men back, I'll handle Seaman Frakes myself."

Cross turned and motioned for Sorsha to follow, then headed off across the deck. Alex fell into line behind them. He followed Sorsha and the captain into the ship and down two levels. The Captain entered a narrow hall that seemed to run the length of the ship, but when Alex turned to follow, he felt the muzzle of a pistol shoved into his back.

"Hello Lockerby," Leavitt's voice came softly in his ear. "I just knew you were going to be trouble."

"I guess you should have killed me when you had the chance, David" Alex said.

"How do you know that name," he snarled.

"I know everything," Alex said. "How do you think I found you?"

"I really don't care," he said, putting his free arm around Alex's neck and pulling him backward down the side passage. "Now you're going to help me escape."

Alex laughed at that.

"Escape to where?" he asked. "We're in the middle of the Atlantic."

Now it was David's turn to laugh.

"You don't think I just picked this ship out of a hat, do you?" he sneered. "The *Tripoli* has a Captain's Launch."

Alex had no idea what that might be.

"It's a little boat that hangs over the stern," David explained in annoyance. "It's not much, but it has a motor. That'll be enough to get me back to shore."

"I can do better than that," Alex said, still walking backwards as

David pulled him along. "Just give me the notebook and I'll help you escape."

Alex didn't expect David Henderson to accept that offer, but he laughed almost before Alex finished saying it.

"I can't do that," he said. "I need that notebook. The Germans will pay handsomely for it, and I'm going to need more than just what the Chinese paid me."

"What about New York?" Alex asked. "Your parents are still in the city."

"That's what makes this perfect," he sneered. "My precious father will burn when that machine finally runs out of fuel and I'll be laughing and rich on the Riviera."

They reached the end of the corridor and David took his hand away from Alex's neck long enough to open a metal door. He stepped back and used his pistol to motion for Alex to go through. Beyond the door, Alex found himself on a narrow catwalk suspended over the stern of the ship.

A small boat hung just beyond the catwalk. It had an engine with a round fuel tank in the stern, and was big enough to have a small area below its top deck. Alex didn't know much about boats, but he didn't relish the idea of being in the middle of the ocean in that tiny thing.

"Get on board," David said.

Alex did as he was told, then turned around as David dropped into the boat after him. He moved aft and grabbed hold of a thick rope that held the boat secure to the *Tripoli*.

"Go forward and take hold of that line," David said.

Alex just grinned at him.

"No, I don't think I will," he said.

"You think I won't shoot," David snarled.

"Actually, I think you would," Alex said. "You aren't very smart."

"Who's got the gun, here?" he said. "I'm more than smart enough for you." He held out the gun, leveling it at Alex's chest. "Now get on that line."

"And if you shoot me," Alex pointed out, "how will you escape? Who will take hold of the line and lower this boat into the water?"

David's face blanched. He clearly hadn't thought of that.

"Also," Alex went on. "Since you're ready to leave right this minute, I know you've hidden Dr. Burnham's notebook here on the launch. That was really very accommodating of you."

David's look of confusion and fear melted off his face and he smiled again. Clearly he'd thought of something at last.

"But if I shoot you, then I don't have to hold the gun," he said. "I can lower both lines by myself."

Alex had to admit, that was a fairly rational plan.

"Yes," he said, nodding with exaggerated sadness. "That would have worked, except for this."

He held out his closed right hand and when he opened it, he ignited his flash ring.

Alex couldn't shut his eyes until the very last second or David might have been tipped off. As it was, he'd been staring right at Alex's hand when the rune went off. He shrieked in furious anger and fired his pistol.

If Alex had stayed in one place he probably would have been hit, but he'd moved the instant the ring burst into blinding light. Stepping to the side, he charged across the little ship's deck and slammed into David, shoulder first. The gun went off again and the bullet hit something, ricocheting with a loud clang.

Alex's vision had barely cleared. He saw David sitting on the pilot's seat in the stern, having been knocked back into the engine. He was off-balance, but he still had the pistol clutched in his hand, so Alex slugged him across the jaw. David's head snapped back, but he recovered, trying to bring the gun up. Alex hit him again and he went down in a heap.

The smell of gasoline assaulted Alex as he reached down and took the gun from David. A gash in the gas tank showed where David's wild shot had hit it. They were both lucky the fuel hadn't ignited.

Tossing the gun overboard, Alex turned around and headed up to the bow. A small cargo box was stowed under the forward bench. Since it was the only place to store anything, Alex knew it must be the hiding place of Dr. Burnham's notebooks. Sure enough, when he opened the lid, he found the missing leather folio inside. Inside that, he found four black notebooks, one yellow one, and what looked like a hundred grand in cash.

"Alex," Sorsha's voice floated down to him. "What's going on?"

He looked up to see her along with Captain Cross leaning over the aft rail two decks above him. Alex pulled the yellow notebook from the folio and held it up so the sorceress could see.

"No," David yelled behind him.

Alex turned, surprised that the spoiled rich kid had shaken off being knocked unconscious so quickly. He was more surprised that David had the foresight to bring a second gun. He stood in the stern, pointing a .38 at Alex, and his eyes were wild. He'd lost his fortune and his wild lifestyle when his father had cut him off, and now that he was so close to getting it back, he wasn't going to let anything stand in his way.

"Wait!" Alex shouted, but it was far too late.

For Alex everything slowed down and several things happened at once. First, David fired his pistol. The gun sparked and flamed as it fired but in the damp air of the North Atlantic, it wasn't enough to ignite the spilled gasoline.

From above, Alex heard the deep, echoing voice that heralded Sorsha's magic. As the bullet leapt from the gun, it met a thick piece of ice that appeared in its path. The bullet ricocheted back, slamming into the engine. This time the spark was enough, and the gasoline ignited in a fireball.

David screamed as the flames engulfed him. They ran along the bottom of the boat, toward Alex, and upward over the rope that held the launch to the back of the *Tripoli*.

Alex turned and grabbed the rope attached to the front just as the back rope gave way and the launch tipped, spilling David, the folio, and the money into the ocean below. Heat and flames rushed toward Alex. He looked up and saw Sorsha looking down at him, her startled eyes wide.

The remaining rope that held the launch to the *Tripoli* was never meant to hold the entire weight of the little boat. With a groan the pulley that held it began to sag. Below Alex, the climbing fire began to lick his shoes and burn his legs.

He gripped the yellow notebook in his free hand, lowering it down by his waist, and then flung it upward toward the sorceress. With the sound of rending metal, the pulley gave way and the burning launch fell. Alex had a momentary vision of Sorsha reaching out and grabbing the notebook with her magic, then he hit the surface of the roiling sea, and it swallowed him whole.

31

THE LEVER

Alex had seen people dive before. They jumped off a platform and fell gracefully, their bodies knifing easily into water that seemed to gently arrest their fall. When the support holding the launch gave way, he had the presence of mind to push off, to get away from where the boat would fall, but instead of landing gently in the water, it felt like he'd been hit by a truck.

Air rushed out of his lungs and before he could suck in more, his body slipped beneath the rolling waves. Alex never learned to swim, and he struggled briefly as his sodden clothing dragged him down into the icy water. The cold seemed to seep into his bones and sap his muscles of their strength. He could see the ship above and the light from the burning gasoline, floating on the surface, but they seemed so very far away.

Blackness closed in around him and exhaustion overcame him. Somewhere, in the deepest, most primal reaches of his mind, he urged himself to fight. He wanted to struggle, to find the will to propel himself upward toward the light of the fire, and the life-giving air that waited on the surface, but the weariness simply wouldn't let him.

He floated like that, suspended in the water, between life and death — heaven and hell. As the all-encompassing darkness began to swallow his vision, Alex became suddenly aware of a light. Not the light of the fire; that had dwindled to a tiny point in his vision. This new light was brighter, and much closer.

Rousing himself, Alex looked down at his body. He'd heard stories of the afterlife, from Father Harry and others, about how the world dissolved into a plain of bright light. What he saw, glowing from beneath the front of his shirt, wasn't any opening to a dimension of light — it was a rune.

As Alex watched, the rune emerged from his shirt, hovering just off his chest and spinning gently. His drifting mind snapped back into focus. He knew that rune. It was an anchor rune, like the kind used to connect an escape rune with a specific location, only this one hadn't been drawn right. It was backwards.

No. Not backwards, but inside-out.

With the desire to see this rune, to know it, came the will to live. Alex flailed, gulping in a lung full of water before he could resist the urge. He began to panic, but then something seemed to grab him by his ribcage. The inside-out anchor rune pulsed and bent as if the center of the construct was tied to an invisible rope that pulled on it. The sensation came again, and Alex felt himself pulled along.

His lungs burned and it was all he could do to resist the biological imperative to breathe. The invisible line pulled again and this time the rune disappeared into his chest, drawn in by the irresistible force. When it touched him, Alex felt himself jerked backward, like a fish on the end of an angler's line. Water rushed around him as his body flew across miles in the blink of an eye and he landed heavily on the rough planks of a wooden floor.

Water that had been suspended around him moments before fell along with him, rushing away on the flat surface. Alex heaved himself up on his arms as the water flowed past his face, coughing and spluttering as he struggled to breathe. He managed three great, gasping lungfuls before his trembling arms gave out and he collapsed back to the floor. His head hit the heavy planks hard and the blackness that had threatened to encompass him in the deep rose up and finally claimed him.

"All right, boy," a strange voice said. "I can't wait around all day, there are things to do. Wakey, wakey."

The voice sounded like Iggy, but the accent was a bit different. Definitely British, though.

Something caustic filled Alex's nostrils and sent a jolt of adrenaline to his brain. He gasped and jerked his head up, which turned out to be a mistake. Pain erupted in his head, pounding relentlessly with the beating of his heart and threatening to crack his skull and ooze out his ears.

"Uh," he muttered as he struggled to open his eyes and keep them open. Dim light glowed in front of him and as his eyes came gradually into focus, Alex could see that he was in a long, wide room. Above him the ceiling sloped down and away from a central ridge beam, meaning wherever this was, he was in an attic. In front of him, about twenty yards away, was a large wooden door, like he'd seen in barns. Hanging from the ridge beam was a bare wire and a dirty lightbulb that cast a yellowish glow over Alex. The air reeked of manure and offal, and from somewhere below, he could hear the sounds of swine.

He tried to move, but couldn't. Looking down, Alex found himself sitting in a plain wooden chair with armrests on either side. Thick ropes wrapped around his forearms, securing him to the chair, and when he tried to move his legs, he found them similarly bound.

"Wha—" he began, but his mouth was dry and he had to force himself to swallow before he could go on. "Where am I?" he managed at last.

"An excellent question," a cultured British accent came from behind him. The floor creaked and a slender man of average height walked into view. He wore a well-made suit, but not an expensive one, with a white shirt, silver cufflinks, and several heavy-looking rings on his hands. His dark hair was longish, as if he hadn't been to his barber for a few months, and he was clean-shaven and handsome. Alex had trouble pinning down his age. He looked to be in his mid-forties, but his expression was that of a much younger man, while his eyes held a wisdom that seemed beyond his years.

"The question you should be asking, Alex, is 'Why am I here?'"

"Okay," Alex said, panting as the simple act of speaking seemed to be draining him of energy. "Why am I here?"

A look of consternation flashed across the man's face, but it didn't linger.

"You're here," he said, putting his hands behind his back, "because despite my best efforts, you keep trying to get yourself killed." He began to pace back and forth in front of the chair. "I'm really quite cross with you, Alex. Of course, spending your life energy to save the people of New York was a noble thing to do, but you seem to think your only option is to die as a result. Good God man, you've had two years to think your way out of that, and what have you done?" He turned to Alex, as if expecting an answer, but when Alex tried to reply, he went on. "Nothing, that's what you've done. You just sat in your little office, helping lots of little people with their little problems."

Alex wanted to point out that he'd done rather more than that, but he wasn't really sure what the Brit was talking about. And his tongue didn't seem to want to cooperate.

"It's been two years since you discovered that little red book on the shelf next to the one where you keep your spare cash," the man went on.

Alex's groggy mind flashed into razor focus, observing the man closely, sifting through every detail he could see. He wore a pocket-watch on a gold chain, real gold, not plated, since there was no tarnishing where the links rubbed together. His shoes were newly soled, but the style was old. None of this really helped, though.

"You've been in my home," Alex said. It wasn't an accusation. The only way he could know about Alex's cache and what was next to it on the bookshelf was if he'd actually been inside the brownstone.

"Well, now you're paying attention," the Brit said, turning to Alex with a self-satisfied smile. "It's about time. And yes, I've been in Dr. Doyle's home. I must confess, some of the protection runes he came up with were very impressive. It actually took me a bit to figure them out."

Alex felt his blood run cold. Whoever this Brit was, not only did he know about the Monograph, but he'd managed to get past Iggy's runes and past Iggy's false identity. Any one of those bits of information would ruin them both if they got out.

"The fishhook rune," Alex guessed, his mind finally running at full speed. "You would have to have put it on me while I was asleep."

"Ha!" The Brit laughed out loud and slapped his leg. "There's the mind I hoped for, very good. Fishhook rune," he nodded, an enormous, energetic grin splitting his face. "That's a good name for it. I think I'll call it that from now on."

"You're welcome?" Alex said, not sure what he'd done that had so amused the man.

"Don't you see?" the Brit said, leveling a finger right at Alex's nose. "You knew what to call that rune because you didn't just see it, you understood what it was. The only way you could have done that was if you had figured out what runes went into its creation. Not just anyone could have figured that out, boy. You've got a great mind for rune magic, and by God, it's time you started using it."

"Who are you?" Alex demanded. "And what is it you want?"

The Brit smiled, not a smile of mirth, but one that looked almost fatherly.

"My name isn't important," he said. "Suffice it for you to know that I am one of those whose hands made the Archimedean Monograph. I expounded upon the work of my former brothers and sisters, expanding it for the next generation. A work I hope to leave to you one day."

Alex shook his head. He didn't know how this fellow knew about Iggy and the Monograph, but he knew a con when he heard one.

"Iggy's had that book for over fifty years," he said.

The Brit's grin turned to one of mirth.

"And who do you think it was that allowed Dr. Doyle to learn of the cursed finding rune in the first place? Who do you think put his feet on the path that would lead him to unlocking its secrets?"

Alex didn't believe it, but one look and he knew that either the Brit believed every word coming out of his mouth, or he was the most spectacular liar in history.

"Doyle was a lot like you," the Brit went on. "He has an amazing mind. I assumed he would do as I had done. That he would devour the

The Long Chain

Monograph, tear it down to its foundations and ferret out all its secrets."

"But he didn't," Alex said. It wasn't a guess. Iggy had impressed upon him many times the dangerous temptations that lay in the power of the Monograph. Temptations Iggy was bound and determined to avoid.

The Brit sneered.

"No, he didn't. Doyle contented himself with sipping from the cup of knowledge when he should have drained it to the dregs. It's why he wasn't ready when the darkness came."

Alex shook his head. He thought he'd been following along, but he must have missed something.

"You've got to be better, Alex," the Brit went on, seemingly oblivious to Alex's confusion.

"What are you talking about?" Alex interjected.

The man looked at him with a cocked eyebrow, then shook his head.

"Have you ever heard the expression that those who don't know history are destined to repeat it?"

"Sure." Alex nodded. "It's a quote from Edmund Burke."

The Brit smiled briefly at that, then his face shifted back to a serious expression.

"Humans never seem to learn, Alex," he said. "Individuals can learn, but as a group, we just keep repeating the same mistakes over and over. It was just over twenty years ago that the shadows of war spread over Europe. They erupted into a conflict unlike any this little planet has ever known. People died on a scale that was unimaginable just a decade before."

"What does that have to do with Iggy or the monograph?"

The Brit looked sad at the question.

"I had hoped he would be ready when next the world teetered on the precipice. Ready to use the knowledge in the Monograph to pull the world back."

"That's a lot to expect from one storytelling doctor," Alex said.

"You say that because you don't understand what's really in the

DAN WILLIS

Monograph," the Brit said. "Dr. Doyle didn't understand, either. He let his fear control him."

"What's in the Monograph is dangerous," Alex said, a bit indignant at the stranger's characterization of Iggy. "There's nothing wrong with avoiding danger."

The Brit shook his head.

"Gunpowder is dangerous, Alex," he said. "Yet you carry enough to kill you twice over under your left arm, right next to your heart. Fire is dangerous. Yet people drive cars that contain fiery explosions inside their engines."

Fire.

Something about that word struck a chord in Alex's memory. Something he'd forgotten.

"The city," he gasped, surging weakly against his bonds. "You have to let me go."

The Brit watched him for a moment, then turned and walked away, toward the wall. When he reached it, he took hold of the barn door and pulled it open. Brilliant sunlight spilled in, temporarily blinding Alex. When he managed to force his eyes open again, he saw a dazzling blue sky and in the distance, the spire of Empire Tower. It appeared to be early afternoon and there was no trace of fog anywhere.

Alex's mouth dropped open and he sagged against his bonds as the burst of energy faded.

"Your efforts to retrieve Dr. Burnham's notebook were successful," the Brit said, pulling the door closed and plunging the attic room back into semi-darkness again. "The ravishing Sorceress and the good Doctor managed to dissipate the fog early this morning."

Something about the way he said 'ravishing' bothered Alex. He was about to ask how the man had known about Burnham's machine, but the answer was obvious — the same way he'd known Alex was about to drown in time to pull him to safety. The man had been watching him.

"Now," he said, walking back to where Alex sat. "The mistakes of the past are returning. A darkness is gathering, the same as it did twenty years ago."

"Are you saying there's going to be another war?" Alex wasn't sure he really wanted the answer to that question.

"Without doubt," he said. "Last time I assumed that it was the folly and stupidity of man that led to war. This time I know better. Dark forces are at work, Alex. They seek a war, they desire it. They exist to rule man, or failing that, to destroy him."

Alex shook his head.

"I don't know what you mean," he said.

"Don't you?" the man said in an amused voice. "How do you explain the sudden reappearance of ancient and long forgotten magics, of alchemy turned to a devastating weapon of disease, of science given the power to burn down whole cities at the flick of a switch?"

Alex felt his blood run chill.

"Yes," the Brit said. "You have seen it. Someone is preparing for war, Alex. They're weaponizing magic and science on a scale never before imagined, and you only know about the little bit you've seen. Think about how much you haven't seen."

Alex was thinking, and it scared him. The Great War had taken somewhere north of thirty million lives. The numbers were so high as to be almost meaningless, and this man was saying that not only would it happen again, but that it would be worse?

"Why are you telling me this?" Alex asked, his voice subdued.

"Another good question," the Brit said in a bright, energetic voice, as if he hadn't just predicted a second global war. "Are you familiar with the works of Archimedes?"

"You mean beyond the Monograph?" Alex asked. "I know he ran naked in the street when his bathtub overflowed."

The Brit tisked at him and shook his head.

"If you'd studied the Monograph more carefully, you'd know that there's a quote by Archimedes on the very first page. It goes, 'Give me a lever and a place to stand, and I will move the world.'"

"So — what?" Alex asked. "Are you telling me you're going to move the world?"

"Yes!" he exclaimed, clapping his hands together in glee. "Finally, you're beginning to understand — and it's about time, too."

Alex wanted to protest. He was pretty sure he didn't understand anything the Brit was saying, not really. Before he could think of a way to say that so he didn't come off sounding dense, the man continued.

"Unlike lesser men, I do learn from history," he said. He was speaking in a loud, dramatic voice and pacing back and forth, as if he were on stage or addressing the legislature. "I was far too lenient with Dr. Doyle, I see that now. I shall not make the same mistake twice."

He turned to Alex, reaching into the inside pocket of his suit coat. He withdrew a pasteboard book that resembled Alex's red-backed rune book exactly, except it had a dark blue cover. Opening it, the Brit tore out a single page and crumpled it up in his hand.

"You don't start out moving the world, Alex," he said. "You have to begin small and work up to it. So I'm going to start by moving you." He held the crumpled-up paper out on his open palm. "Here's a little motivation for you."

With that, he used his thumb to touch one of the heavy rings he wore. Alex saw a spark jump from the metal surface and ignite the flash paper. In one quick motion, the Brit threw the burning paper into the air and it flared into a long flame as it burned and vanished. It left a floating, deep blue rune behind.

Alex squinted at it, trying to recognize and remember every line and symbol. It reminded him of the rune on the bottom of his ghost-light burner, but it was much more complex.

The rune pulsed suddenly, then ignited into a cobalt blue light that was so bright it forced Alex to look away. When he did, he gasped. All around him, in a circle on the floor, were brilliant runes. They glowed the same color as the hovering rune, and Alex couldn't tell if they were naturally that color, or if that was a result of the light. As he studied the runes on the floor, he recognized some of them. There were three life runes joined to linking runes, anchor runes, and others he didn't know.

The strangest thing of all was that none of them appeared to have been written on the floor. They seemed to hover in place, just over the wooden boards, and they would occasionally ripple and move as if they were being viewed through water.

The runes on the floor pulsed like the hovering cobalt one had, preparing to activate. Alex shut his eyes tight as they flared to life, their brilliance dazzling him even through his eyelids. Below him, where he'd heard the swine before, came an unholy noise that raised the hair on his neck.

Alex had seen the operation of a slaughterhouse before. Once the swine were brought into a pen, a worker would hook each pig's rear leg to a chain that would then pull them up into the air. Once they were off the ground, a second man would slit their throats with a butcher knife and their carcasses would be sent into the factory for processing. As soon as the pig felt the pull of the chain it would begin squealing, the sound more than a simple squeal; it was a scream of mortal terror.

It was a sound Alex had never forgotten.

That same sound swelled up from the room below. The rune construct on the floor had three nodes that lifted up as if they were hinged, turning until they were all facing him.

The screaming of the pigs ended abruptly, as if it had been a recording that someone had simply switched off. Around Alex, the three runes glowed with a greenish light, then they shot forward, converging on him. Like the fishhook rune had done earlier, they passed right through his chest.

The sensation was what Alex imagined being hit by a bolt of lightning felt like. Every nerve in his body seemed to burn and his muscles surged, straining against their bonds. It was part agony, part ecstasy, and it filled him up from the inside, forcing the very breath from his body.

The chair to which Alex was tied shattered in a shower of splinters as he simply tore it apart and stood up. Power coursed through him and he shouted an unintelligible battle cry.

As quickly as the sensation had come, it vanished. Alex found himself standing among the ruins of the wooden chair, panting like a racehorse that had just won the derby. His entire body tingled, and he felt invigorated in a way the rejuvenator had never managed.

He felt powerful.

Looking up, Alex found the Brit standing, watching him with his arms folded and an amused expression on his face. Anger flowed through Alex and he took a step forward, determined to get some answers even if he had to beat them out of the man. His leg gave way beneath him and Alex found himself suddenly face down on the floor.

He tried to push himself up, but could barely move his arm.

"What...what have you done to me?" he demanded.

The Brit laughed and shook his head.

"The first time's a right bastard," he said. "Don't worry, you'll shake off the effects soon enough."

"The effects of what?"

"I just transferred the life out of fifty pigs and into you," the Brit said. "It should keep you alive for another year or so. You've got that long to figure out how to do it for yourself." He reached into his trouser pocket and pulled out a large, brass key. "Or I suppose you'll die," he added. "That ought to provide you with all the motivation you need to get studying."

"Why?" Alex asked as the Brit moved to the back wall. He pressed his ornate key against the wood, and it melted into the solid surface as if it were porridge. As the tip of the key vanished, a brass plate with a keyhole appeared beneath it.

"I told you, Alex, the world is on a dark path."

"Right," Alex said. "A lever and a place to stand so you can move the world?"

"Exactly," he said, turning the key. As he did so an ornate vault door melted out of the wall.

"What does any of that have to do with me?" Alex demanded.

The Brit chuckled and gave him an amused look.

"You're going to be my lever, Alex," he said, pulling the door open and revealing a vault beyond that looked like a museum. He winked and then stepped inside. "You are going to be my lever."

He closed the door and it melted away, leaving only Alex and the empty room behind.

THE END

A Quick Note

. . .

You made it. You got all the way to the end, thanks so much for reading my book, it really means a lot to me. I'm guessing you're a fan if you're reading this so I want to ask you to do me a favor. Independent authors live and die with Amazon reviews. Even if you reviewed my previous books, each book counts individually and the more reviews I get, the easier it is to get my books out to more people. So if you would be so kind, take a moment and head over to Amazon and leave me a quick review. I'd really appreciate it. It doesn't have to be anything fancy, just a quick note saying whether or not you liked the book.

Thanks so much. You Rock!

Since this is book 3 in the Arcane Casebook series, I'm going to assume you've already downloaded the prequel novella, *Dead Letter*. If, for some reason you haven't, however, you can get it absolutely free, at www.danwillisauthor.com. *Dead Letter* is the story of how Alex met Danny and the first case they worked together. Get yours now.

So take two minutes and leave me a review on Amazon. And, if you didn't get *Dead Letter* before, grab your free copy at my website (www.danwillisauthor.com).

Also, I love talking to my readers, so please email me at dan@danwillisauthor.com — I read every one. Or join the discussion on the Arcane Casebook Facebook Group.

Watch for Alex's continuing adventures in Mind Games: Arcane Casebook book #4. Available now.

ALSO BY DAN WILLIS

Arcane Casebook Series:

Dead Letter - Prequel

Get Dead Letter free at www.danwillisauthor.com

Available on Amazon and Audible.

In Plain Sight - Book 1

Ghost of a Chance - Book 2

The Long Chain - Book 3

Mind Games - Book 4

Limelight - Book 5

Blood Relation - Book 6

Capital Murder - Book 7

Hostile Takeover - Book 8

Hidden Voices - Book 9

Dragons of the Confederacy Series:

A steampunk Civil War story with NYT Bestseller, Tracy Hickman.

These books are currently unavailable, but I will be putting them back on the market in 2022

Lincoln's Wizard

The Georgia Alchemist

Other books:

The Flux Engine

In a Steampunk Wild West, fifteen-year-old John Porter wants nothing more than to find his missing family. Unfortunately a legendary lawman, a talented thief, and a homicidal madman have other plans, and now John will need his wits, his pistol, and a lot of luck if he's going to survive.

Get The Flux Engine at Amazon.

ABOUT THE AUTHOR

Dan Willis wrote for the long-running DragonLance series. He is the author of the Arcane Casebook series and the Dragons of the Confederacy series.

For more information:
www.danwillisauthor.com
dan@danwillisauthor.com

facebook.com/danwillisauthor
twitter.com/WDanWillis
instagram.com/danwillisauthor
tiktok.com/@danwillisauthor

Printed in Great Britain
by Amazon